The story of a disillusioned American ~~~~ ~~ fierce woman he falls for, and the terrorists who've emb~~~~ ~~ ~~mething in her genome

Nobody can spy on you when you communicate using other people's DNA

FIRST THEY

TAKE

YOUR HEART

Todd Levins

A BLACK CLOUD PAPERBACK

Black Cloud Books
Published by
Bad Sign Publishing
906 North Elizabeth St.
Durham, North Carolina 27701

Black Cloud Books may be purchased for business, promotional
use or for special sales. For information please write to:
Special Markets Department
Bad Sign Publishing
906 North Elizabeth St.
Durham, North Carolina 27701
or email badsignpublishing@gmail.com

ISBN-13: 978-0615791548
ISBN-10: 0615791549

"To dare is to lose one's footing momentarily. To not dare is to lose oneself."
Soren Kierkegaard

For Katie Rehkopf

Acknowledgements

Thank you all so much for your help and support: Katie Guest Pryal, Sharon Elizabeth Wood, Richard Krawiec, Paul Mihas, Joyce Allen, Katie Rehkopf, Leslie Frost, Stephen Peters, Janeen Gingrich, Brendan Love, Stephen Druesedoe, Michael Holloway, Patricia McKenzie Levins, Ray Levins, Andy Magowan, Rose-May Guinard, Natalia Weedy, Mariana Stand Ayala, Romyna Gomez Aguilar, Dana Hopkins, Lisa Hause, Sven Johnson, Emma Allot, Stephanie Wilson, M(a)cGregor Bell, Seth Stephens, Colleen Rigby, Sarah Unger Hamilton, Hernando Sanchez Moreno, Catharine Zivkovic, Lee Sears, Mary Katharine Moore

I

ONE

Sarah's right, Finn muses. She's absolutely right. Finn Barber stands from squatting against a concrete block wall. Above him on a low turret a guard smokes, his arms draped over an AK-47 hung from his shoulders. Finn brushes off the ubiquitous, blood-red Andean sand. He tightens his scarf, and makes his way through the yard—past the knitting women and the men playing cards—to the west hall cafeteria. He's sure his plan is working, it just depends on time; he's not sure he'll avoid solitary confinement, or worse, working the cages, that depends on the warden.

Through a set of double doors Finn files in with the others: shaggy men in sun-faded tee-shirts, women in patched blouses and wide-brimmed hats, and only a few children. He eases down at a scarred wooden table while the masses form a line down the center of the hall and along the back wall. Finn double checks a pocket for the dog-eared photo of Sarah, the one on the Afghani mountain. The wind whips her hair and he can hear her roller-coaster laugh. He wonders if it's his last look. From behind the photo he unfolds the Bukowski poem Eustace gave him. He knows the damn thing backwards, but the handwriting reassures him. *Your life is your life* it begins. *Don't let it be clubbed into dank submission.* He continues, letting the words temper him. Soon the hall fills with people hunched over their bowls and resounds with slurping and crunching. When the line shrinks to just beyond the server Finn joins it. Maybe he'll get lucky with a few gristly hunks from the bottom of the pot.

Swinging double doors beside the kitchen burst open. Two men abreast march in. They're head-to-toe in black: crisp fatigues, knee-high laced boots, knee pads, gloves, elbow pads, and topped with shining helmets. Each holds a stout black baton. Everyone swivels to follow them and those nearby cower. Everyone, that is, except for Finn. He places his tray on the counter, turns his back to the men, and brings his hands together behind him. He repeats to himself that the opposite of love is fear, just as Sarah said. An image shoots across his consciousness: of himself seated in Benjamin's filthy kitchen, the day it all started, that Wednesday in July sixteen months ago, that splinter of time and place which he'd stumbled on, and the only reason he was breathing right now.

The laboratory tedium had become torture. He'd taken off that Wednesday to Friday and had looked forward to a five day weekend without a thought about work. He'd pulled up to Benjamin's house after two coffees and a sausage burrito to stem a nagging hangover, had got out of his car and hopped over a prickly pear cactus. He remembered the front door being half open. He'd pushed inside, past the living room and into the kitchen, called out, shoved a pile of clothes off a chair and sat down at the kitchen table. He could still see the Turkish rug, recently hung on the wall with chunks of plaster scattered on the floor below it.

That morning, like a rough riding Roosevelt stepping from his tent at dawn, Benjamin emerged from his room, except his canvas tent was a bedroom inside a fifties era duplex and it was nearly noon. Cotton pajamas hung below his gut. He grunted and ducked into the bathroom and water flowed in the shower.

Finn flipped through ultra-violet yellowed newspaper pages of an Austin American Statesman. The place stank with a stronger-than-normal tang of anaerobic bacteria. Someone knocked on the front door. Finn picked his way through the living room and opened it. Benjamin's ex-wife, Jessica, stood with their daughter, Sophia. Jessica smiled broadly, genuinely even. He hunched down and gave Sophia a warm hug. He stood up and held the screen door beckoning them in.

Jessica shook her head, "I've gotta run," she said. Her eyes sparkled with something mirthful or mischievous, he couldn't tell. She surveyed the mess and gave a dismayed snort. "It's good to see you." They hugged and Finn leaned back, keeping it formal. Before leaving she pecked him on the cheek, though awfully close to the lips.

A few minutes later Benjamin left the bathroom in swim trunks and a tank top and Sophia ran and jumped into his arms. He carried her to his pickup truck and the three of them left for Pale Face cliffs. Half an hour later they followed a maroon dirt track that wound along sheer limestone fingers jutting out over turquoise Lake Travis. They pulled into their favorite site, empty except for an Hispanic family grilling at the other end. Finn dropped a soccer ball and dribbled around. Benjamin snatched up the bag of hot dogs, buns, beers, and charcoal they'd bought on the way and with the other arm supported Sophia. She clung to a rag doll she'd found in the truck cab. He put her down and plopped the groceries on a picnic table. Then he burst into a sprint toward the cliff edge. Sophia shrieked. He disappeared over the ridge.

A couple of seconds later came the splash and when Finn and Sophia raced to the precipice, bubbles marked the spot where he'd hit. It seemed a hundred feet away. Bubbles rose and vanished and a disconcerting feeling stabbed Finn. It had no act, no idea, no event, no reason associated with it, but it receded when Benjamin burst to the surface taking in a lungful of air.

"Come on!" He bellowed.

"Uh-uh. It's at least fifty feet lower than normal."

Benjamin laughed. "I knew you'd pussy-out." He swam to the cliff edge and began scaling it.

Finn went back to the grill, piled the charcoal in a pyramid and lit it. He cracked open a couple of beers and he and Benjamin passed the soccer ball back and forth. Sophia introduced herself to a girl across the lot.

Benjamin talked about his x.o. (executive officer), complained he was pushing him too fast on too many unsolved cases. He cracked the ball hard directly at Finn's chest. Finn chest-trapped it and dribbled directly at him. He faked right, caught Benjamin wrong footed and nutmegged a pass back to himself between Benjamin's legs. He turned around, grinning, and chipped it to Benjamin with a witch's cackle. Benjamin walloped the ball before it even hit the ground and it sailed over the cliff edge.

"You asshole!"

Benjamin laughed. "You gotta jump now, bitch."

Finn went to the cliff and carefully climbed down on jutting rocks and across a gentle seam. At the water's edge he squatted on a boulder. Wavelets splashed, momentarily staining the limestone before evaporating. The soccer ball floated twenty yards out. A turtle with a shell the size of a car tire breached the surface but then caught sight of Finn and in a single motion disappeared into blackness. Finn lowered himself in and swam back-stroke to the ball. Like a kiddie pool left in the summer sun, the water was not refreshing. Against a cloudless sky turkey buzzards floated on thermal climes, appearing and disappearing beyond cliff walls and for a moment (though it may have been much longer) Finn could have been the only human on earth–except of course, for the boat motors. They were far off but the water made it feel as if their buzzing came from within his head. He thought of Bridgette. He should stop just using her for sex and make her a proper girlfriend. He could grow to love her. Plus, if he were committed to her—or lived with her at least—it would help with the mortgage. But what if he were to quit his job and try for Doctors Without Borders? He probably had enough laboratory experience to qualify for a clinical lab job. If he went with that then he'd definitely be better off single. He imagined bouncing between remote Andean villages in some jalopy. If only he'd trusted himself he could be painting, sketching, doing something creative, rather than trying to figure out how to tolerate the fucking lab. He reached the ball, grabbed it and then swam around to a tiny cove with a shorter cliff and threw the ball up and over. Maybe it wasn't only about trusting himself but also resolution to forge his own way. Anyway, he wished he'd done things differently. At thirty-three he was too old to change now.

Back at the picnic table his cellphone signaled a voice mail. "I can't believe it," he told Benjamin after listening, "My boss needs to see me right now."

"Nice try."

"Really, I'm not playing. This can't be good."

"Seriously?"

Finn nodded.

"Go ahead then. Take the truck."

Finn walked into his boss's eighth floor office in plastic flip-flops, a ripped tank-top, and a damp bathing suit.

She paced in front of a window framing Town Lake. She spoke for a while and Finn caught a few words like "exemplary", and "unfortunate". He'd been laid-off.

He felt relieved, happy even, as if the leash at his neck were abruptly severed.

"You see," she said. "Ultimately it comes down to the investors."

"How much severance do I get?" He blurted. Every second he dallied was precious life lost.

"Well," She pulled the word out like taffy. "That was the investor's decision too." Her face said sorry. "We fought for all of you. We really did."

"How many? Months?"

"Two weeks."

Where's the fucking loyalty! he wanted to shout. "And the two weeks of vacation I have left?" He'd slogged through seven years in that biotech—often going sixty-plus hours a week without overtime—to be dumped with two weeks pay. And on a day off!

"Sorry."

He was free but he had no money. Would he be eligible for unemployment? How much was it anyway? Probably not enough to live on much less take a woman out on a date. Maybe he could get a part-time job. He could do a few contracts with plenty of time in between to enjoy his new freedom. Maybe he would deliver a car like Sal Paradise and Moriarty in On The Road. Or better yet go somewhere where the unemployment money would go far, like to India. He summoned up a camel-packed, multi-hued spice market in a Rajastan desert. He could have an adventure. A tinge of self-involved shame tainted his fantasy. He really should buckle down and use the time like a responsible adult to develop his marketable trades. Like his dad had said 'you're not supposed to like your career. It's a *job*.' He should improve himself instead of acting infantile like Kerouac. He died alone, a cirrhotic-livered madman didn't he? Anyway, what was it that he really *needed*: an ill-conceived adventure in some far off corner, or a life, a job, a career, a stable relationship. He was old now. He had a damn mortgage for god's sake.

"If there's any contract work I'll let you know." She sounded hopeful.

He jumped up. The place felt like a prison. How 'bout you write, 'nothing yet' on a thousand dollar bill every week and mail it to me, he thought. But instead he said, "Thanks."

She said something about an exit interview the following week.

He got in the elevator and began descending. He pulled his hand back about to slap the mirrored wall but the bell chimed. The elevator stopped, and the door slid open. He threw his sunglasses down over his eyes. Some grinning cretin got on. Finn stabbed at the ground floor button about thirty times while silently gnashing his teeth. *Two weeks for seven years. Those motherfucking fucks!* He stomped out into the lobby and through the revolving front door. The heat smothered him.

"Move!" someone yelled from behind.

Finn jerked his head around as he stepped back. A forearm clocked him in the face and everything went bone white.

Two

Youssef knelt, naked in the aubergine light. He recited prayers beside a secondhand mattress lying on the floor, his forehead pressed down next to the base of a oscillating fan. His cell phone buzzed. He fumbled for it on an upturned orange crate, flipped it over, and squinted against the glare. It listed the number as private. He considered silencing it but was too curious about who was calling him at this hour.

"Hello?" His voice crackled.

"Tariq ibn Youssef Al-Momina," a voice spoke in a gruff baritone. Most people knew him as Tariq or Tariq Al-Momina, but his friends called him Youssef. He had not heard his entire name for a long, long time.

"Who is this?"

"It begins," the voice said.

Three years ago, just after he'd arrived in Texas, Youssef received in the mail a letter, hand-written in English, a downtown intersection and time of day printed in black ink on an otherwise blank page. He'd known, of course, to expect it: a location for a meeting whose time would be announced in a subsequent phone call—this one. He had been alert and anxious for many weeks thereafter, but as month bled into month he—a soldier surrounded by polite, smiling enemies—increasingly found himself battling complacency and his own choices. He tried not to befriend Americans, tried not to enjoy himself, tried not to fantasize he was just a another foreign student at a U.S. university. The years fell and he lost a few battles. He proposed to Cemile four months ago when the blue bonnets and those little reddish-pink flowers sprung up in the highway medians, abandoned lots, and front yards.

"It begins," the voice insisted.

"Nineteen," Youssef said reflexively, the proper response. Then silence. He pulled the phone from his ear and saw the call had ended.

This meant the attack had started. It meant he would now be assigned a target and would extract cheek cells from her. It meant the end of his life as he knew it and the first moment of a different one. It meant the chance to become a man, the chance to become a martyr.

Like a fist his stomach clenched itself, and his heart thumped in his chest. He sat on the edge of the bed but felt dizzy. He laid back down and stretched out. This gave him no relief so he stood and paced in his cramped room, and scraped his fingers through his hair. He decided he needed a tea. He went into the kitchen, put a kettle on, and resumed pacing.

These last few years in Austin had not felt like much of a struggle and he sensed a guilt of comfort here, a creeping mildew, musty and nibbling him at the edges. His father used to like saying, "Anyone can do easy. It's through struggle we are defined." He didn't mean it in a driven humorless way. It felt wonderful when he said it. But with so much fallow time Youssef had begun to suspect, and hope even, that his struggle was abandoned. He had begged his father's forgiveness many times.

Two hours later he leaned against a brick building at the designated address—a busy street corner on Congress Avenue six blocks south of the capital dome. High-rises loomed above him. Waiters setup outdoor seating. He watched pedestrians stride by, cars pass, and trucks trundle along, or stop and unload. He hoped Lieutenant Jabaar, or maybe even Malik, would come. Then he realized a blunder he'd made, and a sharp fear surged through him. He dug into his pocket and pulled out his cell phone. He erased all voice mails, text messages, and called and received numbers. Romantic relationships had been explicitly forbidden and he'd nearly gone into the meeting with ample evidence of daily contact with Cemile. He turned off his phone.

Half an hour passed before a white sedan, a Japanese luxury model, stopped. His hopes of seeing an old friend fell when a man he'd never seen before stepped from the back door. With a curt hand gesture the man motioned him over. He wore black sunglasses and was dressed in khakis and a light blue oxford cloth rolled up at the sleeves. They exchanged *Salaams* and with an open palm the man, probably an Afghan or Pakistani, invited him in. As he ducked into the car the man squeezed a meaty hand on his shoulder and guided him. They sat in the rear seats leaving the front passenger seat empty and the driver (he didn't recognize him either) immediately pulled into traffic. The man beside him looked squat and powerful, although Youssef might even have called him obese. His rolled shirt sleeves strained around forearms that sprouted from hands like Baobab tree trunks from the savannas, the ones Youssef used to play on as a child. A thick gold chain peeked out from an open shirt collar. He held out a crumpled cigarette pack. Youssef refused.

"This isn't a test. It's zero hour," the man said, shaking a cigarette from the pack.

Youssef knew to expect that line. "Zero hour," Youssef repeated as per the protocol.

"You call me Ledpaste." He spoke in a gravel voice, definitely the one from the phone call.

"Okay," Youssef said. His name made Youssef think of a table knife spreading a lusterless nugget of lead.

They sat silently while the car meandered through morning traffic and Ledpaste smoked, his sausage fingers squeezing the cigarette. An expensive Swiss watch choked his left wrist and on each hand were heavy gold rings. The driver, constantly turning, moved quickly between cars and buses. It seemed as if they were aimlessly prowling downtown streets. But they must know what they are doing, he thought. He felt awkward and increasingly nervous and wanted to start some polite conversation, just for something to say. Ledpaste stared ahead. He had an immediately recognizable air of self-assuredness and Youssef respected that, but it also made him alert with competitiveness. After several silent minutes Ledpaste's phone rang and he answered it. He said hello and nothing more. Then he turned to the driver. "Fifth and Guadalupe, south-east corner."

A couple of minutes later they approached the intersection of Fifth and Guadalupe. The driver pulled to the curb and stopped beside a line of metal newspaper boxes. Ledpaste stepped out and went behind the car. Youssef turned and saw him putting coins into one of the dispensing boxes. He opened the door, leaned down, lifted up the papers, and took out the bottom one. Back in the car he put the New York Times on his lap. He leafed through it and came to a thin manila folder. Leaning back into his seat he flicked a cigarette stub out the window, shut it, and turned to Youssef. He gave him the folder.

It contained a page of text and a photo.

"This is the target— her specs, home address, office address. This is a photo taken last week." He spoke in Pashto, just like in the *Madrassas* and training camps. Youssef had a hard time following it.

The photo was an eight by ten of a white woman. She was seated, holding an espresso cup in an outdoor café. She wore no makeup. Her cheeks bunched up over an easy smile and above bright green eyes she wore her auburn hair un-brushed and tied with a thin turquoise scarf, silk perhaps.

While Youssef studied the photo Ledpaste pulled out two plastic bags sealed with tape and inscribed with "STERILE" in thick red print.

They each contained a single cotton swab on a thin wooden stick. Ledpaste pushed the bags over the photo. The swabs were the same kind he'd practiced with in the Pakistani training camps four years ago.

His twenty soldier sub-group had trained differently from the other soldiers at the camp. In addition to small arms training, hand-to-hand combat, target recognition, memorization, explosives, reconnaissance, computer hacking, police evasion, and interrogation resistance, they practiced rubbing cotton swabs on their fellow soldier's inner cheeks, then later, on midday streets: stranger's cheeks. The strangers were always female. They practiced approaching the targets and distracting them to get a swab. It was not enough to collect a cigarette butt or a discarded coffee cup, they were told. They needed inner cheek cells.

After the training camps he moved with a few fellow soldiers to London and enrolled in an advanced English language school, honing his skills in the language he had been studying since boyhood. There he received sterile plastic bags and cotton swabs exactly like the ones he now held. But the targets were now young English women. They sent the samples away for analysis and were graded on whether they had extracted enough cheek cells. Not once had Youssef failed. He didn't understand how the laboratories analyzed the samples and he and his fellow soldiers knew not to ask questions. But they speculated in private. He concluded they were training to extract a DNA tag, a confirmation of sorts, from a target infected with a bioweapon.

"Memorize it all. You won't be taking anything with you," Ledpaste said.

Youssef pushed the bag aside and continued studying the photo. Thin, one-hundred and sixty-five to one-hundred seventy centimeters, she had a mole on her lip to the right of her nose, a crooked left incisor, and a thin, hairless scar that sliced across her left eyebrow.

"Your phone, give it to me," Ledpaste said.

Youssef handed him the phone, relieved that he'd deleted everything. He tried to memorize the information while preoccupied with what Ledpaste was doing. He appeared to be searching through call and message histories. Youssef wondered if he suspected anything since they were obviously just erased. Ledpaste returned the phone to Youssef's shirt pocket and patted it.

While Youssef studied the information neither spoke. After several minutes he gave the folder back to Ledpaste. Ledpaste clenched and unclenched his jaws, the muscles above his temples popping in and out. He lit another cigarette then turned and looked into Youssef's eyes. He plucked a loose strand of tobacco from his front teeth and flicked it away. "You have five days from this morning to get the sample. Draw the least amount of attention as possible." He grabbed Youssef's right hand and slapped a cell phone into it. "I'll contact you on this. Be. Ready." He enunciated the last two words slowly and deliberately.

Youssef's cell phone rang from his shirt pocket. He looked at Ledpaste uncertainly and Ledpaste nodded.

It was Cemile. Youssef felt his face flush.

"Am I going to see my little buggie-bug this morning?" she said in a sing-song voice.

"I can't talk right now." He spoke in English.

"You don't have class now. Do you?"

Youssef leaned to his left towards the door and cupped the phone. "I'll call you later."

"You sound funny. What are you doing?"

"Talk to you later."

"Give me kiss, a big smooch so I can hear it."

Youssef hung up. He started to turn his phone off but Ledpaste held out a hand for it. The follicles on Youssef's head tightened as he watched Ledpaste re-dial Cemile. He realized he was breathing through an open mouth and closed it. Cemile answered but he couldn't make out the words.

"Who is this?" Ledpaste grunted in English. "What's your name?"

Cemile said something.

"You tell me yours and I'll tell you mine." He waited a few moments then pulled the phone away and looked at it. Cemile's calls came up "Cemi". He punched a few more buttons and stared at it a while. Was he memorizing Cemile's number? He turned and regarded Youssef steady-eyed and blew out a film of pale gray smoke. Then he looked him up and down. "Are you fucking up?"

Youssef shook his head. He felt as if his stomach were being scraped out. "No."

"Who was that woman?"

"Just a friend, a fellow grad student."

"Her name!"

"Cemilia" Youssef said. He'd dragged out the 's' sound searching for a name.

"Family name."

Youssef stuttered. "I don't know."

"You think I'm stupid."

"No."

Ledpaste stared, projecting himself into Youssef, and Youssef looked down.

"Have you been going to a mosque?"

Youssef shook his head fervently. "No. No way. Definitely not."

"I don't give a rat's ass about your father, or your fucking pissant achievements. Got it! All you've got right now is your mission."

Youssef nodded.

"Whether your family hears you're a hero or some *kuffar* charmed by the soft American life who answers to his fucking cunts, depends on what comes out of *my* mouth. So from this moment on I'm the only one you need to please."

Youssef nodded.

Ledpaste let it sink in. Then he pulled something from his shirt pocket and uncurled his fingers, palm up, exposing two small powder blue pills in a tiny transparent case. "From now on always keep these on you, and swallow one if apprehended by *any* authority."

THREE

Youssef pulled a whistling kettle off the stove and poured the water into a mug holding a tea bag. He sat before a color map of downtown Austin. He made it by printing portions on sheets of paper and taping them together. Felt tip markers and glossy fold-outs of bus routes lay on top of it. He paced, reviewing his plan. He stopped at the tiny window in the front door and peered at the stark blue sky.

The drought was wringing Central Texas into a crusty knot. In over seven weeks not a single rain drop had splashed onto the cracked dirt mosaic of Youssef's front yard. Some said it was the worst drought in seventy years. An unfamiliar gray mutt sniffed around an abandoned lot across the street. Waist-high beige grass choked the empty lot, strewn with branches, cardboard, and plastic bottles. The dog sniffed a rusted bike frame stood upside down on the skeleton of a wooden fence felled by a spring squall. He peed on it.

When Youssef arrived in the United States he'd rented a room in a backpacker's youth hostel and began searching for a place for himself and Jassim, his sleeper cell partner who would arrive six weeks later. He found this cottage on an online classifieds site. The rent was very low and he came to see it that evening. A car sat on concrete blocks in the front lawn and a warped screen door stood open a few inches, tempting him inside. It was a low-ceilinged bungalow on the tail of a dead-end street. The entire place smelled of hot urine and under the bleached light of his flash light the toilet writhed with maggots eating feces. He wanted it. The landlord's pink jowls shook when he laughed explaining he'd practically stolen it at a police auction. It was a crack house piece-mealed from share-croppers quarters thrown together over a century earlier. Maybe, like himself, the original tenants came from a slave trading port on Tanzania's coast.

He plucked the teabag from the mug, returned to the table and reexamined the bus routes. It was Wednesday July 31st, two days after his meeting with Ledpaste. Immediately after the meeting he'd gone to the target's apartment building and was lucky enough she had not left for her office. A red star covered the target's office building in a modest high rise downtown and a yellow highlighter marked the bus routes nearest her house that went there. He scanned his notes until he found comments on the café where she had bought coffee on both Monday and Tuesday before leaving for work. On Tuesday she drove an old and odd car, a Renault, the ten or so blocks to her office, but on Monday she'd taken the bus. He would get the sample on the bus just before a stop. Then he would jump off and leave her, confused but without recourse. If she didn't take the bus he would get a swab on the sidewalk outside the high rise, though this was much less preferable than the bus strategy. Tuesday afternoon he had ridden the bus three times, memorizing the stops. He marked the café with a blue star, and then compared the bus schedule times with the two times she had visited the coffee shop. Already his pulse was racing. He checked his watch. Twenty-six minutes until the the bus passed by the target's café.

"Cemile's here," Jassim called out.

Youssef ran into the living room, cracked a blind and peered through. He cursed to himself and then rushed outside and intercepted her at the bottom of the dirt driveway.

"I left my sunglasses here," she said, marching up the driveway. With a stony expression she looked beyond him.

"Look, I've been writing a paper."

Her gaze jerked to him. "You haven't answered my calls in three days because you're *writing a paper*?"

"Don't be like that."

She held a hand to her face imitating a phone. "Hey baby, I'm writing a paper. I'll call you when I'm done."

"I was in the library researching. I forgot."

"My glasses." She maneuvered past him toward the porch steps.

Youssef grabbed her by the elbow. He turned her, facing him. "I'm sorry. I just need the rest of the day to finish this paper." He gave her a modest smile and slid in between her and the house. "Wait here. I'll get your glasses. I think I saw them in the bathroom." He tried to sound cheerful.

"Who was that man who called me from your phone after you *hung up* on me?" She shifted to climb the porch steps but he shuffled to the side, blocking her.

Youssef looked at the sky and sighed. *Stick to story.* "I was in the library with a study partner and people were giving me stares while I was talking to you. He re-dialed you. He thought he was being funny."

"You're not letting me by."

"I'm not stopping you," he said, still blocking her.

Her mouth puckered.

Youssef exhaled and then stood aside. "Go, go, get them yourself."

She went through the living room and into his bedroom. Jassim sat cross-legged on the couch watching television. He didn't even look over when Cemile came through the door. Youssef saw the maps and bus routes were still on the kitchen table. He blocked the television and Jassim looked up at him saucer-eyed. *What a moron!* Youssef glowered at him and jerked his head toward the kitchen. Jassim jumped up and raced into the kitchen.

"You would tell me if there was a problem with us, right?" Cemile said, coming back into the living room.

"Of course." He sat down on the couch and laced up a pair of running sneakers. "Listen, I really have to go *right* now."

"If there's another woman, be a man and tell me."

"What!" he blurted, with a surprised laugh. "Come on. Don't overreact." He stood up and told Jassim to grab his bag. "Fine, there *is* another woman," he said.

Cemile stood slack-jawed.

"It's my mother. She went back into the hospital Sunday night."

Cemile's face softened. "Why didn't you tell me?"

"I am telling you."

"You make me feel stupid because you're always so secretive. I want to be here for you when you need me. How bad is she?"

"See? This is exactly why. You know I don't like to talk about my family." He hugged her. He pulled back and searched her eyes. Her glossy black hair fell in curls down to the top of her chest, a pink cottony blouse barely concealing the top of her olive-skinned breasts. She wore a pouty frown that made her irresistible. He even loved her jealousy. "I'll call you tonight. Don't worry." He pecked a kiss on her plump cheek. They all left in Jassim's car and dropped Cemile off at a bus stop on Forty Second Street.

Once alone in the car Youssef backhanded Jassim's shoulder. "Get your fucking head on straight," he said in Arabic. They reviewed their plan. Jassim would follow the bus if Youssef boarded. Then he would park on the opposite side of the street after he got off. If the target drove her car Jassim would beat her to the office, leave Youssef at the entrance, and then park two blocks north.

They arrived at the café with two minutes to spare. Youssef sat alone and waited—fifteen minutes, half an hour, an hour—but the target never appeared. He ordered a tea. Jassim shuffled in. As long as it took, he told him, "so get back to the car." He wished he'd been wise enough to suspect he'd have to wait all morning. He would have brought his Malcolm X autobiography.

By noon Youssef was starting to regret this plan. He should have gone directly to her apartment and swabbed her when she answered the door, he thought. However the front desk security guard posed an annoyance. He pondered a plan to distract the guard. A dumpster fire should work. But he still had three days left and didn't yet need such extremes. Jassim texted asking what he would do about Cemile. He didn't respond.

There she was! She stood at the coffee bar sugaring her coffee, in a peach dress, leather sandals, and with an oversize purse over a shoulder. Youssef put down the newspaper article he was reading on pecan pie. The fat purse was good. It would limit her mobility, but Youssef would have preferred a heel on her flat-soled sandals, and a long skirt to a dress. She was gorgeous in a dignified way like the wife of that American president in the sixties, the one who got shot in the head. Her hips and ass protruded in just the right way. He followed her to the bus stop. He had planned to sit behind the target on the bus, but she sat just one seat from the back and the seat behind her was full, so instead, he sat a few seats ahead, opposite the back door. He felt anxious and so recited a few prayers. He had not considered approaching the target from the front when he'd imagined his plan for the bus.

The bus lurched to a halt a block from her office. She got off and he followed. As she walked along the sidewalk he called out to her. "Excuse me. Ma'am?" *Big smile.* He held out a twenty-dollar bill. "This fell when you got off the bus."

She looked confused. "That fell out of my purse? Are you sure?"

"Definitely," he said, still smiling.

She hesitated and then reached for it. "Thanks."

He dropped the bill, shot his left hand under her chin and choked her. With his right he dragged a swab along the back of her throat and across the inside of her left cheek. He pulled the swab from the target's mouth and zipped it into the plastic sterile bag. She coughed and doubled-over. He picked up the twenty dollar bill and then spun and trotted off briskly. He dodged people on the side walk, and through thick four-lane traffic scanned for the dented sedan which Jassim should have parked on the other side of the street. *Simple. Prepare and execute. God is Great.*

Then his head was jerked backwards by his hair, and he abruptly stopped. With his left hand he grabbed the hand on the back of his head, turned around and bent the wrist down fingers upward. He faced his attacker: the target. What a tenacious bitch! She shrieked and knelt down to reduce the pressure on her wrist. He thumped her squarely on the temple with the butt of a palm and she splayed out, keys, change, cell phone, and knickknacks scattering over the concrete. Then he turned and hurried on. Soon she was screaming for help.

The pedestrians stopped as Youssef passed. He thrust a few out of his way. He sped up, peeked over a shoulder and saw some white guy chasing him. He started sprinting, slaloming the morning commuters. His pursuer's shouts mingled with the target's. A would-be hero cocked a timid leg trying to trip him. Youssef easily hopped it. He angled toward a part in the crawling traffic. *Where are you, Jassim?*

A knotty old man grabbed his shirt. Someone crashed into him from behind. Youssef fell to the ground but immediately sprung up facing his attacker: a thin white guy scrambling to stand up. Youssef jumped and piston kicked him in the groin. The man collapsed. A mob began to form. People shouted. A warmth inebriated him. He clutched the plastic bag in his left hand, and with the right reached for a knife between his belt and back. He flipped out a six-inch nickel-plated blade and swung it in a slow arc. "Who wants to fuck with me!" The circle retreated. He bolted and weaved through the traffic, but followed by others. *There is no god but God. God is Great.* He spied Jassim's dusty sedan fifty yards ahead on the opposite side of the street. *Praise be to God!* He swerved around a car, vaulted the hood of another, and landed in a faster-moving lane. A delivery truck screeched towards him. Using the energy of the sliding truck, he bounded off the hood gazelle-like. He landed in the narrow space between the last lane and a concrete construction median. A motorcycle struck him directly but he managed to grab the handlebars. It slung him to the asphalt and the zip lock bag skittered across the pavement. He bolted upright and scanned for the bag. Heads popped from car windows. A burly man in jeans shot out into the narrow shoulder three cars down with another man behind him. They sprinted towards him. Youssef hurdled the concrete median as the man grabbed his shirt. Youssef tore away and dodged cars across the other side of the street. He threw himself into the passenger seat of Jassim's car. "Go, go, go, go!" Youssef grabbed the headrest and turned around looking for pursuers as Jassim squealed off. He didn't see any. "Go three blocks, turn right and park. Walk back along the construction median and look for the baggie. I think it slid out into a lane of traffic."

"Fine."

"Don't act like that. I'd be recognized you idiot!"

They parked on a cross street three blocks south and Jassim got out. Youssef watched him round the corner and disappear. But only a moment later he reappeared. "Cops," he said, climbing into the driver's seat.

Youssef rained down blows on the dashboard and thrashed his head. Eventually he leaned back and ran his fingers through his hair. He didn't say a word more.

Back at the cottage he eased himself onto the love seat, reached over and twisted a whirring box fan toward himself. The neighbor's dog barked through a hoarse throat. He'd been tossed hard by the motorcycle but he didn't hurt particularly—one elbow scraped and his left knee a little stiff. He mulled his predicament. He still had Thursday and Friday to obtain the sample, but he'd attacked the target, and another man, so the police would be looking for him. Also the target was now alerted and could identify him.

"You have some blood on the back of your shirt." Jassim said.

Scenarios of the impending meeting with Ledpaste played in Youssef's imagination. Ledpaste might kill him to destroy a trail the police could follow.

"That motorcycle hit you pretty hard. Maybe you should lie down."

"Shut. up." Youssef said through his teeth. "You're not to say one word about what happened." He paced in the cramped living room like a prisoner. Then he programmed his music player, plugged it into the stereo and flopped back down on the love seat. The music was Moroccan, acappella, and the gentle voices helped him think. He sat still awhile trying to absorb the music, but the neighbor's dog barked incessantly. He got up brusquely and marched outside.

His neighbors, a poor family living under section eight government assistance, always chained their dog in the front yard. Though fully grown she was still just a puppy. Her mud-crusted chain, wound tightly around a tree, held her just inches from the trunk. Her water bowl lay upside down two meters away. When she saw him she bounced spastically, yelping, and wagging her tail back and forth hard enough to whip her sides. He leaned over the low chain link fence and reached for her. "It's okay girl," he cooed. She was mostly pit bull: thirty kilos of muscle and tan like desert sand but with a black muzzle. She squeaked with pleasure when he stroked her. He walked around the fence and through the open gate. He unhooked her and held her down while she strained to jump up, taking swipes with her long mottled tongue. With the other hand he unwound the filthy chain. He tried to think, to plan his next approach to the target. "Calm down girl. Calm down," he said. She lurched and yanked her collar from his grasp. She ran circles in the front yard, her ass nearly scraping the ground. Next she bolted through the open gate. He chased her but she thought it was a game, alternately dodging and stampeding him, making sharp turns just before they collided. He yelled commands at her but she took no notice. Suddenly she stopped and pricked up her ears. Far away a dog barked. Youssef crept towards her. "It's okay girl. It's okay." Just as abruptly as she had stopped she rocketed toward the abandoned lot across the street. The dead grass swallowed her. Only the swaying tips betrayed her path of escape. For a minute Youssef continued calling. She's better off now anyway, he thought, and turned back to his bungalow. He decided he would wait for the target at her apartment.

FOUR

Wednesday evening Finn Barber went to The Elephant Hole, a Fourth Street tavern downtown. Outside, couples and groups sat at wrought-iron tables studded with pints of micro brews. The sun had retreated to the horizon, but still its heat, tangible, radiated from everything. A shortened portico crowned the center of the patio above a half set of stairs leading down. Finn descended into a blue coolness. His name floated out from an outdoor table or maybe he'd imagined it. He turned and saw a woman smiling. Lamplight glinted off her teeth and he thought she was laughing at him. He kept descending. At head height, aqua-tinted windows lined the entire front wall. He leaned against the bar and ordered a wheat beer.

Taking up space a few stools over Finn recognized the deep creases in a leathery neck, Eustace Edelman, a grizzled, stuck-in-amber journeyman on the downtown pub circuit. He'd been kicked out of all the bars in town, hanging out at the few that let him in while waiting for the others to change management. Finn heard that in the seventies he used to fly a single prop around Africa, transporting God-knows-what to God-knows-who. He turned around sporting a serious smirk and nodding his head. It gave Finn the distinct impression that he knew, or maybe understood, something about Finn that even Finn wasn't aware of.

"Finny-boy!" Eustace said.

Finn gave him a nod, a male-to-male head pop. Cutting the same paths as Eustace Edelman bodes real poor for me, he thought.

After getting fired and then smacked-down by a fleeing mugger, he'd come to a split-second later sprawled on the sidewalk while a lithe young woman (the victim presumably) sprinted by in pursuit of her (and now Finn's) attacker. Finn however, had returned to Benjamin and Sophia at the cliffs. He'd been too embarrassed to talk to the police, besides there was no shortage of witnesses. Late-afternoon the three of them returned to town and Finn went home and took a nap before an evening soccer match. He was still in his uniform but with flip-flops. Finn started a tab, found an empty booth, and plopped down facing the bar. He slid the chilled glass across his forehead and massaged a sore quad muscle. Light seemed to shimmer through the blue tinted windows as if rain drops were coursing down them, except of course, there was no rain.

Benjamin ducked inside and descended the stairs talking on a cell phone. He wore a white team shirt covered in grass stains. He had the odd ability to look both young and old simultaneously. A trail of dried blood crusted on the side of his head where he'd split the skin above an eyebrow. "Whatever," he said, into the phone. He threw his keys, wallet, and phone on the table. "I think I heard that fat sonuvabitch's rib crack when I slammed him at the top of the box. The one who swiped you from behind." He pointed to an olive-sized lump above his eye. "Fucker got an elbow in when he went down." He smirked.

"Impressive," Finn said. Even if he was the recipient, Benjamin seemed to thrive off destruction. When they were kids, just nine or ten, he'd convinced Finn to help him roll boulders from atop a long wooded hill behind Benjamin's house. They watched them barrel down the hill, launching off rocks and crashing into trees. With every impact, each splintered sapling, Benjamin's pudgy face grew brighter, his cheering more fervent.

Benjamin plunked himself down across from Finn. "Hey fuck-O, I'm watching your back and you don't even have a pint waiting."

"I handled that defender. I scored didn't I?"

"Pffft! You handled him like that guy on the sidewalk this morning."

"That's low dude."

Benjamin held up the fingers on one hand. "You owe me four pints, dude."

"You're the one employed. You should be buying my beers."

"Do me a favor. Next game do more than jog the first half."

"I had to save my energy."

"Dude, you're waiting to play when you're already playing," Benjamin said.

"I don't want to risk being spent with twenty minutes to go."

"So instead you risk not pushing your limits."

"Hey asshole! News flash. I lost my health insurance today."

Benjamin shook his head and signaled to the waitress. She nodded from across the bar. "I've got something you might be interested in," he said.

"There's a position open in forensics?"

"Nope. It's a woman."

"Like I want anything to do with your sleazy whores." Finn watched a striking olive-skinned woman, a Latina maybe, strut down the steps, smoking a cigarette. She was tall and with tight kinky hair. Her ass bobbed and fell, barely tucked into a white mini-skirt.

Benjamin turned to look too. He turned back. "Oh," he said, laughing, "Mr. Driven Snow. You and Bridgette sure are a vision of purity. Tell her boyfriend I said hello."

"I told you. I'm not sleeping with her."

The Latina stopped at the bar next to Eustace.

"You're waiting until she gets married, then huh?"

Finn felt sucker punched. Benjamin had broken the unspoken rule (yet again) and breached the Jessica incident, the one eons ago between Benjamin's ex-wife and Finn in the back yard of a house party. The host thought she saw Jessica crouched behind bushes giving Finn head. The host told Benjamin directly when he arrived half an hour later. At the time Finn knew Jessica and Benjamin were separating, though Benjamin denied it. The incident exploded into to a drunken, shoving and shouting match, and Finn managed to dissuade Benjamin only through volume and red-faced conviction, that nothing had happened. Though something had.

The waitress put down a pint of black stout for Benjamin. "Seriously," Finn said. "What were you going to tell me?"

"You know my buddy Reece Skully? The jeweler who made my wedding rings?"

Finn shook his head. "Your buddy? You said it was about a woman."

"That was his fiancée who was attacked outside your lab today."

"So you guys are going to help me get revenge on the mugger?"

Eustace was talking to the Latina and soon they were both laughing. Finn thought he saw Eustace look his way.

"She wasn't mugged. The guy took a mouth swab."

"Really? Weird."

"Look," Benjamin said. "It'll just sit in a file, and you're not even working."

"What can I do? I'm a fucking scientist." Finn swigged his beer and then started to chuckle to himself.

"What?" Benjamin said.

"You owe him a lot for the rings, huh?"

"Come on, don't be like that," Benjamin said. "You know DNA and all that shit. What else could he have been after? Just talk to her that's all." Then he smiled. "She's hot as shit, isn't she?"

"You sound like a real good buddy, trying to pawn off his fianceé."

Benjamin motioned for the waitress. "Just give her a call."

"I'd love to get involved with a knife wielding psycho, but I've got to apply to a masters program at UT, fix a leak over my dining room, look for work," *and do whatever the hell I want to.* "And, just a lot of other shit. I've got to figure out how I'm going to pay my mortgage now."

The waitress came by and waited while Benjamin wrote on her order pad. He tore off a sheet and slid it across the table. "I thought you were tired of the lab."

"If I get a masters I'll make a lot more money." Finn pushed the paper aside.

"Take unemployment and work on your painting."

Finn scoffed. "And after six months of selling a few $500 paintings? I'm too old for dreams. I need to buckle down."

Benjamin took a swallow of his stout.

"The things I truly enjoy," Finn said, "painting, soccer—"

"Whoring," Benjamin announced through cupped hands.

"Shut up. I could easily be monogamous."

"Whatever."

"As long as I didn't have to stop sleeping around." Finn drank his beer. "I'm sad though. I can't tell you the name of the last protein I purified but I can tell you that we last played the Internationals in June and the center midfielder, Vito, scored on a through-ball and they won 3-2."

"The highlights of our fucking lives, dude."

"It's the pursuit, the struggle, the uncertainty. They appeal to primal drives, our hunting instincts." Finn felt pretty good about himself, stringing all those arguments together in such a persuasive sentence.

"But this part right here," Benjamin said, poking the tabletop. "Sitting down sore and sweaty and bullshitting over beers, I like it almost as much. It's like I come here to let the high from the game mellow. When that tall Mexican came down the left side and I checked him to the ground. Remember? That hit put me in the game, dude. After that I was gliding on ice."

Finn nodded, "Yeah, the contact. We crave it. Where else can you intentionally slam another man without consequences?"

"On the sidewalk outside your lab seems a pretty good place."

"Fuck off."

Benjamin grinned.

"Maybe you're right. There won't be any consequences for him with the mighty Austin PD on the case."

"Don't make me take your punk-ass down," Benjamin said. Then he slammed his fist down aiming for Finn's hand, but Finn deftly pulled back as if it were a reflex. Benjamin's hand thudded against bare wood and Finn's pint teetered from the jolt. "You got lucky, punk!"

"It's not luck. It's called knowing your dumb-ass since cub scouts."

Benjamin called to the waitress for another pint. "At least tell me this," he said, turning back to Finn. "What genes do you get from dragging a cotton swab in someone's mouth that you can't get from lipstick or a cigarette butt?"

"Do I look like a forensic scientist to you? I don't fucking know."

"Can you imagine even one reason why you would do it?"

Finn sighed, "I wouldn't do it."

The Latina stopped talking to Eustace. Finn thought about going up to her and introducing himself. What would he say?

Benjamin turned around.

"You don't actually look at genes," Finn said.

Benjamin got up. He walked directly to the woman and began speaking to her. She smiled at him. She looked over at Finn and then laughed at something Benjamin said and then she took out a cigarette pack and handed Benjamin a few black cigarettes. At the bar, he wrote on a napkin and gave it to her, said something else that made her laugh, and then returned to the booth.

"What'd you say?"

Benjamin sat down and threw him a cigarette. "They're cloves." He popped one into his mouth. "You got a light?"

Finn shook his head.

Benjamin went back to the bar for a pack of matches. Once, on the banks of the creek that ran behind Benjamin's family's house, Finn had cajoled Benjamin to join him in his first cigarette, a filter-less one Finn had swiped from his father's office. They used the same ones a few nights later to light the gasoline-soaked, rag-tipped arrows that they launched at their evil neighbor's wooden deck.

Benjamin returned, lit Finn's clove and then his own.

Finn sucked in a sweet lungful and eased back into the booth. "Did you give her your number?"

"Maybe I gave her *your* number." He flicked an ash on the floor and turned around for another look.

"Can you imagine getting that skirt off?" Finn said. He took another drag. "I do know this. You don't actually look at the genes to determine identity." He didn't need to tell Benjamin how they nabbed DNA from a reluctant suspect. Detectives like him were the ones who got it. "What really makes us individuals is the space in between the genes. People call it junk DNA, but it's like 97% of the total DNA molecule." He explained that the majority of the human genome was comprised of antiquated genes, regulatory sequences, and viral and bacterial interlopers incorporated eons ago, and bunches of who-knows-what. The waitress brought Benjamin another stout and Finn ordered an Indian pale ale.

Benjamin started talking about police politics of which Finn had no interest. A nagging thought came and vanished, dragging behind it a wake of discontent. Finn sipped more beer, trying to ignore the urge to chase the thought. Eventually Benjamin drained his beer, stood and collected his keys, phone, and wallet. "Give her a call." He pointed to the number he'd written on the page from the waitress' order pad.

"Promise me half the debt her fiancé forgives you."

Benjamin laughed, "If you solve anything then we'll talk. And don't Scrooge on the tip, faggot."

Finn watched him bound up the steps.

After finishing his beer he went to the bar to pay the tab. The Latina was talking with some guy. Finn climbed the stairs and left.

That night, while cooking quesadillas, his phone rang. He didn't recognize the number but answered anyway. "Hi, this is Sarah." The voice was smooth. "Benjamin Black gave me your number."

Finn perked up. "Yeah, you're the woman who gave us cloves at the Elephant Hole."

"No," she said. "I was assaulted on the street today. Benjamin said that man attacked you too."

"Oh, yeah," he said. He heard the annoyance creeping into his voice and switched his tone to something more polite. "I'm sorry about what happened." Though he really couldn't have given a rat's rectum.

"Thanks," she said. "Benjamin said you're an accomplished scientist."

"He got it half right."

"Okay," she said. She wasn't laughing.

"I'm just kidding."

"I see. Listen. I've been thinking. Should I go to a doctor?"

He didn't know what to say. "Why?"

"Could he have been trying to poison me?"

"What actually happened?"

"I was just walking to work..." she began.

Finn smelled smoke. He had wandered into the living room while talking and left a tortilla cooking on an open gas burner. He pulled the phone from his ear and careened back into the kitchen. He Frisbeed the flaming thing into the sink and waved out smoke using the back door. "I'm sorry, the signal's bad. What did you say?"

"That's when I grabbed his hair and stopped him."

"Oh," he said, and she continued talking. He recalled how beautiful she was, her face as delicate as her voice, and her legs as smooth as her tone. And she'd had a nice rack, hadn't she?

"...over the construction barrier and across the street."

"Uh-huh," he said. Suddenly the fire alarm screamed. He jumped out the back door and slammed it shut. "What?"

"Then we went to the police station."

He stalked away from the alarm, towards the back of his yard. She kept talking. "Listen," he said. "Why don't we meet?"

He suggested the next morning at Ooh La Latte on Caesar Chavez, west of Lamar. He didn't ask what time was convenient. He'd meet her at 9:00 A.M.

FIVE

Thursday morning Finn arrived twenty-five minutes late to Ooh La Latte. It sat on a wooded hill a few miles west of the downtown high rises. From the center of a wood deck towered a live oak. Its gnarled branches, several longer than the deck's radius, stretched out horizontally as if defying gravity. A construction crew's pneumatic nail guns hammered a staccato rhythm. They sounded alternatively close and then suddenly much farther away. He climbed steps scanning the deck. Sarah sat alone at a tiny round table. She was undoubtedly gorgeous but not in a mind-blanking, stammering kind-of-way. He shook her hand, rather stiffly, and felt a little guilty for being late but didn't apologize. She lit a cigarette and he went inside to order himself a coffee. While waiting in line he tried to mentally describe her attraction. He came close to finding the words but still they eluded him.

"Think it'll ever rain again?" he said, returning and sitting down. They talked about the heat and the drought. A short navy blue dress hugged her, and her long auburn hair (which she wore in a kind of purposeful tousle) tumbled down her tanned shoulders. From under her mane peeked gold hoop earrings.

"The police aren't going to do anything," she said, though not accusingly, more like an unfortunate fact.

"Who'd you talk to?"

"Some detective. A fat guy, all patronizing."

"Probably, Mulveny. Benjamin knows him," he said.

"I'm sorry if he's a friend, but I gave him the details of the attack and he tells me to call him if I see the perpetrator again and gives me his card. I said if I see that man again I might be calling from a hospital or I might not be calling at all. He thinks the guy's just a whack-job, that I shouldn't worry."

A breeze scurried through the live oak leaves above. "There are two possibilities," Finn said. "He *is* a whack-job, and you might have nothing to fear. Or, he's sane, and you need to be concerned." Sarah blew a cloud of smoke skyward and it struck Finn that they were talking about this anonymous man as if he were a blood-thirsty killer poised for more action. "If he's sane," Finn continued, "The only thing I can imagine he wanted was a sample of your DNA. As far as I know mouth swab DNA samples are usually taken for a rape case or paternity suit. Ever donated or sold your eggs?"

Sarah shook her head.

"Maybe someone wants your DNA to identify you, or connect you to something. It can be used to determine ancestry too. Though usually it's court ordered if a lot of money's on the line. Maybe you're really the postman's kid." He felt foolish for saying that. "Sorry, I didn't mean that."

She sipped her coffee, thinking. "No, nothing like that," she said. "Finn," she said, and she spoke about the man and his eyes. Finn watched her lips and the little peak under the indentation above the center of her top lip. Her upper lip had a nearly invisible veneer of blond fuzz, and beside it a tempting little mole. Her words blurred but he remembered that she talked about the man's eyes and said, "soft" and then "bright and hard." Then he realized how he'd describe her attraction. She made him want to watch her for clues as to what made her so watchable. This made him feel better, finding ideas to define (and therefore understand) her.

"Whatever he wants he'll have to do PCR first," Finn said.

"What's PCR?"

"It takes a little DNA and makes a lot. It can also sift through reams of DNA, find a minute portion of interest and copy it." He told her about an acid dropping, surfing, biochemist named Kary Mullis, who, in 1983 exploited natural principles of DNA and developed techniques to perfect a reaction that (along with flight, releasing the power of the atom, and the integrated circuit) vied for most important human discovery, ever. He was the first in the two-billion-year history of life on earth to replicate viable amounts of DNA outside of a living cell.

She looked unimpressed. "What does that have to do with me?"

"With a mouth swab he'd only get a few hundred cells, a few hundred copies of your genome. That's fine for nature but lab work requires millions of copies of a single gene. PCR makes the copies." He wanted to wax impressive on the splendor of PCR, how, if each DNA base-pair were a letter then the human genome would fill 8,700 books and in fifteen seconds PCR could identify any unique sentence within all those metaphoric books, and copy it. In less than an hour it could make more than one trillion copies, *real shit*, not like a computer sifting through a representation of something and making electronic facsimiles, but actual, real fucking DNA. But she was uninterested and so he only said, "Before doing anything he'd have to do PCR."

"You said that already."

"Oh," he said, feeling self-conscious. He took a sip of coffee.

"I haven't mentioned the most important point," Sarah said. "The motorcyclist that hit him said he dropped the swab down the storm drain."

"Did the police find it?"

"They said they would look for it."

"He didn't get what he came for."

"Nope," she said, without a pause.

"He may return."

"Yep," again, almost before he could finish his last word.

"You have a chance to set a trap and catch him."

"I never want to see him again."

"Do you really think he's crazy?"

Sarah hesitated, "No. He seemed purposeful. But I don't know. I try not to think about it."

"It doesn't matter," he said. She raised her eyebrows curious or incredulous, he couldn't tell. "It's like Pascal's Wager. If you fail to respond, you only get a positive result if he's acting at random. If you do act, you have the possibility of a favorable result either way. You just risk wasting time and effort if he chose you at random."

"Oh no, you're analytical."

Finn shrugged. "Old school logic."

Sarah shifted and exhaled audibly. "This is my life. It isn't a game."

"I don't think it's a game," he said, suddenly defensive. "I'm sorry if I came off like that. The only sure way to find out is for the police to catch him. You do want to catch him don't you?"

"I want him away from me. If that means catching him, fine. If I never see him again, that's preferable."

"Do you have any children?"

"No."

"Do you have any reason to believe that someone would want to prove that you were somewhere. A place that you don't want anyone to know you were?"

She thought for a moment. "No."

"Do you have any relatives that might want to exclude you in a will?"

She shook her head.

"Are you friendly with everyone in your family? Were you adopted?"

"Look, I'm not adopted and I don't know of any contested wills. Besides, it seems a little extreme to attack someone to determine lineage, couldn't someone just ask me for a DNA sample?"

"You need to anticipate his return."

"That's why I'm talking to you," she said in a *duh-no-shit,* tone.

"Who do you live with?"

"I've been at my fiancé's since the attack. I'm afraid to be alone in my apartment. I'm avoiding work, friends, afraid of my usual haunts. He knows where I work, where I buy my coffee. I want to do something but I don't know what, and the way it looks, the police won't be helping. All last night I stayed up listening to wood creak."

"Then you need more information." Finn paused. "You have to lure him back."

She shook her head.

"You only need him to *believe* he'll encounter you."

"You mean *we* need him to believe he'll encounter me."

"Sarah," he said, "I don't know how I can help you. I'm broke, and my time is largely spent looking for work." Though he had yet to spend one millisecond looking for gainful employment.

"I didn't ask you for money."

"No, but—"

"I only asked for your help, and I thought that was why we came to meet. My fiancé runs his own jewelry store and knows nothing about biology or crime solving. Anything you do will be more than he can. I'm in a strange situation and feel very vulnerable. But I want you to do the right thing, for yourself. Wait. Let me finish. I thought you could help me. I'm asking. I don't *beg.*" She stood and turned to leave but then turned back. "I see. It's obvious now. Benjamin lied to me. I was expecting...expecting you to act differently."

Typical, he thought. *That bastard!* "What'd he say?"

"I'm sorry. I'm not mad. I'm just disappointed. He said you'd decided to help me."

He watched her float away and sipped his coffee feeling selfish and aggravated.

SIX

Youssef lounged on a love seat in the target's living room. It was Thursday and he'd dozed all afternoon and into the evening. Feeble sunlight barely illuminated the room now. From the hallway outside the apartment, keys jingled. Armed with his pistol, he padded in stocking feet through the kitchen and to the entrance hallway, between the kitchen and living room. He peeked around the edge and watched the front doorknob two meters away.

He was not authorized to use deadly force but thought the likelihood of shooting his gun infinitesimal. If the target were accompanied, even by more than one person, he did not foresee a struggle if he demanded a mouth swab and went on his way. *Who would risk their life to prevent a mouth swab?* He waited until he realized the sound was coming from an adjacent apartment down the hall.

He crept back to the love seat and laid down. He tried to nap some more but the keys had startled him into an unyielding wakefulness. The autobiography of Malcolm X sat on a tiny table in front of the love seat, Malcolm's portrait, deadly serious, staring back at him. Youssef had brought it to read while waiting for the target. When growing up in Tanzania and the West Bank he never imagined that he would have so much in common with an American. Both he and Malcolm were light skinned blacks, both lost fathers to racist murderers, had mothers go insane, and were sent off to live with relatives far away. Both had relationships with God forged through suffering.

In his jeans pocket a cell phone vibrated and he froze. He couldn't be sure which it was, his or the one Ledpaste had given him. He fished both phones from his pocket and was relieved to see it was only his phone vibrating.

"Tariq." It was his friend Terry O'Brien. "Man, I can't wait for tomorrow." He went on about the upcoming soccer match until Youssef interrupted him.

"I won't be coming."

"Come on, dude. You're our best striker."

"José is not that bad."

"Not that good either. We really need you. Why are you whispering?"

"I cannot play. I am sorry." He hung up.

Youssef laid back down and worried the target would not come home again. He tried to read more of Malcolm X's biography but thoughts that he should be reading the Qur'an and not the word of a man pulled him from the story. Eventually he fell back asleep.

He woke on the target's love seat, his legs hanging off. He'd slept fitfully getting up several times to pace until exhausted, but now sunlight illuminated the room. A cell phone vibrated in a pocket. He fished out the phones again but this time it was Ledpaste. He took a deep breath and released it gently before answering.

"1457 Woodlawn Boulevard, number six," Ledpaste said in Pashto. "Forty five minutes."

"1457 Woodlawn Boulevard, number six," Youssef repeated.

Youssef wanted to rise as a gas over the city and reform anew. But first he wanted to pummel the target, that bitch. He'd pledged allegiance to God, to the *jihad* and now he'd failed. If Ledpaste removed him from the project he would become completely disgraced, a pariah, and God could deny him entry to heaven. He paced the room but then knelt and petitioned God for mercy.

He stood from the prayers and dialed Cemile.

"Cemile."

"Honey, did you finish your—"

"If you don't hear from me by tomorrow you must promise me that you will leave the country."

"Leave the country?"

"Promise me that you'll go home if I disappear."

"What are you talking about?"

"Just promise me, okay?"

"I can't believe this. What are you involved in?" She gasped like she was beginning to cry.

"Just promise. I have to go now. Please promise me."

"You can't call me and tell me this without an explanation."

"Just promise me you'll go home!"

"Is this about your mother?"

"It's for your protection."

"My protection? Who would hurt me?"

"I have to go. Cemi, please, just promise."

"I can't just leave."

"I love you more than God himself," he was surprised to hear himself saying. "It will only be a couple of months."

"You're leaving me?"

"No. I mean if I do, I mean disappear, it would only be a couple months."

"You're leaving me for a few months?"

"No, you would have to leave for only a few months." He was sure that by then the bioweapon attack would have commenced and Cemi would be safely in Turkey.

"This is my home now. I don't understand."

Her refusal infuriated him and he didn't know what to do. His meeting with Ledpaste loomed. He told her he loved her and hung up. He'd tried his best, he told himself. He erased the call, and turned his phone off.

The address Ledpaste gave him was of a smart, terracotta-roofed townhouse perched on a manicured lawn, the last in a set of six. Youssef climbed the brick steps, inhaled deeply and rapped on the door. Ledpaste called to him from inside. He entered a small beige room with gleaming hardwood floors. Ledpaste sat at a plain rectangular wooden table facing the front door in the otherwise empty space. To his right was a white man Youssef had never seen and facing the two men on Youssef's side of the table was an empty plastic patio chair. The white man wore a tie and so Youssef assumed he was not a Muslim. Drawn by a breeze from the closing door, a veil of Ledpaste's cigarette smoke passed and stung Youssef's eyes. Both men stared at Youssef. Youssef felt sick to his stomach, as if he were walking into a gangland hit.

"It's as hot as Pad Idan and we don't even have a fan," Ledpaste said in Pashto, while he dabbed at beads of perspiration on a receding hairline.

"It's very hot," Youssef said.

"Do you have air conditioning at your house?" Ledpaste asked.

"Yes," Youssef said, still standing. Vertigo overwhelmed him. He smiled self-consciously, certain both men stared at the veins throbbing on his temples.

"Cigarette?" Ledpaste said, holding out a crumpled pack.

Youssef shook his head.

"The samples," Ledpaste said, a greasy palm suggesting he put them on the table.

Youssef hesitated. "I failed you," he blurted.

Ledpaste's eyes stalled in an ashen stare. His jaws clenched tight and nostrils widened. He motioned to the patio chair.

Youssef sat.

"What happened," Ledpaste said, changing to English, probably so that the man to his right could understand.

"When I tried to swab her she kicked me between the legs and I had to use force."

"But you did swab her."

"I did, but she called for help and several men attacked me."

"The police are involved?"

"I don't, I mean no." Heat rippled up his body, flushing his face and blotting his peripheral vision.

The other man, expressionless, said something in English but with a strong Russian accent. He had a boxer's nose and looked like a fat pink bug. Prominent sweat stains, rims the color of coffee, sat below both armpits. Ledpaste said something to him in another language. Then Ledpaste yanked a pistol from below the table, pointed it at Youssef's forehead. Youssef stalled, breathless. Deftly, Ledpaste spun the pistol and, holding the barrel, placed it on the table in front of Youssef.

"You did sloppy, amateur work at a crucial stage of our attack, and have attracted the authorities. You have shamed yourself before God and are now a vulnerability." He nodded at the gun. "Pick it up."

Tears welled up in Youssef's eyes. The two men appeared distorted like a distant line of hills through coils of heat. Slowly he reached for the gun. *That corpulent fuck! I should kill them both right now. He cruises around with his kuffar driver living in one of the God knows how many condos and townhouses he owns. He doesn't know sacrifice. He worships gold. He's no true Sharia. Forgive me God, most gracious, most merciful.*

Ledpaste leaned into him, grabbed his hand and pushed the barrel into Youssef's temple. "Do it!" he screamed.

The words came to Youssef as if through water. His hand quivered. He twisted his face away from the muzzle. Tears rushed down his cheeks. *If I killed them I would have nowhere to hide.* He applied pressure slowly, steadily to the trigger. He squeezed his eyes tight. *God, few are chosen yet I am one. You showed me the straight path but I failed you. I am a true believer. I fear you. Please show me mercy and throw your wrath upon Ledpaste.* An image of Cemile's face filled his mind's eye, but trailed by a terrifying thought. *I'll never have sex with the woman I love! Please God allow her into heaven.* Her lifetime would be but a moment to him in paradise and then they would make love for eternity. *God, you gave me life and now I come back to you. There is no god but God, and Mohammed is his prophet.*

Then he pulled the trigger. A click. Nothing more.

His eyes widened like an infant's.

Ledpaste smacked him across the temple with an open palm. His head snapped and he crashed to the floor.

Tariq ibn Youssef Al-Momina was born in Dar Es Salaam, Tanzania to a Palestinian father and a Tanzanian mother. When he was sixteen, many years after his father's death, he learned his father had been a member of a short-lived Palestinian Liberation Organization splinter group named Black September. Black September was known above all else for kidnapping and sacrificing eleven Israeli athletes during the 1972 Olympics in Munich, Germany. Israel responded with the vile Operation Wrath of God, assassinating leaders, organizers, creators, and the three remaining soldiers of Black September. The very last man assassinated in that operation was Youssef's father. After his father's death, life became very difficult for his mother and four siblings. Initially his father's two wives supported one another but Youssef's mother increasingly sank into depression, shuffling around a filthy kitchen unable to care even for herself. An aunt took care of his mother while Youssef and a brother were smuggled into the West Bank, Palestine, to live with an uncle. There his father towered above mortals. Aunts, uncles, and cousins recited his habits and sayings, everyone aspired to be so convicted and courageous, or at least meet with such an honorable death. Youssef spent dusty days absorbing the rhetoric of struggle and duty, the obligation to fight for the nation that was barbarically stripped from his grandparents. He yearned to be warrior, and one no less glorified than his father.

His older brother, Mohammed, had dismissed his zealotry. As teenagers, the two of them would sit on their front steps early in the morning watching the neighborhood come to life, greeting their friends and neighbors passing on foot and bicycle, Youssef brushing his teeth and spitting into the smoldering trash heap next to the front steps.

"Look where it got him," Mohammed would say. "He was selfish when he should have thought of the family. Mom tried to raise us all alone and poor, and it made her go mad."

"Don't ever call Dad selfish! War requires sacrifice." Youssef said. "If nobody were willing to fight then the Israelis and Americans would destroy us."

"How do you think we're living now? We're in a big refugee camp. Our Arab brothers won't even give us land to call our own."

"They shouldn't have to. We already have our own land. If they give us land they only aid the Israelis."

"Don't be stupid," Mohammed said. "They don't give us land because they don't want us. Nobody wants us. So we try to fight a war that's unwinnable."

"You're the one who's selfish," Youssef said. "You'll get a degree in Italy, make a lot of money and pretend to forget about the people here. Your people. Exiled, abandoned, futureless."

"It's not our war, Youssef. I'm tired of the bombs. I'm tired of dead friends. I'm tired of everybody crying and yelling, shouting at Jews when there are none around. You know who my enemies are? You want to know? The Muslims who tell me to fight, and die in *Jihad*. The best thing you can do is escape."

"So you want the Palestinians to disperse like stray dogs to the corners of the earth? You're a coward!"

"And you're an idiot! We wouldn't have to live in this shit-hole if Dad had seen the futility of dying for nothing. We'd all be together at home in Tanzania."

At the age of nineteen Youssef joined an exchange program between Al Qaeda and Hamas, one of the thousands of young Palestinians in military schools in Iraq, Pakistan and Afghanistan. At the age of twenty Youssef prepared many months before following a mid-rank Hamas member into a restaurant bathroom. Many considered the man a traitor for discussing limited disarmament with Israel. Youssef slit his throat while he urinated. Later, he showed the man's I.D. to a sergeant he'd trained under and this impressed him and several officers. Youssef received a promotion into an important and highly secretive operation to be executed America. That was twelve years ago

Youssef climbed to his feet.

"Pulling that trigger was the only thing that saved your life," Ledpaste said, stabbing a finger in his face. He was on the same side of the table but Youssef didn't remember him coming around.

Youssef hung his head. *Thank you God.*

"I have saved your life today but it won't happen twice."

Youssef knew that not Ledpaste but God had spared his life, even if through a instrument as crass and disgusting as Ledpaste.

"We planned for failures like you. I will call you as soon as I have information on the contingency target. Now get the fuck out!"

Youssef wobbled out the front door of the townhouse feeling vacant. He passed many minutes this way, uncertain the number of blocks he had walked. *Thank you God, for still having a purpose in me. Thank you for showing me the straight path*. He would fix his error. He would be redeemed.

. . .

What Youssef didn't know, was that he was now alone. Sleeper cells had awoken in seventeen places throughout the United States.

At 1:53 a.m. Tuesday July 30th, in Chicago, Lauren Jerrell, an Egyptian Studies Ph. D. student at Northwestern, sweated, and gyrated to thumping hip-hop beats on the second floor balcony of a crowded dance club. A young Afghani man grabbed her, vigorously kissed her, and then spat into a sterile baggie while vanishing between dancers. Nobody noticed. Lauren never went to the police.

That same day at 3:35 p.m. in Center City Philadelphia, Samantha Peters, a representative in Near East sales with a multinational drug company, joined a young Iraqi male in the elevator after lunch. Before she reached her floor he overpowered her, swabbed the inside of her cheeks and left her startled and alone in the elevator. She phoned security but they only produced fuzzy video footage of him. The Philadelphia police filed a misdemeanor assault report, and promptly forgot it.

On Wednesday, July 31st, a young man approached Romyna Gonzales Aguilar, a movie production assistant, at her West Hollywood cottage. He explained that he was working on a project at UCLA to determine the incidence of a DNA mutation that conferred resistance to H.I.V. and asked her to give a cheek cell sample. She hesitated but when he explained he was Nigerian, how the virus ravaged his people, and that one day her help may lead to a cure or vaccine, she cooperated. They chatted, Romyna excited about the coincidence that she had traveled in Nigeria three years earlier.

By 2:15 p.m. Thursday, August 1st all the sleeper cells but one had collected the cheek cell sample. Only the Austin chapter had failed to deliver its cheek swab.

SEVEN

After Youssef left Ledpaste's condo he wandered past apartments with trimmed lawns, junk strewn bungalows, and eventually, shops and offices. When he climbed aboard the bus to return home he was sure of neither how much time had passed nor what he'd thought of during that time, though certainly his father's and mother's faces had been floating across his mind's eye—and especially Cemi's, and even Mohammed's once or twice. When he shuffled into the bungalow, Jassim looked up from watching television. Youssef went directly into the kitchen and began washing rice. Jassim followed him.

"What do we do now?" Jassim asked.

Youssef filled a saucepan with water and put it on the stove. No sisters, aunts or wives here in the United States to cook for you. He didn't mind though. He found cooking calmed him and allowed him to think.

"What did they say to you?"

"New target." He snapped. He wondered whether he'd been exposed to a biological weapon through the target. For Cemile he feared he was now contagious. However, he doubted that he could be contagious so soon. During training he'd quietly investigated his role. He had spoken to several soldiers who were part of the opposite end of the operation from him: the dosing groups. Their job was to identify a traveling American female and infect her with the agent (a clear, watery liquid in an eye-dropper bottle). They usually worked through a restaurant that catered especially to foreigners. Once they'd identified a recipient they would serve her the food with a smile and a few drops of the agent, and always on a cold dish: a salad, fruit, or in a drink. The dosing groups were scattered from Lagos to Jakarta and every one that Youssef had spoken with described these exact same methods. Others on his end of the operation, the receivers, were at English language schools in England, Australia, and Canada, and were training just as Youssef was. He believed they were practicing for the real attack when they would confirm infection of a biological weapon. While the beef browned he took his noon *salat*. He begged God to protect Cemile. *She is innocent*, he prayed.

He never dreamed of having a love marriage. When he was just a boy, his mother said he would have a love marriage only over her dead body. As a boy he wondered about who he would marry and whether she had been born yet. Then later, at the training camps, he knew he would never live long enough to get married. Cemile caught him off his guard though. Love for her had trounced him like malaria, made him feverish and dizzy. Sometimes he would shake with self-loathing, wishing he would never see her again, fearing the consequences of their relationship. Other times he couldn't be away from her. After three years of inactivity in his sleeper cell he allowed himself the luxury to fantasize about a future and when the hill country wildflowers began blooming last spring he arranged a camping trip to the Lost Pines wilderness. Just before dusk on their first night he asked her to marry him. She jumped up onto him wrapping her legs behind his thighs and they spun tight circles laughing until they became dizzy and crashed into the soft pine straw. She thought he was just another civic design graduate student and, for that moment, so did he.

Cemile must be terrified now. He should call her immediately, but he didn't know what to say. He wondered if he had already endangered her. *I should have sent her away on Monday, right after Ledpaste called me. It's stupid to procrastinate.* The aroma of cooking rice began to mix with the scent of cumin in the beef. Youssef turned on his phone for the first time since meeting Ledpaste in the condo. He had five missed calls from Cemile. He called her.

"Praise be to God! Are you okay?" Her voice sounded like paradise.

"I'm fine. I'm fine."

"What's happening?"

"I'll come by. I'll tell you everything."

"No. You have to tell me now. What's going on?"

"The danger has passed. Don't worry. I'll tell you when I see you. I can't talk about it on the phone."

"I'm coming over right now."

"No! I can't see you right now. Please trust me. I'll come over soon. Bye."

"Wait!"

"Everything is fine now. I love you." He turned off his phone and called to Jassim to come and eat. Youssef piled the rice on one plate and the beef on another. They sat on pillows at a squat wooden table. The phone Ledpaste had given Youssef rang.

"Come back. Now," Ledpaste said, and hung up.

"I need your car," Youssef said to Jassim. "And don't eat until I get back."

As Youssef crossed the thick grass to the stoop of the terra-cotta roofed townhouse Ledpaste opened the door. "Rita Meyer," he said. "10 South 3rd street, apartment number 403." Youssef repeated it and Ledpaste handed him another sterile baggie containing a swab and shut the door.

Back at home Youssef and Jassim sat cross-legged to eat. They rolled little rice balls, dipped them in the beef gravy and pressed chunks of meat into them.

"Did we get a new target?" Jassim asked.

Youssef nodded. He ate quietly and formed a plan to approach the contingency target. His tactic would be utterly direct. He would lure the target to the door of her apartment, grab her, swab her, and be done. No fooling around. No complicated plans or intricate cons. No knives, no fights.

"What's the plan?" Jassim asked.

"You wait here."

Jassim smashed a rice ball onto his plate with a thumb.

In an hour I'll have reclaimed my reputation, Youssef thought, and done God's work. Then I'll protect Cemile. He washed the dishes, stuffed the baggie and swab into a pocket, and took a bus to the target's apartment.

The teal and white building was five stories tall and rectangular, with the apartments facing into a banana plant strewn interior courtyard and a swimming pool. He zigzagged past balconies climbing an open stairway that began in the courtyard. He knocked on apartment number 403. The door popped open, held by a security chain, and a white middle-aged face peered through the breach. "May I help you?"

"Good afternoon. My name is Michael. I've come to speak with Rita."

At the mention of Rita's name the woman's expression took a quick turn. Her brows pointed down at her nose, she gave him a sharp stare, and pursed her lips. She paused, wiped her hands on an apron and unlatched the chain. "Who are you? How do you know Rita?"

He couldn't understand why she suddenly acted suspicious yet had unchained the door. He wondered whether Ledpaste had given him a complete set of information. Then he remembered his psychology trainer's advice in the camp. *Be vague.* He'd drilled it into them when lecturing about interrogation. "A friend of mine recommended I speak with Rita about my upcoming trip. She's been near to the place I want to visit and I hoped she could give me some advice. My friend gave me her number but it must have been wrong. "

The woman's look softened. "Rita passed away."

He stood motionless, slack-jawed. He thought of having to tell Ledpaste that Rita was dead.

"She's my daughter." Rita's mother misunderstood his reaction and with a false kinship of grief patted his shoulder. Moisture laid on the surface of her eyes anxious to form a tear. She suddenly sobbed with a gasp. Youssef leaned in awkwardly and hugged her.

"I'm sorry." He patted her back feeling scared and lost himself. "When did she pass away?"

"December 7th. It was a car accident." She wiped tears with her apron.

"My deepest condolences for your loss Mrs. Meyer." After several moments he said, "I must be going now."

"Won't you come in and have some iced tea?"

"No, I'm sorry. I really must go."

She stood in the doorway dabbing tears. "It wouldn't be but a moment. I didn't expect anyone and you came and asked for Rita and I just couldn't stand to be alone now."

He looked back at her wretched face. "I really must go. I don't have any time." But as he said it he began to think: C*ould this bitch be lying to me*? *Why would she invite me in if she were lying?*

"But you were fixing to speak with Rita?"

"I came to schedule a time to meet when I could speak longer."

She pulled him gently by a shoulder. "I've some refreshing mint tea and its air conditioned inside. I drink it sweet but I have some unsweet if you'd prefer."

They walked down a narrow hallway towards the kitchen. They passed a hall table covered with flowers, and framed family photos, several of a plump, smiling young woman, whom he could only assume was Rita. The kitchen was steamy. Something cooked in a large covered pot on the stove and he smelled bread baking. She took butter from the refrigerator, heavy oatmeal bread slices from the counter, and put it all down in front of him. She offered him bread and began buttering a slice for herself. He regretted agreeing to come inside, but buttered a slice anyway. He could verify Rita's death online back at home.

From the refrigerator she pulled a glass pitcher of dark brown tea with several lemon slices floating in it. "Sweet or unsweet?"

"Sweet."

They ate the bread in silence. After finishing she spoke. "It was just so awful, so sudden. She was gone just like that. I had corn on the cob waiting for her, and she was dead and stupid me, still cooking." She cried more, wiping her tears. "It shouldn't be like that. She should have buried me."

"I lost my father when I was eight," Youssef said.

"My dear son, I'm so sorry."

"He was executed."

"Goodness gracious!" The pot on the stove bounced its lid with steam.

"It happened in Dar El Salaam at his favorite café. I was there. He was playing chess with a friend when two men came up to us. One of them said his name, Ahmed, and when he looked up they both rolled down ski masks and shot him. They shot him twenty or thirty times. I remember one of them screaming over the blasts. Afterwards he said something threatening to me but I couldn't understand it. Then they ran to a car at the corner and that was it. Just like that. He was dead."

The pot lid continued to hiss and rattle. As if shaking off a trance, the woman stood, removed the lid and stirred the pot. "Bless your heart."

Youssef's lower lip trembled and he looked at his watch. "May I see a window?"

"A window?"

"Yes. I'm Muslim. I need to know which direction to pray. The stairs got me turned around."

"Of course. You can pray in my bedroom."

But then standing, Youssef said, "No. I must go." He rebuked himself for coming inside and becoming emotional. He felt entirely inept and impulsive. He would have to explain yet another failure to Ledpaste. He should never have talked about his father. Still, maybe the woman had tricked him. He sniffled, wiped his eyes, and went directly towards the front door. His heart thudded against his ribs. Ledpaste, that fucking pig, may kill him now. He felt dizzy, and realized that he was taking in air in large gasps.

"Michael, please sit back down. You've worked yourself up something awful. You've gone through a horrible tragedy. We both have."

Youssef swiveled, trembling. His eyes were full of tears and he saw her as if looking up from the bottom of the sea. "You, you don't know tragedy! You don't know sacrifice!" He turned and stalked down the cramped hallway. He swept his arm along the table, sending the framed photos and flowers crashing to the floor. He got to the door and fiddled with the chain, the deadbolt, and the handle lock. "How the fuck do you open this thing!" Finally he hurled the door open. He slammed it shut with all his might and it bounced off the jamb with a discordant, metallic ping, swung back open and smacked into the wall. Bounding down the stairs, he emerged beside a patch of banana plants, her sobs echoing softly off the courtyard interior four stories below.

EIGHT

Finn was dreaming a dream of those who somehow, or for some reason, feel doom. He felt it in the loss of his job, in the endless cars, and in the hours before dawn when he'd fret about his future. But, then again, maybe it was these dreams that imparted such a feeling in his waking life and not *vice versa*. In any case, he was dreaming.

He lay face up in a meadow below a sky darkened with squadrons of low-flying, knife-winged bombers. Like immense buzzards the planes' wing tips nearly touched as they passed, merging into black clouds on the horizon. Sunlight danced upon his face between shadows of the bombers but the heat seared him and he shifted side-to-side hopelessly trying to escape it. Sarah stood above and leered down at him, a stiletto heel on his chest. He tried to sit up but couldn't. The drone of the engines was intolerable, mesmerizing, and buried everything. Abruptly, trap doors on the planes fat fuselages swung open and they belched bombs, tens of thousands of them. They tumbled end over nose until the tail fins caught the air and they were slung to the ground at steep angles. Suddenly the planes broke formation, and like bats, swerved erratically in all directions. Then came tight, sharp, arrhythmic impacts followed by deep explosions.

He jumped up with a start and a dull pain drove into his brain through his right eye. "Oh God." Sunlight dappled throughout his bedroom on pale, fuzzy shadows of trees leaning in the breeze. A ceiling fan swirled above him. He untangled his arm from a white bed sheet, and reached for a vibrating phone on the nightstand. It was Sarah. "What time is it?" he asked her. He'd spoken to her last night. *Had he been drunk when he called?* He said he would help her. That, at least, he remembered.

"Listen," she said.

But he couldn't. He felt like he'd been dragged behind a truck. His elbow throbbed when he started to prop himself on it. He saw numerous small cuts on both of his palms and felt mysterious wounds on his back. A woman stirred beneath the sheet next to him and memories from last night came back like a stack of photos chased after a gust of wind. He'd been out with Benjamin just for a beer. One pint turned into another, and another, and they abandoned the pub for a discotheque. He remembered a brawl. He was almost certain the woman next to him was Bridgette. She exuded sex, that was for sure. He hoped he'd used a condom.

"...You see?"

"Yeah."

"Yeah? That's your response?"

"Wait. I mean, what?"

"What time is it?" Bridgette asked, from beneath the sheets.

"What time is it?" Finn asked.

"Eleven," Sarah said.

"Eleven," Finn said.

"Eleven!" Bridgette flung the sheets aside and jumped up.

"Call me back when you can talk," Sarah said. She sounded aggravated.

"Wait! I can talk." He stood up from the bed but then sat back down, struck with nausea.

Bridgette collected her clothes from the floor. "Jesus, I'm an hour late," she said. Then she shut herself in the bathroom.

"What happened?" Finn said to Sarah.

"Not on the phone. It could be tapped. I think I'm nearby. You live downtown right?"

"Yeah."

"What's your address? I'll stop by."

"I could meet you. At Ooh La Latte again."

"Don't worry. I'm not staying."

"If it's tapped I shouldn't give you my address, right?" he said, thinking that she'd gotten a touch extreme.

"Oh yeah."

"How about I give it to you in pig-latin."

"Just meet me at that, well, I don't want to say the name now."

"But I already said it."

She exhaled in frustration.

"Here's my address," he said, and he gave it quickly as if speed would confound a tapper.

He opened the bathroom door. Bridgette was in the shower.

Naked, he went into the kitchen, filled and started an automatic drip coffee maker, and then made toast. He tried to recall a dream but couldn't. Only a sentiment remained, one of being trapped. Then he remembered Sarah's face above him while she stood on his chest. Its obvious meaning was unsurprising. Back in the bedroom, the bathroom door was open. Bridgette sat on the toilet peeing, a towel wrapped around her head. He climbed into the shower.

"Did you miss a breakfast date?" She mocked.

He thrust his head into the cool rushing water. "Can you hand me some aspirin?" He massaged his scalp. The shower curtain slid over. He peeked from under the water and held out his hand. "Three, please."

She tipped the bottle into his hand. He popped the tablets into his mouth and swallowed them using shower water. Bridgette flushed the toilet and went into his room.

"Coffee's brewing," he said, though immediately regretting it. He didn't want Sarah to see Bridgette leaving like this.

"You were fucked up," Bridgette said.

Finn turned off the shower. He ran his hand across the top of his head, squeegeeing the water from his hair. "Towel please!"

She picked her towel up off the dresser and tossed it to him. "I think you smashed that guy's windshield." She ran a brush threw her hair.

He covered his head, toweling it, and couldn't hear what she was saying. The revelation that he'd smashed a windshield frightened him. He remembered dancing with her, kissing her neck, and trying to tease down her blouse. Then later he was struggling with three or four frat boys that had surrounded her on the dance floor while he'd left to buy more drinks. He had yelled for Benjamin. He stopped thinking about it, not wanting to remember. When he pulled off the towel Bridgette was gone. He grabbed a pair of soccer shorts off the floor and hiked them up while praying to God to give him power to never repeat a night like last night and to keep him free of H.I.V. While brushing his teeth he inspected his face. His bloodshot eyes stared accusingly at him. At least he didn't look quite as hideous as he felt.

"Your date's here," Bridgette called out from the living room. The screen door slammed.

"I'll call you later," he said, though he probably wouldn't. He went to the front door, waved to Bridgette, and held the screen door for Sarah. She looked distraught.

"He's been in my apartment," She said, coming inside.

"Would you like a coffee?"

She shook her head. They went into the kitchen and he poured himself a mug.

"He was waiting for me in my apartment."

"How do you know it was him?"

"I don't know it was him, exactly. I just know that someone was in my apartment and he currently tops my list of suspects."

He wanted to roll his eyes but refrained. "Was anything taken?"

"Not that I could tell."

"Yeah, hard to prove a negative." He sipped his coffee and sat down on a stool. "What evidence did he leave behind?

"You don't trust me? Don't you think I would have a sufficiently sound reason to say unequivocally that someone was in my apartment?"

"I'm just trying to understand." He massaged a temple. It was less for comfort and more for communication.

"That man was in my house and we must decide how we'll react. And don't start pouting just because I am not explaining to you the details."

"I'm not pouting, I'm hung-over." He had no stamina for bickering. "Did you tell the police?"

"The cat shit under the bed."

"Excuse me."

"The cat shit under the bed. She never does that, unless a stranger's there, and for a long time. She's extremely timid. I just went by now to pick her up and I'm never going back."

"Did you ask the security man if he saw anybody different coming in alone?"

Sarah's cell phone rang. She answered it and then turned from the phone, "I have to go now. Think about our next move. She gave him a small, but sweet, peck on the cheek and a one-armed hug. A plump tit pressed against his chest. "I'll call you later," she said. She left, her slender legs taking graceful steps like a giraffe.

He went into the living room, stretched out on his couch and closed his eyes. Thankfully, the headache was receding. Yesterday morning Sarah had said she wanted him to do the *right thing*, whatever the hell that was. The right thing. As if it floated in the eternal abyss of the universe, known and understood by some impartial god. And, as if among the infinite possibilities of actions, only one was correct— correct forever. He didn't want to tangle with a violent man. Her beauty, and, more than he could admit, fear that he was actually a coward, had driven him to help her; and he knew it was selfish. However the fear of being a coward didn't bother him as much as not being bothered by his selfishness.

NINE

National Security Council

Al Qaeda, the Taliban, Egyptian Islamic Jihad, and Hamas, among many other militant Islamic terrorist groups, had abandoned electronic communication for organizing attacks. They used the Internet more than ever but rarely for anything beyond propaganda and recruiting. Because of this electronic silence, a capable and brave informant was worth thousands of deciphered emails, translated phone calls, and software engineers, even soldiers. A trustworthy spy with deep connections was worth innumerable lives.

On Friday, August 2nd at 1:07 p.m. Troy Stanley, the National Coordinator for Security and Counterterrorism, received a report created by his highest level Al Qaeda spy. It described a three day terrorist meeting that had ended the previous Sunday in the bucolic mountains of the Taliban controlled Swat Valley province in Pakistan. The spy had been present as part of Al Qaeda forces responsible for defense and security of the meeting. Troy was floored by the groups and individuals cooperating, some ideologically incompatible and without a history of contact. After finishing the report he poured a whiskey, sat down, and immediately called the White House Chief of Staff requesting to speak directly with the President of the United States.

The report began with the trip to the village where the meeting took place. On Thursday July 25th the spy was one of many Al Qaeda fighters packed into open air cattle trucks in a convoy of jeeps, trucks, pickups and dusty sedans. The Al Qaeda fighters were stopped mid-journey and commanders told them to surrender all electronic equipment. After collecting cellphones and portable music players the commanders did something only a few of the Al Qaeda fighters had experienced and only before nearing extremely high ranking men. They were strip searched, which included a rectal examination. The fighters climbed back onto the cattle trucks and rumbled on. After many hours they clanked across a swaying suspension bridge spanning a deep, craggy valley. On the other side, scattered across green undulating hills, and tucked between the valley and looming glaciated mountains was Mandal Dag, a modest village of squat huts and pastures of goats and sheep.

As the Al Qaeda fighters arrived and setup canvas tents, trucks of armed Taliban and Laskhar-e-Taiba guerrillas crossed the bridge. Then came rigs with rocket propelled grenade launchers, and Chinese "Cherry Bombs" (portable heat-seeking surface-to-air missiles for protection against everyones' greatest fear: American drones), sniper rifles, mortar tubes, night-vision goggles, and flak vests. The spy had never seen so much advanced weaponry in a place so far from battlefields or supply lines. The following morning the Taliban exploded the center of the suspension bridge rendering impassable the only road leading out. Half the villagers were forced to cram with their families into relatives' houses, becoming human shields and leaving their huts available for the gathering. The gathering was conducted in a series of two or three hour, small, focused meetings throughout the day, five or six people at a time, and with the evenings open for any unfinished work. Everyone had Kalashnikovs slung across their backs and many had two or more bodyguards. Translators scrambled from hut to hut speaking in Pashto, Arabic, Russian, Persian, English, Spanish, and French.

Although not privy to the meetings the spy listed identified attendees.

Hezekel Gradau: Gray bearded and turbaned with an ever present black kefeyet, the most powerful warlord in southeastern Afghanistan, probably living in Tora Bora.

Sadeed Nuhrani: Warlord in the opium-rich Helmund province in South Eastern Afghanistan. Sixty-five percent of all Afghani opium passed into Pakistan through the Helmund province. Suspected of fighting a proxy war against the United States by shunting hundreds of millions of dollars in opium profits to Al Qaeda, the Taliban, and other militants.

Dahoud Gradau (street names: Ledpaste, Seven): Secular Muslim Indian, now residing in Pakistan. A stout, barrel-chested man with an imposing voice. Liked expensive gold jewelry, cigarettes, and usually wore sunglasses. Born in Mumbai where he built a powerful and feared crime syndicate, the "D-Boys". There he led a lavish life, dated Bollywood stars, hosted parties where famous cricket players, artists, and musicians bragged about their invitations. Had half the Mumbai police force on his payroll. In '93 he was put on India's most wanted list and fled to Karachi where he made connections to Laskar-e-Taiba, a militant Islamic terrorist group. He was fingered as the orchestrator of the Mumbai terrorist attack in 2008 and fled to Dubai. There he built rackets on organized labor before coming under too much pressure and returning to Pakistan. The Pakistan government officially denied his residence in the country.

Ibrahim Ubaydah ibn Basiri: Commander of Egyptian Islamic Jihad.

Saleem Rafiq Nuhrani: German educated Pashtun Afghan with a PhD. in biochemistry from the University of Berlin. Son of Sadeed Nuhrani, opium warlord in the Helmund province.

Nizar Al Hakim: Head of Al Qaeda-Iraq.

These were just the people that the spy could identify but among them were unknown Russians, Indians, Eastern Europeans, Africans in long robes, and neatly shaved Latin Americans. The spy suspected several men of being Russian government bureaucrats. One man was a sub-director in the Colombian guerrilla organization the FARC. Many of the unidentified non-Muslims recognized Muslim militant leaders, shaking their hands, hugging and smiling like old friends.

In the evening on Sunday, July 28th the meeting broke and everyone hiked down a steep and rocky mule path to a meandering river and then back up the other side, reaching the road in the early morning hours. The meeting attendees were whisked away in waiting cars while the security forces unpacked the mules and loaded the missiles, rocket propelled grenades, and other weaponry onto trucks. They slept a few hours and then set up encampments on the other side of the river where they waited three days (without cellphones) for cattle trucks to come and trundle them back down the crenelated roads on which they'd arrived. The spy said it felt more like detention than waiting. The report ended with the spy concluding that this was a mid to late stage organizational meeting about a strike in Europe or the United States. Immediately after arriving in Islamabad the spy had begun writing the report. He stayed up all night writing and sent it immediately after finishing.

The United States President was in Germany when Troy Stanley reached the White House Chief of Staff. The Chief of Staff called back saying the president had agreed to convene the National Security Council in three hours. Troy took the most conservative security strategy and advised against having the President connected even via the secure video links. Only four of the eight NSC members were able to attend with such short notice: the Secretaries of State and Defense, the Director of National Intelligence, and the Chairman of the Joint

Chiefs of Staff.

The Director of National Intelligence agreed to immediately set intelligence gathering on the terrorist summit attendees as her department's overriding priority and would request any international intelligence connected to the terrorist meeting. The Chairman of the Joint Chiefs of Staff would immediately mobilize three special forces platoons into the Swat Valley province, deploy two army regiments to the Afghan border west of Swat Valley, and increase drone surveillance on terrorist training camps in the region. The Secretary of State would meet with the Pakistan president to authorize any drone bombings and the special forces platoons, and to set warrants on all the identified attendees and any suspected attendees, in hopes of catching some that may have not yet left Pakistan. The Secretary of Defense would organize domestic intelligence searching for evidence of terrorist activity. They classified the terrorist meeting as a nine on a scale of ten of terrorism threat but agreed not to tip their hand and kept the terrorism alert level at the current yellow.

TEN

This is what's happened: It's Friday afternoon. Finn's mopping his kitchen's cheap linoleum tiles and trying to alleviate his hangover with more caffeine. The phone rings. It's Sarah. He hesitates answering it thinking how much she frustrates him. Among things he can't express, he thinks she can be pushy and testy, but also graceful, and smart. On the phone she says she has some ideas and he invites her to stop by after work.

He regretted her being witness to the end of his drunken hook-up with Bridgette, but not because it was drunken or a hook-up. Sarah had a fiancé (of who knows how many years) and all Finn could muster was a few hours oiling his dick with his drinking buddy, Bridgette. He did like her, however. She was good-looking, funny, and smart but he didn't think he could ever love her, but he wasn't certain. Apart from a teenage infatuation (what now seemed like a movie clip watched long ago) he'd never been in love. He knew well how lukewarm romances ended. Bridgette's pull on him mirrored a woman's he dated the year before, a Brazilian au pair eight years younger than him. He had mentally tabulated her qualities like an entry in the Merck Index of chemical substances. PHYSICAL DATA: slender but voluptuous, APPEARANCE: brown, syrupy, REACTIVITY: low (highly stable), THERAPEUTIC CATEGORY: purported aphrodisiac at low doses, sedative at high. But, no matter how he wrote it, the entry always ended the same way: Dissolves easily.

A year ago he'd gotten the Brazilian pregnant. Had he been just a couple years younger he would have asked her to have an abortion. Instead, he had begun to fantasize of falling in love and having children. He asked her to keep the baby and she agreed. Three months later he wasn't sure what upset him more: that he had stopped holding out for real love or that she'd lost the baby.

It was dusk when Sarah arrived. He was in his backyard garage, underneath his car, and trying to loosen a bolt securing the alternator. "Over here," he yelled out when he heard gravel crunch beneath her feet. When she came over he shimmied out from underneath the engine. He leaned in and greeted her in an armless hug, holding his grease streaked hands back from her. Her hair hung loosely but a black dress clung to her. Her face seemed to beckon him, drawing him towards her buttery lips. From an old lever-handled ceramic fridge he'd rebuilt he pulled a Hefeweissen beer, gave it to her, and then opened one for himself. While she strolled around the garage looking at the paintings from his disastrous Central American trip, he leaned over the engine with a socket wrench, thinking about how damn alluring she was.

"That's an incredible drawing," she said, inspecting a large pen and ink hanging on the wall. It was a portrait of a woman with a precipitous stone temple towering behind her. "Heads rolled down that."

"What?"

"Tikal. They did ritual sacrifice there."

"Oh yeah," he said, in a flat tone (Impressed she'd identified it but not wanting to let her know.) "That woman's a farmer who lived nearby. Her husband took me on a hike into the surrounding jungle and I stayed a few days at their house." Sarah said something and he imagined a time long ago where a seething sea of people chanted below the temple, an obsidian-knifed priest and his prey, perched above.

"Don't you think?" she asked.

"Huh?"

"That's why she seems intense."

"I suppose," he said. "She told me the Mayans abandoned the city during a war of succession between two brothers." He jammed his arm down into a tiny hole next to the alternator and rubbed his fingers over the metal parts feeling for a hexagonal bolt head. "But some historians claim a disease ravaged the peninsula and emptied the cities."

"The Mayan writing system's been deciphered. It ended suddenly, the writing, that is."

Finn looked up from the motor. "You've been to Tikal," he said, stating and not asking.

"I studied archeology."

"Ahh, an archaeologist."

"Now I'm doing large-scale art preservation."

"You work for a museum?"

"With a non-profit. We're restoring a standing Buddha in Afghanistan. The Taliban shot it up with mortars and tanks back before 9-11."

"You've been to Afghanistan?" Finn asked, feeling envious and hoping that she hadn't. He thought Buddha preferred sitting.

"I was there only a year ago but it feels like a lifetime." She stood with her face inches from his sketch, inspecting it "Oh!" she said, and turned back to him, "You drew it." She looked back to the sketch. "Did you do it at the ruins?"

"First I made small sketches and then later this piece."

"You certainly have talent."

He shrugged. "Thanks. What was it like being in a war zone." He knew he wouldn't tell her how impressed he was, that he wouldn't even have the courage to go to a war.

"It sounds strange, but it was beautiful. Bamiyan, where the standing Buddhas are, or were, carved into a cliff face, is a cozy little village of stone houses in this lush valley. I never saw any fighting there."

Finn wanted to know how dangerous Afghanistan was, what the people were like, how they treated the invading Americans, what their sense of humor was, what sports they played. He wanted to know the cuisine, the landscape, and more, but he felt emasculated that he'd left the country once and only to come skulking back while she'd gone straight into a goddamn war zone.

"Are you into Meso-American art?" She asked.

But her courage aroused him too, and he imagined her screwing him, on top, with her hands clawing into his chest and face, her breasts shaking as she spoke, *fuck me you scared little baby, fuck the woman who's more man than you.* "What? Yeah, when I was twelve I read a book about Paul Gauguin," he said, "And his travels around the pacific and Caribbean and how he painted as he journeyed. I decided that's who I wanted to be, but my parents steered me on the upper-middle-class, status quo path."

"Probably thought you'd become some drug-addled flake."

"Oh, I'm addled all right." He found an alternator bolt head and then blindly tried to slip the socket over it. "I had my nonconstructive rebellion phase."

"Yeah?"

"On my SAT's I just picked random answers. My dad hit the roof."

"How long did that phase last?"

"Last? I'm just hitting my stride, baby." He pushed the socket hard onto the bolt head. "Damn it."

"What'd you do?"

"The socket fell into the engine."

"No, I mean after sabotaging your SATs."

"The day we graduated high school Benjamin and I took a road trip west with our graduation money." He told her about camping out by fields of corn on their way to Alaska, about the night they picked up a pair of alabaster-skinned, Midwestern beauties and laid, crammed on

Benjamin's car hood, the four of them, with dance-hall music drifting from the open windows, sharing dreams, a bottle of whiskey, and a bag of mushrooms. "We made it to Alaska and found jobs in commercial fishing."

"Sounds like an adventure."

"Our freedom only lasted about three weeks." He shined a flashlight down into the engine compartment and looked for the socket. "And the fishing ain't like on television. Newbies work the canneries, some days fourteen, or sixteen hours straight. We gutted, and bled the fish. At the end of my shift every inch of my body ached. I remember being so hungover but not being able to take a break. A couple of times I puked on the floor while I worked, right into the ankle deep blood and guts."

"Gross."

He kneeled down and looked under the engine. "I wanted to quit but Benjamin convinced me not to. I can still remember the feeling the moment I clocked out on the last day of that first season. I had $9,000 bucks in the bank. Eighteen years old: no rent, no bills, no job. It was pretty heady."

"And you blew it all."

He shimmed back under the car. A sudden urge to be alone struck him and he stopped awhile. His breath bounced back to him off the motor case. He worried if he was really that predictable and uncreative. "Would you mind shining the flashlight down while I look for the socket?" She came over and he groped around on the top of the plastic oil pan shield. "How'd you know?" he asked.

"Eighteen years old: no fear, no experience, no sense."

"Even now it still hurts to admit it." He couldn't bring himself to tell her the truth. The socket glinted in the flashlight beam and he snatched it and crawled from under the engine. "Benjamin went home to his girlfriend and I grabbed a sketch pad and schlepped around the backpacker-slacker circuit in Mexico, and Guatemala. I fancied myself a modern day Gauguin but I really just made bad sketches. Mostly it was a blur of drinking, drugs, and sex."

Sarah raised her eyebrows and took a swig. "At least you had the lifestyle down."

Again, he squeezed his arm through the hole. This time he popped the socket onto the bolt head. He grabbed the wrench and attached it to the socket.

"But the sketch of that farmer is wonderful."

"I did it years later, when I first moved to Austin and was trying to become a professional artist."

"This too?" She asked, looking up at his watercolor of an old grizzle-voiced convict, prison bars before him.

"Uh-huh," Finn said.

"Who is he?"

He was part of his project on prisoners, he told her. She said that she liked it, that it had a depth and an ambiguity she couldn't describe but that made her want to stare trying to feel it. Finn thanked her though to him the paintings had long ago blended into the background. Sarah's noticing them had exposed raw feelings of regret for ignoring his talent, for not having had the faith, or courage, to take the adventures it offered.

He left the wrench on the socket and suggested they leave.

But now she was sifting through photos spread across his work bench. *Damn!* He regretted not having put them away before she arrived. She held up a photo. "You were so cute with long hair."

He went to a sink and quickly washed his hands. "My sister said she'd scan my old photos for me so I was culling the good ones.

He went over and began to collect the photos into a pile. She swatted a hand and took photo he was about to pick up. "Oh my God. Is that Benjamin? You two look crazy."

"That was two days before he went to Iraq," Finn said, leaning in for a good view. He remembered Benjamin roaring with exuberant excitement, his entire body quaking. He was different when he came back.

Then Finn saw an exposed photo he didn't want her to see. It was on the other side of her. He hesitated but then reached across her ready to stash it in the middle of the pile he was collecting. He was almost home when she grabbed the corner of it.

"Who are they? They're beautiful." She looked up from the photo.

For a moment they held opposite ends of the photo looking into one another's eyes. Then she tugged it from him and pulled it close, inspecting it. He didn't need to look. He knew every detail of that fucking photo: Pablo, leaning back, arms circumscribing a black, upholstered, curved booth seat, mirrored sunglasses pushed up on his short cropped hair, and staring down at the top of the Spanish girl's large tan tits nestled in a push-up bra and white frilly blouse. "He's the reason I never finished my Gauguin inspired quest." Finn had taken the photo the last night he ever saw Pablo. (That's what he called himself though he was a white American.) The photo seemed to change each time he looked at it (Pablo's swagger seeming to grow). Pablo would have been saying, *Guero!* (his nickname for Finn) *let's have another round, rich boy!* While Finn snapped the photo Pablo must have had the plan to rob him already laid out. "I only spent a thousand of the 9,000 bucks I earned in the canneries. Pablo spent the rest." *It still hurts, even now, to say it.* Finn thought Pablo and that Spanish chick probably spent the rest of the summer living it up, fucking and drinking, laughing, eating, traveling, and all on his tab.

"I'm sorry," she said.

Finn piled the photos together and dropped them in the shoe box with the others. "It's all right." He put the box in the back seat of his car so he'd remember to mail his selection to his sister.

They went to the porch and listened to the radio from weathered wicker chairs. Sarah struck a match and a lazy August breeze tugged at the flame. The sulphur flare cast shadows of her lashes across her forehead like little horns. But what he really liked was how the flare fattened the crisp curve in her upper lip drawing on the cigarette. Even her little lip-mole cast it's own shadow.

"Wireless surveillance cameras," she said. "Would you install some in my apartment?"

Finn sipped his beer. "I guess."

"Can you do it right away?"

"I think I can do it in the morning. Excuse me," he said, and went into the living room and played reggae through the stereo. He returned and listened to the heavy bass meshed so well with the darkness and humidity. "How are you? Are you able to sleep?"

"You'll put the cameras in tomorrow morning?"

"Yeah, yeah, I'll do it."

She nodded, and took a deep pull on the cigarette. "I feel like a nervous child. I'm constantly afraid he's lurking nearby, and more afraid at night. She paused and walked to the edge of the porch. "I thought I had never seen him before in my life, before the attack. But later I realized I first saw him a couple days earlier at the café I go to before work. He was there again the next morning, *and* the day he attacked me. He'd been following me three days, Finn. Being stalked is scary enough, but then to be attacked... And today I find out he's been in my apartment. Look, I know we've argued, but I feel comfortable with you, like you won't judge me. I can be honest with you."

"I can't even figure out my own life." He took a swallow of beer.

"I've had some asshole boyfriends. Let me tell you. But even when they were being aggressive, I knew them. But this man. I have no idea of his motives or limitations. He can fight and he didn't hesitate to level me, *or* you."

Thanks. "You've known a lot of violent guys?"

"I've been threatened, man-handled, beaten, stalked, chased, raped, and drugged. But I'm no saint either."

"Jesus. Being attacked by any guy would be upsetting."

"Not really."

"Really?"

"A couple months ago Reece, my fiancé, he and I had an argument and I went out alone. I was broke and just wanted someone to buy me drinks and listen to me complain. I went to a neighborhood bar and some preppie guy bought me a martini. We had polite conversation but nothing more. After a while, I left the bar and headed back to my apartment on foot. A few minutes later Martini Guy pulls up next to me in a Mercedes. He offers me a ride and I say no. He became very persistent and I finally gave in."

"You just got into a car with a complete stranger?"

"People stop being strangers once you meet them."

He watched her as she talked, her posture, her emphasis on certain syllables, her cadence, the way she dragged on her cigarette, her sips of beer, and realized that they combined to mesmerize him.

"When I get into the car he immediately starts to patronize me. *Why didn't you call a taxi?* He says. I told him I didn't have any money. He questioned whether I really liked my fiancé. Then he pulls away his shirt and has his dick hanging out. It was stiffening. He begged me to jerk him off and I refused. Then he grabbed my hand and we fought over it but I managed to pull it back."

"Oh my God."

"He offered money, and when I said no he slammed on his brakes and kicked me out of the car."

She took a long drag on her cigarette and he found himself getting a hard-on from the description of the man's uncontrollable desire. Men are so simple, he thought. "And that was it?"

"I refused to get out of the car."

"That's crazy."

"He thought I was a poor pitiful girl that he could exploit. He offered me a ride and I was determined to make him honor it. We argued and shouted. He was ashamed, and aroused, and getting more emotional and I saw he might have been angry enough to hurt me. So eventually I got out."

"That was gutsy."

"Not really. I was never frightened. Nervous, definitely, but I'm not naive. I knew there could've been problems when I climbed into his car.

But other problems could have happened simply by continuing to walk alone that late, and I'm not the type to hole up and avoid life because there may be danger. I've lived in a war zone for God's sake. He was just a lonely horny boy who didn't have the charm or patience to get a girl." She paused and he thought she was going to add a comment about crude and frustrated men, or men in general. But she jerked up, stood, and walked to the edge of the porch and back, "But, Finn, this man pursuing me, he's," she dragged on the cigarette and blew smoke out in tight stream. "He's, he's... I don't know. He's different."

ELEVEN

Saturday morning Youssef woke, said his prayers, and squatted down at the kitchen table with a cup of dry tea leaves while waiting for water to boil. By the age of sixteen desire to join the global *jihad* had plunged a tap root deep into him, and by nineteen he'd given his *Bayat*, his sacred oath of loyalty to the *jihad*, to Imam Ibrahim Al-Madri at his Pakistani *Madrassa*. He and four others had given their *Bayats* that day. The Imam stood before them reading aloud from the Qur'an about their duty to God and to all believers, that all killed in God's name were alive at his side. Youssef felt the presence of his father and was certain he would be proud of Youssef's accomplishment. *I will redeem your death*, he prayed. *I love you, Dad.* Then he thought of Ali, and other friends that had died in the fighting in the West Bank, and prayed to their ghosts and families. He thought of the Jews and Americans who killed women, the elderly, and children, and vowed their death. The Imam placed his hand on him and blessed him.

Yesterday, a block from the contingency target's apartment building, Youssef threw himself down on a bus-stop bench and tried to formulate a plan of action despite his mind seething from his failures. He decided he would send Cemile home: safe from him were he (or were he to become) contagious, and safe from the attack. Only then would he go back to the original target's apartment. He would get the swab this time. He wouldn't tell Ledpaste the second target was dead.

At home he searched the Internet for a flight from Austin to Ankara, Turkey. He called a local travel agency and booked the flight through them. Using a credit card he made a cash withdrawal at his bank, went to the travel agency and bought the ticket with the cash. The flight was due to leave in five hours, today, Saturday, at 1:00 p.m.

The kettle whistled. Youssef got up and poured steaming water over his tea leaves.

Jassim came into the kitchen rubbing his eyes.

"I need your car keys," Youssef said.

"Did you get the sample yesterday?"

Youssef shook his head. "We have more work to do."

Fifteen minutes later he was parking at Cemile's apartment, four blocks off Guadalupe, across from the University. It was a two story rectangular complex with a pool in the middle and sixteen apartments surrounding it. He rapped on the door and Cemile's roommate answered. She was brushing her hair and yapping on a cell phone. "Cemile's in class," she shouted over music and scurried back to a bathroom, out of view. Cemile's roommate was an attractive white, Christian, girl from Atlanta, Georgia. She seemed to always be talking on the phone, or texting. He sat down on the couch. She crossed a hallway to her bedroom and came out a few moments later, a backpack slung over a shoulder. "Don't forget to lock the door if you leave," she said, lifting the phone from her ear.

He tried to focus on how he would approach the first target again. It would be considerably more difficult this time. His thoughts jerked, unbidden, to Cemile. Thinking of her gone away made him pace the living room, feeling queasy. *Focus.* He had to completely surprise the target and in a private place this time. He yearned to suck on Cemile's fat lips, strip her down, lay underneath her and stare at her breasts. He imagined her nipples were the color of dark chocolate, though he couldn't be sure. He used to fantasize about his wedding day, for the first time he'd be inside of her. But now he knew he'd have to wait until heaven. He imagined her outlined in brilliant white light, her coal black hair falling over his face and chest. He kneeled down and pressed his head to the floor. *God, from which all life and all things begin, let your will be my wish. I am your humble servant.* He continued praying for himself and Cemile and then climbed onto the sofa laid down and slipped into a doze. The rattle of keys in the front door snapped him from sleep. He sat up as she entered.

She ran over and threw her arms around him. She felt cool and smooth, like polished glass.

"I have a surprise for you," he said.

"You're not going to tell me what happened?"

"let me give you your surprise first. "

"First, tell me what happened."

"I want to take you on a trip for a couple of days."

She crossed her arms, leaned back and surveyed him. "Why are you avoiding telling me what that phone call was all about?"

"I borrowed money from some guys I shouldn't have. They may have known about you. I *had* to be cautious."

She sat shaking her head at him. "I can't believe it."

"Jassim helped me get a bank loan and I've paid them. It's over now. I know I never should have done it. I believe God will forgive me. I hope you will forgive me, too."

"You made it sound like these men could have killed you."

"They were very angry. They could have kidnapped me until someone paid. They might have come looking for you."

"You paid it."

"Yes."

"No one will come looking for me?"

"I paid it all."

"With more money you borrowed."

"From a bank. It's interest free for nine months. I will have paid it back by then. Listen, I've arranged for us to go on vacation to Corpus Christi."

"Are you gambling?"

"I was borrowing money for my mother's medication and treatments."

She hugged him, "Why didn't you just say that?"

"I never should have borrowed from these men. But I didn't have time and—"

"I could have helped."

"Look, I lied the other day when I said my study partner re-dialed you trying to be funny. The man I owed money came with a thug and they threatened me and anyone close to me if I didn't pay. Then you called and he took my phone from me. I avoided you. I was worried they would follow me."

She shook her head looking at him doe-eyed. "All this scares me. Are you sure you paid them everything?"

"Yes. Let's forget all this and take a trip to the beach."

"Classes just started."

"The first few days don't matter. You can skip." He eyed her from her softly curving legs to her dainty neck and a fear shot through him, that he would fail and God would bar him admittance to heaven. Then he would never make love to Cemile.

"Why are you looking at me like that?"

"I already rented a condo right on the beach." He pulled her close to him. Really they were as good as married. They had a verbal *nikah*, nothing was signed that's all. "I thought you would be excited after all this." He kissed up her arm to her neck.

She pushed against him. "Yousi."

He pulled on her blouse.

"Stop it! It's *haram*."

He fell onto her and she sunk into the couch. He pulled up her blouse and kissed her stomach and then up toward her breasts and the dark chocolate nipples.

She wiggled out from under him and stood over him.

"It's not forbidden. We have a verbal *nikah*," he said looking up from the couch.

She groaned. "It's just a few more months then we can make love all day. God will bless it then."

"You don't understand," he said.

"Of course I do."

He jumped up. "Everything's so tidy for you. You want to be with me and so we're getting married."

She looked confused. "Yes. I love you."

He held the back of her head and kissed around her neck and along toward a shoulder.

She pushed him back and tried to search his eyes while he craned for another kiss. "Don't you love me?" she asked.

He groped her hips and ass. "Cemi, I'm completely in love with you. That's not it! It's that sometimes there's more than one rope pulling you."

"What are you talking about?"

He kissed her lips and she pecked him back. She was softening. "Come on baby, we're as good as married."

"What do mean about the ropes?"

He pressed his hard-on against her belly but then maneuvered around and behind her.

"Stop. That hurts."

He thrust her face-first against the wall, desperately mouthing her neck and shoulders. She struggled and he humped her ass through his jeans while clawing at her belt and pants. She kept saying something, but he pushed her harder against the wall. Finally he thrust her pants down and then undid his own. They fell to his ankles. Digging his hands into her ribcage, he hoisted her up and then down onto his cock. Her pussy was dry, but he pushed and soon squeezed into her. He fucked her pumping urgently. Her head thumped on the sheet rock wall and her tight little olive-skinned ass rubbed against this stomach. Soon he rose into a heavy euphoria, and all his senses melded. "I love you," he chanted. "I love you." He loved God, and her, and himself. He came and came and pumped and came and then put her down and then stood back swaying, drunk from the orgasm.

Her eyes were red and she hit him on the shoulders and face with her tiny bunched hands. "What's wrong with you!"

He collapsed onto the couch.

She began to weep.

Fast food franchises zipped by as Youssef drove down Ben White Boulevard, Cemile in the passenger seat. He yearned to move, to get Cemile safe, to get the swab, not sit in that damned car. "We'll find an Imam and get married. First thing. I promise." Cemile stared ahead mutely, refusing to look at him. He took an exit for the airport.

"You promised to take me home."

"Please. It's a surprise." At the airport taxis, buses, and pedestrians moved along the departure terminals to their right while they motored along in the left lane. Youssef scanned the airline names.

"I'm not going anywhere with you," she said.

He pulled to the curb. He couldn't look at her. "Cemile, this is it. You must go. I bought you a ticket to Ankara. It's dangerous for you here, very dangerous."

Her face contorted. "Stop it. Take me home."

He made himself look into her eyes, brown-black and nestled behind delicate lashes. "Everything will pass in a couple months and you can come back. Make it easy on us and do this quickly, please."

"Easy on us? What are you doing? Whores? Drugs? I don't even know you."

"Every moment you're here you're in more danger. Trust me. Trust my love for you that I wouldn't do this unless there was no option."

"What do you know about love!"

He held out her ticket. "Take it."

"No!"

"Do you want to die!"

There was a sharp rap on the glass. A large bald white man in a dark blue security uniform leaned in towards Youssef and spoke through the half open window. "The passenger must disembark or you must leave."

"It will be just a moment."

"It's not a parking lot. Move it or lose it." He grabbed a radio on a belt clip and popped his eyebrows up looking for Youssef's response.

"We're unloading now, sir." Youssef opened the door, stepped out and walked around the back of the car. He felt the guard's gaze. He smiled at the guard, opened Cemile's door, leaned in and whispered. "There are things I cannot discuss with you. You are in danger with me here, now. I'm sorry, but everything will be all right if you do as I say. It's just a couple of months for your life. You were not meant to die here." He gently pulled on her arm and managed to get her standing.

The guard strode away. Youssef tried to hug her but she glared at him through raw eyes and let her arms dangle at her sides. He kicked the door shut with his foot.

"You fucking rapist, lying piece of shit! You're taking me home. We're through." She turned and opened the door.

Then he seized her by the throat, dug his fingers in the sinewy muscles running up and down it, and spun her facing him. Her eyes were aghast. She tugged on his wrist and made a wet gurgling sound. "You will die if you stay. I'm doing this because I love you," he spat, through clenched teeth. He jerked her away from the car and threw her towards the terminal. She stumbled back wary of him as if he were a rabid dog. In his periphery he saw the bald guard walking back towards him.

TWELVE

Late Saturday morning, Finn installed cameras in Sarah's tidy one bedroom apartment. Each small oval unit, both camera and microphone, was the size of a pecan. It sent a wireless signal to Sarah's home computer, allowing for constant surveillance. He hid them in the bedroom, kitchen, and living room. Then he walked through the apartment imagining himself the intruder to see if he would spot any cameras. He tried a couple times before realizing he could not be objective. At least he thought they were well hidden. He worked fast hoping not to run into the man chasing Sarah; in his back pocket he carried a telescoping police baton Benjamin had given him, just in case. Before leaving he stopped at Sarah's dresser and lifted a framed photo of her and a friend, in bikinis on a Caribbean beach. Sarah's tits were barely contained by a red crochet top. Was that a aureole? God its so big! He held the frame to his nose trying to see through the loose weave, but still wasn't sure if he could see it. He paged through several books on a shelf in the living room and then found a diary. Thinking better of snooping, he snapped it shut, but then reopened it and began reading. At first he skimmed the words hoping to find a tidbit before guilt reined him in, but then he slowed. She was in Afghanistan and wrote of the cold, the poverty, the friendliness of the people, the fear of the Taliban. But, she was very excited to be there. He felt pangs of regret, and envy that he'd not had the courage to forge a life of his own like she had. She seemed intelligent and supremely willful. Once, he had begun forging a life from his aspirations but it sank before it could sail. It's too late now, anyway, he thought (at thirty-three I ought to be thinking of a family and settling down, not going off on adventures). He called Sarah.

"Everything's installed," he said, while sprawled on the bed and still reading her diary. She wrote of her troubles with Reece, her uncertainties over their compatibility. She mentioned another man, Jean-Luc, and her growing feelings for him. He was working in Afghanistan with a French non-governmental organization. They'd had a fling that became more.

"Thank you so much," she said. "You don't know how good this makes me feel."

"It was easy."

"It's not that," she said sounding frustrated. "I could have done it myself. It's that someone's helping me."

She wrote that she thought she was falling in love with Jean-Luc and didn't know how to reconcile her feelings between him—though she was certain it was just a tryst—and Reece.

"We're in this *together*."

Tucked between the pages was a photo of her and Jean-Luc hugging on a hilltop, chiseled and barren mountain peaks framed them. They were laughing and a strong wind blew their hair and Sarah's scarf.

"Listen, I'm meeting a friend at Gueros. You're welcome to meet us tonight around nine."

Jean-Luc had signed the photo on the back, *Sarah, mon petit lapin.* It sounded cute, whatever it meant: my little something. "Is your fiancé going," he asked.

"Why? You scared of him?" She laughed. "Later gator." She hung-up.

The photo filled him with its sharp chilled air and the feeling of being halfway around the world in a strange warring land with nothing to lose. He closed the book like someone who's trying to quit smoking stubs out a 3/4ths cigarette. Then he left.

All day he felt anxious and eager to meet Sarah at Gueros. *Gueros* meant Blondie in Mexican slang, what Pablo had called him. Pablo, the American party boy, the one he'd met in Mexico City fifteen years ago on his Alaskan-fishing funded and Gauguin-inspired trip to build his art portfolio. He'd hung around Finn like a gnat and Finn knew he was trouble but they had a good time chasing women and drinking and Finn thought he was keeping his distance.

The day everything fell apart Finn woke at one o'clock in the afternoon overcome with nausea. He remembered being painted in a sheen of sweat. He jumped up and fumbled with the door before realizing that in his drunkenness he hadn't even bothered to lock it. He lurched through searing pools of sunlight and vomited on a floating turd in the communal toilet. Back in his room he collapsed on the bed. He couldn't recollect anything past the ninth beer. He decided breakfast would help and went to Pablo's room and knocked on the door, but he didn't answer.

At three o'clock he stood outside a bank at an automatic teller. "What the hell!" he said aloud. The automatic teller told him he had insufficient funds for his withdrawal. He had $7,800 the last time he'd withdrawn money, two days earlier. He punched some buttons accessing his most recent withdrawals. He scared the people in line behind him by screaming when the computer screen displayed a $7,700 withdrawal at 9:30 that morning at that *very* bank. He flew inside, past a line snaking from the tellers to the entrance. He couldn't understand it. His debit card and passport, both required for such a withdrawal, were exactly where he always kept them. He shouted at a teller in pidgin Spanish, "I am rob! I am rob here this morning!" A security guard raced over to control him. "You rob me. You fucking rob me here, here." A woman, a bank manager, escorted him down a hallway to an office. Fifteen minutes later she handed him a photocopy of his passport, debit card, withdrawal slip, and a grainy still from a video of him making the withdrawal. He was wearing a floppy hat and sunglasses. "You're wearing the same shirt, sir." she said, looking smug.

Pablo. He'd even gotten lucky with the fucking shirt. Or maybe it wasn't luck. Finn only had three shirts and Pablo knew his favorite. Finn called his parents. They bought him an airline ticket and the next afternoon he skulked back to their house in Philadelphia, where the cold gray skies and Yankee stares reminded him of his failure every waking moment. It wasn't long before he succumbed to his parents urgings, and enrolled at Virginia Tech studying biology. After college he followed Benjamin to Austin with the idea of re-kindling his dream of being an artist. He collaborated in a series of watercolors of prisoners, where below each portrait was a paragraph written after an interview with the prisoner. The show was well received and he began thinking about his next project. Slowly, though, life and work encroached, and now, he hadn't painted in over five years.

At 9:30 that evening he walked to Gueros. The kitchen was open and surrounded by a bar in the center of an expansive hall lined with booths and tables, all packed. From speakers a man wailed out a Ranchero just below the clamor of conversation, laughing, and clanging pots. Covering the walls were colossal sepia-tone photos of banditos (probably old stock of Pancho Villa's gang) with shaggy moustached frowns, wide sombreros, and chests crisscrossed with bandoleers. They posed, solemn, before overturned and bombed rail cars.

His sweeping glance snagged on a sultry brunette. She sat with her back to him on a bar stool and wore tight blue jeans. He loved the way they hugged her ass. It was full, and stuck out in just the right places. And from behind he could see the sides of her tits too. *Oh my God, I would so fuck that.* Just then he realized it was Sarah.

He walked over and Sarah introduced him to her friend, Eli. The women drank dark Mexican beer and their teeth showed when they laughed. He ordered a gin and tonic from the bartender and pulled up a stool. He watched Sarah's adorable crooked teeth and the mole below her nose. The women chatted, and a sense of freedom floated around them and their conversation like a haze and he wondered if it was really there and if they felt it too. He would ask them, he thought. 'Cause if they feel it, it must exist. But then he dismissed the question as absurd. He let them talk, thinking of how he wanted to know more about Sarah. *If only she wasn't engaged.* Eli stood and left for the bathroom and brought him out of his thoughts. "All the video files connect to the Internet through your computer," he told Sarah. "And rout to mine where they're stored. That way they can't be stolen if someone finds the cameras."

"How will you scan all the footage?"

"Any noise or motion activates them. Oh, and I also put your television, a couple of lamps, and the stereo on timers to make your place seem occupied, in case he's watching."

"Thank you so much," she said. "It's so creepy to think he's watching."

"As soon as possible we need to go to building security and tell them you're hiding from a man stalking you, and that you want him to believe you're still living there. Where's Regis?"

"It's Reece, and he's busy. He's moving his jewelry store and has a lot of work to do."

"If I were him I wouldn't let you go out alone."

"I never come here and besides the guy couldn't sneak up on me now since I know what he looks like."

"No, I mean I wouldn't let you out alone looking as good as you do now."

She shook her head and told him to stop it. She wasn't laughing.

"How'd you end up working in Afghanistan?" he asked.

"I've always loved art and architecture. After my undergraduate in archeology I got a masters in art restoration. I was looking for something exciting and with travel and I found this project in Afghanistan."

He suspected she had an upbringing that fostered her creative development and had been expected to go into art. "Are your parents artists?"

"No. My dad's in business and my mother's a dabbler."

Maybe her parents had not expected her to study art but her dad was probably a wealthy investment banker and covered all her costs. He bet she could have studied Inuit tusk carvings and her dad would have bankrolled it. "I would have liked to study fine arts but I was afraid of taking on so much in student loans," he said.

"Ohh," she sighed. "Don't get me started on student loans." She took a sip of beer. "How'd you become a scientist?"

"When I was eighteen I was pressured into making a choice. Funny how the decisions of youth stick with us, huh? Aren't your parents afraid of you going into a war zone?"

She smiled. "They know better than to try and sway my decisions about life. They knew it was exactly what I wanted and any criticism would have been transparent as nothing more than fear. And my mother always said *the opposite of love is not hate, it's fear*."

He nodded contemplating her mother's wisdom.

"Now," she said. "It's moot. Long ago I accepted the risks and committed to the job."

"Aren't *you* scared to go into a war zone?" There, he'd asked it.

"Sure, but there's no true safety net in life."

Eli sat back down. "The toilet is so disgusting," she said, wrinkling her nose.

Finn had hoped he would find something in Sarah's story that was absent in his, that would justify his own lack of adventure. But he'd only found a begrudging respect for her decisions and actions, and one that highlighted a weary dissatisfaction of his own.

They ordered another round of beers, told stories, and laughed. Later he suggested they go across the street and listen to a live band. While the women gathered their things he began strolling to the Guero's entrance. The restaurant was packed, not an empty table. As he worked his way to the front door he had a powerful but fleeting feeling that everybody and everything had halted while he continued walking. As if it had occurred during a blink. It reminded him of something but he could not recall it and that annoyed him. But the essence of the feeling lingered and he imagined himself walking through the restaurant, everything silent and everyone frozen in time except him.

The three of them crossed the street to The Electric Company, a deep and narrow bar. At the back a frantic three-piece churned out scalding riffs over a thunderous back beat. "I keep tripping over the same stone!" the bassist wailed. Beer and crushed cans flew at the musicians. Occasionally someone rose up, crowd surfing. Finn, Sarah, and Eli sat on bar stools above a floor strewn with plastic cups, and beer cans, and had to yell into each other's ears to be heard.

When he leaned in close to Sarah he didn't smell perfume, he smelled a subtle acidic but pleasant fragrance of sweat and skin, but not entirely. There was something there that was hers only. He was grateful Reece was busy. When she stood and went to the bathroom he followed her. The hallway to the bathroom began at the back of the bar and curled around, behind the stage. He went to the men's restroom finding himself wanting badly to kiss her. He hurried in the restroom, left, and leaned against a wall watching the band along the side of the stage. The guitarist grimaced and poured sweat, working himself into a frenzy with a brawny, sinister solo. Finn moved back when he saw the bass player pick up a sledge hammer single-handed. He played a simple bass line with his left hand and began slamming the sledge hammer against a flattened metal trash can along with the beat. The thick crowd shook and cheered. Then the guitar solo de-crescendoed and the guitarist motioned the crowd back. Finn craned to see.

Sarah left the bathroom and he grabbed her hand and forged a path through the crowd. Once it began to thin he turned and whispered in her ear. "Kiss me." Her soft, smooth, cheek caressed his face. He leaned back and looked into her eyes. She stared at him and he tried but failed to see the meaning behind it. He leaned towards her but she turned her head. "Please, just one."

She shook her head.

The rejection didn't surprise him. He shouldn't have tried. She's engaged for God's sake and he was quite buzzed. Just then, with a soft thud, the bar ignited in a hot amber light. He jumped and saw a fireball rising from the stage in front of the guitarist. The band chugged in a locomotive rhythm and the guitarist stomped on something sending up another fireball. The crowd seemed ready to tear the walls down. When they rejoined Eli, Sarah leaned in and said something to her. The heat from the fireball reached them. Sarah leaned towards Finn and asked him to go outside with her. Maybe she did want to kiss him...that's it, she just didn't want Eli to see.

Outside she turned to him. "I can't believe it. You're supposed to be protecting me from a mysterious attacker, and you know I'm engaged, and you pull this shit. I should stop everything right now."

"Okay, okay, I shouldn't have done it," he said, and then tried to apologize but the words got tangled up.

"Forget ungentlemanly," she said. "It was disrespectful and could undermine my relationship with Reece, and our working relationship."

"But the beauty and your charm and beguiling."

Sarah laughed. "Oh no, Mr. Man. You will take responsibility for your actions. Drunk or not. I have to think about whether we can continue working together."

"I swear I can be trusted. I won't make any advances. I promise." He clasped his hands together. She narrowed her eyes at him and shook her head. Then she pushed past him and back into the bar.

They ordered another round of beers, and the band quit. Sarah spoke to Eli about a road trip through Northern Mexico, about wide canyons, ferries, and Indians who ran for days kicking a little ball. Perhaps it was the alcohol but everything seemed to swirl about his mind: gleaming and laughing teeth, his former bench in the lab, the martini man wrestling Sarah to jack his enormous cock, the Brazilian ex-girlfriend's dead baby, his empty bank account, his looming mortgage, the attractiveness of Sarah's face. Someone turned on an amplifier and a jarring electronic blast pierced through ambient-folk background music. It drove him outside.

He stared at the phallic neon sign in front of a motel down the street and a sense of urgency rushed into him as if, he thought, quoting Morrison, *With the sudden fury of a divine messenger.*

"Let's go," Sarah said slapping him on the back. He walked the women to their cars and then strolled home alone under clear skies, his feeling of urgency melting away under the cricket's and cicada's drone, and his flip-flop's metronome slap.

...

On Sunday evening the sun shone in at a low angle over a rickety spare bed and across the hardwood floors to Finn's bare feet. An oscillating fan blew on him. Before him a computer sat on a broad desk he'd fashioned from an old mill house door. All weekend he'd intermittently checked the cameras for activity. Because the television and stereo came on with timers he found two audio-triggered files with a duration of one hour and ten minutes each Saturday afternoon.

Expecting to see only the two timer-triggered files, he now checked again; but instead found more than thirty. He drew in a sharp breath. He leaned into the monitor and opened footage of the first saved file. A tall, thin, young, black male hurried past the camera in the kitchen. He still couldn't tell if it was the man who'd attacked him and Sarah. After four minutes without movement the man reentered. It was him! Finn had a detailed image of him rummaging in the refrigerator. He removed a milk carton, sniffed and then sipped it. Finn dialed Sarah.

"We've got him!"

"On camera?"

"I'm watching video of him going through your refrigerator, right now."

"Right now?"

"The video's three hours old. I'm watching it for the first time now."

"Do you have a good face shot?"

"We've got enough to pin him with breaking and entering and with your testimony we'll get assault too."

She said she was on her way and hung up.

Files from all three cameras, capturing the intruder passing from room to room, showed that he had waited in the apartment for more than five hours. Finn's excitement waned sharply after scanning more than twenty files of empty frames initiated by a cough, sniffle, or shuffle. Cameras activated by sound or motion looked like a good idea on paper but produced hours of empty video.

He opened a video file from the bedroom. For two minutes the man paced, speaking on his cell phone. The cords of his jaw muscles twitched, and his nostrils flared, yet his voice (In Arabic probably) conveyed none of the fury. He threw the cell phone onto Sarah's bed and continued pacing several minutes before stopping at the dresser and inspecting several photos of Sarah. He grabbed a framed photo. It was the one of Sarah and Eli in string bikinis on a Caribbean beach. He unzipped his pants, fixated on the photo and began to masturbate. He leaned back furiously pumping his cock erect and holding the photo up to his face. Finn stared, his own temper flaring. After a few minutes the man moved the photo down, held it in front of his cock, and splattered it with cum, moaning, and thrashing his head. Finn leaned back in a squeaking swivel chair. That fucking bastard!

Then, with a growl, the man slammed the photo down on Sarah's dresser. The frame's glass exploded and Finn jumped back. The man left the room and Finn fast-forwarded. Several minutes later he reentered the video. With his back to the camera he searched over a nightstand across the room. Then he moved to a short bookshelf. He swept off trinkets and threw a few books down. He was obviously searching for something. He turned around and scanned the room while facing the camera. Abruptly he stopped and marched directly towards the screen and reached for it. The video image skewed. It pointed vertically showing nothing but Sarah's popcorn ceiling. Seconds later the image whirled and then Finn jerked back again when the man's face loomed on the monitor. The man peered down, eyebrows taught. Initially it gave Finn the impression they were scrutinizing one another, but then it struck him that the man was looking directly into him (could he see his soul?). The man clenched his jaw, screwed up his lips and screamed something at the camera.

The image bounced around and finally rested, showing the ceiling fan cutting lazy circles. In the background the television played. The timers must have made him suspect cameras, Finn thought. He realized he should review the two files started by the television and stereo—the only ones he'd skipped. After several minutes the man returned, and an eerie serenity constructed his expression. "Sarah," he said like buttermilk, "you can accept your role or fight it. If you cooperate you will never again be bothered by me. If you choose to fight, and contact the police, sacrifices will be made." Then he dropped the camera again. The file was enormous. Finn fast-forwarded until he realized the sweeping fan was activating the sensor. He was reviewing the footage a second time when he jumped in his seat from a knock at the front door. It was Sarah.

"Some new footage has come up," Finn said.

"What is it?"

"It's not pretty."

Sarah's expression turned serious. "I want to see everything."

"I'm just preparing you."

"I want to see it," she said, not missing a beat.

They walked into Finn's office and he played the refrigerator video.

"That's him!" She said.

Next he cued the file of the phone conversation where the man paced and spoke in a foreign language. "Omar, a friend of mine from Egypt, speaks Arabic," Finn began.

"That's not Arabic," she said when the video started. "It's Pashto. Its spoken in Afghanistan and parts of Pakistan." She stood, dialed her cell phone and went outside to Finn's porch. In the waning light he could see the cherry of her cigarette swoop up and down as she walked back and forth. Something about its glow and its slow arc felt comforting. He continued reviewing the video searching for clues. "I have a coworker that speaks Pashto," she said, coming back inside. "He's coming over right now." When they reached the part where the man smashed her photo, she covered her mouth, inhaling sharply. After hearing the man's threats, she stood up. "Sacrifices? What the hell does that mean? I came here feeling triumphant and now I'm terrified again." Her voice quavered and she verged on crying. "You should've hid the cameras better."

"Come into the kitchen and I'll cook you dinner," he said. "Your friend will be here soon." Finn sautéed chicken breasts for soft tacos while choping tomatoes at the kitchen table.

"He could be connected to my Afghani restoration work. But how?"

"We'll know a lot more when we have a translation. He didn't know microphones were in the room when he made that call."

Her colleague, Abdul, a young Pakistani from Islamabad, arrived an hour later. He gave Sarah a friendly hug and, smiling warmly, shook Finn's hand. "My family immigrated from Islamabad to the United States when I was fifteen," he said. "Pashto is my first language."

"You two worked together in Afghanistan?" Finn wondered if they'd ever slept together.

"We've both been to Bamiyan, working on the Buddhist architecture project, but not at the same time."

Sarah gave Abdul a summary of the situation and they all scrunched up around the computer monitor and played the man's phone conversation.

"It's Pashto," Abdul said, "But he's not a native speaker. I can't place his accent, though."

Finn reversed the video and they listened to Abdul translate while Sarah jotted it down in a notebook. The man entered the room speaking on his phone.

"Yes sir, I've already been to see her."

"Well, yes and no."

"Stop," Abdul said, "his Pashto is rough, so there may be mistakes."

Finn wondered if he meant mistakes in translation or mistakes by the speaker.

"Go back," Sarah said. "Stop. That bag, on the bed, it's the same as the one he used after swabbing me." It was a clear bag with "STERILE" inscribed across it in fat red letters. They couldn't tell if it had a swab in it. They continued.

"She's dead," the man said into his phone.

"Her mother, she told me."

"In a car accident."

"I checked the obituaries." The man held the phone from his ear, clenched his jaws, grimacing, before bringing it back to his face.

"We will get the DNA message."

"Yes, yes. I'm currently continuing with the first target."

"A few."

"I'm in her apartment." The man listened, held the phone away from his ear again. He pulled the phone back to his mouth. *"Yes sir,"* he said, and hung up. He whipped the phone against Sarah's bed and it bounced off the mattress several feet high.

"Who's dead?" Sarah said, "And what the fuck is a DNA message?" She paced about the room.

Finn turned to Abdul, "Are you sure you got the line about the DNA message right?"

They replayed the video and Abdul said, "he says, 'We will get the DNA message'. The phrase 'DNA message' is definitely there."

"So I have a fucking group of Pakis searching for a DNA message in my mouth? She turned to Abdul, "I'm Sorry, I'm just..." She covered her face with her hands and leaned her elbows on the desk.

"Sarah," Finn said. "Rethink your last trip to Afghanistan and try to make any connections with shady characters or strange incidents." He rubbed her back. "I can have Benjamin email Detective Mulveny this video footage."

"Wait! This is my fucking life here." The woman who worked in a war zone looked scared. "If I go to the police sacrifices will be made? What does that mean?"

"I don't know," Finn said. "I don't know." The video scared Finn too but he felt as if his courage, no, as if his very character were at stake; like it was shoved onto a stage. He could not, would not, let fear take over in front of Sarah.

THIRTEEN

Sunday evening Youssef bumped along on the city bus. His heart still thumped from a four block jog from the target's apartment to the bus stop. The target had set a trap and he'd fallen for it. But he thanked God he'd been spared capture by the police. However, he'd been caught on camera and surely the police would soon have his photo. Ledpaste might regret letting him live if he found out he had been caught on video. He was running out of time, too. It all made him very nervous.

The bus stopped and a hunched-over whiskery woman managed her way up the steps next to Youssef. He stood and helped her into his seat, and remained standing. He reviewed what he'd done, looking for mistakes: Once he'd suspected there were cameras, he searched the living room where the target's computer had been. He'd found one there and one in the bedroom. Then he had hacked into her computer and searched for video footage but there wasn't any. This meant she was storing the video on a remote computer, and that put him at greater risk every moment he dallied. Hurrying, he'd opened Internet files, copied stored account I.D.s and passwords and emailed them to himself. Then he erased the browser history, the cache, and the cookies, and logged out. He doused the broken glass and semen with ammonia he found under the sink, mopped it up with toilet paper and flushed the wad. He concluded that he'd been careful enough once he'd detected the cameras.

The bus ground to a halt and he got off at the main branch of the public library, a few blocks from the capital dome. At the library he logged onto the target's email account and got access. He skimmed through emails in the inbox and sent folders. One, received yesterday, interested him. It was from a woman named Melissa Taylor. Her mother had died and she announced the funeral in the email. He could lure Sarah to this woman's house. He would use the drug Burundanga on this Melissa. The Colombians had shown him how to use the powdered drug on a cross-training visit to his military camp. In Colombia they used Burundanga to kidnap or rob people. It steals people's willpower to oppose you, they told him. The real beauty of the drug, they said, was its retrograde amnesia. As long as you use it within ten minutes of meeting the person, they'll never remember you.

Youssef went home and found Melissa's address online. In the bathroom closet he dug around for the wax paper wrapping the Burundanga powder. He hoped it was still potent after all these years.

The next morning, Monday, as he was preparing to leave someone knocked on the door. "Africa!" called a man. It was Bob, his neighbor next door. Youssef opened the door and went out onto the porch.

"You seen the puppy?"

Youssef shook his head.

The man craned his neck trying to look into the house. "You wouldn't steal him would you?"

"No way."

"Bring him over if you see him then," he said, and began limping around the porch, trying, not so subtly, to look in the windows. "He's been gone a week. My grandbaby's throwing a fit."

Youssef knew the dog was female.

"Do me solid brother."

Youssef didn't know what he meant.

"A favor. See, I can't walk to the store." He pointed to his left leg. Youssef had looked at it many times but never let Bob see him looking. Now, though, he looked. Below the knee it had no muscle, just a bone wrapped in leathery hide, a blue flip-flop jammed on the shrunken foot. "Truck's in the shop."

Youssef checked his watch.

"Come on. I be quick."

Youssef relented and they climbed into Jassim's car and left. "Were you in the war against Russia?" Youssef asked. "The one in Vietnam."

"I's in a war. Never knew who it was against."

"Why did you go then?"

"Don't you know nothing! Government pulled my number. Lemme tell you. Back then black men like you and me, we was worth less than we are now. And our women, well, they got it worser."

Youssef had wanted to ask about his leg so many times but couldn't. He drove trying to gather courage for his curiosity. He parked at the convenience store and Bob went inside. He came back with three 40 ounce bottles of malt liquor. Youssef started back home and Bob drank a long gulp. "Your leg, you got that in the war?" Youssef asked.

He regarded Youssef a moment, then he clicked his tongue, once, loudly. "Don't know what the hell I was doin' over there. I didn't give a rat's ass if them slopes killed themselves. And besides, this country never brought nothing but misery and slavery for me and my family and there I was laying the only thing I got on the line for it. I got stuck on recon patrol. One night we got into the shit. We's in the jungle and so couldn't see much but when the shooting stop you could just hear them brothers moaning. I was shot up in the gut but keeping my mouth shut. Then those sneaky motherfuckers come out and I hear a man scream like a baby in a vise, and then a gunshot. I'd liked to shit my pants. I knew what they was up to. People'd said to save bullets the Viet Cong would chop a downed soldier with a machete and shoot him in the head if he so much as blinked an eye. So right then I made a promise to God and myself that I wasn't coming to see him and I wasn't gonna move no matter what they did to me. They sliced the calf half off and I didn't make a peep, and here I am." He took another long gulp and eyed Youssef. "You smart, Africa. You in school. You know them computers. Don't never go to no war, son. Do everything you can to help it 'cause it won't help you none."

Youssef left the car at the house, pocketed the Burundanga powder and walked to 38 1/2th street to catch a bus for Melissa Taylor's house.

Sitting under the shade of a tree he watched the house from across the street. After two hours a white station wagon pulled into the driveway and a chubby white woman got out and began unloading bags of groceries.

"Excuse me ma'am," Youssef said, approaching. Gently he unfolded the wax paper.

The woman turned around.

"I'm lost. Could you help me with my directions?" He held the small square of wax paper as if it had notes on it.

"Sure."

When she was close he blew the powder on her face. He stood back and waited while she coughed and cursed him. Eventually she stopped.

"How about we have some tea," he suggested.

"That sounds wonderful."

. . .

Finn woke early Monday morning, the sun having already started its cruel inspection of the Central Texas hill country. The pristine blue theater spread unending and careless without a wisp of a cloud. Finn's worries: his lack of employment, family, wife, and money, and anwsers for Sarah, all shrank under the magnitude of it all as if God were reducing them against his splendor. He was overcome with a feeling that all was possible and everything was right. In other words, the world was his.

He turned on the shower and waited for the tepid water from the main-line below the street to push out the hotter water in the shallow pipes running to the house. In a few months he would look back on all this with nostalgia, he thought. But Sarah was getting married in a few months. He doubted the wisdom of devoting so much effort to ultimately see another man have her. He had his own life to concern himself with. He had to admit the fact Sarah was in a relationship created a nice barrier, one from which he could observe and experiment without being obligated to commit. But her fiancé should show some damn gumption and do something for the woman he's going to marry. However, in his neglect he'd left a crack in which Finn could insert a wedge. Plus he relished being with her too much to stop now.

The water was still hot, but bearable, and Finn stepped into the shower. The man had said *DNA message*. What the hell was a DNA message? And how was she carrying it? She'd been to Afghanistan and the man had spoken an Afghani dialect. Maybe they were fanatical Muslims looking for a message from God: the second coming of Mohammed or some crazy shit like that. Maybe Sarah had stumbled through an emergent disease, and fearing an international crisis, someone was trying to hide it. Epidemiologists were always spouting doomsday bullshit like an imminent pandemic from a mutated avian or swine virus. Or, maybe she had some genetic peculiarity that the man wanted to sequence (a message in the form of a genetic mutation).

But a true message is deliberate, he thought, and DNA encodes information, that's its purpose. It could easily store any message you wanted. Base-pair combinations would have to be assigned letters, that's all. The problem wouldn't be retrieving the message (With the right PCR primers that would be cake walk) it'd be inserting it into someone's genome in the first goddamn place. Retroviruses, like H.I.V., sometimes inserted their DNA into the host's genome, but this was random or at least hard to control. And without knowing the exact location of a DNA message the PCR primers couldn't be made to retrieve it. So that man must already know something about what he's looking for, something about the sequence of Sarah's DNA message.

Finn stepped from the shower, wrapped his waist with a towel, and went to the kitchen to make coffee. He wandered through the house mulling the attacker's phone call, how he'd attacked Sarah, and his ultimatum to her. One thought percolated up and Finn was both struck by it and angry it had not come earlier: the attacker found the cameras and therefore may have looked on Sarah's computer trying to find the video files. Her system was password-protected but the man could have stolen her computer in an attempt to trash the videos. If he could hack in, he would find information that would lead him to Sarah.

Finn realized the camera in the living room faced Sarah's computer. All he had to do was check the final video footage from the living room and see if the computer was still there. Simple. He called Sarah. She didn't answer and he left her a voice mail message.

He went to his computer and searched through the video files. The last file was triggered by the television he'd put on a timer. He had ignored it yesterday, assuming it nothing more than the TV, and then had forgotten to go back and check it.

He raced through the file in fast forward. Nothing moved but the TV blared. From a tiny desk behind an overstuffed love seat the corner of Sarah's black monitor poked out. Next to it stood an unpainted pine bookshelf, stoic against the wall. Several times Finn stopped scanning to watch the man do nothing more than pass through the room. Then at minute forty-three the man entered again.

He strode to the bookcase, inspected it and then hurled the books to the floor. He spun, lifted the laptop, and with a forearm swiped the desk of papers, pens, and books. He replaced the laptop, and looked over the desk. Like a wolf distracted while gorging, he jerked his head up from the computer desk and looked across the room. He strode to another bookcase (where the camera was hidden) and disappeared from view off the right side of the screen. *I'm so fucking stupid!* He must have discovered the camera and now had Sarah's computer. *Come on Sarah, call me.*

Things thudded and crashed. The image swirled and ended blank white. Then the man's face appeared above bending closer. For some time Finn and the man stared at one another, again. Although the man's expression was flat it carried a hostility that gave Finn the sensation of being hunted. Then the man stood, pulling away from the camera, and lifted a leg, the black heel of his shoe suspended above. The heel grew encompassing the screen in its blackness.

"Shit!" He snatched his phone, and ran to his car. While driving to Sarah's apartment he called her twice on the way. She didn't answer.

At Sarah's apartment complex the security guard looked up listlessly from over a paperback. "Here's my cell phone number, Finn said. "Call me if anyone you don't know enters. Call me first and then the police if this man enters." Finn pushed a printed image of Sarah's attacker across the counter.

"I saw him yesterday."

"I know. Whatever you do don't let him know you're suspicious," he said, and jogged down the hallway.

Dalmatian spots of black forensic fingerprint dust dotted the apartment. Sarah had decided to tell the police. Finn tiptoed down the tiny hall between the kitchen and living room. He caught a glimpse of movement to his left, shuddered and then cursed himself when he saw it was his reflection in an oval hall mirror.

Books, magazines, and papers covered the floor in Sarah's living room. One bookshelf lay face down with two lamps next to it on the ground, their shades twisted and dented. The computer, surprisingly, was still on its small desk. He typed in the password and checked the video download connections. The video process was set correctly and seemed undisturbed. He relaxed. He guessed he had overestimated the man. Next Finn opened an Internet browser, expecting it to ask him to restore the last session, his email site. Unless Sarah had used the computer he'd been the last to use it while installing the cameras, on Saturday, two days ago. The computer did not ask him to restore his last session. He checked the browsing history and it was absent. He knew there had been a browser history when he had installed the cameras. He dialed Sarah and he got her bubbly recording, again. "Hi, this is Sarah," she said over laughter and music. "You know what to do."

"Sarah, its Finn. Call me immediately when you get this message."

He scanned the hard drive and cache memory for clues but found nothing. Then his phone rang, Sarah calling.

"Has anybody used your laptop since Saturday?"

"I haven't used it in nearly a week."

"We have some serious problems. I think that—" He heard no background noise. "Sarah? Sarah?" The line was dead.

. . .

Inching ahead on Interstate 35 in what must have been a hundred-car-line to her exit, Sarah felt testy and impatient. Finn had called, hyper and going on about when she last used her computer and then she lost the signal. She felt relieved when he called right back, except that it wasn't him.

"Hello? Sarah?"

"Who is this?"

"It's Melissa." She wasn't such a close friend and Sarah thought it odd she was calling.

"I'm so sorry about your mother." She didn't know what else to say.

"I just feel so all alone. I don't feel I can fully share my grief with even John. I'm calling to see if you could, I mean, would you mind coming over and just talking for a while?"

"I know this sounds callous, but I'm having some problems, you couldn't possibly imagine. I'm really sorry. I just can't now."

Melissa paused and Sarah expected her to accept her refusal, begrudgingly maybe. "It would just be a few minutes. I really need someone now."

Sarah felt like imploding.

"It would mean so much," Melissa said.

"Maybe," she said stalling for an excuse. "When this blows over." It struck her as absurd that she needed a reason beyond a violent psychotic stalking her.

"It's just that you're the second person to reject me this morning and I've made cookies and coffee, and—" She inhaled quickly as if she'd started to cry and then stifled it.

Sarah suddenly felt selfish. "Okay, okay. I'll stop by."

"Thank you, so much. I'll be waiting."

Pinned in by traffic, Sarah felt claustrophobic in her car. But it was more than that. She felt vulnerable. She remembered how the Los Angeles police had pinpointed O.J. Simpson in 1995 using his cell phone signal. Maybe that psycho had such a device and was zeroing in on her right now. I shouldn't use my phone, she thought.

FOURTEEN

"Can you pronounce Wagner but would rather listen to Gaye," read the title of Sarah's webpage. Accompanying it was a photo of her in a red toboggan hat, the sun brightening a careless smile. In the background a waterfall splashed down a small cliff studded with flowering cacti while to her left the ocean frothed through perforated boulders.

A feeling came to Finn, swiftly but gently like a balloon, the kind treasure hunters inflate at ocean depths to haul their discoveries to the surface. The fluorescent hunter-orange balloons, eerily out of place in the clear black of the deep cold water, shudder as they hurtle up crossing thermal climes, thousands of bubbles racing ahead. He sat a few moments staring into her green eyes. He wondered who had taken the photo, who Sarah was smiling for. It struck him that he wished she were smiling for him. A few bubbles broke the surface of his consciousness and he was aware of the feeling but not yet understanding it. I've only known Sarah three days, he thought. And then, without doubt, he knew the bright orange globe was just below the surface and rising fast and he was in awe of it. He needed not guess what it hauled.

He wondered how he could love her after only three days. Is a treasure stumbled across after only three days of searching less a treasure than one found after years of hunting? "Yes," he said aloud, still staring into her eyes. The torment of the quest gives appreciation of the rarity of the fortune. But I've been searching ten years or more and only now just discovered Sarah. While savoring the sensation of loving her, he realized he didn't care about her past or her future. He didn't need to get to know her better, or move in and try things out for a while, or see how things would work out, and frankly he felt stunned, even overwhelmed by it.

His eyes swung from her photo to the date below listing the last time the account had been accessed: August, 4th, yesterday. He called her and connected.

"When did you last open your webpage?"

"I don't know. A few days ago. Yeah, Friday evening before I went to your house."

"Really?"

"Yeah."

"Are you sure?"

"I said yes."

Think, he thought, *think*.

"What's going on?"

The man must have accessed her stored passwords and account IDs on her computer. He could have accessed many of her accounts. What would he look for, Finn thought—information on where she was staying. He'd look in her email, yes, that's where he'd look first.

"What's your email password?"

"Huh?"

"Your email password."

"Guinevere, the i is a 1. Why?"

"We need to talk, now. Where are you?"

"I'm in danger, aren't I." The calmness of her voice surprised him.

"I don't know."

Finn thought she whispered, *Typical*. "Where are you?" he asked.

"I'm in my car. I'm going to a friend's house in Round Rock."

"Don't."

"Her mother died. I'm just going to console her."

"Seriously, thirty minutes, max. Okay? Sarah? Sarah?" Silence. "God-damn-mother-fucking-piece-a-shit-phone!" He dialed her again and got voice mail. He slammed his phone down and opened Sarah's email account. He didn't need the password after all, both the account ID and password were stored. He didn't know what he was looking for but the in-box seemed normal. All the messages from the last two days were unread and no messages had been sent in the last two days. Browsing the saved folder he didn't see anything that could help the man find her. There were two files in the trash folder. The topmost was from a Melissa Taylor announcing her mother's funeral that Sarah had referred to. Finn relaxed but kept reviewing. Above the trash icon were words, "Trash Emptied Every 1 Day." He stalled and then made the connection in a meteoric second.

. . .

The sun cast a furious brilliance across the car roofs filling the highway and service roads. Sarah crawled forward a car length. A bead of sweat coursed down her forehead, over her eyebrow, and into her eye. The salt stung and she squeezed her eye tight. Her burning eye, the spotty cell phone coverage, the traffic, the searing sun, the man hunting her, the missed presentation to the major donors of her Afghanistan project, Finn's cryptic call, her apathetic fiancé, the brakes pulling right, squeaking, and reminding her of how shitty her car was, and Melissa's annoying insistence, all hung on her simultaneously. And then she lost it when some asshole pulled his shiny 4X4, double-cab-extended-bed-dualie-pickup into the small gap she'd inadvertently opened at the head of a massive exit ramp line. She leaned on the horn. "You dickless inbred yokel!" A chubby pink hand emerged from the driver's side and held up its middle finger. *Perfect,* she thought.

Melissa's house was a modest one-story cottage with a pebbled driveway. A rose-covered trellis led to a porch strewn with elephant ears and ferns. She parked behind Melissa's car. Half-way to the front door her phone beeped, signaling an incoming text message. Melissa opened the front door.

. . .

Finn called Sarah and left her a message, telling her not to go to Melissa's. Then he dialed 911.

"What's your emergency?" a female voice said.

"Hello, yes, I need police presence, at the residence of Melissa Taylor."

"Okay, what's the emergency."

"Someone's in imminent danger!"

"Is someone hurt?"

"Not yet. I mean, no."

"Excuse me?"

He hesitated. "There's a break-in happening right now."

"What's the address sir?"

"At the house of Melissa Taylor."

"Are you there?"

"No, I just spoke with someone there on the phone."

"Okay I'm looking up the address. 402 Virginia Drive, Round Rock, John and Melissa Taylor."

"That must be it. Please, send someone immediately."

He called Sarah again, and left her another voice mail. Then he collected his things and sprinted out the door, past the security guard, and to his car. As he drove he typed Sarah a text message, but noticed just after he hit the send button it that he'd mistyped and the auto-fill had completed it.

. . .

"I am so glad that you made it," Melissa beamed. Sarah thought her expression weird after the panic on the phone.

"Just a moment," Sarah said, looking at the text message. It was from Finn. *It's a trial!* the message proclaimed. She couldn't make sense of it. He was really beginning to piss her off.

"Come on in. I've got tea and coffee."

Then a second message beeped. *It's a trick!* The message said.

Sarah froze. She gazed at Melissa, standing by the open screen door, with a toothy smile smeared across her face.

"Come on," She said in a tone too cheery for someone in mourning. Sarah took a cautious step backwards. A languid breeze floated along, not a single bird song in it. A deep-throated engine punctuated the silence. The vehicle came from Sarah's right, down and behind the crest of a small hill.

"Sarah, what are you doing?" Come on up.

Sarah turned and bolted, a pair of over-sized sunglasses sailing off her head.

FIFTEEN

arah followed a police secretary to Detective Mulveny's open door. Behind his desk he reclined in an aged-crackled leather chair and took a bite from a brisket sandwich. Several strands of coleslaw, stained crimson with sauce, squirted out.

"Sarah Dougherty's here to see you," the secretary said.

He wiped his fingers and mouth with a napkin transparent with grease. "Come in," he said.

"He tried to lure me to a friend's house," Sarah said. "He tried to attack me again. He almost got me. He could have killed me. He had a gun this time. I had to stop a car on the street."

"Whoa." He brushed a strand of coleslaw from his shirt where the buttons pulled taut lines over his belly. "Take a breath and have a seat." He sounded tired.

She told him how she barely escaped and how Finn had texted her a warning.

Mulveny responded by running his tongue slowly across his teeth and leering at her breasts. "Miss Dougherty, I'm going to have Detective Saunders get the details on the incident," he said, standing. "You look like you could use a glass of water. Sit tight." He left the office.

Gingerly, she rotated her left wrist. Already it was swelling from the fall in the woods. She couldn't understand how that man had convinced Melissa to lure her there. She was so grateful that Finn had warned her, but couldn't understand that either. Surprisingly, she hadn't lost her phone in the attack but the battery had died. She lifted the receiver off Mulveny's desk phone. From the hallway behind her came loud talk and the occasional burst of a cop radio. She dialed Finn's number.

"Hello?"

"It's me. I'm at—"

"Oh my God! Are you all right?"

"Yes, I'm at the police station."

"I thought he had you."

"Where are you?"

"At Melissa's. Your car's here. I've been running around screaming your name."

"How did you know it was a trap?"

Finn explained how he discovered the man had hacked Sarah's computer and email account, and read the message from Melissa. All of this sank her heart. The man had managed to break into the apartment, breach private email accounts, manipulate friends, and elude the police. He was a true demon, and he remained free, waiting for her. She was not free.

"I'm waiting to make my statement. Come meet me here."

"Where's Reece?"

"Just come."

Detective Saunders mustache bristled above his thin lips. He looked at her sternly, under the soulless glow of the fluorescent lights, and threw questions at her with barely concealed aggravation. In the leafy New England town where she'd grown up the cops directed cars under broken traffic lights, or hauled in fourteen year-olds who'd stolen Daddy's car. They did not sit on the other side of a cheap plastic table in a windowless room directing hostility at a woman seeking refuge. "What happens after Melissa comes out the front door?"

"I can't believe this. I came here for help, for God's sake. Why are you making me repeat everything?" She had already told him how Melissa lured her there, how Finn warned her at the final moment, how, as she tried to flee, a screen door on the side deck exploded and that man erupted from it, hurdling the rail headlong towards her. She told him how she plunged into a patch of woods and negotiated vines and stumps, how she shot onto a small street in front of an oncoming pickup-truck, how she forced the driver to stop and then jumped into the bed, and how, as that man tried to scramble into the truck bed with her, she hammered his fingers with a crow-bar she'd found in the truck bed.

The door to the tiny room opened, and detective Mulveny entered and whispered into Saunder's ear. "We'll be right back," Mulveny said. The sight of a familiar face should have relaxed her but Mulveny's expression offered no comfort. A moment later Mulveny returned and placed a small digital recorder on the table. He stared at her impassively. "Let me get this straight, Miss Dougherty. On Wednesday, July thirty-first, a stranger, who is looking for a DNA message (he made finger quotes in the air), accosted you and swabbed your mouth. Then, as this stranger flees he gets in a fight with Finn Barber. On Saturday this very same stranger breaks into your apartment, getting past security unnoticed and enters your apartment without damaging the door. While he waits for you, he masturbates to a photo of you. You captured him on camera because you thought he might come to your house, and you were right. Today he's after you again but he doesn't catch you because Finn comes to your rescue. He calls 911 and reports a bogus breaking and entering (a serious crime, by the way). He gives this false report because he divined with his superhero powers that your mystery attacker would be at Melissa's. Mulveny stared at her.

Sarah sat, her arms crossed over her stomach. "He broke into my email."

"You're a very beautiful woman."

"So what!"

The detective looked at her unflinching. "I'm not saying this didn't happen. I just don't believe you're being forthright about your connection to the stalker. I think you know him."

"I told everything to Detective Saunders, exactly the way it was."

Mulveny raised an eyebrow. He left the interrogation room leaving the door open. In the hallway he colluded with the other detective and several police officers. It reminded her of when she once went to her father seeking solace. She was seven or eight and something she'd done had scared her. Now she couldn't even remember what it was. However, she could clearly remember her father dragging her by an earlobe, furious over what she'd done. A paratrooper, all muscle and knuckles, he was a demigod to her then. She'd never anticipated him not being the safety she'd expected.

"Sarah," Mulveny said, coming back in, "The officer who responded to the call at Melissa Taylor's found her alone and she claims nobody was in her house with her. He says she'd been drinking or possibly high on painkillers, understandable considering her mother's death."

"Maybe that's why she can't remember the man being in the house with her."

"May I offer something that makes more sense?"

Sarah glared at him.

"You go over there to console your friend Melissa. There's this man stalking you—an ex-boyfriend, a fling. I don't care. That's not important. He follows you there and surprises you. You call a friend, a neutral party, Finn, because you can't let your fiancé know about him. So Finn makes the 911 call, lying in order to get the most rapid response from the police. Your stalker, now infuriated, chases you and just barely misses getting a hold of you. Both you and Melissa are terrified of what he would do if you brought charges directly against him, and I don't blame you. He sounds like a real fucking nut-job."

Mulveny leaned into her, barbecue sauce on his breath. "But lying to the police won't help us catch him. And believe me, when we catch him he'll wish he never'd met you." He smiled smugly.

"I'm not lying."

"We'll get him on simple and felonious assault, and possibly attempted murder, and we've got witnesses. He won't be free for years —plenty of time for him to simmer down. And if you want to keep your fiancé out of the loop that's up to you. We'll take a private deposition. It'll never see trial. Cowards like this always take a plea. What do you say?"

She closed her eyes. "There is nothing more I would love than to give you his name. But I told you the complete truth. I don't know him."

Mulveny regarded her wearily. "Fine, you talk to Melissa and get her to corroborate your story, then we can move forward." He stood, the buttons on his polyester-cotton blend struggling to contain his gut.

SIXTEEN

Sarah waited for Finn at the police station. After he arrived they drove—with a police escort—back to Melissa's to pick up her car. Melissa remained cheery, offering them cookies and tea as if nothing had happened. She claimed not to remember any man running out her back door, nor even having seen Sarah earlier. Finn suggested they go somewhere unexpected. They dropped Sarah's car off at Finn's house. She got a bikini from the trunk and they drove to the trail-head for Campbell's Hole. Finn called Benjamin and told him to straighten out Mulveny. Finn worried over her the entire ride. "Can I get you anything? Cigarettes? Something to drink? To eat?"

"No, no." she responded. "Fine. A pack of Pall Malls."

Soon they parked at the trail-head and hiked down a root strewn dirt path to rapids where water boiled up through porous limestone making dozens of marvelous little Jacuzzis. She ducked behind some bushes and slipped on her red crochet bikini. When she returned she saw his camouflage shorts and ragged tee-shirt lying on the bank but did not see him. Across the creek a large group drank beer and passed a joint, laughing and chasing one another in the loose sand. Nearby a couple embraced and kissed, only their heads above the foamy water. She stopped knee deep in the crisp jade water and scanned for him, but still couldn't find him and it agitated her. She shuddered when he burst head-first up through the bubbling water. Drops rolled off his hair and stubbly beard as he climbed onto a rock above a particularly furious froth. He wore only a pair of black boxer shorts. His body was lean, lanky even, with shoulders that umbrellaed out over butterscotch skin. The center of his chest was sunken in but not overly so and had the effect of making his pectorals look thicker, and wonderfully menacing. He stood up on a rock and then dove, disappearing into the churning bubbles. She climbed in to the compact Jacuzzi with him and for a long time, and without the need to chat, they let the turbulence massage them.

Back at Finn's house she opened her email and changed the password, and then she created another email account on a different web site. Her despair waned and in its place came indignation, and then rage. She wanted to stab that degenerate right in the fucking heart. Who was he to threaten her? The reason she felt so despondent was her lack of control, she concluded. I could turn this tragedy on its ear, make him the hunted, she thought, Finn and I could go looking for him, just like he's doing me. I could post his photo all around town and on the web, and when we find out who he is I'll turn him in. Fuck the detectives! She strode into the kitchen where Finn was washing a food crusted pile of dishes. But instead of saying anything she surprised herself by watching him. He was in bare feet and an old miserable tee-shirt, and his messy coffee-hued hair stuck up at random. His broad shoulders stretched the round holes in his tee-shirt into ovals.

"We're going to hunt him," she finally said.

"Huh?" Finn said jerking around.

"What do we know about him? And don't say he likes to jack-off to me."

"I wouldn't. I'm certain he didn't like it."

"Don't you like jacking off to me?"

"Me, I love it."

"Yeah I bet. Get used to it," she said. "So he's lived in America and probably Pakistan. What else?"

"He looks Northern African or Middle Eastern, but possibly Indian, or Latino.

"Wow, you're so helpful."

The doorbell rang.

"I'm sure that's Reece," she said.

"Come in!" Finn yelled, drying his hands.

Reece strolled into the kitchen and gave Sarah a lazy hug. "Finally meeting my silent partner in the jewelry store," he said to Finn. "With you keeping her busy I've had my most productive week yet." He reached out to shake Finn's hand and smiled, though it looked contrived.

Sarah was nervous that meeting for the first time Reece would feel threatened by Finn and act obnoxious or jealous. So far, he was in character.

"I'm not the one keeping her busy," Finn said, looking over at her.

She gave Reece a look and his smile wilted some.

"How's the mystery going then, mod squad?" Reece asked.

Finn seemed not to know how to answer.

Reece looked soft and tedious next to Finn. He seemed like a bitter penguin, in his white oxford cloth shirt and black slacks, shuffling from one foot to the other and treating Finn contemptuously. While Finn, in his tattered tee shirt, cut-off army pants, and week-old beard, looked raw and reckless. And, he was smart enough not to be dragged into an argument with Reece's taunts. Finn was attentive and it was such a pleasure to have someone care for and worry about her. Reece was so confused that he actually thought he was getting credit for helping her through this turmoil. Because he'd asked Benjamin Black to help her out and Benjamin had sent Finn, Reece thought he could take credit for doing something. But while Finn was saving her from being attacked at Melisssa's house, Reece had been fretting over the wiring to his display cases. He'd hadn't even asked her how she was yet; he'd been so eager to brag about his jewelry store and get in his jabs. He'd probably not thought of her all day. That fucking store. That's all she's heard about from him the last six months. About how rich it'll make them and how Reece will become a respected and recognized jeweler. *You're gorgeous, courageous, and intelligent,* he'd told her when he proposed marriage. Although it sounded like a complement, she was growing convinced he was most pleased by how her qualities reflected well on him.

"Come on," she said to Reece. "Let's go eat." In the driveway Reece put his arm around her shoulder. She turned and peeked back at Finn, who stood at the front door and watched them leave. He flicked his wrist in a wave. "Let's walk," She said. "We can find a place on Congress."

Reece, sighed. "I'm too tired to walk."

She didn't feel up to an argument and got in his German sports car, the one he loved, but with the payments he loved to complain about.

"Absolutely crazy at the shop," he said. "Finally got the wraparound display case finished and now the workstations are wired and ready to fire up. And the employee insurance is all dialed in. Gotta stay on top of these things or you'll end up paying big-time in the end."

"Good," Sarah said. To be fair, she had yet to tell him about today's attack, but Reece knew the man had been in her apartment, and had threatened her. "I was attacked again today," she said.

"Oh my God." He stopped the car and looked her over. "But you're all right?"

"He had a gun. I barely escaped by flagging down a truck."

"I can't believe it. Who the hell is he? Are you sure you don't recognize him at all?"

She couldn't believe he was asking such stupid questions—again. They'd been through this the day after the first attack. She'd gone through hundreds of her photos from parties looking for a glimpse of the man, and had called friends hoping for clues. "Am I sure I never saw him before?"

"Yeah."

"Yes," she said, "I'm sure!"

"Jeez, I'm sorry. I was just trying—"

"Don't you think the police would have him by now, if I knew who he was?"

Reece started driving again and they went three blocks to a tiny burger joint. "The important thing is that you're all right," he said, as they went inside. It was sharp and clean with chrome stools, black and white checkered floor tiles, and cool, grease laden air. They sat on high stools at a round table and ordered from a grotesquely cheerful waiter in a red-checkered shirt. Reece took a swallow of beer and began complaining, first about the price of gold and then about taxes. She watched, incredulous. But then she had a moment of clarity and began to feel relieved. She thrust her hand into his face holding her thumb and forefinger an eighth of an inch apart.

He shut-up and leaned his face back.

"I am this close to getting up and walking out of your life *for-ever*," she said. "It's becoming clear that your store is more important than your bride-to-be."

"Relax."

"Don't fucking tell me how to feel! How can you be so self-involved that you'll continue whining about your store after what happened to me today?"

"It's our future."

"Hello! There may not be a future if this guy gets a hold of me. He broke into my email account and we have to assume that he now knows who you are."

"You didn't tell me that."

"I'm telling you now."

"This is a big problem."

"Finally, your getting the idea."

Reece shook his head.

"We have to stay in a hotel tonight."

"A hotel?"

"I'm sorry, when I ordered psychotic, violent stalker I forgot to select my fiancé's house as off limits."

"I didn't mean it that way."

"I have to leave town and hope this simmers down. I'm not too hopeful though considering his persistence, but maybe it will put me out of harm's way and give the police a chance to make some breakthroughs. Anyway, we could use it as a chance for a vacation. How about South Padre Island?"

"But I have work lined up solid for the next five days."

"Then reschedule it."

"But, its, I'm so close to opening."

"So you'll have me go off alone for your stupid schedule?"

"Don't be like that. I'm just being honest and emotionally accessible, like we said in therapy. Voicing our concerns, right? You go ahead and nobody will know where you are but me. When the work is done I'll join you. I'll stay in a hotel here."

"I know you think I'm a tough person, smart, self-reliant, and all that. But I'm still a woman, Reece. I'm not going anywhere alone right now." She glowered at him. "If I had known you were so egotistical, I would never have dated you." It reminded her of a night last year when, alone at home she'd heard a prowler outside and had first called him and then the police. He was working late, a five minute drive from their house. The police came in three minutes and Reece didn't show up for another fifteen. He claimed that he knew the police would arrive sooner and saw no need to rush. "This is how you protect the mother-to-be of your children? You know what?" She stood up from her chrome stool. "You do whatever the fuck Reece wants!" She smacked her beer bottle. It clattered across the table toward Reece and he jumped back. The bottle fell and smashed on the floor. Everyone turned to look but she didn't give a fuck.

She stalked out of the restaurant and then took off jogging down the side walk. At the first side street she turned left toward Finn's house. Reece yelled to her. It sounded like he was at the restaurant entrance. She darted down an alley, and half-way down the block went up a set of stairs and through a restaurant back door. It smelled of grease and beef and two Hispanic cooks looked up in unison from their frying pans at a gas range. She held a finger to her lips. In Spanish she said, "I'm sorry. Someone is following me," or so she hoped. (What she really said was, "I feel like something, Someone I follow.") She whipped out her cell phone and dialed Finn. The two men continued staring and stirring in unison. First the police skepticism, she thought, and now Reece's egotism. Finn answered.

"Hey," he said.

"Can you come pick me up?"

"Yeah, of course. What's going on?"

"You need to come right now if you're coming." A call from Reece beeped.

"What's going on?"

"I'll tell you when you get here. Pick me up in the alley, at the back door of," She turned to the cooks, "*como se llama*?"

"Nana's," they said in unison.

"The back door of Nana's"

"Are you all right?"

"Just come on." She hung up and turned off her phone. She cracked the back door and kept watch on the alley. Finn was there in under a minute. She turned back to give the cooks a smile before clambering down the stoop. They both returned an identical wide smile. Once she assured Finn she was okay he asked where she wanted to go. She didn't care. "Go, go. Just go." She didn't want Reece trying to charm her right now.

They drove silently for several minutes.

"Sarah?"

"Yes?" She glanced at Finn. He looked nervous, like he was going to say something serious. "What?"

"I'm not saying this just because I just felt it now, or to take advantage. But I do feel it. I mean, what I'm about to say, I know, as well as feel it. And it does come at a time that looks opportunistic to me, but that's not it. It's an opportunity but I'm not being opportunistic. You see? It's just a coincidence and—"

"I have no idea what your saying."

He worked his lips as if pushing the words out.

She was annoyed. "What!"

"I'minlovewithyou." He blurted it out like one word. He looked boyish, with big lashes. His expression was earnest if not downright dumb. He blinked, mouth open and looked at her with anxious eyes, like some brain-dead oaf. Everything that had happened to her in the last week: the attack on the street, her missed presentation to the donors of her Afghan work, the man breaking into her apartment and email, Melissa's betrayal and the terrifying chase outside her house, the suspicious police, the fight with Reece, and the need to go into serious hiding—she could top-off with Finn, a man she'd only known four days, telling her that he was in love with her, and looking childishly sincere to boot. She exploded into laughter. She tried to stop but only laughed harder. He looked offended and she doubled over. He pulled to the side of the road and she hacked breathlessly. He stared ahead tight-lipped and silently indignant and she convulsed wiping tears from her eyes.

"I should never have told you." His voice wavered.

She gasped for breath. His lips were scrunched up in a cute pout. She wished he would just laugh with her but his ego was too involved. She erupted into another fit. He opened the door and began to get out. She grabbed his arm laughing. "Don't you see?"

"No, I don't see. Drive yourself. I'm walking."

She laughed even harder. "I don't even know where we're going."

"I meant you can drive yourself to my house and get your car."

"Get in, you idiot!" She yanked at his arm. She managed not to breakdown at his sullen face.

He drove them to a tavern called The Door, and went directly to the bar still pouting. It was Spartan with a wrap-around bar and a hand-hammered copper counter top. Two pool tables book-ended by couches sat at the far wall. He ordered two beers, a working-class brand, not that fruity shit Reese preferred. On the way back he stopped to chat with a disheveled and greasy-haired older man, who kept looking back at her with a filthy grin. Probably a washed up musician. God knew Austin crawled with them. They rented a pool table.

"It's this horrible situation and all its stress," she said, "and we've only known each other four days." She played not trying to win, but preferring to watch him gracefully stalk around the table sinking the balls. Slowly, the beer put her in a state of careless euphoria. "Nobody's ever told me they love me quite like that."

He looked at her skeptically and she shrugged and said she didn't know what else to say.

After several games they were drinking, joking, laughing, and touching. "You should have seen your lips," she said, "they stuck out a mile." Three mangy musicians prepared on a cramped stage in front of the bay window and the bar filled with people and excited energy. The more she laughed and drank, touched his arms, shoulders and chest, and felt his muscles, like tightly wound rope, the more she wanted to take off his clothes. Then without warning they kissed, gently at first but then urgently, groping and squeezing one another. People bumped into them, but she didn't notice.

She pulled back and looked at him. His jaw was angular and his lips full and slick. She swayed gently back and forth, uncertain where the high from the beer left off and the one from the kiss began. He stared into her eyes. Then he took her hand and dragged her back to the car. While swerving home he kissed her neck, ears and lips. His kisses shivered into her ear and coursed through her body like tiny electric jolts. At his house he dropped the keys on his porch and they continued kissing. He pulled off her shirt and tossed it away and threw his on the ground. Hopping on one leg he strained to remove his pants and underwear but then he slipped and crashed to the porch floor. She sprang on top of him, kissing and biting his lips and neck. Then he stood and opened the door to the house. He cradled her and laid her on the sofa with her ass hanging off and her feet on the floor. He ripped off her bra and she kicked off her shoes. He kissed down her neck and sucked on her aureoles and erect nipples. Next he moved to her navel while he yanked on her pants. She kicked and he pulled, and one pant leg stuck on her ankle. When he finally got it loose, he stumbled backwards and the pants sailed onto the floor behind him. He jumped back toward her, pulled off the last of her clothing and pushed his mouth onto her crotch. She moaned. He nibbled her clitoris until she couldn't stand it.

As he climbed on top of her Reece's face flashed through her mind's eye. "No, I shouldn't."

"Not now. You can't say that now. Please, please, please, please, please, please."

"I shouldn't."

"just a bit." He rubbed his erection, pushing apart her labia.

She writhed, inhaling in gulps. Her head was the clean black sky.

"You like that," he breathed into her ear.

"Okay, just a little. Just the tip."

"Yeah, just a bit."

"Just the tip, just the tip, just a little. Give me a little." It felt so good.

They tumbled to the floor. He put the head of his cock in her but she held his hips keeping his distance. For a long time he pumped in and out just the head. He bit and tugged on a nipple. Suddenly he thrust deep into her. "Oh, you're hitting my spot! You're hitting my spot."

He threw the coffee table aside and a glass broke on the floor. He pushed up onto his knees and she held her own head up and watched him piston in and out of her. Fat drops of sweat fell from his nose and chin and ran down the sides of her neck and breasts. Time accordioned in and out and they writhed across a rug and onto the hardwood floor. Ten, or just as easily forty minutes could have passed. Somewhere in the folds of the moment she'd had three orgasms. Another one came rushing towards her like a wall of water in a tidal river and she dug her fingernails into his shoulder blades. Everything went double, then triple, and she shuddered, shook, and yelled while he came inside her, thrashing and bellowing and banging hard up against her uterus. "I love you. I love you. I love you," he breathed into her ear. He collapsed on top of her and she slung her arms out on the cool pine floor. Almost immediately he drifted off and for some time she tenderly kissed his neck and a cheek. Later she woke with a start, worried that Reece would come looking for her there. Finn's head lay on her chest and he'd drooled on her. She wriggled from beneath him and pulled on her panties. She tried to put on her bra but the clasp was broken. After fishing car keys from her jeans she went outside and searched in the darkness but couldn't find her shirt. She parked her car three blocks away and jogged back wearing only her panties. She pulled Finn off the floor and they climbed into his bed and slept twisted together.

SEVENTEEN

Early Tuesday morning Youssef parked Jassim's car at the head of a long and narrow gravel driveway. It meandered through scrubby woods to the target's fiancé's house, a white guy, a jeweler, Skully, Reece Skully. Youssef knocked loudly on the back door and waited. He knew Reece wasn't there. He was at his shop. Jassim was watching him from a bench across the parking lot.

Youssef knocked one more time. Then he smashed a pane of glass, reached in and unlocked the door. Inside he found a bunch of mail for Reece Skully's store and then, finally, a card sent by the target's mother, mailed from a Washington D.C. Suburb. It had been mailed to the target's apartment. He dialed Ledpaste. "They live in D.C.," he told him. He gave Ledpaste the parent's address.

Half an hour later Youssef and Jassim sat in Jassim's car, parked in front of Reece's jewelry store in a North Austin strip mall. "This is your job," he told Jassim. "If he's seen any video footage he'll recognize me." Jassim got out, and went to the store. The store was not yet open to the public so Youssef was relieved when Jassim went in through the unlocked front door. From the driver's seat he craned his neck to see around the glare on the plate glass windows fronting the store. Reece stood behind a display case speaking to a man with a full leather tool belt, probably an electrician. Youssef's heart accelerated. He double checked the safety on his Glock. Reece turned from the electrician and to Jassim. *Careful Jassim.* The electrician went through a doorway to a rear workshop where a flickering glow circumscribed a woman soldering, her back to them. Jassim darted between the display cases and whipped out his pistol. He leaned in close to Reece. Youssef clapped. *Excellent!* Reece jerked looking to the back of the store and Youssef thought he could see Jassim press the pistol into his ribs. The two of them walked to the front door, Jassim behind him. Youssef started the car.

An hour later the three sat silent in a miserable old motel on the east-side. Blindfolded, Reece sat on the only chair in the room, Jassim and Youssef on corners of separate double beds facing him. Youssef stared at stains on the dull green carpet while Jassim pointed his gun at the man. Youssef was going to fulfill his mission this time and that could mean killing. He didn't want to do it, but it wouldn't bother him much, just like he was sure it hadn't bothered a single Jew when they'd killed Ali.

Ali had been selling tickets in the bus station the day Youssef arrived in Jenin, in the West Bank (four months to the day after his father had been murdered at the café). When his mother had gone crazy the family had decided to move him and his brother Mohammed to live with their uncle. Youssef arrived cursing the place in Swahili and swearing that he'd be back in Dar Es Salaam within the week. A few days later Ali gave him a walkie-talkie. Youssef hid it in his bedroom and the two would stay up after bed time swapping stories over static, Youssef in his broken Arabic, and Ali with the occasional word of Swahili that Youssef had taught him. From then they were inseparable, until the day Ali died.

That day came back to him in sharp focus. He and Ali were outside his uncle's concrete shack playing soccer in the street with a bunch of other twelve-year-olds—a couple eight-year-olds relegated to goalkeepers. He and Ali criss-crossed through defenders on their way to the goal. But nobody ever took a shot. A deep rumble came faintly from far away and then quickly crescendoed into a heart-pounding roar. Youssef froze next to Ali on the dusty street. Gunfire popped and men yelled, a few carrying rifles and running from house to house. The roaring thing rounded a corner and careened at them, swift and muscular like a dinosaur. It was six-wheeled, black-armored, and with a swiveling turret atop. Wherever the gun pointed debris and dirt jumped off houses. Something warm spread down Youssef's legs. He looked around. He was alone. A woman in an open window twisted her face, her hands out between metal bars, begging him to come to her. Something chugged like an elephant's rumble. A thin cottony cloud of smoke jetted by. He woke up deaf, and buried in debris. He wandered through rubble, the sound coming back like someone turning up the volume on everything very slowly. Then he saw Ali's mother, wailing and holding Ali, like a piece of wilted lettuce.

Youssef rubbed at the carpet stains with his shoe and gestured for Jassim to remove the blindfold. Youssef held up a baggie inscribed with the word "STERILE" and containing two cotton-tipped wooden swabs. He explained to the man that he would use these to scrape the insides of his fiancée's cheeks. The man looked back, nodding, his eyes rimmed red from his crying fit in the car. "Now we wait," Youssef said. He checked the phone that he used to speak with Ledpaste. The signal was strong. Time passed silently except for a dripping faucet. It was nearly time for *salat*. He thought about blindfolding Reece again and kneeling to pray quietly in the room but he decided against it. Instead, he closed his eyes and recited his prayers mentally. *It is not me but God that kills. There is no glory but through God...*

Later the phone rang with an unknown number. A man, speaking English with a Hindi accent, told him he was going to put someone else on. "Mr. Dougherty?" Youssef said into the phone.

Reece's eyes bulged.

"Where's Sarah!" Mr. Dougherty yelled through the phone. "You better not hurt her. I swear—" he was cut-off and Youssef heard yelling and banging.

The guy with the Hindi accent got back on. "I am sorry. He is ready now to speak."

Coughing, the target's father got back on.

Youssef hit the speaker button. "Mr. Dougherty, tell Reece, what is happening."

"We've been kidnapped, Sandra and I. There's two of them, they're Indian and—"

Dougherty was cut-off again and Youssef quickly switched out of speaker mode and put the phone to his ear. "Is that all you need?" the Hindi voice asked.

"Yes, thank you."

Reece's lip trembled and he looked pitiful.

"Everybody's going to be fine as long as you do exactly as I say," Youssef said. "If you get the police, or anyone else involved, or try anything strange, Sarah's parents will die. It's not worth it. It is only a mouth swab. You are going to call Sarah and tell her about her parents, then you will meet her at the volley ball courts in Zilker Park. All this will all be over in an hour."

. . .

All night Sarah and Finn alternated between sleeping and fucking. In fact, she was on top of him when the tinny intro of Marvin Gaye's Sexual Healing came from the living room, again—the fifth time in the span of two minutes. Surely it was Reece freaking out. But, why had he waited until the morning?

Sarah got up off him and came back and sat down next to him listening to a message. Her face contorted and she looked shocked. She snatched a tee shirt off a chair, yanked it over her head, and bolted from the room.

"What'd he say?" Finn called to her.

"I have to go," she yelled from the living room.

Finn got up and went to the bedroom doorway.

"I have to go. I'm done hiding!" She pulled her sandals from under the coffee table.

"I was just curious."

"You can't help me anymore! Did you hear me?" The veins bulged in her slender neck.

"I, I hear you."

She yanked the front door against its frame. "Goddamn it. how the fuck do you open this thing!" He helped her and she threw it open and went running down the street. Her car wasn't in the driveway. He stood behind the screen door, naked and puzzled. Then he got an idea and ran into his bedroom and threw on a tee shirt, shorts, and flip-flops. He jumped into his car and drove the direction she'd run. At the end of the street he saw her car take a right turn.

EIGHTEEN

Peeking from behind a tree in Zilker Park, Finn watched Reece walking towards Sarah. She was at least a hundred yards from him beyond a pair of volleyball courts. When Reece reached her, he hugged her. Then he swabbed her. *What the hell!?* Finn searched for a way to disbelieve it. How had that bastard forced Reece to do his bidding? He bet Reece hoped to give the man what he wanted and return to normalcy with Sarah. They hugged again and then Reece jogged away from Sarah and toward the edge of the park. Sarah jogged back to her car. Finn put a forearm on the tree and for a while leaned his head on his arm, wondering what to do. He took out his phone and dialed.

"Benjamin. It's me," he said. "I need your help."

"Call me after lunch."

Keeping an eye on Reece, Finn hurried towards his car while speaking, crashing the words together. He told Benjamin they may have a chance to catch the man.

"Now?"

"Yeah, right now. Where are you?"

"North, near Breaker Lane."

"Damn it! That'll take twenty minutes."

"I'll be there in eight." Benjamin hung up.

Reece hailed a cab and Finn followed in his car. The taxi stopped in Zilker Park parking and Finn pulled into a nearby slot. Three and a half minutes later the taxi pulled out and went east. Finn followed. They passed the Mexican restaurant with the purple octopus on its roof, and the barbecue houses with picnic tables packed with nine-to-fivers on lunch break. They turned left and came to the wide, murky Colorado River dragging itself underneath the South Lamar Boulevard Bridge. Concrete construction barriers blocked all but two lanes of the bridge: one north, one south. Dense traffic crammed onto each one. Heat rose from the black asphalt like translucent smoke. As Finn nudged onto the bridge, five cars behind Reece, Sarah's attacker jogged by toward the taxi. "Holy Fuck!"

The man stopped and talked to Reece through the taxi window.

Finn re-dialed Benjamin.

"Four minutes," Benjamin said, answering.

"He's here. The guy who attacked Sarah. He's here, right in front of me!"

Through the window, Reece handed the man the baggie with the swabs and the man trotted away, toward the other end of the bridge. Finn dropped the phone on the passenger seat. *I've got to stop him before he gets away.* He grabbed his face in both hands and then ran his fingers through his hair.

Do it. Do it. Do it. Go!

He needed to wait for Benjamin. He couldn't leave his car there in the middle of traffic. *There's no time.* He yearned to burst from his car, cocky and resolved, but he didn't know what he would do if he caught the man, or what weapons the man had.

Do it!

He gnashed his teeth, and pounded a fist on the dashboard. He felt as if he were a rubber band being pulled in both directions but going nowhere. The traffic inched forward. Benjamin shouted something through the phone. Now half way across, the man loped along between cars and the construction barriers. Finn decided he would tackle him and hope to get the baggie, or an I.D., or a cell phone, anything to identify him. But, the man knew how to fight. Finn hung-up his phone. He hesitated then jerked his hand toward the door handle. The man was three-fourths of the way across now. He had a knife when he'd attacked Sarah and right now Finn had flip-flops and 37 cents. He breathed and exhaled through pursed lips. Then he decided that he would do it. He would—

Stop thinking! Act! The car ahead rolled forward several feet. He cracked the door. I'm doing it, he told himself. *I'm doing it.* He threw the door open and put one foot on the pavement. The man was at the end of the bridge now. The single lane coming towards them was immobile with cars and trucks. Just then a scrawny dark skinned man scurried along the other side of the bridge passing Finn's car, no other pedestrians in sight. He shouted something, "Yusif!" (or was it "Joseph!"?). He shouted it again and Sarah's attacker stopped and turned at the end of the bridge. He looked. Finn looked. The other man pointed and waved his arms in a deliberate motion like an air traffic controller but without the flags. Finn's phone buzzed. The display showed it was Benjamin. He didn't answer it and jerked his gaze back to the second man, who yelled something and then the man who'd attacked Sarah spun 180 degrees and launched into a terrifying sprint. He ran directly at Finn.

The second man turned and sprinted as well, still on the opposite walkway. It seemed a gossamer membrane, an amniotic wall, connected the two men. Certainly heat rose from the bridge in vapors, but the wall (whose edges rose into infinity) moved along with each man. Although he could see through it, beyond it, he knew it was an illusion, that what he saw was nothing he could grasp.

"I'm here. I'm here." Benjamin said into the phone. Finn had answered the phone without realizing. Then Finn understood why the men had turned around. Across the river Benjamin's white patrol car, heading west, flashed between trees and snaked around crawling cars. He caught a glimpse of pulsing white lights but the sirens weren't on. He pulled his foot in and clicked the door shut; he wasn't sure why. It just happened. On opposite walkways the two men hurtled towards Finn. They dragged the amniotic membrane behind them like a portal to another world, one Finn would soon be in. The man jumped a concrete barrier and continued in the construction lane. "I'm stuck!" Benjamin shouted. His patrol car turned facing Finn at the other end of the bridge, but sardined by cars, a narrow walkway, and concrete barriers. "Which one is he?"

"On the right. I mean, Your left," Finn said, though it didn't sound like his voice.

Something glinted in the man's pistoning hand (a knife blade perhaps?) He zoomed at Finn, ever closer, the horrifying wall straining to keep pace. "Stop him!" Benjamin barked into the phone. Finn froze but he wanted to throw the man down and tear the baggie from him. The baggie swung in his right hand as a rush of plastic. Benjamin's voice seemed far away. At the end of the bridge he climbed from his patrol car and chugged toward Finn like a bag of concrete, while Sarah's attacker bounded around cement barriers. Three cars ahead he jumped the other side of the barrier and landed in the walkway. An image filled Finn's mind, of himself, on the ground and bleeding out from a bubbling chest wound. The man was only one car ahead now. If Finn jumped he could still stop him.

But instead of jumping out he only swiveled his head as the man shot by. The man shouted to the other one, now parallel to him. Finn glanced across the bridge and then back, craning his neck around to see Sarah's attacker reach the end of the bridge and careen left. A gap was open in front of Finn and the next car. A distance he couldn't measure. Someone honked behind him. The other man dropped off the bridge too, but went the opposite direction. Finn pulled ahead.

Benjamin barreled up, panting. "Which one?" he said. But he may have said, "Why didn't you stop them!" or anything for that matter. Finn pointed over his right shoulder. "Come on," Benjamin said, and bolted. Finn sat like a stone. The time had passed and he'd froze. But then he jumped from the car. Benjamin was twenty yards ahead. He gained on him. They cut through cars, and up on to the sidewalk and stopped at a massive intersection at the end of the bridge: Twelve lanes of traffic and three pedestrians. None were Sarah's attacker. Benjamin backhanded Finn's chest. "You fucking pussy. You let him get away!"

For a moment Finn was quiet. He wanted to say that he didn't want to be killed by some Paki obsessed with Sarah's saliva, but instead he said, "I'm sorry."

"We could have had him!"

"I guess it's over now," Finn said. He jogged back to his car. The southbound lane inched by while in front of his car, in the northbound lane, a huge gap had opened. People honked. Several stood outside of their cars, and talked on cell phones. Reece's taxi was gone.

He climbed into his hatchback and eased it into gear. People shouted at him. He couldn't remember if Benjamin had walked back with him. He drove as if under a spell. He called Sarah. She didn't answer. When he got home he plopped down onto his recliner. Amongst strands of broken glass next to the skewed coffee table lay Sarah's bra. He wasn't certain what had just happened. He found an old box of bran cereal at the back of a cupboard, poured himself a bowl, and chewed on the stale flakes. Slowly but steadily he began to understand there was nothing for him to do.

He called Mulveny. "It's Finn Barber. Has Sarah Dougherty called you?" Mulveny said she hadn't and asked if her stalker was up to something.

"Her fiancé gave the man the mouth swabs."

Mulveny mumbled something like he was grateful that maybe this entire circus would be over now. "We almost had him, Benjamin and I," he said. "I tried to stop him but he had a knife."

"Well, if you do talk to her," Mulveny said, "Have her call here so that I can close the case."

Finn hung up. He thought about what he'd told Mulveny, that he'd tried to stop him. *And hadn't he?* He'd done everything he could short of committing *hara kari* on Yusif's dagger. He'd followed Sarah, called in Benjamin and chased Yusif until he couldn't even see him anymore. He'd even left his car and blocked the bridge. If Reece was determined to capitulate to that man and had convinced Sarah as well, who was he to stop them? He just wished she would call.

He dozed, trying to ease his hangover, but sleep was fitful. Eventually he gave up and read a short story by Roberto Bolaño. It was a story of a young man, B, and his father. The two seemed to care for one another, and they had a type of spiritual or visceral connection but it was faulty. The father was more wild than the boy and tried to make him drink and whore with him, but, as always, with caring. The father was a boxer and found an ex-cliff diver to drink and share lies with. B got drunk with the two men in a decrepit bar. Later, outside, he received a blow job from a prostitute while a chained pit bull bore his teeth at him. Inside, at a card game his father won money and lost friends. The prostitute noted that B loved his father, and she warned them to leave or something bad would happen.

Finn wasn't sure how he felt after reading it. He kind of slammed it down onto the coffee table from where he lay on his couch. He felt lost he finally decided, more lost than he'd ever been. But strangely, it wasn't a sense of being lost accompanied by a panic to orient himself. He knew being lost always generated this deadly panic. This time he felt lost accompanied only by a sense of wretchedness. The story hadn't helped either.

The phone rang and he slid it off the coffee table. It was Mulveny. Thank God! Sarah had probably called him.

Finn answered but Mulveny didn't sound pleasant.

"Is Sarah all right?" he asked, suddenly afraid.

Mulveny was sending a car for him. He'd explain everything at the station.

II

"We were successful," Youssef said into the phone. "Finally," Ledpaste responded. "It's taken you nine days to get one lousy mouth swab. Put Jassim on." Youssef gave Jassim the phone.

"Yes? No. But we have the sample," Jassim said into the phone. He looked worried. "Until Youssef got the swab. From the fiancé, on the bridge in very heavy traffic. I was rear cross-point-cover when a police car came from the northeast. Yes sir. I don't know. No sir. Sir?" Jassim turned to Youssef, "He wants us to come immediately."

"I know," Youssef said, "I know."

Jassim drove them west down Enfield Drive. They passed over the parched bed of Shoal Creek and climbed a hill shaded by pecans and evergreens. "Turn there," Youssef said. They passed manicured lawns of townhouses and apartment complexes dotted with pear cactus and rose bushes. Ahead, a frail girl wearing a pink helmet rode a pink bicycle with training wheels and red and white plastic tassels fluttering off the handlebars. A flabby man struggled behind the pale waif. She wobbled along. It reminded him of the communal bike he learned to ride on, a multi-colored mutt piece-mealed together with junk-yard scraps, him perched above barefoot and shirtless and dodging broken concrete, dogs, mule carts, and cars. "Here," he said, pointing to a row of terracotta-roofed townhouses.

Youssef started up the brick steps with Jassim behind him. He was thinking about his insane mother and his brother in Italy studying engineering, and Cemile in Turkey, furious with him. He wondered whether his mother would understand he was gone if this meeting with Ledpaste was the last this world had for him. His brother would see what he'd done for their people now. Sweat droplets stippled his shirt. He turned and regarded Jassim, and Jassim stared back nervous. He rapped on the door. Ledpaste opened it and ushered them in with a wave of his arm. He looked grim. He was neatly dressed with black slacks, a crisply-ironed shirt, and a pair of sunglasses pushed up on his head. The air was hot and hung with the stale smell of cigarettes. The small wooden table and its chairs sat unmoved from the week before, but Ledpaste had added a leather recliner, side table, and a large plasma screen television on a stylish, brushed steel table. On the television a muted soccer match played. The edge of a cardboard bullet box poked from a trash can next to the TV.

"You're late," Ledpaste said in Pashto.

"Today, or in general?" Youssef asked.

"Don't get clever with me now."

Youssef pulled the baggie out of a front shirt pocket and placed it on the table. He looked at Ledpaste impassively trying not to show pride in his success nor shame in his delay. He had erred in his first attempts to get the swab but he also knew he had an exceptional target, exceptional in her persistence, her strength, and the people who came to her aid.

"Sit down," Ledpaste said. He picked up the baggie and went around a broad column and into the kitchen. He put the baggie in a drawer. Jassim and Youssef sat down. Youssef felt anxious but resolved to accept his fate now. *Those killed in God's name are alive at his side.*

Ledpaste returned, studied both of them and paced on the other side of the table. "You've finally brought me the cheek swabs but you've broken protocol," he said looking at Youssef.

"But, *you* authorized the kidnapping."

"I'm not talking about that." He paused. "You think you're a maverick don't you?"

"No." He wondered why Ledpaste was asking him that.

"You think you can pull the wool over my eyes?"

"Although I am ashamed for my delay I have now performed as required."

Ledpaste chuckled. "I'm not talking about your performance either, although that's highly questionable." He placed both hands flat on the table and leaned in, "I'm talking about your woman."

Youssef felt as if his stomach had jammed up into his lungs. He looked at Ledpaste trying not to change his expression.

"Nothing clever to say now? Cemile Yilmaz," He sang her name. "She goes to the university with you."

"She's not my woman, she's a fellow student." The words jammed a little in his throat. "What does she matter?"

"She matters because she's your fianceé and you broke protocol. No. Intimate. Relationships." He slammed a fat hand on the table. "What the hell is wrong with you!"

Youssef felt flushed, and dizzy. "She was just a friend," He said. "I used her for sex. She knows nothing."

Ledpaste leaned in close smelling of cigarettes and beer. "You think she's waiting for you in Ankara?"

Oh God, he knows where she is. "I swear in God's name she doesn't know anything."

Ledpaste looked at Youssef as if he'd claimed to be God. "I'm responsible for the entire Southwest. From Louisiana to fucking California!" He turned his back to them and stepped away, but then came back calmer. "If you think for one fucking second that I'm going to let that gutter slut put us at risk, then you've seriously underestimated me. And you've totally underestimated this operation. The rules and expectations were very clear!"

"It's just that it was nearly three years before I had contact. I thought I could just sleep with her and fool her into thinking I wanted—"

"You think I'm a fucking bitch you can manipulate!" The veins stood out on his neck and his flushed face shook. "I cannot risk having to answer as to why I didn't act when I knew you violated protocol. It doesn't matter what she knows. It matters what I know, you dumb fuck, and I know she's your fiancée." He violently swung his arm as if sweeping Youssef away. "Now, get out!" He turned and went to the kitchen.

Youssef's chin trembled. "But she's innocent."

From the kitchen Ledpaste glowered at Youssef. "You destroyed her innocence. *You* put her in danger and *you* chose not to tell her. Now I told you. Get the fuck out!"

"Don't you even think of touching her."

Ledpaste laughed, throwing back his head. "Don't be stupid." He reached behind his back and pulled out his Glock pistol and leveled it at Youssef. "Think I would tell you if you still had a chance to save that cunt?" From a drawer he pulled something and slammed it flat-palmed on the counter top. He pulled his hand away revealing a large gold hoop earring, Cemile's. "You tried with the ticket to Ankara. I suppose she thought you were just fooling her."

Everything beyond and around Ledpaste blurred as if he were at the end of a long tunnel. Youssef's thoughts vanished. He riveted on Ledpaste, a point of clarity in a sea of dusky images. He breathed through his mouth. Ledpaste shouted something.

He sprang directly at Ledpaste as if nothing lay between them, not a table, nor a chair, nor a counter top. A strange sensation, that he was acting simultaneously in the present and past, overtook him, as if he were able to reflect upon his actions while experiencing them. Ledpaste pulled the pistol towards himself and fidgeted with it. Youssef leaped over the wooden table in a fluid movement except that he clobbered his head against a lamp hanging above. It didn't feel like he'd hit his head, but rather like it had only been forced aside. He landed on the other side of the table and with one stride only the counter remained between him and Ledpaste, still fiddling with the gun. Ledpaste looked up, his expression of hostility gone now.

Youssef found himself suspended above the counter, both feet forward, and hurtling directly at Ledpaste. He struck him squarely in the chest with both feet. Ledpaste's sunglasses sailed away. Youssef's lower back bounced off the edge of the counter and his head snapped. He felt the pressure of the counter-top against it. Ledpaste's arms splayed out to his sides as he crashed back into cabinets. A cabinet door splintered behind his head. Youssef bounced onto the kitchen floor. Ledpaste stumbled forward and Youssef jumped back to his feet in front of him. He drew his neck back and head-butted Ledpaste's face. Teeth bit into his forehead. Ledpaste collapsed. His eyelids flickered. Youssef scanned for the gun but didn't see it. Instead, he snatched a thick, square-bottomed olive oil bottle from the floor. With breathless grunts Ledpaste squirmed to sit up, blood rushing down his lips and chin. Youssef swung on his face. The bottom corner of the bottle struck the top of a jowly cheek. Ledpaste covered his face with his hands. The next blow smacked a hand and he pulled it back. Jassim yelled something. Youssef spun the bottle and drove it straight into the bridge of Ledpaste's nose, then his forehead, then his eye, then his cheek, then his mouth. His hands fell to the floor. Youssef pounded some more, until the bottleneck cracked and the bottle bounced on the tile floor and shattered. Ledpaste lay still.

Slowly Jassim's shouting registered. "Stop! Stop it!"

Youssef stood over Ledpaste trying to catch his breath the way a child tries to resume a rhythm after a tantrum. Ledpaste's face was a mess of pulpy flesh, blood, and oil. Jassim had stopped shouting, and all Youssef heard now was his own panting, and Ledpaste's raspy breath struggling in his throat.

"I love her. I love her." Youssef said. He stood above Ledpaste, straddling him.

Jassim stood in the entrance to the kitchen, his hand covering his mouth.

Please God don't let Cemile be dead. Youssef could see her face the last time she'd pinched his lips together and said, *Gimme a big smooch,* while laughing her stupid snorting laugh. He had just spoken to her a couple days ago, days so close he could touch them. Youssef didn't care if he himself died. He didn't want to die though, but he didn't care. They weren't the same. But, Cemile, he never fathomed her dying, and he cared deeply that she did not die. He had planned that her lifetime would be but a moment for him waiting in heaven, where they would reunite and she would tell him about the attack, and her life and the world afterwards.

Then the front door swung open and inside stepped the fat, bug-eyed Russian, the one with Ledpaste when he'd made Youssef put a gun to his own head and pull the trigger. The Russian glanced around and then quickly shifted his gaze between Jassim and Youssef. For an impossibly long moment nobody moved, not even breathed (except for Ledpaste's rasp). Hot blood seeped into Youssef's mouth. The Russian raised his hands palms forward, showing that he meant no harm, and kicked the door shut behind him. On the floor to Ledpaste's left, poking from beneath the refrigerator, lay his Glock. Ledpaste sputtered.

"Who is he?" Jassim asked in Arabic.

"No talking," the Russian said, in English.

Slowly, the Russian walked toward them. "Over there," he said to Youssef, pointing to the far end of the kitchen. "And, you, go there," he said to Jassim, and pointing to the television.

Youssef nodded for Jassim to obey. And they both did as they were told. The Russian came around the column at the end of the kitchen counter and then halted staring at the mess. He regarded Youssef and then looked back at Ledpaste. Ledpaste's chest rose and dropped. Youssef still held the dripping neck of the olive oil bottle. The Russian kicked the Glock and it slid away from Youssef and across the kitchen below a pantry door. He stood over Ledpaste mumbling to himself.

"Well," he finally said, looking up at Youssef. "Don't start anything you can't finish," and backed away from Ledpaste.

Youssef searched the man's eyes and then looked over at Cemile's earring on the counter top. The Russian followed his gaze. And then Youssef could see written on the Russian's face as clear as the blue sky. Cemile was gone.

"Turn up the TV as loud as it will go," the Russian said to Jassim.

Jassim raised the volume and the T.V. filled the condominium with trebly noise. Excited men commented on a soccer match over a mixture of cheering, drums and whistles. Youssef leaned down and let his rage flow into his fingertips. Double-handed, he clamped Ledpaste's neck just below the chin and squeezed his throat into his spine. One eye, bulging and unseeing, swam as if a fish in a bowl. The other blinked, looking at Youssef. Ledpaste sputtered and vibrations quaked through his body to his feet and fingertips. A television announcer yelled. People cheered and pounded drums. The announcer bellowed,

"Gooooooooooooooal!" Sometime later Youssef released his grip.

The Russian leaned down and checked for a pulse. Then he stood up and pulled the baggie of swabs from a drawer and jammed it in his shirt pocket. He walked into the living room and lowered the T.V. Volume. "We're leaving, *now*." He marched Youssef out the back door, Jassim ahead of them.

The back door opened onto a small railed, wooden deck a few feet off ground. They straddled the railing and climbed to the ground and then around the side of the condominium to a parking lot. "Come back in two hours," the Russian said to Jassim, "And if the police aren't here, clean up and take the body out after dark. Put it somewhere it will be unnoticed for at least a month. No lakes, no rivers." The Russian gave Jassim a key to the condo and his cell phone number.

Youssef was still panting and his heartbeat throbbed. Cemile couldn't be dead. It just couldn't be. He took out his cell phone and dialed her Texas number. Maybe she would check voice mail from Turkey. The Russian peered down a narrow path and swung his head back and forth looking at the parking lot. Cemile's voice-mail answered and Youssef begged her to call him. He licked a forefinger and rubbed blood from a few keypad buttons.

After Jassim pulled out the two of them left in the Russian's S.U.V. Sunlight glared off the windshield, the windows, the chrome molding, and even the dashboard. As if he were sitting behind one of the little waterfalls in Campbell's Hole, tears dropped a curtain across his vision. Then a drop escaped down his cheek. He brushed it away and squeezed out the others, wiping them off his face in one quick motion. He sniffled but then coughed trying to cover it up and then the tears were back. He turned toward the window.

"I am sorry about Dahoud." The Russian said.

With his head in his hands and still facing the window, Youssef tried to muffle his sobs. Sloppy tears splashed off the armrest. The car turned and then stopped. The man didn't speak and Youssef heard him flick a lighter and then smelled cigarette smoke.

Youssef wiped off tears and tried to sit up straight. They were at a stoplight. "Is she really dead?"

The light turned green and they rolled forward. "I can tell you this. He was a sadist. He put the operation at risk with his violence."

Suddenly Youssef felt trapped. "Stop the car."

The Russian looked at him nodding, maybe in agreement or maybe just in acknowledgement. He placed the cigarette between his lips, glanced over his right shoulder and pulled into the right hand lane.

"You are free to go but you're not entirely finished. There are a few threads to clip."

"I don't fucking work for you, *kuffar!*" Youssef bellowed in his face.

The Russian stopped the car against the curb and spoke calmly. "Ibrahim Al-Madri, he gave me my authority directly."

Youssef, now half in and half out of the car, abruptly turned back to the man.

"You pledged him your *bayat,* huh? Look, there's not much left to do. With your work today," he patted his shirt pocket holding the baggie of swabs, "The operation can proceed to the next stage. I can arrange for you to speak with Al-Madri if you'd like."

Youssef stared at him.

The Russian leaned over, opened the glove compartment, and removed a brown paper bag. Holding it toward Youssef he said, "These are the vials. Deliver them as usual. Remember, you're God's child and you're still a soldier."

Youssef stared at the brown bag without reaching for it. Slowly he shut the door. He turned away and left.

He passed many hours wandering, wandering. He was around the university. Eventually the downtown left him. He left Cemile many voice mails. Then it was dusk. He crossed a bridge. Throngs of people gathered on a lawn below. School-girls screamed as swarms of bats sprouted from under the bridge and dipped towards them. Above a shimmering sliver of sun the bats formed black clouds to the horizon. He felt utterly alone and collapsed in the grass. He trusted the grass with his tears. For Ledpaste, killing Cemile was revenge for him allowing police involvement. He knew it. He had told Reece not to call the cops. Why hadn't they fucking listened? He wanted to find the target, tear the bitch apart, and leave her to die slowly. He swore he would dedicate his remaining life to finding Sarah Doughtery and making her understand her mistake and regret it for the rest of her short life.

What Youssef didn't know was that the bug-eyed, pug-nosed Russian was Nikolai Kotesky, Scientific Director of the current attack against the United States. Seven years ago Kotesky's boss, Valentin Sanchiev, then president of applied research at the Russian Academy of Sciences, asked Kotesky to prepare a confidential plan for an immense, though hypothetical, biological attack against the United States. It was an attack to be carried out by Islamic fundamentalists in collusion with Russian scientists using old Soviet bioweapons technology. It was a defense program designed to test the possibility that disgruntled Russian germ warfare researchers, many now unemployed and impoverished, could sell bioweapons technology to Islamic fundamentalists, and possibly ignite a war between Russia and the U.S.

The United States, after September 11, 2001, vastly improved its surveillance of electronic mediums: short wave to Ham radio, all forms of Internet communication, and telephone voice and text transmissions. The CIA used custom, artificial intelligence software and quadrupled the number of specialists sifting through the morass of data. The U.S. government fortified border security, visa verification, and foreign intelligence and by 2007 it had incarcerated many key terrorists and many suspected terrorists as prisoners of the War on Terror.

Like bacteria under an antibiotic assault, terrorist groups fragmented, became less virulent, and were annihilated. But a few groups with traits conferring resistance to detection, grew, immune to the increased vigilance. The extraordinary pressure selected for groups that were cohesive yet de-centralized, powerful yet small, and more sophisticated yet less dependent on electronic communication. Here's what it came down to: a silent war was occurring, of which the average American was haplessly unaware, and this silent war was far more dangerous than the overt wars in Afghanistan, Iraq, and Iran. The American civilians were the targets, yet unlike soldiers they were blithely ignorant they were on the front. Julius Caesar claimed the soldier's most important weapon was the spade. The American civilians had no spades. They had not even trenches.

. . .

Moscow, Seven Years Earlier

After eight months on the bioweapons project, Kotesky, during a trip to Moscow, knocked on the door of his boss' cramped office. "Come in," Sanchiev called out from behind a dreary metal desk. In his mid fifties, slender and graying, he looked the part of the well-mannered scientist. He was surprised to see Kotesky, greeted him warmly and invited him in. They spoke politely, Kotesky tense, thinking about when to state what he came to say. He believed that the defense department program studying a hypothetical terrorist attack using Russian bioweapons technology was a ruse. He suspected

Sanchiev wanted to sell bioweapons technology to Islamo-facists. As they chatted, a prickly sweat broke out underneath his arms. He deliberately thought about his facial expression, tried to keep it confident but nonchalant.

Kotesky knew if he were correct and tried to resign from the project he would be assassinated. He had too much knowledge now. He could also be killed if Sanchiev and collaborators thought him a threat to them or the project, or considered him untrustworthy. However, if Sanchiev and others planned to sell the bioweapons technology, he would be indispensable as long as he was deeply involved. That, and the fact that he couldn't deny a tiny part of him fantasized about flexing the plans he'd spent a lifetime developing. Sanchiev must have had some trust in him, enough to bring him in, Kotesky believed. Now he relied on this belief.

"This biological attack is no defense program," he blurted.

Sanchiev's eyes opened wide, but then quickly he regained his composure. "The program is top secret. Only two people beyond us know it exists. It must be that way to be effective."

Kotesky looked Sanchiev directly in the eyes with the most serious expression he could muster. "You can trust me one hundred percent."

Sanchiev pursed his lips.

A bead of sweat slid down Kotesky's armpit. "I'm in," he said.

Sanchiev looked at him sternly. "What you are implying is treasonous. Now, if you will, I have work to do."

Kotesky left the office feeling faint. He'd exposed himself and received no answers. After two nights with a .45 under his pillow and waking at every creak of a floorboard, Sanchiev called him in for a meeting downtown. In a dim bar with cracked floor tiles and scarred wooden booths Sanchiev told him that he would soon be given all the information on the project, and that Sanchiev and the two others needed his help and so concocted the defense department story to test him out.

"The capitalists want to pretend we never existed, never revolutionized warfare," Sanchiev said, pounding the table with a finger. "They want to forget everything we accomplished." He swigged vodka from a slender glass. "And then they expect us to crawl away and retire on that shit they call a pension. Do you know what a scientist with your talents and intelligence would earn in the United States? You'd be a goddamn national treasure. I guarantee you that. And look at what we've become."

"Those systems are functional."

"Look, some fundamentalists want to buy a system we made. That's a far cry from deploying it, or even trying to deploy it, especially for them."

"What do they want?"

"They're interested," He paused. "They want to use Plan 3-27."

"Whoa," Kotesky exhaled, and leaned back. Plan 3-27 was a colossus, and it had been his life for an entire decade.

"I know, I know," Sanchiev said. "I never dreamed of negotiating with those fuckers. But the U.S. now has Afghanistan, Iraq, and are drooling for Iran, and who-knows-what after that." He swung an arm. "Uzbekistan? Kazakhstan? You want to cross Yankee blockades just to visit your family?" He stared at Kotesky intently. "I need you to hammer out the deal with the Muslims."

Kotesky swilled his vodka.

"Don't worry Nikolai, the only biological attack those goat herders could launch would be a few cases of hoof and mouth disease. But in their failure the United States and the world will acknowledge and respect the power of the weapons we developed. And us, well, we won't need those government pensions."

"But that system..."

Sanchiev held up a finger. "I know, I know. You remember Tarasov. Yeah? He laughed a little. Hey, I'm not trying to piss you off. I'm telling you because I don't want you to worry. We're setting him up as the main fall." A gentle smile bent Sanchiev's lips. "How about that?"

"Fine. But that system was created with many safeguards against failure."

Sanchiev's smile vanished. "Then you definitely won't have to worry about those Yankee blockades."

. . .

Kazakhstan, Six Months Later

"Uncle Sam," Kotestky said, in English. "Has an impeccable record of intelligence." He sipped a steaming cup of coffee in a leafless park in the town of Oral, in northern Kazakhstan, six months after his meeting in the bar with Sanchiev. He sat at a bench with his contact, Saleem Rafiq Nuhrani. Around them the stone-gray sky merged with the earth. Saleem, an Afghani and Islamic fundamentalist, represented the Taliban, Al Qaeda, and a few other militant allies. He had studied

⌐ in Germany and now lived in Kabul, Afghanistan.
ghtened his coat's fox fur collar against his neck and
some coffee. "They cracked both the Nazi and Japanese
ᴄᴏᴅᴇ. ⌐orld War II and they may have lost the war entirely if not for
one phrase: "No more fresh water on Midway Island."

"I am not interested in a history lesson," Saleem said.

"My point is simple. Weapons are mere tools. Strategy and planning supported by intelligence wins wars. And if communication is intercepted or compromised then all the strategy, planning, and intelligence in the world is worth shit."

"Another sales pitch?" Saleem asked.

"You should buy more than what you're asking for. You cannot just ask for the bombs, guns or planes. You must ask for effective means of disseminating them, using them, *and*—and this is what most people don't realize," he leaned in to Saleem. "Hiding them." He swallowed some coffee and dragged on his filter-less cigarette. "In Ethiopia there's a wasteland of Russian tanks, fighter planes, and artillery. We sold them to the Ethiopians in their war against Eritrea, but the Eritreans bombed them as soon as they came off the container ships. Dumb fucking Africans never even used them once." A breeze flipped one of Kotesky's fur coat collars down to his shoulder.

"I don't think I'll have a problem hiding a few vials of viruses." Saleem said.

Kotesky nodded. *He looks so damn young and clean-cut for a Mohammed freak.* "Look, an operation such as this will be vulnerable at many levels but especially at the planning stage. All communications are vulnerable. The Yanks will infiltrate, incarcerate, torture, maim, and murder. They have no limits and they have the best intelligence. If just one goddamn Jihadist gets loose lips on his cellular we lose our operation, and our lives, and maybe our families."

Saleem had stood up. "I will not sit here and listen to you blaspheme Islam."

"Calm down. I speak impetuously." He was about to say that the Muslims treat their women like shit and have to beg their God all day long, but he didn't. He didn't care too much about insulting Saleem. He was a goddamn Russian. If this snot-nosed shit, one university degree removed from stirring lentils over charcoal, didn't want his technology someone else would. "I'm not prejudiced," Kotesky said. "I don't give a fucking rat's ass if you pray to Jesus-Ali-Mohammed-Buddha." Kotesky patted him on the shoulder, "Come, sit down. We are allies now. You had to ally with America to beat us and now you should ally with us to crush them. Then we can resume fighting each other, eh?" Kotesky chuckled. Saleem sat reluctantly, and Kotesky continued. "Sure you can hide a few vials of smallpox, maybe even the plans and men to disseminate it. But a small attack with a contagious virus will be nullified in a few weeks with quarantines, medical care, blockades, vaccines,—all that shit. Even a slight head start from intelligence or spies will smother it. It's even possible they have companies that can develop new vaccines within days. Listen, 9-11 taught the Americans. Any big attack now needs a new form of communication, and deployment: a whole new strategic paradigm."

"We can handle all that."

"You have an effective sleeper cell network system, I'll give you that. But if you want to work with us, we demand brand new cells with absolutely no electronic communication until the launch of the attack."

Saleem laughed.

"Then I ask you this: What would you gain by mounting a massive domestic strike—the scope of which I will soon detail—and not removing all possible security weaknesses before starting?"

Saleem looked at him skeptically, angrily even. "I'm sure you can tell me."

"You may save the three years of work it takes to create new clean cells only to find later, when the strike is ready, that it has been detected and dismantled." He dragged on his cigarette and let the sharp air haul the smoke away. He looked Saleem in the eyes. "We won't collaborate with you to end up being captured, along with our families, and tortured and killed by the Yanks."

"I have come to secure a deal for the technology," Saleem said. "We can manage the process. If you don't trust us then sell it somewhere else."

"I trust you can handle the process," he said, though he didn't. "It's which process you handle, I'm concerned about. We have a system that will work very well for a sleeper cell network. The system has several key qualities," he continued, without letting Saleem interrupt. "One: Messages can be sent that will have an infinitesimal chance of being intercepted. Two: Even if they are intercepted they have a minuscule chance of being decoded. Three: They can be sent across borders with zero risk of detection. And four: Once initiated only a few key people can stop the attack."

Saleem looked interested. "I'm not making any decisions," he said.

"DNA," Kotesky said. He told him that he had refined a system of inserting DNA into the inner cheek cells of any person. A virus would insert its own DNA, along with foreign DNA, into any human. "So," he said, "Taking advantage of billions of years of evolution we can hide, in any human host, an undetectable DNA sequence, or in other words, any information we want."

"How do we infect the carrier?"

"Spike their food or drink. Pop it into some tourist, international businessman, who ever the fuck you want. They go back to the United States, and *violá* you've got an untraceable, undetectable, and unknown message to everyone but the person waiting for it."

Saleem took out a notepad.

Kotesky continued. "The carrier will be entirely unaware they are infected. In the foreign DNA will be encoded information as well as pieces of a virus, and the viral DNA from seventeen carriers will be joined creating an intact viral genome. It meshes perfectly with Plan 3-27. As you know the immensity of the human genome makes it inconceivable that someone could discover and decipher a message encrypted in it. But with the right primer pair finding the metaphorical needle, trivial."

"How long is the message retrievable?"

"A minimum of five years, and it could be much longer."

"What virus do you use?"

"A baculovirus."

"A baculovirus? That's an insect virus."

"Yes, but strangely enough it can infect human inner cheek cells. And here's the best part: since it is not a natural human pathogen, humans have no antibodies that could attack it and prevent infection of the message. Everyone is a potential carrier. The message crosses national borders and sits dormant in the mouth of some unsuspecting sap. All you do is get an inner cheek scrape, or even saliva. That's also possible with a deep kiss." He took a drag and blew out a cloud of blue smoke. "Before you get any ideas. We've worked years developing a baculovirus sub-species which is extremely effective. I'll give you a few weeks to think about it but now I need the list of names you promised."

"First the secret to the attack," Saleem said.

"First the names."

For a long time Saleem looked off toward distant gray hills. Then he opened a briefcase and pulled out a single sheet of paper. On it he began to slowly write names. Kotesky looked at the sheet. "Oh no, no, no, only three."

"You said Five."

"Five: me, you, and three others you choose. I told you that," Kotesky said, lying. Sanchiev and a couple other Russians also knew. He lifted his eyebrows and held the paper for Saleem to take back. "Three or no deal."

Saleem took it and with a pen marked through two names and handed it back.

Kotesky folded it and put it in his pocket. "If I suspect that anyone other than these three know, then everything will be immediately and irrevocably canceled. Understand?"

"Okay. The secret?"

"Understand?"

"Understood."

Kotesky cast about and then back to Saleem. "Any effective biological strike *must* have four characteristics." With pudgy fingers he counted them off: "Surprise, multiple and simultaneous initiation, the ability to overwhelm the systems designed to contain its spread,—medical, civic, or military—and, unless you want to be a victim, a geographical limit. Plan 3-27 has all of these. It comes in two distinct waves. First there's a decoy attack. In addition to diverting resources and focus it will give adjacent countries time to halt travel, seal their borders, and minimize the spread from the true onslaught that will come several weeks later.

Saleem scribbled notes and asked scientific details and Kotesky proudly supplied them.

"Saleem," Kotesky said, standing to leave, and poking a finger into his chest. "You follow my instructions and this baculovirus system coupled with Plan 3-27 will knock those war-mongering, carbon-spewing, Mickey-Dee-eating motherfuckers back into the stone age."

TWENTY

Ten minutes after Mulveny's call a police sergeant arrived to escort Finn to the station. Cops mulling outside Mulveny's office hushed when Finn neared. Benjamin was among them. An officer spoke to him and Benjamin was listening with a look of angry defeat. Without time to say anything Finn passed holding his hands up in a what's-happening gesture. Benjamin shook his head. Inside Mulveny's office a man in a navy blue suit and yellow tie sat across the desk from Mulveny. The sergeant ushered Finn in and left, shutting the door.

The man in the suit started, "I'm—"

"Is Sarah all right?" Finn nearly yelled.

"Yes. Yes," Mulveny said, motioning for Finn to sit.

"I'm detective Brian Deyermand, a federal agent," the man in the suit said.

"You found the man who attacked Sarah?" Finn asked.

"No suspects have been apprehended."

"Did you get the baggie with swab in it?"

Mulveny held his hand up for Finn to relax.

"What's your relationship with Sarah Dougherty?" Deyermand asked.

"What's happening?" Finn asked.

"Before you leave," Mulveny said, "You'll know everything, but we need to do this first."

The agent stared at Finn.

Finn took a deep breath and exhaled. "I was helping her with the problem of the man stalking her to get her saliva."

"And your relationship to her fiancé, Reece Skully," Deyermand asked.

"I met him once."

"When did you first meet Sarah Dougherty?"

"Why is this a federal case?"

"Mr. Barber, I only have a few more questions and then I'll try to answer yours," the agent said. "When did you first meet Sarah?"

Finn wondered if the man meant yours singular, meaning only the last question, or if he meant yours, plural, meaning all of them; because he had a shit-ton. Could you really fall in love in three days? And if you truly could, was it a good idea? Had he betrayed Sarah? Was he a coward? Was he betraying her right now?

"Well?"

"Six days." He glanced at the man's watch, "six days, four hours and eighteen minutes ago...approximately."

The agent gave him a deadpan look. "How did you know Sarah was going to Zilker Park?"

Finn thought about telling the cop he'd followed her but it sounded awful, like stalking. Plus, it would lead to the next question: Where did you begin following her? Which he didn't want to answer. "Did you say you've spoken with Sarah?" Finn asked.

"I didn't say. How did you know she'd be at Zilker Park?"

"I'm sorry but I can't answer any more questions until I've spoken with an attorney."

The agent nodded pensively, clicking his tongue. Mulveny shook his head and two of them looked at each other, silently deliberating.

Mulveny spoke. "This is a double homicide case now." Finn felt as if his insides had been doused with a bucket of hydrochloric acid. He tried to ask who but only huffed and stammered. "Sarah's parents were murdered this morning in their home, outside of D.C. They were kidnapped and executed and it's connected to Sarah and the mouth swab."

"Where's Sarah?" He imagined her the last time he saw her, in the park jogging away from Reece, her lanky frame bouncing awkwardly.

"How did you know she was going to Zilker Park?" the agent asked.

Finn regarded him. "I feel sick."

"These first hours are crucial."

"Sarah's safe now," Mulveny said, sternly, "But she may not be out of danger as long as those men are loose."

Finn stopped, and looked at the federal man and tried to push his mind through the clamor of confusion. "She left about ten a.m. and I followed her."

"In your car?"

"She got a voice mail message and started acting strange, and then immediately left. She wouldn't tell me what it was all about. I assumed it was Reece."

"Left where?" He scribbled in his notepad.

"My house," Finn finally said.

Deyermand looked up and then back down to the notepad and kept writing. "Can you think of anything else you'd like to tell me that may help our investigation?"

"The man who attacked Sarah, his partner called him Yusif, or maybe Joseph—more likely Yusif. "

The detective scribbled. "That's good, that's very very good."

"You should look at the video in Sarah's apartment. He's Yusif."

"I've been through that."

He was ten feet from me. I could have stopped him. I'm a coward. Finn began to exhale and inhale and he knew he was not on the edge of a precipice but had cascaded over it. He was rushing away from the past and into the unseen. The agent asked a few more questions and Finn seemed to be answering them. *I'll never be anything but a coward.* Before leaving he gave Finn his card and offered his hand but Finn didn't take it. Even though they were on the same side, for some reason it didn't feel right. He stood to leave but Mulveny motioned for him to sit.

"They were really executed?"

Mulveny nodded.

"Where is Sarah?"

"She's under emergency protective custody. Only the U.S. Marshals know where."

Finn's mind felt like one long space between thoughts.

"Who could have known it would come to this?" Mulveny said. "It's the strangest case I've ever seen in twenty-eight years. Look, I'm fixing to nail those fucks, and we're gonna. We just have to be persistent. These things take time. Now we've got the feds helping. We'll get 'em. Get yourself some rest." He offered his hand and Finn wasn't sure why he needed rest. Mulveny looked him in the eyes. "One thing I can tell you is: These guys ain't amateurs."

He wanted to tell Mulveny that he'd had his chance and blown it. But he wasn't certain. Sarah hadn't called the police before she'd met Reece at Zilker Park so Mulveny couldn't have been expected to help. She'd screamed at Finn not to interfere but he had, and now her parents were murdered.

TWENTY-ONE

National Security Council

11:13 a.m. Wednesday, August 7th

The National Security Council met in the tank, a windowless, surveillance secure room in The Pentagon on Wednesday, August 7th, five days after their emergency meeting, the one held after discovering a terrorist gathering had occurred in Swat Valley, Pakistan from Friday, July 26th to Sunday, July 28th. Three of the four members that attended the first meeting, The Secretary of Defense, the Director of National Intelligence, and the Chairman of the Joint Chiefs of Staff were now joined by the President, Vice President, Secretary of the Treasury, and National Security Advisor, in other words, all NSC members, except the Secretary of State—who had immediately flown to Pakistan after the emergency meeting.

Three special forces platoons had moved into Swat Valley and two army regiments sealed the Afghan border to the west, but no terrorist meeting attendees had been captured. Using his spy's descriptions Troy Stanley, National Coordinator for Security and Counterterrorism, had emailed him hundreds of photos of potential attendees, concentrating on the Russians. The spy identified only a single match, Nikolai Kotesky, before Troy lost contact with him. The spy's body was found yesterday, dumped in Mingora, Swat Valley. Only a few strips of skin remained on his back. When Troy read the email he collapsed at his desk. He'd grown to love that boy (he was only twenty-two) almost like a father. He wiped tears from his cheeks; he had a presentation to give.

Troy went into the tank and began without any comments, no small talk. He put his flash drive into the computer and projected a file photo onto an 8'x8' screen.

Nikolai Kotesky: A Kazakh national. Bald and usually wearing a disheveled beard or just scraggly sideburns. Fat, bug-eyed, gruff, and dragging on a perennial cigarette, his file photo looked more like that of a long haul trucker than someone connected to an international terrorist meeting. He'd been chief scientist at VECTOR, the State Research Center of Virology and Biotechnology, but was now a director in the

Russian Academy of Sciences. VECTOR was most famous for being one of the two repositories of the human smallpox virus along with the CDC in Atlanta.

Troy explained that smallpox was the first scourge on humans to be eradicated in nature and now only existed in highly guarded vials in these two places. With a thirty percent fatality rate it was a prime candidate as a bioweapon, and excepting a few health care workers, all Americans were susceptible—either unvaccinated or with an outdated vaccine.

Kotesky and another Russian, Valentin Sanchiev, had co-managed a Soviet open-air chemical and bioweapons testing site on the Aral Sea—Vozrozhdeniye Island—in present day Kazakhstan. There they tested plague, Q fever, and smallpox, and purportedly buried tons of weapons grade anthrax on the island. In the late 90s, Kazakhstan, then independent, allowed the U.S. to inspect the site. The inspectors, Troy explained, had found a dusty and lifeless island, growing in the shrinking Aral Sea. Telephone poles for tethering animals went on for miles, buried at one-kilometer intervals, like spokes, in straight lines from the lab.

Kotesky's whereabouts were unknown. However, the Director of National Intelligence noted that three years earlier Kotesky had flown into Los Angeles and then left four weeks later from Miami. Hearsay was that on the trip he'd made contact with the North American gang MS-13.

MS-13:   It plied the usual gang trades: drugs, extortion, racketeering, prostitution, but they had a reputation in human trafficking. Rumor was, for twenty-five grand they could get anyone a clean visa. The Miami chapter president, Hernando Gonzales Sepulveda de la Vela, had been arrested on January 8th with false German passports and fake social security numbers. Troy put up his police booking photos. His forehead, cheeks, neck, chest, shoulders and arms were dappled with a patchwork of blue-black tattoos. His head was shaved and his expression stern while he stared at the camera, as if taunting it. He stood shirtless with his arms spread wide, parallel to the floor, a tattoo, *sicario* (slang for assassin), arced across his stomach in Old English font. He'd served prison sentences for drug possession and assault, but had beaten a case of multiple homicide when the witnesses were gunned down outside a strip-mall. And, Troy added, the MS-13 Miami chapter was the defacto lead chapter, making Sepulveda the

United States MS-13 boss. Kotestky had most likely met with him.

In Sepulveda's most recent arrest the counterfeit passports and visas were authentic enough that it took two weeks of cross checking names and numbers before federal agents could confirm they were indeed fake: Three German passports for males, who, from their photos looked to be Middle Eastern. The men remained unidentified.

When Troy finished they switched to planning and separating responsibilities. The President would immediately request from the Russian Prime Minister a warrant for the arrest of Nicholai Kotesky, a detainment order on Valentin Sanchiev, and a cooperative effort between Russian Federal Security Service and U.S. intelligence in finding them. He would also immediately arrange meetings between U.S. Armed Forces Medical Intelligence (AFMIC) and Russian Ministries of Defense and Health and press hard for an open exchange of all biological weapons data and knowledge. The National Security Advisor would coordinate the dissemination of millions of Ciprofloxacin pills from the national pharmaceutical stockpile for anthrax treatment, and the disbursement of smallpox vaccines from the U.S. stockpile of 390 million doses. He would also initiate the emergency smallpox vaccine plan to prepare the entire U.S. population for vaccination. The Secretary of Defense would coordinate the Office of Homeland Security, the Federal Emergency Management Agency, the CDC, Fort Dietrich AFMIC, the National Guard, and the individual state's Offices of Emergency Management as they instituted the bioweapon civil defense preparedness protocols. The Secretary of State, now in Pakistan, would pressure Islamabad to find and arrest Dahoud Gradau (a.k.a. Ledpaste), the Indian mobster present at the terrorist gathering, and Saleem Rafiq Nurhani, the biochemist son of the Helmund province warlord, also present at the gathering. The Director of National Intelligence would organize FBI SWAT for bioweapons defense, manage all new intelligence, and continue pursuing terrorist meeting attendees. The Chairman of the Joint Chiefs of Staff would manage the defenses on the border between Afghanistan and Pakistan west of Swat Valley. Troy Stanley would coordinate with the Defense Advanced Research Projects Agency (DARPA) and a biotechnology company, Maxygen, in readying an experimental system for creating instantaneous vaccines to genetically modified superbugs.

Before going home that day Troy pulled a file on Operation Top Officials, a biological weapons preparedness drill run in the waning days of the Clinton administration. The exercise was created to test the ability of the United States to respond to a lone terrorist's release of *Yersinia pestis*—pneumonic plague—through the fresh-air ducts of the Denver Center for the Performing Arts. One Saturday in May the role-playing started as "victims" filed in to local emergency rooms. Only after five hundred people had checked into local hospitals and twenty-five were marked dead was a public-health emergency declared. By day's end on Sunday emergency supplies of antibiotics had arrived, half the nation's ventilators were in Denver, and eighteen hundred cases of plague were reported with over four hundred casualties. On Monday the CDC urged the Colorado Governor's office to quarantine but state officials refused without provisions for food transfer and without the people or resources for enforcement. By Tuesday the exercise organizers declared that the epidemic had spread beyond control. The report estimated 3,700 cases and 950 deaths, and this had only been a drill of a single, isolated release and with a crude weapon. Troy hurled the study to the floor. He switched off the lamp in his office and for a long time sat in the dark, images of the boy's skinless back consuming him.

Twenty-Two

Lance Matterson

4:31 a.m. Friday, August 9th

In his University of Texas at Austin lab Lance Matterson sat leaning forward and staring anxiously at a computer screen before him. He rubbed his eyes and swallowed a mouthful of cold, bitter, coffee. Computers, monitors and humming servers cramped the windowless cinder block room. Capital letters, representing one of the four DNA bases, filled the screen in front of him like unpunctuated gibberish. He read the letters sliding a pen point across the monitor screen to keep his place. "A-T-C is p, T-C-T is o." He spoke the letters aloud in triplets and referred to a handwritten code on an index card designating each letter of the alphabet to a triplet. "C-G-C is s, C-T-A is t, C-C-T is space, T-C-T is o, G-C-T is f, G-C-T is f." He scribbled the deciphered text on another index card. A-A-G is i, T-T-G is c. He checked the time. It was 4:32 a.m. He was delirious with exhaustion. He just wanted to get the damn thing done (and get paid, yo!).

In two weeks Lance would begin his senior year at the University of Texas at Austin studying cellular biology. Lately, most of his time passed as innumerable hours in Dr. Cooper's Zoology laboratory working on his independent research project and plotting sigmoidal curves of enzymatic efficiency versus temperature. Soon classes would interrupt this tedium, but for now the interruption was a three day project PCRing, deciphering, and mailing off a DNA fragment—his small part of a large project studying DNA stability.

The DNA stability project was a scholarship requirement. He didn't mind the work, although it was difficult and he had hardly slept for the three days it took to complete. These detours were infrequent enough— about twice a year—and he was paid a generous bonus based on his speed and accuracy. Otherwise he felt like any other senior: anxious to graduate and excited over the promise of his boundless future.

His scholarship, funded by the Russian Academy of Sciences, was not like any the other students had. It stipulated he work without interruption once receiving the DNA samples and primers for the stability study. That meant PCR amplifying, sequencing, decoding,

PCR amplifying again, and finally, mailing the second PCR product to one other scientist—and all without a break. He now approached hour thirty-seven.

Six years earlier he'd read about the scholarship online. After several emails and a phone interview he had a plane ticket to Russia. Leaving the airport his burly mother clamped him in a hug with her farm-hardened forearms, but on arrival in Saint Petersburg Ivana, a svelte, gorgeous blond with clunky English laid her cheek on his and planted a peck just in front of his ear. He and Ivana took a taxi through the slushy streets. She pointed out buildings and statues and he smiled not listening, high from the strangeness of it all. They crossed over a gaping, black river to his hotel room with a whirlpool tub. Below his balcony the river dragged along shadowy hunks of ice. He watched his breath condense in the air, thinking that for his first trip outside of West Virginia he'd done pretty well.

The following morning a fat, bald man reeking of cigarettes and reading from a computer sat in a musty office listed on Lance's itinerary. When Lance arrived the man stood and greeted him warmly in a heavy accent and introduced himself as Nicholai Kotesky.

He licked a finger and flipped through the pages of Lance's application. "You scored very high in the biology exam. Your high school must have a good science department."

"Not really, I just read a lot, and love the outdoors and animals."

"An autodidact. Very good." He cleared his throat. "Mr. Matterson your abilities and interests make you an attractive candidate for our scholarship program." The man explained that Russia was attempting to reach out to its democratic allies, create scientific collaborations. "We want to create early connections with young scientists who want to learn our language and culture and foster lifelong collaboration. We think this is the best way to sustain peace and prosperity." The program would begin with two years of language, history, culture, and biology courses at the University of Saint Petersburg. Next, he would enroll in a biological baccalaureate program at an accredited U.S. university. He would be required to conduct his own independent research and contribute to one of several collaborative studies. The opening that Lance was applying for would participate in a Russian study of DNA stability and sequence reproducibility.

"We are interested in understanding DNA as a long term data storage device and how human and experimental error, and natural mutation, affect the sequence. It is a molecule designed to store data, just like a computer, but it can last for tens of thousands, or possibly millions of years." He slapped his computer. "We are far behind God." He laughed at himself and Lance joined in self-consciously.

"You will sequence specific pieces of DNA. You will also replicate particular regions of DNA and send them to other scientists for sequencing and they will repeat the process. Of course all of this will come much later after you have taken the preliminary course work." He explained that this would allow them to determine error and mutation rates. Lance would also get the chance to travel to conferences in France, Spain, and Britain.

The man leaned back in a creaky leather chair and regarded Lance. "This is a six year program and you must commit for the entire duration to be accepted. This is an opportunity for you to get an exceptional education, make important scientific discoveries, and contribute to an international collaboration. You have four more days to enjoy our lovely city, our food, and our hospitality while you decide. Think it over carefully."

Lance paced in his spacious hotel room, wandered the city, and slept very little trying to decide. In the end he couldn't refuse the wonderful, if not intimidating, opportunity. Back home on the family ranch clamping milking suctions to a cow's nipples in the predawn he'd fantasize about Ivana, the milky blonde, and about the superiority he'd feel, an international scholar walking among the ordinary.

By his sixth and last year of the scholarship program, and senior year at University of Texas, Lance had grown skilled at processing the DNA sequences for the stability project. It was always the same routine. He received a package with a cotton swab, on which was the DNA sample. Then, a thin but muscular black man (he'd never told Lance his name) would find him within a day or two and personally hand him the PCR primers and the cipher (Why the hell they couldn't just email the primer sequence to him, he didn't know). Using the PCR primers he was given, he would amplify a portion of the sample DNA, and then sequence it. With the cipher he would decode an address *and* a second set of PCR primers which he was to make himself—and only himself. He was to make the second set of PCR primer in two pairs, a dummy—or decoy—primer in each one. He was to discard the dummies and use the remaining pair to amplify another portion of the sample DNA. He was then to destroy the second PCR primers and any evidence of its sequence. (All the secrecy seemed over the top and why the hell they couldn't just email him the address he didn't know that either.) He guessed they made him decipher the sample address to see if any DNA mutations would occur making him fail to mail it correctly—

though it seemed an awfully inefficient way to observe DNA stability. He would mail the second PCR product to the deciphered addresses in a sterile baggie identical to the one the swab arrived in and that was that. He supposed the next student in the chain would receive some of this sequence on a swab and the chain would grow one link, eventually returning to him four to six months later.

A couple times, out of curiosity, he'd sequenced the DNA fragments that he'd mailed. One turned out to be a portion of the equine testosterone receptor, and another was part of the human actin gene. Long ago it had begun to bore him and he never sequenced mailed fragments again.

A week after he mailed the sample he always got his performance report, rating his speed and accuracy, and—the best part—a fat check based on his rating. He began to rely on this money, getting anxious and often in debt if more than seven months passed between samples. On his second test he'd decoded one of the mailing addresses wrong and didn't earn a fucking penny. On his fourth or fifth test he'd wasted two days unsuccessfully trying to do the second PCR before discovering he'd made a mistake deciphering the primer set. He missed three car payments after that mishap and from then on sequenced and deciphered everything twice.

Yesterday, Wednesday (Well, technically two days ago now) Lance sat down at his lab bench and in middle of the counter top, sat a small, brown cardboard box addressed to him. He opened it. "Awesome," he said aloud on seeing the swab. He wanted to break his record of $7,534.54, which he'd achieved last year. His BMW raised enough eyebrows among his classmates. Just wait until they see him in a Porsche! (leased, though he wouldn't tell). He threw the box out, but then picked it back up. It had an Austin postmark. Of the others, he remembered one shipped from Miami, one from Nashville, and one from D.C., but never one from Austin. He shrugged and tossed it back in the trash. The swabs were his DNA templates but he could do nothing without the primers. He stuck the baggie in a -20° Celcius freezer and left for the day.

"Lance Matterson?" A dark-skinned man, Indian or Middle-Eastern, standing outside the zoology entrance, had spoken. Lance didn't recognize him.

"Yeah?"

With a latex-gloved hand the man pulled out a sterile plastic baggie with red lettering: the same kind the swab always came in and the same kind he mailed his PCR samples away in. Although surprised to see this unfamiliar face, Lance reached out for the bag. This wasn't the tall, muscular, black man who always gave him the primers and cipher. It was the first time someone different had done it. Otherwise, as usual inside the bag were two tiny plastic vials. He plucked out a vial and swiveled it between a thumb and finger. One tube was marked A and the other B—the primers for the swab DNA. Next the man handed Lance a 3 X 5 note card, the cipher, handwritten, neat and crisp.

"Burn these after you use them. Do you understand everything you are to do?" The man spoke in a sad monotone with an accent Lance couldn't place.

The tall, black guy always gave him the cipher handwritten, crisp on a note card, always told him to burn everything, and always asked him if he understood.

"Yes," Lance said.

The man turned and started to walk away.

"Hey," Lance called out timidly. The man turned around. Lance held out his hand. "My name's Lance." He wanted to ask him who he was, why the other man hadn't come, what their role in the project was.

The man looked down at Lance's hand and then brought his eyes back up. Then he turned back around and left. Just like the tall, black guy, this guy wouldn't say anything beyond his scripted lines either. Although curious, Lance always ended up forgetting about it. Before the man disappeared behind a building he looked back at Lance. Lance waved but the man did not wave back and Lance felt stupid and quickly put his hand down.

Now, at 4:32 a.m., thirty-seven hours later (only one of which was sleep), instead of sitting on a barn stool and massaging cow's udders he sat in a cramped computer lab, gulped coffee, and massaged his eyes. In Russia he'd been instructed to manually decipher the test DNA sequences and never to store the deciphered text on any computer, phone, or hand-held data storage device (to exclude automated errors in DNA reading, they'd told him). He rechecked his decoded scrawl: *Use following 2 primers: 5-CCTAGGCGCTTATCTGTCCG-3, 5-GCATGCTTACGTAACTCGG-3. PCR amplify a 19.6 KB fragment. Purify and mail 1 microgram to the following three addresses: Post office Box 7549 Chapel Hill, NC 27514...* Two more addresses followed, one in Athens, Georgia and one in Pasadena, California. *What the fuck!* Usually he only sent one micro-gram to a single address. Now he'd have to purify three times the amount of DNA and send it three different places. This better not be a trend. Or, maybe he'd get paid three times the amount. *Yeah right.* He went to the Biology building, used his card-key to unlock the door to the DNA Sequencing and Synthesizing Facility to make the second primer set. He still had plenty of time before the sequencing lab technician, Gogan, would come in exactly at 8:00 a.m.

TWENTY-THREE

Over the next few days (was it weeks now?) time became a gray fog, it twisted and blew around Finn. He drank. He was good at drinking. He drank with Benjamin. He drank with strangers. An afternoon blended into a morning, into dusk, into a stifling evening, into an iridescent afternoon.

He was in a bar again, drinking. Just like that. Transported like in a spell, or in A Christmas Carol by the ghost of Christmas yet to come. Benjamin was there. Benjamin was not there. Things became dull, but not in the uninteresting sense. He tilted toward the bar for another beer. He held onto a man who didn't look used to supporting anyone or anything. In a splinter of a moment the floor hit the ceiling, and next, the street the sky. He breathed the cool dry night air. Cool was good and night covered everything. People pulled on him, laughing people, people with drinks. Laughing was good. He pretended with the laughing people. They said they were Good People. Someone spoke of rum, others of fast cars and fights. Bars lurched by with people at quaint tables, proper people, safe people. People who made safe rational decisions, Finn thought, like me. People with weighing scales in their fucking heads. Thoughtful scales with a tray on each side: one for pros, one for cons. "Fucking pussy!" Shouting felt good but the words didn't come out as neatly as he imagined them. Good People liked when he shouted. They shouted with him. A smart motherfucker grabbed at Finn, leaned over sharp wrought iron trying to show for his little bitch. Finn told him so. Finn was dexterous, always had been. Fast like a rabbit motherfuckers. As fast as he could have been on the bridge chasing Yusif, he thought. The Good People joked. One proved her lack of panties. One smeared on lipstick, sloppy over stubble. They laughed. They shouted: for sex, and rum, and cocaine!

Then they were in a white van. Just like that. They took turns hard, tires squealing in pain. From speakers, blasted Damien Marley's syncopated chants. They had bottles of rum and the floor of the van was cool corrugated metal. Tools—some sharp, some dull, but all deadly—swung overhead. Cool coolness. He pressed himself into the chill. The spells kept coming. Now they were on a balcony. Someone was on the railing, the city far below. Above glowed mean neon lights.

"I'm a golden devil!" she shouted, her arms out wide as if on a crucifix, or perhaps for balance. Was she balancing the good against the bad, he wondered, just like he'd done. Someone pulled her back with the tail of her shirt.

A grinning Good People opened a piece of wax paper. Finn had never smoked base. They all smoked it from an eye dropper. They smoked it on the balcony. It smelled like tires burning, and tasted like nothing he'd ever wanted to taste. He expected a rush but felt nothing, or maybe he felt a burn. Something left him with the rush of milky smoke, something inside him was inexorably drawn out with it.

He was on a couch inside. Strawberry lips took his flaccid cock into her mouth. Another Good People whipped out a donkey-dick and stroked it to half-mast. His face was determined. He concentrated on his stroking and the strawberry lips sucking off Finn. Finn concentrated on the lips as well, his cock stiffening. Rum burnt him behind his right eye. Burnt, burning. Burning was bad. The lips reached a hand up and twisted Finn's nipple. The pain rearranged his thoughts. He saw the Strawberry lips for what they were. He slapped them off his cock. He wanted to slap the lips all the way across the fucking city. He went to the balcony, his mind blue and red and getting more red all the time. The Lamar Street Bridge lay below right where he'd been not so long ago. There's the bridge, he thought, and time didn't matter. It couldn't change, never or ever. People shouted behind him. He heard the strawberry lips. There was the bridge, across the river less than a mile away, but maybe across the universe. One of the Good People was not acting so good. Finn held on. Voices surrounded him, sharp voices, like hammers on iron. His limbs were a tangle and no longer his. The others, now they were red too. He needed to escape. He moved his limbs but they didn't respond like he thought they should, and he laughed at the Good People. However, he wasn't laughing at them but rather impossibility. His mind went from red to black.

He heard birds chirping and opened his eyes from beneath a bush. The left side of his face throbbed, the skin taut like a pregnant belly. He ran his tongue across his lip. It was swollen and crusted with salty blood on the corners. He pressed his fingers lightly against his left-side ribcage and found a painful area. His balls ached as well and he tenderly stuck a hand down his pants. He winced. His right testicle was three times its normal size and a tap of his finger sent bolts of pain into his abdomen. Suddenly nausea erupted. His stomach contracted and vomit bubbled up into his mouth and down his chin and neck. Panting, he wiped it away, sticky strings coming off with his hand.

TWENTY-FOUR

F inn got up from his wicker porch chair and went into the kitchen. He wore only cut-off army pants. He opened the buzzing refrigerator and grabbed a beer. The beer was cool and beads of sweat popped out when the hot air swamped it.

"Hey there little buddy, you don't mind the heat do you," he said to the beer, rubbing it on his forehead. He shuffled back to the porch and threw himself in a hammock, his ass just scraping the porch tiles as he swung. He looked over at one of the frayed wicker chairs. It was in that very chair one month ago that Sarah lit a cigarette and told him of her idea to put cameras in her apartment. There must be some way to reach back four short weeks, when, in that chair, her copper skin glistened in the streetlight, and no one had died. It seemed that somewhere in the ether hung a prayer, that if recited exactly, would appease God and he'd move Finn back just one shitty month. He took a swig and pushed off the ground swinging himself. He was a coward and because of that the parents of the only woman he'd ever loved had died, and he would never see her again. He didn't know how to get beyond it.

"You don't," he mumbled aloud.

This was the very porch where they'd laughed and where he'd first wanted to strip her and kiss her entire body. He meant less than nothing to her now; he meant worse: loss and death. He would forever be that hideous mistake. Before he'd only been unfulfilled: an unfulfilling job, unfulfilled aspirations, and unfulfilled love. Now he was hopeless. She'd shown him who he wanted to love and he'd destroyed everything. He guzzled the beer. He wondered what was worse: being alone physically, or alone spiritually while the people around you created an illusion that you weren't.

He turned and caught sight of his reflection on a pane in the porch door. *You'll always be a pussy. You'll never stand up for what you believe.* Why did he insist in fulfilling other's expectations while hiding his true desires? Why did he play it safe? He mocked himself in a nasal whine. "I'll study biology. It'll be my safety net. And then I'll try painting. Where did that get you, huh? And Sarah, she's engaged for God's sake. Even if you hadn't pussied out she wouldn't have left Reece for you. You're stupid, naive, weak, and worthless, and you deserve to be alone!" He whipped his beer bottle at the pathetic face staring back at him. The window burst and he flinched. Saber-like shards stood where the pane had been.

He rolled out of the hammock and stepped hard directly on the broken glass, grinding the ball of his foot in it. In the living room he collapsed on the rug, and thrust his head in his hands. "Okay God, I give up," he yelled. "You win. You win." He fell over and laid fetal for a long time. Eventually he pulled himself up and into the kitchen and slid another beer out of the refrigerator. He spun circles drinking it. Back in the living room he threw himself down on the couch and stared at the ceiling fan in the dark. Time passed. Benjamin startled him from his stupor.

"Finn!" He came into the darkened room, and glanced at the broken window and the blood splotches on the floor. "Damn, dude." He eased himself into a chair next to the couch, and regarded Finn. Then he jumped up and went into the kitchen coming back with a couple more beers. He put on a John Lee Hooker album and sat back down. Pulling out a fat joint from his breast pocket, he snatched out stray strands from one end. "Nabbed it off a speeder." He lit it. "I know you're going through hell now."

Finn stared at him and drank his beer.

"I know you may not believe it but you should try and trust a more objective point of view. It's over. It gets better from here, even though you can't feel it now."

He offered the joint and Finn took it and smoked a lungful. Blowing out a cloud of sweet smoke he said, "Remember when you stole your old man's fire-fighter emergency light?" They'd done it the summer before their senior year of highschool.

"We pulled that Guido over in the Camaro."

"We weren't afraid then," Finn said.

"We were stupid. Who knows what Sarah and Reece were mixed up in. And you definitely don't know what motivated those men to kill her parents." He took the joint from Finn. "You couldn't have known the stakes. If she'd been totally open—"

"She told me not to interfere."

"I'm sorry I ever got you involved," Benjamin said.

"I know it's stupid, but I love her, now more than ever." They sat in the darkness the singer's voice floating through the smoke, *I had a good start but women and whiskey tore it down—women and whiskey ain't no good for me.* An orange ember swung back and forth between them. "I need to know what those men were looking for."

Benjamin pulled on the joint and the cherry grew an angry red, illuminating his face. "Two people were killed. This is bigger than your curiosity."

"Executed. And over what?"

"That's not your job." Benjamin talked about police politics and his daughter, Sophia, though the words couldn't penetrate Finn's never ending loop of thought. It started with the simple question of how he could have acted so that everything would have ended perfectly, and then it divulged into an orgy of possibilities. It was like looking back five moves on a chess board and imagining how the potential present board could differ from the actual present board. More precisely, it was impossible.

Benjamin stood. "I gotta go. Listen, you know you can call me anytime man." He shut the door behind him.

Finn slid another beer from the fridge and dropped back onto the couch. He watched the fan drag out lazy circles and drank. At least he had one piece of good news: his former boss at a biotech company, Larry Harken, was now a biochemistry professor at UT and had offered him some part time lab work. He picked the roach off the coffee table and smoked it while staring at the broken glass shadows like fangs in the street lamp's jaundiced light. He got another beer and cut a lime to squeeze into it. Then he took the knife and pushed the tip into his pectoral and dragged it down across his stomach. He did it several more times, each time pushing harder and going deeper. It didn't hurt as much as he'd imagined. He was about to start on the other side of his chest but instead, walked outside, still holding the knife. The clouds reflected crimson light from the city and the air seemed to suffocate him as if he were breathing through layers of cheesecloth. He took air in large gasps and his heart began to pound. Images consumed him: Sarah's parents full of gaping bullet holes, their brains pureed, guts hanging out of exit wounds, them writhing in agony as the killers stood above shooting endlessly. Then he was overcome with an urge to stab himself. The more he tried to banish the thought the more powerful it grew. It exploded into images of cutting his own wrist, gouging out his eyes, slicing off his penis, plunging a butcher knife into his anus. He hurled the knife across his yard and ran into the bathroom and looked into his eyes. The pupils nearly enveloped his blue irises. He ran out of the bathroom and out the front door. He dialed Bridgette.

"Bridgette, its Finn. Listen, I need...Finn!" Ambient noise, voices, and music were compressed by the phone.

"What?" she yelled.

"Just come over to my house now. It's an emergency!"

"An emergency?"

"Come now!"

"Okay, okay. I'm coming."

He couldn't shake the thoughts of cutting himself. He thought he should call 911 but then decided against it. He would wait. He dialed Benjamin but he didn't answer. Huffing the dense air, he walked until he just lost sight of his house and then turned back. He did it a few more times until he saw headlights bob into his driveway. He jogged back and found Bridgette at the front door. "Hey."

She spun around. "Jesus Christ! You scared me. She wore a clinging black dress (a lot like the one Sarah wore when she first came to his house) and high heels and smelled of smoke and sweat. "What the hell happened?" she said, recoiling from him.

"I think I'm Oding."

She looked at him sternly. "This better not be some sick joke. You'd made me leave a good party."

"I swear," he said. "Benjamin brought this weed over and I think it was spiked with something."

She frowned at him.

"I'm serious."

"What is that?" She waved a finger encircling his chest.

He looked at the blood trickling from the diagonal slices down his torso. "I cut myself on a rose bush," he finally said.

She furrowed her brow and then gave a little snort. She opened the front door and went inside. "You're not getting a pity fuck out of me."

On the couch she put her arm around his shoulder and he liked the way her body was smooth without edges, like butter. His pulse dropped. He told her about Sarah, how he loved her and how he'd gotten her parents killed. He told her how everything of Sarah's worked differently than his, how her mind operated through a foreign and mystical process, as if it were a completely different mathematical function from Finn's "If you put the same set of variables into both my mind and Sarah's you'll get drastically different conclusions," he said.

"I get it. You love her," she said. "I wish someone loved me that way."

Finn shut-up and leaned his head on her shoulder. "I'm a coward, a complete coward. I fucked it up. I fucked it all up."

"It's gonna be all right. Everything's gonna be all right," she said.

But it wasn't all right.

When they crawled into bed he felt a little better, the curve of her back and ass melting into his pelvis.

Two days later at 4:00 in the afternoon He lay in bed naked reading, an oscillating fan purring back and forth. He hated air conditioning. It made him feel like a god damned flaccid zoo animal that wouldn't last a single breath in nature. His phone rang.

"Hey Stem Cell, let's grab some beers." It was Benjamin. "It'll cheer you up," he sang.

"Fuck off."

"Meet me at The Door." He hung up.

Finn lay back down. He hadn't been sleeping well at night. Nighttime was when he got lonely and his dreams invariably ended with Sarah. It seemed that every dawn after a few fitful hours of sleep he awoke with images of her. She screamed at him, insulted him, or worse, ignored him. He took a shower and walked to the bar running his fingers through his wet but still greasy hair—he'd run out of toilet paper, soap, and now, shampoo.

He went inside The Door and leaned against the cool copper bar top and ordered a dark beer. "Finny!" Eustace Edelman, the grizzled old bastard, called out to him. He was hunched over the bar a few stools over. Benjamin walked in and Finn caught his eye.

"Later Eustace," Finn said. Thank God, he thought. Benjamin sure saved me from a lot of blathering. They moved to a pool table in the back and Benjamin ordered nachos. Then he placed pool balls in the triangle one by one. "Things getting any better?"

"Jesus," Finn said. "Wait. One day I'll look back on this and it will all feel like—"

"Hey! I'm just being positive." Benjamin shook a pool cue in his face. "You're lucky I put up with your bullshit."

Finn slapped the cue away. "Put up with my shit. I'm the only friend you got, dude."

"It just gets worse and worse and might never get better. How's that?"

"Much better, thank you."

"That's right. Don't listen to all the people telling you it'll get better."

"*You're* the one telling me it'll get better."

"I just told you it would get worse."

"That's because I made you."

"At least I'm trying to help, dude."

Finn laughed. "Don't bullshit me. You just didn't have anyone else to drink with."

"You want me to be brutally honest?"

"If you can't trust your friends who the fuck can you trust?"

"Don't try to change your feelings. Let the anguish and hopelessness express itself because it will never subside unless you let it."

Finn might have thought he was being sarcastic but he looked serious. "And you should know," he said. "Because that's what you did when you were responsible for the death of two innocent people?"

Benjamin's upper lip twitched. "Sometimes you act like you're the only person in the world."

Immediately Finn regretted what he'd said. He knew Benjamin had a hellish time in the Iraq war and had come home reckless and careless, and wouldn't talk about it. "I'm sorry, man, I, I wasn't' thinking."

"I guess I hoped there was an easier way for you," Benjamin said. His phone rang and he answered it. He looked disappointed saying, "Okay, okay, yes," and "I'll be there, yeah, yes, ten minutes." He said he had to go look after Sophia.

"You hop around like a damn flea, dude. What am I supposed to do now?"

"It's my daughter." He gulped some beer and threw a few bills on the table. "Buck up Fuck-o you'll get through it."

Finn slouched down into a couch next to the pool table and drank his beer. He felt it brace him. Maybe he should go to one of the hipper bars and try to pick up a disaffected woman. At least he'd have someone to help him sleep even if he did dream about Sarah.

"Finny boy." He looked up and saw Eustace Edelman standing above him all crinkled, sporting a smirk and cradling a pool cue. The bartender put down a heaping plate of nachos on a table at the end of the couch and Eustace snapped up the top chip covered in jalapeños and onion. A long cheese string stretched out behind it and sour cream dribbled onto a few fingernails, black grime jammed under their rims. "You fixing to play or cry in your beer?" he asked in a West Texan drawl while crunching the chip.

"Rack 'em up then." Finn said, snapping his hands up.

Eustace broke the balls with a sharp crack like rifle fire. "What happened to those tits with legs I seen you in here with a couple weeks a ago?"

Finn regarded him harshly. "I don't know."

Eustace considered Finn and then nodded, perhaps understanding. A current of hostility lingered from when Benjamin had been there. But it wasn't just hostility towards Benjamin, or Eustace now, but rather humanity. It felt like an undertow and he suspected Eustace felt it too and was toying with him. Finn leaned over and shot. "Is it true you used to fly all over Africa?"

Eustace nodded and smiled, "The first time I put down in Kenya I had to dodge lions just wallering on the runway, big fat ones."

"What'd they do when you landed?"

"Shit. Them lions didn't even twitch a tail and I didn't know how in God's name I was going to get out. Every twenty minutes or so a car passed and I'd wave like a damn fool to stop 'em. Then we'd just yell at each other."

"Couldn't they just pull up to your plane?

"Nope, there's a wooded ditch between the runway and the road, and the closest we could get to one another was about thirty feet. And I had valuable luggage. Ain't no way I was gonna leave it there or try to make a run for it neither. Ever see a lion attack? I'll tell you. It's a terrifying sight. What'd I do? I sit in that goddamn plane all night, until someone come back in the morning with a shotgun and scared 'em off."

"What'd you do in Africa?"

"In my early years I run diamonds up from the Congo to Holland. Did that until I found out how far the Congolese would go to get them diamonds."

"So you got scared?"

"There was always fear nearby in the type of business I was in, in Africa."

"I mean you got too scared to keep going."

He looked at Finn like he'd asked him to switch his beer for milk. "I got a little lead poisoning in a dust-up at a pit-mine. Spent seven-hundred and thirty-two days in a Congolese *penitentiary*. I was a marked man in the diamond market after that. Let me tell you. Fear is a gauge. It directs your attention. It shouldn't never make decisions. Just as many men as I seen run at the first shot popped I seen dead ones who tried to shove fear down their own throats trying to prove something to someone, themselves mostly. I didn't care how I made my money and I had no beef with those D-boys. The day I got out was the last day I put foot on Congolese soil."

"So you came back to America?"

"You're talking to Eustace Edelman! You let the fuck-up stand, then you stand to be the fuck-up, boy."

Finn laughed.

"After that I tried my hand at coffee, ranching, some post colonial politics, you know."

"Interesting," Finn said, wondering about the politics. "You must have seen lots of things."

"Seen 'em. Done 'em. Learned 'em."

"I certainly could use some wisdom right now," Finn said.

"Pfttt. Son, men don't get wise. If they live long enough they learn all about how they done wrong, and their regrets just pile up, long with their habits." Eustace held up his beer and gulped what remained in his pint glass. Then he wandered around the table surveying the position of the balls. "So you're hurting for the girl, huh?"

Finn nodded.

"She ended it I gather."

"Her parents were killed because of me."

"Ummm," Eustace raised his eyebrows. He leaned his pool cue against the table and moseyed over to the bar. He came back with two pints and gave Finn the dark one.

"I thought I was helping," Finn said. "I really thought I was just helping."

"Who killed her parents?"

Finn shrugged. "Don't know. We don't even know why they did it."

Eustace scrunched his face up and stared at Finn. Then he walked around the pool table. He sized up a difficult shot and then leaned over and took it. The cue ball knocked hard into the seven, which banked off the side and then bounced directly towards the corner pocket he intended. But it ricocheted back and forth inside the beveled edges and came out a few inches in front of the pocket.

Eustace looked at it for a moment and Finn thought he would curse it having barely missed sinking it.

Eustace turned toward him bouncing his bristly eyebrows. "Hah. Got yer pocket blocked, cowboy!"

Finn took his shot. He smacked the cue ball and it crashed into the ten and they both careened wildly across the table. Before the ten ball had stopped the cue fell into a corner pocket. He flopped down and ate a few chips.

Eustace came over rocking the cue ball in one hand and grabbed a chip with the other.

"Does she blame you?"

"Wouldn't you?"

"Don't know the specifics."

"They told her no interference from anybody and I secretly followed her."

Eustace rolled the ball in his hand and Finn had an impression that everything was taking place a long time ago, that Eustace would warn him not to follow Sarah but he would be fated to repeat the mistake. He felt Sarah would walk out of the bathroom door any moment. He focused on that image knowing it wouldn't happen but believing it could if he concentrated hard enough.

"You fixing to let her get away with it?" Eustace said.

"Her?" He thought Eustace must be drunk. "You mean them."

"You gonna let *her* get away with blaming *you*?"

"It's a federal case now. Her parents weren't nobodies. They'll find out who did it."

"I'm not talking about who did it. I'm talking about understanding what happened." Eustace nodded his head. "Police solve murders not mysteries. That's the only way you can hope to stop from being blamed or more importantly, blaming yourself. People want to know if they should condemn or condone. And they do not want to know if they're deceiving themselves. They want to categorize, put others in a nice box so they can fool themselves into thinking they understand 'em: animal abuser, schizophrenic, alcoholic, bi-polar, borderline, businessman, kleptomaniac. They really don't have the time to understand someone. And God save you if you empathize with them. If you really want to understand what happened you'll have to find out for yourself, cowboy."

"I should have just stayed out when she told me to."

"Now your getting wise." Eustace said, chuckling.

"Huh?" The old bastard was really beginning to piss him off.

"Storing away those regrets." Eustace took another hunk of chips, hung his head back and opened his mouth skyward. He lowered three chips covered in sour cream, salsa, and cheese into his maw, flecks of stale beer foam in its corners. "How's that doing you?" he said stuffing in the corner of a chip.

Finn ground his teeth. "Believe me, I've thought about it plenty. If I start nosing around now, I could put Sarah in danger again. That's a risk I won't take."

Eustace placed the cue ball on the table, gauged the angle and distance for his shot, and hit the cue ball with a measured force. The four ball strolled into the pocket. He regarded Finn. "If I could live over again I would try to commit more errors. I would run *more* risks."

Finn didn't respond.

"That's Jorge Luis Bores," Eustace said. "How you know she's not still in danger?"

Finn closed his eyes and exhaled. "The man got a cheek swab. That's all he wanted."

Eustace frowned. "Damn! Her parents were murdered for a lousy cheek swab? What the hell is that?" He knocked a couple of balls in and then missed one. "Well, I guess there's nothing for you to do 'cept cry in your beer."

A feeling of imminent injury filled Finn, that serious damage, maiming, dismemberment, lay await for him like a drooling hyena in the night. Though he had to admit he'd never seen a hyena, much less a drooling one waiting to pounce.

Eustace was digging through slips of folded and wrinkled papers. He handed a couple to Finn.

Moments, by Jorge Luis Borges, was printed at the top of the first one. Above the name was written in a sloppy scrawl: Whore—hay Lou—ease Boar—hayes.

If I could live my life over again
The next time I would try to commit more errors

He glanced up at Eustace suspecting a ploy to distract him from the nachos. He sure was cramming them in fast.

I would run more risks
travel more
contemplate more sunsets
climb more mountains, swim more rivers
I would go more places that I have never been
eat more ice cream and less beans
I would have more real problems and less imaginary ones

"Your shot, cowboy!"

Finn jerked up from the poem.

"Keep 'em," Eustace said.

"Thanks," he said smiling. For a moment he felt a type of clean goodness like a clear rushing river. "Really, thanks a lot." He folded them and took a shot.

TWENTY-FIVE

Monday, September 2ⁿᵈ

L ate Monday morning Finn sat at his lab bench trying to concentrate on pipetting liquids into tiny plastic vials for a series of DNA plasmid purifications. It was his first day working at the University of Texas lab for his ex-boss, Larry Harken. Outside, the sun yellowed everything into a hopeful brilliance, but with none of the positivity filtering through to Finn. He wanted to leave the lab, leave town, leave his regrets, but there was nowhere to hide. He pulled out a photo of Sarah in a white mini-skirt leaning up against a green-pastel plaster wall in some provincial Mexican town and hung it from his lab shelf. He'd stolen it from her apartment when he'd rigged up the cameras. He thought of the morning he woke up next to her, their bodies intertwined so tightly he didn't think it possible they could have gotten closer. He stared into her tiny face in the photo and couldn't help but believe God had taunted him.

He squirted the first liquid in a series of three and a white precipitate floated to the top of the plastic tubes. *Dammit*! He'd mixed up the order of the liquids and ruined all twelve samples. He sat staring at the tubes and cursing himself. Three hours wasted! He left the lab and went to a campus café. While strolling, a sensation of the vastness of the universe struck him, of the earth being an invisible speck in it, and him being indistinguishable among the seven billion other humans. With this came the feeling that nothing existed that judged him, no conscience aware of him but his own. It felt awfully lonely. He passed beneath swaying pecan trees and by the time he reached the café the vastness feeling had left him, but the loneliness remained. He ordered a coffee and a banana muffin and sat down across from a pretty girl reading a textbook.

If he'd only listened to Sarah and stayed out of it, he thought (and If he'd never met her he wouldn't be the wiser nor the worse). *No. I'd be worse*. He wouldn't change meeting her for anything. This thought made him feel a little better, but not much. He repeated the thought to himself as much a belief as a reinforcement of a hope, a hope that someday he could look back on all this without self-pity. Eustace hadn't consoled him like others, told him everything would be all right. Now he couldn't even regret properly without that grisly face poking into his conscience and asking how the regretting was working out for him.

"The fuck should I do then?" he said aloud. The girl looked up at him and he smiled and dropped his head. *The sterile baggie.* The thought seemed to come from nothing. *Find out who ordered that make of baggie and you find Yusif.* He remembered the baggie in the video and on the bridge, the one Sarah had pointed out. But there could be hundreds of places that ordered those, he thought, plus I don't even know who manufactures them. He reconsidered the thought. In Austin only the universities, hospitals, clinical labs, and a handful of biotech labs would order sterile baggies. At least it was something to do other than regret.

He went back to the lab and searched the index of a thick catalog. He glanced through the eight page section of "sterile sample bags" looking at the photos. He went on to another catalog, and then another. In the fourth one the red letters and bold font jumped out at him when he flipped a page. He opened his email account where he'd stored the videos of Yusif. He opened the video of Yusif talking on the phone and compared the bag on Sarah's bed to the one in the catalog. He zoomed in on it. It looked like the same one. It felt invigorating like a tiny victory. For a moment Finn was a young Eustace Edelman striding into daylight, released after two years in a Congolese shit-hole. In the video Yusif's face was determined, as it had been on the Lamar Street Bridge, when he'd shot by on the walkway. *I'm coming after you Yusif,* he murmured. *Finn Aaron Barber's coming after you, motherfucker.*

"Our databases don't work that way, sir. I can't crosscheck shipments by location based on an item. You need a recipient," a polite woman in customer service said into the telephone.

"But that's exactly what I'm looking for."

"Besides, I am pretty certain we don't release information on our customers."

Finn silently debated himself, only the hiss of transmission on the line.

"Sir?"

"I'm a detective with the Austin Police department. This is a double homicide investigation," he said.

"Oh," she paused. "Okay."

"You can remove any financial or extraneous information. I just need the names and addresses of places in and around Austin that received these bags within the last year."

"Well, ah, okay, ah I'll need to check with my manager."

"My name is Black, Detective Benjamin Black."

"Okay Mr., Detective Black."

"I'm going to fax you information verifying the case number and investigation," Finn said. "You take it to your manager."

He hung up and went into the cramped break room. He pulled a soggy slice of pizza from the refrigerator and chewed on it while thinking about the Benjamin situation.

"You kill me. You really do," Benjamin said over the phone.

"You said I could call for anything."

"I said you could call me *any-time,* not for *any-thing.* Your asking a lot, man."

"I'm not asking a lot. I'm asking you to *risk* a lot. That's a fundamental difference."

"The difference is I'm doing the risking, not you."

"Dude, if you just make up a case number, I'll handle it. You'll never hear about it again. Besides, if it ever comes up I'll admit to forging it."

"Fucking-A you'll admit it."

"What's the problem? I'm moving on, just like you suggested."

"This isn't exactly what I had in mind."

"What? You imagined me letting the fuck-up stand?"

"No. More like something that didn't involve me risking my career. Look, I've gotta go."

"Don't be so dramatic."

Benjamin exhaled and Finn waited quietly. "This is the last favor you ask from me over Sarah. All right?"

"So you'll do it?"

"The last favor."

"Fine. The last favor."

"I'll get to it this afternoon."

"Hey. Fax it on official letterhead. And remember, replace your cell phone number with mine."

Tuesday, September 3rd

The next afternoon he received the list. It contained nine recipients: two hospitals, three clinical labs, a UT zoology lab, a doctor's office, a tattoo parlor, and a business. He felt disappointed although he didn't know what he'd expected. *Fucking Yusif's name on it?* He printed out a map to the business, the oddest on the list. Then he dug through saved emails until he found one with an attached photo of Yusif, a still shot from just before he had sniffed the milk in Sarah's refrigerator.

He left work early and drove by the business (In a south Austin strip-mall). Storefronts, marked with block letter generic signs, squeezed together in front of swaths of asphalt. Beyond stood cheerless personal storage units surrounded by razor wire-topped chain-link fences. He parked seven-odd slots from the business, Cardinal Design Works. Their web page had looked eighty years old and mentioned they did custom design work, whatever the hell that was. A few people came and went from nearby businesses. Two stores to his left two men leaned over an open hood of a tow truck.

He sat in his car mustering, mustering his courage to openly ask questions, to expose himself. He hadn't figured out what he would do if he ran into Yusif. He started to feel sorry for himself but then stopped. Eustace was right of course, though he hadn't said it in so many words. Finn's pain came from the loss of a chance with Sarah, and the guilt and regret at having blundered, and barely from empathy for the loss of her mother and father. How dare he pity himself when it was Sarah who'd suffered the tragedy. He looked to the sky, full of cottony clouds, as if God were up there somewhere.

He climbed out of his car and went over to the two men, one black and one white, at the tow truck. The black man, his grease smudged hands hanging past the radiator, lifted his eyebrows, the only indication either gave that Finn was not an invisible specter.

"I'm looking for my brother. I think he may be working nearby." Carefully watching his expression he showed the black man the photo of Yusif. "He's my half-brother," he added.

"You a cop?" the black man asked.

"No."

"Must be a lawyer then," he said, and glanced at the photo. He looked Finn up and down and then met his eyes. "Ain't never seen him." The white man shook his head and Finn didn't think he'd even looked at the photo. Thanks, he told them. The men turned back to one another.

Slapped across a tinted glass storefront in stick-on letters was Cardinal Design Works. Finn went inside. A chubby woman with peppery hair grinned at him from behind the front desk. Beyond her a hallway ran back to a warehouse stacked with pallets of five-gallon buckets.

"Can I help you?"

"I'm looking for my half-brother. A friend of his said he may be working here."

"Okay," she said, eagerly. "What's his name?"

"Yusif."

She shook her head. "Your last name?"

"Ah," Finn said, stalling. (Already a ragged hole in the plan.) "Come to think of it he's probably not using his real name."

"Oh," she said, surprised.

"He's shooting meth and skipped probation. This may help." He put the photo on the desk. As before, he kept careful watch of her reaction.

She picked up the photo and held it at arm's length "No," she said. "He hasn't worked here, at least not in the last four years." Her eyes were earnest.

He drove home, the buoyant enthusiasm from yesterday deflated.

TWENTY-SIX

Wednesday, September 4th

The next morning Finn woke feeling reinvigorated. He wasn't sure why he felt that way but he welcomed the feeling. While waiting for coffee to brew in the break room, he crossed off Cardinal Design Works and looked over the remaining recipients. He'd eliminated the only recipient for whom use of the sterile bag was not evident, and so decided he would check the rest, doing the easiest first: the Cooper lab in the UT zoology department.

Back at his lab desk he searched the Cooper lab on the UT website.

Larry came by, a sheaf of papers packed under an arm. "How'd the experiment go?"

"Not good. The plasmid purifications didn't work."

"What do you mean?"

"I think the reagent kit is bad," he lied. "I'm having a replacement sent."

"You overnighted it?"

"Yep."

"Let me know as soon as you get the results." Larry hustled through the door and into the hallway.

Finn searched for Yusif in the directory of students working at the Cooper lab, but found no photo of anybody who even closely resembled him. He read a summary of Dr. Cooper's research focus—the rapid and recent disintegration of the world's coral reefs. Web links listed abstracts published by his students. Leaning back in his desk chair he tried to hatch a plan to enter and peruse the Cooper lab. He went to a paper published in the Proceedings of the National Academy of Sciences by an undergraduate, Lance Matterson. A publication in PNAS was a big stick any scientist would be proud to carry, not to mention one yet to earn a degree. Lance had made a new chimeric protein—a combination of two proteins.

Finn hatched his plan.

He printed out a photo of Yusif, folded it and pushed it into his back pocket. Moments later he was in the zoology building in front of Dr. Copper's office. He took a deep breath and knocked.

Professor Cooper slouched behind a large computer monitor at a broad desk covered with scientific journals, reams of paper and coral skeletons. He looked as if he'd been tossed about by waves himself.

"I'm Finn Barber, with the Harken lab," Finn said. "I'm here to speak with Lance Matterson." He cast about for the sterile baggies but didn't see any. "I'd like to get his advice on making a chimeric protein."

"Yes, Yes," Cooper said, cheerily. "He's probably feeding cells." He led Finn through the laboratory and into a small rear room, nearly filled with a shiny, stainless steel, sterile hood for culturing cells. A young man sat at the hood holding a pipette and a clear plastic flask, his back to them. His nose pressed against the glass partition that hung two-thirds of the way down the front opening.

"Lance!" Cooper yelled over the drone of the hood. The man turned and Finn saw he was just a kid. He wore jeans and beat-up leather cowboy boots. "You have a visitor."

The kid smiled. "Just a moment."

Cooper and Finn walked out together and Finn surveyed the lab.

"He's the most dedicated undergraduate I've ever had, and his thesis is better than half of my grad students'. I'm not surprised you'd seek his help. Are you a post-doc with Harken?"

"What?" Finn finally said, engrossed in scanning the lab for a sterile baggie. "Yeah, yeah, I'm a post-doc."

The kid came into the main lab, and Cooper introduced them and left. The kid pulled off purple latex gloves and shot them like a rubber band into a trashcan ten-odd feet away. He asked Finn how he could help him while sifting through a pile of loose Styrofoam boxes. Still surveying the lab Finn said something about reading his paper. He used words like brilliant and cutting-edge. The kid slurped it up. "I'd like to make a chimeric RNA polymerase, combine it with a G-protien coupled receptor. Would you give me some advice?"

"No problem." The kid grabbed a Styrofoam box and took it over to a black container sitting on a lab bench. He opened it and white carbon dioxide vapor drifted up and over the edges. He pulled out angular chunks of dry ice and placed them in the box.

"That sounds great," Finn said, looking around.

They walked over to a freezer and the kid opened it. He pulled and pushed on tiny fluorescent plastic racks full of vials. "What species?" he asked.

"Huh?"

"What species are the proteins from?"

Finn surveyed the freezer. "Human," he said.

Lance took a vial and nestled it in the dry ice. He brought it to a lab bench and Finn followed. Lance twisted a monitor to face him and started clicking keys on a keyboard. "What's your email address?"

Plastic bags, papers, pens, tape rolls, cardboard boxes, pipettes, vials, flat-screen monitors, keyboards, and tubes, covered the bench-tops. Then suddenly, like a camouflaged cat being recognized, a plastic baggie stood out from the sundries, a clear zip-lock baggie inscribed with "STERILE" in diagonal, red capital letters. Reflexively Finn reached for it but then jerked his hand back thinking he didn't want to put his finger prints on it.

"Your email address?"

Finn chuckled. "Hey," he said, lifting a pipette from the bench top. "I use Eppendorf pipettes too. Who's bench is this."

"It's mine," the kid said.

Finn dropped the pipette, dug into his back pocket and whipped out the photo of Yusif. He unfolded it, and tapped Yusif's face. "Ever seen him?"

Lance glanced between the photo and Finn as if to see if he were serious. Finn locked onto his soft blue eyes. The kid lowered them back to the photo and they stayed there a second or two. Then they darted to the bench-top before meeting Finn's again. "No," the kid said, but he dragged the word out and the pitch rose at the end as if asking a question.

Finn turned to where the kid had looked. The baggie. "Why'd you look at that?" He asked, pointing at the baggie.

The kid looked concerned, or maybe confused. "I don't know," he stuttered. "I looked there 'cause you looked there before you showed me the photo."

Finn couldn't tell if he was lying. "Are you sure you've never seen him?" He tapped the photo.

"I'm sure," he said, without looking. "How do you know him?"

Finn looked around for a box of gloves. At a nearby lab bench he yanked out a single latex glove and put it on his right hand.

"Are you with the Russian Academy of Sciences?" the kid asked.

Finn picked up the baggie.

"Hey! You can't do that." he said moving towards Finn.

Finn held the baggie down and behind him, positioning himself between it and the kid.

"I'm doing it," he spat through clenched teeth. He wanted to say it was evidence in a double homicide. He wanted to say, *Tell that fuck Yusif, Finn Barber's coming for him,* but instead he swiped the photo off the lab bench, turned, and marched back to his lab. With a clip, he hung the sterile baggie inside a cabinet, careful not to let it touch anything else.

He strode into Larry's office. Larry sat, squinting at a computer monitor, ear buds jammed into his ears. On a peeling laminate stand next to him bubbled a murky fish tank, covered by a scrap of cardboard. "Larry, Lawrence!"

Larry looked up and pulled out the ear pieces.

"The baggie. I have a baggie and I think it's the one used to hold Sarah's mouth swabs." The week before, when Larry had offered Finn a temporary research project, Finn had told him all about Sarah, the man hunting her for the mouth-swabs and her parents' executions.

"How do you know it's the same one?"

"The guy who had it. I showed him a picture of Yusif and I swear he knows him. Of course he denied it."

"How do you know the baggie didn't just come from the same supplier that the man who attacked Sarah got his baggie from?"

"It *did* come from the same supplier. I had them send me a list of local recipients. When I put the photo of Yusif on his desk it startled him and he looked at it a few seconds. But, get this, before he looked back at me he looked right at the baggie. It was no coincidence."

Larry picked up a straw and chewed on it. "Did it have the swabs in it?"

"No. But he got upset when I took it. Why would someone care about an old bag?"

"I care about my old bag."

"Come on. I'm serious."

"What if it's because you have a heightened sensitivity to the baggie. He looked at it because you had been staring at it. And he had a use for it. I don't know. If it hadn't been connected to a murder and Sarah—"

"Murders," Finn said.

"Fine. Murders. Then, you wouldn't have even noticed it."

"Exactly. If no one had died then I wouldn't have noticed it. It could be connected to a double homicide so I'm obligated to investigate even if I have doubts. Look, I just wanted to let you know what I was doing, in the interest of full disclosure."

Larry hung his head back and sighed. "If you go to the police with it you keep me out of it. I just made associate professor and if I'm fingered as part of a failed witch-hunt I'll never hope to make full tenure. I'll look bad enough just by association with you."

"They couldn't get a warrant anyway without fingerprints," Finn said. He went to his desk and phoned Benjamin.

"I know your not calling for a favor," Benjamin said, answering.

"Has anyone gotten the swabs that Yusif dropped in the run-off grate?"

"Now what are you doing?"

"Asking a question, not a favor."

"That was over a month ago. It's long gone by now."

"In the last month have you seen a single drop of rain?" Finn asked.

Benjamin grumbled something.

"I need one of your wedding rings."

"What?"

"Just to borrow," Finn said.

"Hey moron you think Jessica would give that back. It was probably pawned long ago."

"Just call her would you?"

"I see. Your trying to squeeze a few more blow jobs out of Bridgette."

Finn hung up. He called around city services until he spoke with someone who had storm drain access, and then he laid all he had on him: His wife dropped her wedding ring yesterday see?, a present from her great-grandmother Catherine, bless her heart, she'd hidden it through the holocaust. And he and the wife were terrified, terrified a flash flood would wash it away any moment. Weren't they due one?

Three hours later, in front of Sarah's architect firm, traffic rumbled overhead while a city employee waved a flashlight over debris below the storm drain: branches, leaves, a doll's head, plastic bottles, Styrofoam cups, and then, the red block lettering—"STERILE"—the bag seemed to only be there in a dream. Sticks, like brittle bones, cracked under his feet and he snatched up the baggie while pretending to find the wedding ring Jessica had loaned him. With the man distracted by the ring, Finn stuffed the baggie into a pocket.

Back at the lab he called Benjamin. "No questions. Now I need a favor."

Eventually Benjamin agreed to have forensics fume both baggies with ruthenium tetroxide—the most sensitive method to reveal latent fingerprints on plastic surfaces.

Finn drove to the police headquarters and met him in the parking lot. He told Benjamin that forensics only needed to match the prints on the bags (an easy job).

Benjamin said he *wouldn't* call when he had the results.

Finn went back to the lab and tried to re-purify the plasmid DNA he had destroyed two days ago, but couldn't. Like a child on Christmas Eve, neither his body nor mind could contain his electric anticipation. Soon he'd have the evidence that would lead the police to the murderers. He was sure of it. Everything felt right. But he wanted the information this minute. He paced the lab, gave that up too, then put on his running shoes and shorts and jogged to the campus gym. He did squats, pull-ups, and bench-presses until a giddy high seeped into him.

When he went back to the locker room he saw he had a message from Benjamin. He paced waiting to hear it. "Hey Sherlock" he said. "There's two sets of prints on the bag from the sewer and one from the lab. None match. Stick to cell jockeying. I am impressed you found the bag, though. We're keeping it as evidence, obviously. Oh, and I didn't tell Mulveny what you're up to. But you owe me. 'Cause now *I* owe favors to forensics. All right. Later. Wait, where's the swab? You're done poking around, right? Right?"

Finn crumpled onto a bench and hung his head in his hands. He felt betrayed by his certainty. When he lifted his head right next to him some old bastard was toweling off his nuts. Finn jumped up and went back to Larry's office.

"The prints don't match," he told him quietly.

"I'm sorry," Larry said looking sober. "I really am."

Finn knew he meant it, but he also knew what he wasn't saying: that he was glad they wouldn't have to pursue a murderer at UT and threaten Larry's academic tightrope walk.

Finn moped across campus toward his car. It didn't matter, he thought. He needed to pursue whatever lead he had and he was doing it. This consoled him some but a forgotten anxiety nagged him. He probed a little looking for the memory but then stopped, preferring to ignore it. He'd managed to find the make of the bag, get a list of local recipients, and was eliminating them one by one. So why didn't he feel better? He could go to the clinics, and hospitals, and nose around, ask questions, that wasn't difficult. The problem, he realized, was his emotional response. The kid's reactions in the Cooper lab had sent him down a chute of rapids and he'd expected to be dumped into a revelation but only found the cliff walls opened in to just more meandering river. The only way he could tolerate it would be to emotionally detach. But his emotions were what drove him.

As he crossed a street towards a sprawling parking lot, he fished his keys from a pocket. He felt a folded piece of paper and pulled it out, not remembering what it was. *Of course.* It was Yusif leering into Sarah's fridge. He put the car key into the lock and something in the back seat caught his eye: the shoe box of old photos. Sitting on the top was the photo of Pablo smirking, in a black upholstered booth with an arm around his hippie girl-toy. Then the forgotten anxiety clawed it's way through his subconscious. He shook his head at an audacious revelation he just then understood.

Pablo, the American party-boy who cleaned him out so many years ago in Mexico City.

Only a few weeks before that photo was taken Finn had left his first summer stint in the Alaskan fishing industry, flush with cash, and on an epic adventure to sketch Mayan and Aztec ruins, before heading home to include them in his art school resume, his hard-earned baby steps toward a career as a free artist. At the time Finn had seen himself as a victim of Pablo's, and without options—that he had no choice but to crawl back to his parents. But it struck him now there had been choices, and crucial ones (and that his heart had been closed to them). He could have chosen to pursue Pablo.

Through the car window Pablo beamed at him. While a flock of grackles screeched in a nearby tree Finn studied himself with growing shock. It hadn't even occurred to him before. He could have taken small jobs and made Pablo his project. He wouldn't have been too hard to find. Those bohemian circles drew large but narrow arcs. Even if he had gone as far as Argentina Finn could have tracked him down with his only photo of Pablo. It was likely that in one of the backpacker hostels he would have run across someone who had seen him. At the time, however, Finn thought attempting to find Pablo and reclaim the remaining money a fantasy of self-indulgence and a whining ego. Now he saw it much, much differently.

Not only had he lost an opportunity to step aside from his family's cocoon, to bolster his confidence, and self-esteem, to steer his own future, and join a God-given adventure in search of the roach that had robbed him, but he also lost the chance to prevent someone else from falling prey to Pablo. It wouldn't have been even remotely selfish. People would have helped him, too. They've all been down. Some would have lent him a sympathetic hand, a few free nights in a hotel, a job for a week hauling coffee with mules maybe. A plate of rice and beans—the kindness of strangers— that's how he understood it now.

He crumpled Yusif's photo with a single fist and pounded it against the roof of his car, over and over again, denting it in several places. He spun and hurled his key chain at the car next to him, and howled.

Yusif was Pablo reincarnate.

Pablo's theft of $7,700 dollars seemed negligible compared to

Yusif's murderous violence. Right? Here was the deal: Pablo stole way more than money. He'd stolen Finn's self-determintion, fifteen years of his life. But even worse than that, Finn had let him. The problem was never Pablo. The problem was Finn. He couldn't have controlled Pablo anymore than he could have controlled his own birth, but he could control, nearly one-hundred-fucking-percent, his actions and reactions to Pablo. His choices failed him. And no failures are free. They have their prices just like success. But their prices are always higher.

That diamond-smuggling old prune, Eustace Edelman, was right. Life's not about avoiding mistakes. It's about how you respond to them, how you manage them, and ultimately, how you fix them. When Eustace said *If you let the fuck-up stand then you stand to be the fuck-up* he'd left out the part that a fuck-up thrives off the life it's robbed from you and if that fuck-up is serious you can be damn sure that one day it will come back, and stare into your puny, frightened little eyes, and will be much, much more ambitious, but you'll have less to spare. Yusif wouldn't settle for taking a few thousand lousy bucks and leaving Finn terrified of his own heart. He wanted Finn's life, his lover, his soul. He'd come for everything.

TWENTY-SEVEN

Thursday, September 5th

The next morning Finn was in the lab when Larry arrived. Finn followed him into his office. "You have the results on the plasmid preps?" Larry asked, sounding upbeat.

"They must have done PCR on Sarah's swabs," Finn said.

Larry considered Finn. "You're not going to let this go."

"Matterson, the undergrad in the Cooper lab; I know he recognized Yusif's photo."

Larry drew a deep breath and let it drift out.

"We don't need the baggie to prove anything. They did PCR and therefore they have primers. We just need to find the primers."

"You can't get the primers without asking the very people you suspect are connected to a double homicide."

"I thought this out last night," Finn said. "We get a record of the PCR primers that Cooper's lab ordered in, say, the last year, and re-synthesize them. I've got Sarah's swab, the one Yusif dropped the first time he swabbed her. So we can test the primers."

"How'd you get the swabs?"

Finn smirked and tapped a finger on his temple.

Larry chewed on a plastic stir stick and drummed the fingers of one hand on his desk. "No. No. No way. If this leaks and I'm caught snooping around and accessing another lab's primer orders, my career will shit the bed."

Finn's smirk vanished.

"If you do it, you go through Cooper."

Finn reinvigorated, "Really? Wait, Cooper could be involved."

"Dude, Cooper was purifying proteins before you were sucking your mama's titties."

"Okay. Okay. Fine."

"I'll call him in this afternoon so we can finally put this to rest."

They discussed the logistics and then Larry phoned Cooper.

That afternoon Professor Cooper appeared in the laboratory doorway. Finn led him into Larry's office, kicked aside an empty cardboard box and offered him a plastic lawn chair. He chose to stand.

Larry explained the murders to him and why they wanted a year's worth of primer-pair sequences. He plunked down the fax of the sterile baggie recipients. "We're just going down our list. It's nothing personal: old-school trial and error."

Cooper nodded. "Why aren't the police involved?"

"Police here aren't doing a thing since the murders were in D.C. And in D.C. they don't seem to be doing too much. We'll go to them if and when we have solid evidence," Larry said. "We've got nine local recipients on the list and we've eliminated a few. It's probably nothing more than a coincidence that your lab turned up."

Finn tapped on the filthy fish bowl. A tail flashed in the murk.

"It's not standard procedure to go back over orders and cherry-pick primers." Cooper said. "This may take several weeks. We order from a lot of places and I have seventeen researchers."

Larry held out his hand, indicating Finn. "He can help."

Cooper turned to Finn. His face reminded Finn of a balloon blown up too tight. Finn nodded at him and Cooper turned back to Larry. "What sequence are you looking for?"

"We don't know. We only want to eliminate the primers used in your lab. We'll confirm that they don't amplify any DNA from Sarah's cheek swab, and then move on down the list. "

"Doctor Cooper," Finn blurted, "This is a federal case of assault, kidnapping and double homicide, executions actually. If we go to them with this evidence, they'll come in with a blanket warrant, and seal your lab." Out of the corner of his eye he saw Larry cringe. "And they'll dismember it looking for clues." He thought it unlikely, based on their scant evidence, but it sounded impressive.

Cooper looked at him slack-jawed.

"When we find out who received that baggie," Finn said. "We can go to the police with a single suspect. No black-eye for your lab, not to mention its funding." Finn licked his teeth. His heartbeat surged.

"Look, Paul," Larry said soothingly. "We're trying to do this as quietly as possible."

With flared nostrils, Cooper stared down Finn. "I have nothing to hide. And I won't withhold any details of this conversation from the police."

"This is completely legal," Larry said.

"Just send us all the primer pair sequences your lab ordered in the past year and we'll have them re-synthesized," Finn said. "But we need them tomorrow." He didn't look at Larry.

"If you are being anything but entirely forthright, I will

immediately go to the police," Cooper said, raising a finger, "And the Dean. Now, I must get prepared for a lecture." He regarded both of them sternly, and left.

Larry looked at Finn impassively, or maybe it was a disappointed look.

That evening Finn opened his email and (like he always did) scanned hungrily for one from Sarah. He shifted in his chair to take the pressure off a rib he'd bruised in the fight on the balcony weeks ago. It ached dully, radiating down to his hip and up to his shoulder. He tried to feel grateful that he was making progress in Sarah's case, but the chance they would discover a mysterious primer set that would only amplify something in Sarah's mouth seemed beyond remote. However, most importantly, it was infinitely better than regret.

He clicked open his email inbox and scanned through the spam. One was from an address he didn't recognize but titled: *Benjamin, new address*. He read the first sentence and froze. He stood up and spun in tiny circles with his head in his hands. He sat back down and kept reading.

Finn, It's not Benjamin. It's me. I'm not supposed to contact you but email is definitely safer than cell phones. I created this email account just to contact you (Obviously I'm not using any old accounts). I used Benjamin's name so you would open it. So I know it's you, tell me the song on my cell phone for voice mail.

He typed: *Sexual Healing*, and sent it. He stood up, turned circles, and pumped his fists furiously in air.

That night he hardly slept, repeatedly getting up to check his email. At 8:12 a.m. she responded: *Find me on instant messenger at 9:00 with this email.*

While he brewed a pot of coffee visions of her filled his imagination: the first time he'd seen her, at Ooh La Latte sitting alone and waiting for him, draped in a thin blue dress, her hair hanging down into her cleavage. And the last time he'd seen her, as she jogged away from Reece (on her endless tan legs) in Zilker Park . She *was* hot in a lose-your-mind-kind of way.

He paced, continually checking his computer.

Hey, she wrote at 8:51.

He stared at the three letters for a long time. Would she vilify him? He sat down to type, but then stood and paced some more.

Finn?

It's so good to hear from you, He quickly typed, *I'm so sorry.*

Entirely sorry. He hit "Enter", sending it, but then seized his head with both hands realizing he'd just apologized for causing her parents death with, "I'm so sorry. Entirely sorry."

I'm glad to hear from you too.

Thank God! She'd ignored his milquetoast apology. *How are you?* he wrote, but thinking it a moronic question.

Physically, I'm fine. Emotionally, it's torturous.

He wanted to apologize, but do it right, kiss her painted toes and beg her forgiveness. He typed an apology, erased it and retyped, and then moved some sentences around, re-read it and thought it sounded corny. He felt her staring at the phrase "Finn Barber is typing a message" flashing in her instant messenger window. *With every molecule of my being I regret interfering on the bridge. It's my fault your parents died. If I could exchange places with them, I would. I apologize with all my heart.* He didn't like it but finally pushed "Enter" and waited.

Finn, I've had a lot of time to think. I know you heard my warning but had no idea of the risks involved. You were acting in the best faith. Ultimately you were trying to protect me.

He felt like crying. *I tried to be a hero.*

Were you looking for glory?

The question surprised him. He did want glory, though not in an It's a Wonderful Life kind of way, but through her trust. *Honestly,* He wrote, *I only wanted to be your hero.* Man, he was getting cornier by the minute. He watched the instant messenger program flashing, "Benjamin Black is now typing a message". Suddenly a sharp fear coursed through him, fear that he was not writing to Sarah but someone posing as her. He tried to think of something only she could know.

They may have killed them anyway, she wrote, *we'll never know. I knew the stakes and didn't explain them to you. I never imagined you'd follow me.*

Where's my birthmark? He wrote.

He waited, one second, two, three.

Your right butt cheek. It's me, don't worry.

She was wrong. It was his left butt cheek. Did she deliberately get it wrong as a signal that someone was making her email him?

I mean left.

Whew. Okay.

My parents were held hostage and threatened with death if I didn't cooperate. I made the mistake of trusting the enemy. The circumstances may be a complex knot to untangle but they pulled the triggers, not you or me.

Finn was reborn. With just a few simple words she had loosened the grip of the murderous tentacles of guilt. He wanted to scream to her that he loved her. First he typed that he loved her but then erased it, thinking he shouldn't say it now.

The police say I should wait to see anyone I know until they have solid suspects in custody, She wrote. *But I'm withering by degrees. Will you come see me?*

He couldn't believe it. He jumped up pumping his fists in the air and shouting. Y*es, yes, yes, yes!!!!*

How's this Sunday?

He thought about the work at the lab, wondered what he would do if, before Sunday, he found the primers used on Sarah among the list that Cooper was to give him? But then he dismissed anything but going directly to her. O*f course.*

I'll buy you a ticket. I shouldn't tell you where I am. I'll make another fake email and send you the carrier and time of flight. Get the ticket at the terminal.

What about Reece?

Forget Reece.

I'll send money for the ticket.

It's easier if I buy it. Look, I'm warning you, I've been hit by an emotional tsunami. Last chance to back out.

I won't leave the computer, waiting for your email, he typed.

She disconnected.

That wondrous but evasive feeling that life was magical, limitless, and held spectacular secrets, surged in him. He ran throughout his house whooping and jumping.

Then he showered, and went to the lab. He'd been there only half an hour when Cooper arrived looking dour, and handed him a printed copy of the primer list. Whistling to himself, Finn used a computer to crosscheck the primer sets for similarity to the human genome. With Cooper's research focused on ocean coral his primers should not recognize human DNA, or more precisely, Sarah's mouth swab. This is what Finn expected, and the computer cross-checks supported it.

He bounded up the Biology building's concrete stairway in twos and threes. On the fourth floor he marched down the hall to the DNA Synthesis and Sequencing Facility. A thin Indian man wearing a deep-blue turban spoke to him while pipetting into a tiny trough at one of the DNA sequencers. "Samples on the tray to your left. One micro-gram per mil." He didn't look up.

"I have twenty-seven primer sets I need made, and, even though everybody probably says this, it *really* is an emergency."

"Email me the file and you should have them by this afternoon," he said, still pipetting.

"Excellent. Thank you very much."

The man turned to him and gave him a curt nod.

He probably has the same expression after he shits, shaves or fucks, Finn thought. A sharp nod. A job well done—or in this case, to be well done.

That afternoon Finn watched colored lines crawl across a graph on a computer monitor. The PCR thermo-cycler added a digit for each cycle, 6,7,8... on the horizontal axis, and the colored lines, each representing a separate experiment, notched forward along it. The vertical axis represented the amount of PCR product, that is, the creation of new DNA. Each cycle took a little over two minutes and for now all the colored lines crawled along the baseline, no measurable PCR product. At cycle twenty-one the fuchsia colored positive controls—using coral DNA Larry had begged from Cooper—began to rise from the rest, as the PCR product was being detected. This is what Finn expected. It told him that the reagents and experimental conditions were good. Soon the machine neared the last few cycles: ...28, 29, 30. Nothing but the positive controls rose. The machine stopped at cycle thirty-five. Only the positive controls had worked. He spent the rest of the night trying different conditions and only the positive controls ever worked. This meant the experimental conditions were fine and none of the Cooper primers recognized any DNA from Sarah's mouth swab.

It was dark outside when he finally left the lab. The air was on him like an instant fever. He stared at the quarter moon. He must have been wrong about that kid and the baggie after all. "Fuck it," he said aloud. It didn't matter anymore. Larry was right, he'd done an admirable job. He'd followed his lead at the Cooper lab and that was the best he could do. Before seeing Sarah in three days, he might check off the tattoo parlor or the hospital, but now there was no urgency. The police would get Yusif eventually, a little voice told him. *Besides, let's be real. I'm a cell jockey, not a detective.* He decided to go to the campus bar and relax with a beer before going home. Behind him the door swung open and the guy from the DNA facility stepped out. Without the lab coat and safety glasses, Finn almost didn't recognize him. "Working late?" Finn said.

"I had a lot of extra work today."

"I'm sorry if you had to work late because of me. Let me buy you a beer." Immediately Finn regretted it, considering he might get nosy about the primers.

The man appeared to weigh the offer for a moment and then, as if shaking off a doubt, gave Finn a curt nod.

Que será será, Finn thought. "I'm Finn, by the way," he held out his hand.

The man shook it, "Gogan."

"Oh. Like the French impressionist," Finn said.

"Pronounced like it, yes. But usually I'm the one who says that."

They chatted while walking. Finn remembered hearing "Calcutta" and "opportunities" while he thought of coincidence. Only two days before he'd made the connection between Pablo and Yusif and now here was a man with a name pronounced identical to the artist who'd inspired his disastrous Central American trip. It seemed to be just a coincidence, but maybe it meant something deeper. He liked that.

The bar was austere. Wooden booths lined three walls below ceiling fans hung from long extensions. The place hummed with conversation. Finn ordered a couple pints of stout and they took seats at a booth.

"You were raised in Calcutta?"

"My father was a rickshaw puller. We were very poor, and there were six of us, but we had much love. My father encouraged all types of education and many of his clients gave him books which he passed to us. We had a small space in a house full of rickshaw pullers and their families, but it was cozy and friendly. Many had it much worse than us." He told Finn how he earned a math scholarship to Purdue University when he was sixteen. And now he could send enough money to his family for a mortgage on a small house.

He was grateful he could do this and Finn respected him for his confident pride. Finn asked him how he felt living in the United States so far from his culture and family.

"Uncles, aunts, cousins, they all suffered so that I could become an American. They sacrificed without the promise of change. You were lucky enough to be born an American, but my family knows the price to become one." He took a sip of beer. "Let me ask you a question, Mr. Barber." His statement had an uncomfortable tone. "Why did you re-synthesize the primers from the Cooper lab?"

"I didn't tell you they were from the Cooper lab."

The man laughed ever so slightly. "Why did you re-synthesize them?"

"Hmm," Finn said, stalling for inspiration. This is what you get, he thought, for doing what feels right without thinking. "Well, I'm collaborating with Cooper. I wanted to discount batch-to-batch variation, you know. So I had you remake them all at once." He thought the lie sounded pretty solid.

Gogan looked at him seriously. "I hope I can trust you to be honest about my work."

"Certainly."

"My previous synthesis of these primers wasn't good?"

"No, absolutely. It's not like that. No. Nothing was wrong. Like I said, batch-to-batch variability."

"The re-synthesized primers, I am just delivering them, without knowing really why." He paused. "Just like a rickshaw puller." A sly smirk curled towards his cheeks.

Finn chuckled but really regretted coming now. Gogan knew he was lying. "Look, it's just that I'm not at liberty to say what experiments we're doing. You know, it's a privately funded project and we signed non-disclosure statements. All that bullshit." *Much better.*

"Then I suppose I am at no obligation to tell you what I know."

Finn turned serious. "What do you know?"

"I too am under bullshit agreements."

"I hope you're not joking."

The man raised his eyebrows. "I do not mean to upset you, Mr. Barber."

"I'll be less upset if you tell me what you mean."

Gogan stopped and took a sip of beer. "Why were two primer sets excluded?"

"Excluded? No. We remade all the primers used by the Cooper lab in the last year."

"All but two sets."

"No. Cooper gave me a list of all the primers ordered by his lab in the last year."

The man shook his head making tiny clicking noises. "When I saw the list of primers were all previous orders from the Cooper lab, I checked them against all the primers ordered under the Cooper account. You requested all but two pairs made within the last year. He stopped and wagged two fingers in the air. "And those two pairs. I did not make them."

Finn scowled. "Who did?"

"Someone from the Cooper lab. They were on his account."

"I mean who, in particular?"

"I don't know."

"How can you not know?"

"The lab is accessible anytime with the right card-key. Sometimes grad students or post-docs work late and want to make primers. It doesn't happen often but it happens. I had to dispose of many chemicals contaminated by hurried and sloppy biologists, so I prefer that people wait for me to make them. I am very vocal in requesting people use it alone only under real emergencies. I suppose that is why the person that made these primers immediately deleted the entries."

"Deleted? If they were deleted, how do you know about them?

"I programmed the DNA synthesizer to back up the primer sequences in the case someone *accidentally* deletes one."

"Someone impatient made it and didn't want you to know about it."

"With this back-up program I find out. But the most detailed info I can get is the lab the primers were billed to. I am no control freak for anything other than the quality of my own product. I could care less what they do as long as they follow standard operating procedure. Which, of course, they never do."

"Or someone didn't want anyone to know the sequence," Finn said, though more a thought aloud.

"What did you say?"

"When were those two sets made?"

"A month ago."

"A month?"

"Yeah."

"Together?"

"At the same time."

"I need them right now."

"Is this a real emergency?

Finn's expression softened and he even laughed. "Yeah."

The man took a sip from his glass, still nearly full, and then stood. "I must be going to the wife now."

"Do you work Saturdays?"

"Sometimes."

"Can you make those primer sets first thing in the morning?"

"Can you tell me why you are re-synthesizing all those primers, first thing in the morning?"

Finn stood and they shook hands. He wouldn't tell Gogan shit. "All right," he said. He thought he'd move to the bar and have one more beer before going home. "But I'll be waiting for the primers."

"I'll be waiting for the story."

TWENTY-EIGHT

Saturday, September 7th

"Have you heard the news?" Larry asked. Finn sat at a lab bench in front of the PCR thermo-cycler waiting for the results of the two deleted primer sets that Gogan had remade. A hangover headache throbbed behind his right eye.

He turned from the computer monitor. "Huh?"

"Smallpox. They think there's a case in Chicago."

"Terrorists?" Finn asked. Finn knew epidemiologists claimed smallpox had been eradicated in nature, with the only known surviving viruses at the Center for Disease Control in Atlanta, Georgia and somewhere in Russia.

"Not conclusive yet," Larry said.

Finn didn't know if he meant the terrorists or the smallpox, or both.

"How'd the experiments with the Cooper primers turn out?"

Finn turned back to the computer screen. The data from the two deleted primer sets ran in real-time. Fuchsia, the positive control lines, were the only ones that worked. He hadn't told Larry about the two deleted primer sets that Gogan found—probably just a grad student in a rush after all. "Just the positive controls," he said.

"Hey, you did your best, man."

"I guess," he said. The experiments were empirical and objective, but he felt betrayed by them nonetheless. It made sense that someone would delete primers that could recognize DNA important enough to murder for. So using these two sets he'd been more hopeful than with the first twenty-seven primer pairs Cooper had given him. Evidently his imagination had gotten the better of him, and it made him feel childish for having the audacity to hope.

While chewing a banana muffin and waiting for aspirin to erase his headache, he forced himself to ponder an oddity about these last two primer sets, one he'd noticed after cross-checking them against public databases for hits (DNA sequences they recognized).

Each PCR primer in a pair should give search results similar to its partner. They should bind to (recognize) DNA very, very close to one another, in relation to the gargantuan size of most genomes. Almost always this was within the same gene. All of the primers from the first set of twenty-seven did just that. But these last two primer pairs did not recognize any known sequences well. The top hit on the first primer in pair one was: Mus musculus (house mouse). The top hit for its partner primer: Arthroderma gypseum (some fungus). They didn't even recognize sequences from the same fucking kingdom. The second primer pair was no better. It was as if they were fake.

Pair one
5-CCTG<mark>CCTGCAGG</mark>TAAGTACG-3

5-CTGAGCCTGATATTTCGGCC-3

Pair two
5-CCTACCATCCGGTTCATAAT-3

5-TTACGCCTGCAGGATCCGC-3

He looked over the primer pairs again. Then he recognized a palindrome, a tell-tale sign of an enzyme cut site—CCTGCAGG—(In the first primer in set one).

Specialized enzymes clip DNA at these cut sites and others join pieces of DNA at those same cut sites. By engineering a primer with a cut site a biologist can PCR amplify the DNA and then clip it with the enzyme that recognizes that specific cut site. Then, using receiving DNA cut with the same enzyme, the biologist, like the old film editors working manually with cellophane, simply splices the PCR product into the larger DNA.

This particular site was a long one, and a rare one. He searched online and found a *Streptomyces* bacteria made the enzyme that recognized that site: SbfI. Then he used an online program and searched for cut sites in the second primer in set one. He found none that were useful in splicing. It confused him. An enzyme cut site on only one primer in a pair was nearly useless, you need it on both ends of the PCR product—hence, on both primers. Trying to insert it into a larger piece of DNA would be like putting a one-armed woman into a chain of hand-holders.

Next he searched set two for DNA cut sites and found an SbfI site, right there in the goddamn middle of the second primer. He backed his chair away and paced in front of the computer. *Jesus Christ.* Maybe the two primers with the SbfI sites were meant to be used together, and the other two were dummy primers, distractions for anyone they weren't intended for.

He hurried back to his lab bench and prepared another set of experiments mixing the two primers with the SbfI sites.

An hour later he saw the lime-green line of Sarah's swab sample notch upward at cycle twenty-five along with the fuchsia positive control. He threw back the lab stool. "I got you motherfuckers!" He leaned into the monitor. "Now you're fucking with Finn Barber!" Spittle flecks stuck to the monitor and refracted the light like tiny prisms. To his right a Chinese grad student stood wide-eyed, holding a rack of test-tubes. He smiled self-consciously, "Hi." Then he decided he would do another experiment to either weaken or bolster the results. "Could I get a mouth swab?" he asked her.

From neighboring labs he managed to get more than twenty mouth swabs.

Two hours later he marched into Larry's office. "I got a fucking hit, Lawrence." He slapped a print out of the raw PCR data. "That one, the fuchsia line, it's my positive control. It comes up at cycle twenty-four every time. The lime-green one comes up right along with it. It's Sarah's mouth swab, an average of six replicates. All the others are swabs from twenty-one students I got this morning, done in duplicate. Not a blip on any of them but every one of Sarah's pegs out."

"I thought you'd tested all of the primer pairs?"

"I had. But these two primers are combined from two pairs."

Larry frowned and then looked at the data, for a while. "Did any other primer pairs work?"

"Not a single one, and I ran them twice in duplicate."

"What do you mean you combined two pairs?"

"The tech running the DNA synthesizer found two primer pairs in the synthesizer log billed to the Cooper account. They weren't on the list Cooper gave us. They were made a month ago and deleted."

"Who made them?"

"We don't know, but they knew the Cooper lab password."

"Why did you mix two primers from different pairs?"

"One primer in each pair has an Sbf I site, so I mixed them. Someone really didn't want this primer set to be discovered."

"If this is real, it's incredible."

Finn bounded up the steps to the sequencing lab. An effervescent high distilled into his head. When he entered, Gogan, hunched over a machine and holding a pipette, turned around. "I got a hit," Finn said breathing hard. "I need it sequenced. As fast as you can."

"I'll be done here in just a moment." He turned back around and pipetted blue liquid into holes in a machine.

After Gogan left the bar last night Finn knew he wouldn't tell him a thing. He didn't need to know. But without Gogan's help he wouldn't have known about the deleted primers. It was simply foolish not to collaborate with him, plus, even if he didn't need to know he deserved to know now. He considered the possibility that Gogan was somehow connected to Yusif but then dismissed it. Finn liked him, he felt trustworthy and he was resourceful and intelligent. At some point you've got to rely on faith.

Gogan stood up from the machine and put the pipette down.

Finn looked directly into his eyes, black pools, like the *cenotes* dotted across Mexican jungles. "Gogan, if I tell you what I'm doing your life may be in danger."

"You can tell me but you'd have to kill me?" He laughed.

"It sounds like a joke but it's true. Maybe you should think about it for a couple of days. I can get someone over in biochemistry to sequence it."

"You are serious?"

"As smallpox."

"I survived the slums of Calcutta. I can survive this."

Finn explained everything. The first attack on Sarah, the man breaking into her apartment, his mention of a message in her mouth, his threats, her narrow escape from Melissa's house, the chase on the bridge, and the kidnapping of Sarah's parents and their murders.

"I'm so sorry," Gogan said.

"You understand you cannot say a word of this even to your wife."

Gogan looked skeptical

"Okay, only your wife." Finn gave him a tiny plastic tube—the PCR product to sequence. "Did the person who made the primers leave any clue to identify themselves?"

"The only data I have on those primer sets is its charge to the Cooper account and the time it was made. I will get the records for the card reader-door lock just before the primer was made."

"You can do that?"

"I will tell campus police someone made primers that night and I found expensive broken reagent bottles in the morning."

"The more I know you, Gogan, the more I like you."

"You don't know me yet."

"Call me when you have that sequence. Forget everything else." They shook hands and Finn felt an intense connection to the man. A feeling that if he had to lay his life down for Gogan he could and would. He, Gogan, and Larry were in it together now.

TWENTY-NINE

Finn's phone rang. He'd fallen asleep on the couch. He leaned forward and fumbled for the stereo remote control. The sun set while he napped leaving the living room painted in dying streaks of indigo. He muted the music and answered the phone.

"Finn," It was Gogan. "I sequenced the PCR product. It's Interleukin-4, human."

"The gene didn't mean much to Finn, although he knew it was part of the immune system. He felt let down, as if he'd expected something obvious, the sequence screaming out, *look, here's why we chased Sarah through the streets and killed her parents!* "Why would someone want Sarah's Interleukin-4?"

"It's not *her* Interleukin-4. Remember, those primers don't recognize anything in the human genome."

"Yeah, right, right," he said absentmindedly. A dream he couldn't remember had seared an impression into him, a hot iron momentarily laid on muslin. With Gogan's news he struggled to make connections. "Maybe those primers only recognize something in Sarah's DNA? That would explain why nothing came up on a human DNA search."

"Impossible. In the genome Interleukin-4 has way too much junk DNA mixed in. This PCR product is 500 bases, just the essential gene. No introns."

"How much of the gene is it?"

"The whole thing."

"The whole thing! It's only 500 base pairs?"

"Less. One end has a promoter."

"Why the hell would someone want to PCR an Interleukin-4 gene?"

"This is not the question."

"Huh?" He bristled at Gogan's smugness.

"How did a spliced human interleukin-4 gene get into Sarah's mouth? *That* is the question."

"Hmm," Finn said rubbing his eyes.

"The campus police gave me the I.D. from the card-reader door lock to my lab. Just before those primers were made, Lance Matterson, an undergrad, entered."

"I knew it!" Finn jumped up. "I'll call you right back." He pulled out his wallet and scattered business cards across the coffee table. He plucked out the F.B.I. agent's card—the one who'd interrogated him with Detective Mulveny after Sarah's parents were executed. The phone rang a million times before a man answered.

"Yeah," the voice was tired.

"Detective Deyermand?"

"Yeah," the voice sharper now.

"This is Finn Barber. You questioned me in Austin about—"

"I remember you." His tone said get on with it.

"I have a lead. A student at the University of Texas received the swabs."

"Name?"

"Lance Matterson."

"Hold on." Deyermand repeated it while writing. "How do you know he has the swabs?"

"It's not easy to explain."

"Easy or not, you'll have to."

Finn cleared his throat. "Well, to get anything meaningful from a mouth swab you have to PCR amplify—"

"Hold on." He spoke to someone else but Finn couldn't tell what he said. "Listen, Mr. Barber, this smallpox outbreak has us running in circles. I don't mean to be callous but don't expect anything until this quiets down. Does Matterson suspect you know anything?"

Finn paused considering a lie. "No," he said.

"You'll have to come in and give a written report. I'll give you a call when this is all over, thank you."

"Wait," Finn said. "He might suspect something." He thought he heard Deyermand sigh, or maybe blow out a lungful of smoke.

"Don't do anything and don't go near the suspect. I'll call you in a few days."

Finn sat back down on the couch feeling deflated. He was quiet a moment before realizing how mad he really was—mad that the F.B.I. didn't have the resources to deal with a single smallpox case (and only a suspected one at that) while also investigating the murder of Sarah's parents. The idea that punk undergrad in Cooper's lab was connected to the murders and still free seethed inside him. He decided he would collect the primers, the baggies, and the swabs and take them down to Deyermand right now. Because they didn't have time didn't mean he had to stall as well. While driving to the university Gogan called.

"Listen to this," Gogan said. "Expression of mouse interleukin-4 by a recombinant ectromelia virus."

"Ectro-what?"

"In 2001 some Australians spliced Interleukin-4 into the mousepox virus trying to weaken it. But they accomplished the opposite. They made it hyper-virulent. With the Interleukin-4 mousepox they infected immunized mice and it, quote, *resulted in significant mortality due to fulminant mousepox.*"

"What's fulminant?"

"Explosive."

"Are you saying this is connected to the smallpox case?"

"One hundred percent of the mice died, vaccinated mice."

"How related are mousepox and smallpox?"

"Very."

He thought about the Middle Eastern men chasing Sarah down to get a mouth swab, her parents murdered for it, her trips to Afghanistan, the man in her apartment speaking a Pakistani dialect. "Jesus. Sarah's infected with a smallpox super-strain." *She could be dying right now and I could be just days behind.* He felt like a leper, invisible viruses peeling off and riding on dead skin flakes. He pressed his lymph nodes below his chin. They weren't swollen and he felt fine. He flicked on the interior light. The skin on his arms looked normal, no blemishes. If they'd infected her with smallpox what did they want with her after that? Maybe they were checking to see if the modified virus had successfully infected her. But then he realized it couldn't be. He was nearly certain smallpox had an incubation time of less than a month and Sarah's mouth swabs were older than that. And she was still healthy, or so she'd said on instant messenger. It had to be her. She knew his butt-cheek mole.

"...Finn," Gogan called through the phone. "I'll Make a set of smallpox primers and look for the virus in her mouth swab."

Finn said okay though it felt like someone else speaking. He hung up. While scrolling through his cell phone contact list, he steered with his right elbow, and shifted with his left hand. He took a wide turn and slid into another lane. Someone blared their horn. He jerked the wheel and careened back into his lane. The phone on the other end rang.

"It's part of this smallpox attack."

"What?" Agent Deyermand said harshly.

"The information I have says the murder of Sarah's parents is connected to the smallpox attack. They were looking to see if she'd been infected with a genetically modified smallpox virus."

"You better think twice about what you're saying. I *will* arrest you if this is bullshit."

"I'm coming to San Antonio right now."

Finn threw down the phone, yanked the steering wheel, and U-turned across the four lanes of Congress Avenue. Then he dialed Gogan and told him he was going to see the F.B.I. in San Antonio.

The sun set completely as he plunged south. An hour later he exited the freeway for downtown San Antonio as gusts of black wind hauled in air pungent with rain. Green reflective street signs hanging across the intersections swung wildly forcing him to stop and piece together the snippets of names. As he turned onto the street of Deyermand's office the sky exploded with lightning and thunder. Moments later rain lashed down sideways, in alternating heavy and super-dense torrents. He crawled along the four lane street blind to even the lines and deafened by pings of ricocheting hail. Finally, among high rises he found the detective's building. He parked on the street and sprinted under lightning strobes, through shin deep water already coursing into storm drains. The storm belched Finn into the entrance of the federal building. A security guard opened the door for him at the last moment. He was a big startled-looking guy. Finn shook off the rain while the man talked excitedly about storm as he escorted him to Deyermand's office.

Deyermand looked younger and stronger than he remembered. His hair looked greasy from not washing, slicked down and pushed forward like a Butch Cassidy mug shot. Finn explained what he and Gogan had found.

"Let me get this straight. Interleukin-4, a *human* gene, inside a smallpox virus would make it resistant to the vaccine." His not so cordial veneer seemed ready to splinter.

"If smallpox reacts the way mousepox did."

"So, the only solid evidence you have that this is related to the smallpox attack is from a scientific paper that showed Interleukin-4 strengthened a mousepox virus?"

"The men who attacked Sarah spoke in Pashto; they're probably Al Qaeda; they murdered to confirm this sequence was in her."

The detective exhaled and turned to the window. Rain still pelted the panes but the storm was already dying. "God knows we need this," Deyermand said.

Finn couldn't be certain if he was talking sarcastically about the smallpox outbreak or the strange twist with interleukin.

"The rain, I mean," he said turning back to Finn and rubbing his hands through his hair. "I don't have the kind of clearance or contacts to make this easy, but I'll try to confirm if Interleukin-4 is in the smallpox DNA from the case in Chicago, well, provided it is indeed smallpox. I'll also have Sarah tested for smallpox." He wagged a finger in the air. "I'll put my neck on the line but you and your friend have to make triple-certain of your results. If we find weaponized smallpox the whole freaking country will go ape-shit. Do you understand? We can't make a single mistake."

Finn nodded. "I'll go directly to the lab."

"No, you will go directly to a hotel. You'll be escorted there, locked in and guarded, and will stay there until we get the lab results on Sarah and the smallpox sequence. Don't look shocked. You're lucky. The only reason I'm not putting you in a detention center is that, God forbid, if you're right I can't put others at risk." Then Deyermand opened a desk drawer, fished out a plastic Ziploc bag and held it open in front of Finn. "Drop your phone in here. Your room will not have a phone. You will have no contact with anyone but your guard."

Finn took his phone from a pocket. He gave him Gogan's number and Deyermand wrote it down.

Deyermand stared at him like a man in a duel. "Get some sleep," he said, an absurd thing to say.

"Okay," Finn managed.

THIRTY

Sunday, September 8th

After a sleepless night, Finn heard a knock at the door and the guard entered. He had Finn's phone with detective Deyermand on it. A short-tempered Deyermand told Finn that they had not found interleukin-4 in the confirmed smallpox from the case in Chicago. It was *Variola major* with no genetic abnormalities. Also, Sarah's smallpox test was negative. Before hanging up he sharply warned him not to further interfere in the murder investigation. Finn drove back to Austin feeling moronic but relieved, thanking God that Sarah was not infected with weaponized smallpox. He called Gogan. "Sarah's clean."

"Where are you?"

"I feel like a conspiracy theorist."

"I need to speak to you."

"About what?"

"Not on the phone."

Whatever, Finn mumbled to himself, determined not to let Gogan's secrecy puncture his buoyant mood. Though they'd been wrong about the Interleukin-4, he would be with Sarah in less than twelve hours and they had a solid suspect in her parents' murders. The smallpox would probably be like the anthrax scare a few years back: a few cases quickly forgotten. "I'll meet you at the Brain Café" he said. "I'll be there in an hour."

The café was crammed with electrically colored outsider art and dry-rotted wood. Cartoons of Technicolor brains in various shades of neon and pastel chalk were scrawled on a blackboard behind the counter. It listed drinks like "Anti-Febrile Cerebral", "Straight to the Amygdala", and "(I wanna) Party on your Pituitary". He joked with the cashier, ordered a coffee with a shot of bee pollen, and an omelet. He sat down at a minuscule round table in a side room beside a couple discussing the smallpox outbreak. Smallpox with no genetic modifications, Finn thought. He listened to the woman talk about international flights being canceled while worrying if his flight to see Sarah would be affected.

Gogan entered, practically marching. His beard was a wiry black mess, and without a turban his rich black hair hung down nearly to his waist. Finn stood. They shook hands and then he found himself hugging and thanking Gogan, asking if he was alright and apologizing for the F.B.I. agents that had quarantined him in the lab overnight. A gawky teenage guy plunked down Finn's omelet.

"I found something this morning after the F.B.I men left," Gogan said, sitting down. "At the beginning of the Interleukin-4."

"Yeah?"

"It has a promoter, to turn the gene on."

"So do all genes? Would you grab the salt, please." Finn gestured to another table closer to Gogan.

"It's a viral promoter on a human gene." Gogan leaned forward putting the shakers down, and in a colluding voice, hardly a whisper, said, "a smallpox promoter."

Finn looked over at the couple chatting next to them and then turned back.

"One hundred percent," Gogan said.

"But that's not what they found," Finn said. "The smallpox case is *Variola major,* no interleukin."

Gogan whispered, "Someone is intending to create an s.p. super strain."

"No," Finn spit through his teeth. "Interleukin's not there."

"But what else can the s.p. promoter on the interleukin-4 mean?" His whisper rose.

Finn squished a piece of omelet under his fork.

"It's the only logical conclusion," Gogan said.

"But," Finn shook his head trying to think of something to counter his claim. "Are you sure?"

Gogan nodded. "Sarah is connected to the smallpox attack but is not infected. We must call your F.B.I. Agent. "

"You wouldn't if you'd heard him this morning."

Gogan pulled out his cell phone. "His number?"

Finn huffed.

"Our country is under attack," Gogan said.

Finn opened his wallet and threw Deyermand's card down.

Gogan dialed. "Voice mail," he said. "Agent Deyermand. I have new evidence that Sarah Dougherty and the murder of her parents is definitely connected to the...the current events." He left his name and hung up.

Finn jammed two forkfuls of omelet into his mouth. He chewed deliberately, still coming up with no way to refute Gogan's evidence.

Sarah's adorable lip-peak (or whatever you call it) pecked into his imagination. He wanted to nibble it. He needed to pack for Sarah's and leave for the airport by 4:00. Gogan and his insistent clues. *Damn him!* Then a solution came to him. They wouldn't wait for Deyermand to call back. They'd go to San Antonio and explain the latest evidence. Deyermand would have to see the logic. They'd be back in Austin by 2:00 and he would pack and leave with a clean conscience that he'd done everything possible. Simple. "We need to see Deyermand, *now,*" he said while stuffing his mouth with omelet.

Outside they looked back and forth between Finn's dented hatchback and Gogan's tar-black luxury coupe looking as if it were spit-shined.

"What's with no turban?" Finn asked, as Gogan pulled off the service road and sped onto Interstate 35. Keeping his eyes on the road Gogan spoke: "I put it on this morning like I always do but after the smallpox outbreak yesterday I couldn't bring myself to walk out the door wearing it." They shot from the outside lane over the middle and into the slow lane, hurtled past an eighteen-wheeler and then ricocheted back to the fast lane. "To tell the truth, I was scared." They zoomed up within three feet of a white sedan and Gogan braked hard. Finn grabbed the dash board and then scanned for cop cars. "Once, early in the morning," Gogan said, "after leaving a dance club downtown, I separated from my friends and went to my car. I was alone on a deserted section of third street. Three guys coming down the opposite side of the street started yelling, 'Osama, Osama!'. I yelled the first thing that came to mind." He pulled in the middle lane and passed a truck pulling a horse trailer.

"What'd you say?"

"Yo mama, yo mama!"

Finn laughed.

"Then they put me in the hospital for three days."

Finn stopped laughing.

"I believe you call it a beat down," Gogan said.

"I'm sorry."

"Don't be. I became an underground Sikh superstar, made the two main papers in Calcutta."

When they pulled up to the F.B.I. Offices, the building looked much different than the night before. It shone bone white in the stark sunlight. "I'll be right back," Finn said, jumping out. He passed by the guard (a different one) and through the metal detector, and went up to a man at the front desk. He was thick-lidded, bald, and looked bored. Finn asked for Deyermand.

Slowly, the man swung his gaze up from a computer monitor. "Name please."

"Finn."

"Fin?"

"Yeah, like Latin for the end, but double-N. Barber."

The man typed one-fingered and then looked back to Finn.

"It's urgent," Finn said. The man dropped his gaze below the counter. A mouse clicked and he dragged his eyes back up. "He'll be in Monday."

"We've got to find his house," Finn said, jumping into the car. He accessed the Internet through his phone and soon they were winding through suburban neighborhoods, houses more monstrosities than homes. They passed one fronted by a colossal porch with thirty foot tall pure white colonnades and five ceiling fans hung down on long extensions. "Back up, that's the one," he said.

Finn knocked on the front door: a huge one, forest green and with a long curved brass handle. When it swung open cool air poured out and a slender blond woman, thirtyish stood with a wet paint brush in her hand.

"Yes?"

"Is Brian Deyermand here?"

"Who's asking?"

"Excuse me." He offered his hand. "I'm Finn Barber. Brian is working on a homicide case I'm involved in. I'm a witness."

She didn't shake his hand. "Brian's sleeping," she said narrowing her eyes. "He hasn't slept since Thursday. He doesn't work from the house." She put a hand on the edge of the door.

"I'm sorry but I must insist you wake him."

She drew her face together in a sour pucker.

"A lot of lives are at stake here."

She hesitated as if she was going to say something but then thought better of it. "And you mean to tell me with so many lives at stake that none of the other 7,000 agents can help you until Brian gets enough sleep to function?"

"That's exactly what I'm telling you."

"I don't believe you."

"We've found evidence that shows that the homicide case is undoubtedly connected to the smallpox outbreak. Brian has already been working on it." He shifted from foot to foot trying to get a view of the foyer.

"Oh. Her looked changed to something between amused and annoyed. "*You're* the guy who kept him up all night."

"But we have new evidence. And I—"

"I won't wake Brian for anything short of an act of God."

"This may qualify."

"Get off of my porch." She swung the heavy door closed.

As the door slammed shut he snatched the brass handle and pressed the thumb latch, pushing hard against the door. It sprung open just as the deadbolt jutted out into the air. The woman stumbled backwards. "Brian!" Finn shouted up a staircase that curved against the foyer wall.

"Get out!" She slapped him with the paintbrush and pushed him. "Get out!"

Paint stung his eyes. But still he managed to block her thrusts and step into the threshold. "Brian!" The next thing he knew she was on him and swinging a long black tube at his temple. He pivoted, and threw his right arm up. The blow crashed down on the middle of his forearm. He howled, scrambling backwards and she swung again. It was a heavy, black, metal flashlight. She caught him in the ribs with a glancing blow off his elbow. He retreated across the porch and she held her ground just outside the doorway, flashlight raised, and breathing heavy.

Then, behind her came Deyermand, like a savage-king, a pistol in one hand and naked, save for a black eye cover hanging on his neck. He hurtled down the foyer steps, taking four or five in a bound. Finn's breath stuck in his throat. Deyermand blazed through the doorway his pistol leveled. Finn threw his hands up.

"Are you okay?" Deyermand asked the woman but while riveting his eyes on Finn. "What the fuck Barber!"

Finn spewed the words. "The-smallpox-has-it's-weaponized-there's a promoter on the IL-4-it's a-hundred percent—"

"Are you out of your fucking mind!" Deyermand came directly at him, scarlet-faced and wild-eyed, pointing the pistol at his chest.

"We have more—"

"We checked the DNA," Deyermand said. "*There's! Nothing! There!*" He enunciated each word. Breathing hard, he stared at Finn for a long moment. He looked over at Gogan's car.

"But this is new evidence."

"Let me clue you in, buddy. After you there's a thousand more waiting to tell us that their neighbor's building a bomb in the basement, that their co-worker is plotting to poison the water cooler. It's nut-jobs like you that end up helping the terrorists."

"Get the fuck off of my porch before I arrest you," the woman said.

Deyermand trained the gun on Finn's heart.

From the porch the couple—Deyermand covering his crotch with a hand now—watched Finn back away and get into the car. Gogan backed down the driveway. For many minutes they drove with just the gentle whirr of the air conditioning. At a long stoplight their eyes met. "How did it go?" Gogan asked.

Finn looked at him flabbergasted. Gogan looked back solemn. Then a lone chuckle bubbled up from Finn. Gogan joined him and soon they were both buckled over. Gogan could hardly drive. Each time they calmed down an attempt to stifle a laugh would start it all over. Finn held up a hand in front of him palm down, and it shook like a twenty-year boozer with the DTs.

"I hope you didn't hurt her," Gogan said.

"Fuck you. That flashlight was the size of a sequoia." Finn rubbed his throbbing right arm. It was already beginning to bruise. He thought about Sarah and a knot in his stomach—that had been there since he'd eaten—tightened in increments. He stopped laughing. He folded down against his legs.

"Are you okay?"

"Just get out of here, away from this traffic. We need to be moving." His thoughts became specters. *You're paranoid. There's no weaponized smallpox.* They hovered around him and took turns darting at him. *You'll never do anything right. You'll always be a coward. You're broke and you're aimless. You're a failure. Sarah won't truly forgive you. You're an alcoholic. You can't leave to see Sarah with what you know now. You'll never see her again.*

"Pull over," he blurted.

"Here?"

"Right here. Right here. Stop!" Finn's stomach knotted. Gogan turned onto a side street, and with cars whizzing by Finn climbed out onto a small grassy island in a sea of asphalt. He paced in tight circles and then leaned against a light post, hanging his head. Nearby a suburban shopping mall parking lot gleamed with endless rows of parked cars. The specters intensified their attack. Gogan left the car and put his hand gently on Finn's back, and for a moment Finn felt a little better. He paced in the strip of grass. "What time is it?" he asked.

Gogan grabbed him by the shoulders and stopped him. He looked him in the eyes. "Finn, only you and me know what is happening. You and me."

"I don't even know where Sarah is, where I'm flying."

"You must believe what we have found."

"What are 'you and me' going to do, huh? Save the world?"

"We have to do something."

"I'm such an idiot. I should never have gone to Deyermand's house. I just wish I'd never gone out on that bridge."

"Then we would never have discovered the weaponized smallpox."

"Who are we? Starsky and fucking Abu!" Finn broke away and paced again.

"If you must see Sarah I cannot stop you."

"What the hell are you going to do?"

"I am going to find Lance Matterson."

"You should go back to India. Protect your family."

"I will *never* abandon my country."

"You think Matterson'll give you a flow-chart for the smallpox attack?"

"I don't know."

Finn thrust his hands against his face and rubbed it. He stalked around the island of grass and then onto a gravel lined drainage ditch. He needed to stop giving the specters a stationary target. He needed to think. He followed the ditch along a field of asphalt to a strip-mall. From there he took another drainage ditch along a service road to a convenience store. He went inside, grabbed a forty ounce beer, and stood in line to pay. "A pack of American Spirits," he said when it was his turn. Outside he cracked the bottle and lit a cigarette. He tried to imagine what Sarah would do in his place. He tipped up the brown-bagged bottle and swallowed several mouthfuls. A man with a homeless-tan and an over-sized flannel shirt sidled up to him asking for money. He gave him a twenty. He so desperately wanted to see Sarah, to dissolve into her like salt into steaming water. But if he went to see her now and ignored the obvious clues that Deyermand dismissed as paranoia, eventually his betrayal would be no more hidden from Sarah than from himself.

But if he stayed and Yusif and the terrorists were still on the hunt to kill her, if one of those vulnerable was Sarah herself and he sacrificed her for nameless masses, he would never, ever forgive himself. It was a risk with an outcome not to be pardoned. He drained half of the fat tear-drop-shaped bottle in several long swallows. The cigarette unbalanced him. He put the bagged beer on top of a newspaper dispenser and dialed Gogan, his thoughts congealing if not his determination.

"You are doing the right thing," Gogan said.

"Please don't say that. Look, I'm about a quarter mile from where we stopped."

"I am on the highway going to Austin. I am not turning around."

"You won't come back and pick me up?"

"I am proud of your thoughtful decision-making but I am certain the terrorists are not delaying for you."

"How am *I* supposed to get back?"

"You are a competent man. You will figure this out." Gogan gave him Lance's address. "Get guns, weapons, anything to subdue or kill somebody." He hung up.

Finn drew hard on the cigarette. Here he was, outside a filthy San Antonio convenience store swigging a forty on a seemingly normal day, though in the midst of a terrorist attack, but without the jet-fuel fireball explosions and collapsing towers. Watching the cars stop and gather behind a stoplight, Gogan's last words echoed in his mind. Chrome rimmed windshields dissected the sunlight. Drivers swayed to music or spoke on cell phones. He was standing in a war zone, and it was no exaggeration, but nobody knew it and they were all vulnerable. He flicked the cigarette in a high arc over several cars in the parking lot and time fragmented its motion. Did the ends justify the means, now? He considered jacking a car. Though, practically it was a bad idea, forget the fact he didn't have the guts.

He marched to the store, withdrew four hundred dollars from an ATM and returned to the curb. He surveyed the cars stopped at the red light and spied a man in a pickup truck, unshaven and wearing a tee-shirt with the sleeves crudely cut off. He tapped on his passenger-side window and the man leaned over and rolled it down. "I'm in a horrible bind. A friend stranded me. He's left to kill himself. I need to catch him before he gets home to Austin." It spewed out before he could think about it. "I have four hundred bucks. I don't have time for a cab."

"Why don't you call the cops?"

"If he sees the cops at his house he won't go near it and if they come after he gets there he'll shoot himself before they get in. I know him. He'll at least talk to me." Finn stared at the man. "We'll have to break a few laws. I can look for another ride."

"Get in," the man said

The stop light held a steady red. Above the engine rumble a radio announcer said there was a second suspected smallpox case. The man chewed on a lip, turned and looked over his right shoulder. He pushed the gear-shift into first, and pulled onto the grass. Then he punched it to the stoplight. "Don't get pulled over," Finn said.

"You gotta go at it whole hog," The man said, turning to Finn while gunning the engine. "You fixing to save him or not?"

"Yeah," he said, "I'm fixing to save her. I mean, him."

The man ran the red light, shooting across four lanes of traffic through a narrow break. Finn held on. He reached for the seatbelt, then thought better of it and let it go. Blazing north the man talked the entire way. Only snippets managed to penetrate Finn's harried thoughts: things like "pill-popper", "personal transformation" and "results are proportional to effort".

Once in Austin they rushed down Congress Avenue and Finn directed the man a block from Lance's apartment. When he jumped down he pulled out the four hundred dollars and laid it on the passenger seat. "You don't know what good you've done."

He looked at the money in disgust. "I did it for you. For whatever bind you got yourself in. Remember, there's more people like me than whoever's chasing you." He slipped a twenty out of the pile. "That's enough for gas. They smacked hands hard in ghetto handshake, Finn ashamed he'd offered the money. Through the man's hot, calloused palm, Finn felt, no, knew, knew their lives were separate but the same, knew that he loved him.

"You don't have a gun do you?" Finn asked sheepishly.

The man shook his head.

"Anytime, man, anytime," Finn found himself saying, though he didn't know what it meant and felt stupid. He stuffed the bills back into a pocket, and sprinted towards Lance's apartment. When he got close he dialed Gogan. "I'm here," he said, panting.

"I told you you are competent."

Finn waited on the corner of Congress and Eva for Gogan to pick him up. "My friend Benjamin, he's a cop, he might be able to help," Finn said, jumping in. "And he's got guns."

THIRTY-ONE

Finn opened the front door to Benjamin's apartment. "Benj!" He stepped inside. Plates, crusted with dried remnants of food and crushed beer cans covered a footlocker between a futon and a plasma screen television. The television was perched on a rickety child's school desk beside the front door. A dented-shade table lamp sat on the hardwood floor next to it. A old rock and roll song, Soulhat's "Bonecrusher" punched through a boom box squatting in the corner.

In the kitchen Benjamin stood with his back to them. He inspected the insides of a few coffee mugs plucked from amongst plates, egg shells, fruit skins, mayonnaise jars, and paper towels strewn across the counter top. Finn plopped himself down at a tiny round table and Gogan sat next to him. "This is Gogan. He works with me at the U.T."

Benjamin looked over his shoulder. "Um." He turned back around and a coffee bean grinder whirred.

Finn gave Gogan a nervous look.

Benjamin put a stainless steel kettle on the stove and turned the burner on. It popped to life with a soft thump. "Can't drink like I used to. These fucking headaches 'bout make me insane."

"Make it strong. I didn't sleep either," Finn stood up and fingered a Kevlar vest hanging from a fat rusted nail next to the refrigerator. "Listen, man, I need to ask you for help. I need, we need, your help. Some crazy shit has come to light. I mean, it sounds crazy but it's real."

"What are you blathering about?"

"I know this is sudden and extreme but we don't have much time, and I want you to know that I wouldn't ask a favor like this if I didn't have sufficient cause and—"

"You already used up your last favor."

"The men who killed Sarah's parents have something to do with the smallpox outbreak."

Benjamin looked as if Finn was telling him to wear a thong.

"Gogan and I have solid evidence." Finn said. He told him about Lance Matterson, Lance's secret primers, the Interleukin-4 gene from Sarah's mouth swab, and the Australian scientists' super-mousepox with mouse Interleukin-4. He told him how Deyermand had quarantined him in a hotel all night, and kept Gogan in his lab while he double checked the interleukin gene from Sarah's mouth swab. "Deyermand looked for Interleukin-4 in the DNA of the smallpox isolated from the woman in Chicago. He didn't find it," Finn said. "And, thank God he didn't find smallpox in Sarah."

"Tell me something I can't figure out," Benjamin said, and disappeared through a doorway leading to the back of the apartment. Water splashed on a bathtub. "You wouldn't be here if he did."

Finn followed and stood in a tiny hallway leading to the bathroom. "It would have ended right there except..."

Benjamin pulled off his pajama bottoms and climbed into the shower.

"this morning, after Deyermand let me go—"

"I can't hear a word your saying!" Benjamin yelled over the splashing water.

Finn moved to the doorway. "Gogan found a smallpox promoter sequence in front of the Interleukin-4. It signals the virus to use the gene. There's absolutely no other reason to have it there unless you plan on putting it into smallpox. The men who killed Sarah's parents are trying to weaponize smallpox, make it immune to the vaccine."

Benjamin stuck his head out, massaging shampoo onto it. "Why are you telling me?"

"Deyermand doesn't believe me."

He pulled his head back in." Go to his boss then."

"Deyermand threatened to arrest me. He thinks I'm paranoid."

"Are you?" The words came out garbled with water running over his lips.

"No!"

"Then why didn't they find Interleukin in the smallpox?"

"All right, that part doesn't make sense."

"And why isn't Sarah infected with smallpox?"

"Fine," he grunted. "That part too, but, I'm telling you. They're connected. We just don't know how. The Middle Eastern guys chasing Sarah, the murders, the smallpox outbreak, and then the Interleukin connection to mousepox, it must fit somehow."

"What about the student who made the primers?"

"Matterson."

"A white boy? An American? An undergrad?"

"Timothy McVey was as corn-fed as they come. Look, We're not second-guessing the evidence. We're following it. The point is we're losing time and nobody's doing anything."

"Hey Mr. Holmes, have you considered the possibility Deyermand's lying to you?"

Finn snapped his head back. "No. He'd have to quarantine me."

"What if he did find interleukin in the smallpox, and with no evidence of smallpox in Sarah, he could let you go because you haven't come in contact with it."

"No way. He'd want to keep me guarded if we're right."

"So you may not be right?" The water cut off.

"Damn man. Who's side are you on?"

Benjamin slid the curtain on its hooks, stepped out of the shower and rubbed his head with a hand towel. "He wouldn't want to keep you guarded, dumbass, he'd want to monitor you and find out where you're going, if you were lying about anything. You're all worked up, you're not thinking straight. I'm sure he's got a GPS on your car right now."

"We're in Gogan's car."

"He's probably got one on Gogan's and your boss'. It's a good thing you're not a detective. Now *I* can expect a visit from the Fed's, thanks a fucking lot."

The kettle belted out a raspy whistle. Finn went into the kitchen, pulled it off the burner and poured steaming water over the coffee grinds.

Benjamin came in, barefoot, a crazy-eyed cartoon lemur on a threadbare beach towel wrapped around his waist like a sarong. "Are you certain Sarah had the Interleukin gene with the smallpox thingy?"

"Positive." Finn said, turning to Gogan for confirmation.

"One hundred fucking percent," Gogan said.

Benjamin looked between them. "How similar is smallpox to mousepox?"

"Close enough that the Australian scientists debated for several years before publishing," Gogan said.

Benjamin pushed aside dishes and onion skins. He opened a cabinet, pulled out a pound of sugar and plunked it in the cleared space. Fruit flies scattered like mobile freckles. He sugared the coffees and handed them each one.

"Think Mulveny would talk to Matterson?" Finn asked.

Benjamin scowled. "Highly doubtful. Mulveny wouldn't put his pension on the line for Mother Teresa. He's two years from thirty, dude." Benjamin sat down with them. Orange shafts of sunlight cut through the kitchen windows, steamed from the shower. He looked haggard.

"It does not matter," Gogan said, "We need action not more

talking."

This seemed to amuse Benjamin. The light emphasized his crow's feet and his gray flecked stubble. He blew steam off his coffee, and sipped it. "You fucking slay me," he said to Finn.

"That kid's a few miles away," Gogan said. "He did something and he knows something, and it pertains to weaponizing smallpox."

"Pertains to weaponizing smallpox," Benjamin mocked.

"Look, we're the only people who know this and believe it, and we need your help," Finn said.

Benjamin worked his lips in a way that made Finn uncomfortable.

"We need help interrogating him," Finn said.

"I could lose my career, and my pension, everything." He thumped the table.

"For asking questions?"

"For interfering in a federal case. For illegal detention. News flash! Otherwise known as kidnapping. You don't just knock on a door and ask a suspected terrorist a few friendly questions."

"We cannot do nothing while we have a lead on someone involved in the smallpox attack," Gogan said.

"Why don't you give the kid a break?" Benjamin said. "Maybe he was just in the wrong place at the wrong time."

"Can't we just wait for him to drive somewhere, pull him over and go from there?" Finn asked.

"What was I thinking?" Benjamin said in mock reconsideration. "He'll spill everything when we stop him for seven over in a thirty-five."

"Let's get the guns," Gogan said to Finn.

"Whoa, don't want to hold up Charles Bronson here."

"You don't get it," Finn said. "This is war."

Benjamin leaned back and guffawed.

"This is wasting our time," Gogan said.

"In my book," Finn said, "friends sacrifice for friends."

Benjamin's bloodshot eyes fixed on him. "You wouldn't know sacrifice if it was up your ass doing cartwheels." He stalled in a half-snarl that Finn remembered seeing a long time ago, a time he couldn't remember, or maybe he could but it wasn't clear now. Benjamin pointed at Gogan, "What do you have on the line, huh? You might do a little time for interfering in a federal case, or maybe probation if you kidnap this undergrad and he actually turns out to be a bad guy. And you," he turned to Finn, "Mr. Play-It-Safe. You come here talking big, trying to show your raggedy-ass sidekick that you're hard. But I know you're here just to assuage your conscience. I'm sure you're saving your energy. You always have a backup plan. How 'bout I help you along then? I'm not fucking arresting that kid!"

Finn stared at him while biting the insides of his cheeks.

"I would be deported," Gogan said, "Never to fulfill my dream of becoming an American."

Finn stood. "Let's go," he said to Gogan. Gogan went through the doorway and Finn followed, but then he paused and turned back to Benjamin. "I'm done with backup plans." His chin trembled. "For your information I've got everything on the line now, everyfuckingthing. You're right. I've spent my lifetime pondering the consequences of my shit choices, wallowing in regret, endlessly considering and reconsidering like some terrified idiot trying to create the perfect life but I'm creating nothing 'cause I'm too scared to do anything without a net." His voice choked. "I'm in love with Sarah, one hundred percent and finally, thank *fucking* God, finally for once in my life I don't give a fuck what that means or what that brings." His voice warbled. "I promised myself I'd do everything in my power to figure out what's going on. I'm not going to let her down. I'm not going to end up single and sad like you. Although I have a ticket waiting for me at the airport to see her, I can't go. I can't go because right now we have no time to waste and one lead. And we're following it, regardless of anything and everything. And definitely not because you're pussying out."

Benjamin looked determinedly nonplussed. "You're the man."

"Yeah? What kind of fucking man am I? The kind that let's some motherfuckers attack the woman he loves, kill her parents, and stand by like a fucking eunuch! How could I ever face her again? Will I take the risk into my own hands or pawn it off onto someone else 'cause I can't man up? 'Don't worry baby-doll. The cops will help you.' That's a big comfort. If Mulveny had taken the case seriously in the first place her parents wouldn't be fucking dead, and they might even have Matterson in jail." Finn's voice found a solid base and touched off from it. "Now the feds are doing the same shit. Everyone seems to have an excuse but I don't have one. If Sarah's hurt or worse, and I've played it safe, waiting on the feds. I swear to fucking God if that happens, no, uh-uh, that can't happen." Spittle shot from his mouth. "I'm telling you I'd rather die going whole hog against these motherfuckers than get through this thinking I spent one iota of energy digging myself a trench. Fucking pussy-ass Deyermand puts a gun up in *my* face. I'll kill a motherfucker. I DON'T GIVE A FUCK!" His body quaked.

Benjamin put his coffee down and began slowly clapping with a disgusting phony grin on his face. "Great. Really emotive. You should show that one to Toastmasters."

"You're a fucking cunt!"

Benjamin threw his chair back and it cracked against the wall. He charged him with terrifying speed and Finn couldn't help but flinching. Benjamin poked a finger into his chest. "You come up into my house with your tough act, spouting cockamamie bullshit theories. Fuck you! I'm responsible for Sophia and her future, I've dedicated myself to doing something no one ever did for me, being a real parent. It's called sacrifice and commitment, something you don't know shit about. You can talk all you want but I know the real Finn Barber. And the real Finn Barber always looks for the easy way out. And he always pretends he has no choice. You wouldn't last a heart-beat in war. I'm the one who doesn't want to end up like you—the nutless fucking wonder!"

Finn swatted his hand away. "I bet you and Sophia have real heart-to-hearts after you've been up all night snorting an eight-ball off some escort's tits."

Before he knew it Benjamin had bulldozed him through the doorway. Finn tripped over the lamp, tumbled and thudded down onto his hip. He jumped up cursing Benjamin and kicked the lamp. His foot went clean through the shade and shattered the base. For a moment he danced, trying to shake the lampshade from his foot. Then he turned to the television and lifted his leg high, poised to piston-drive it barefoot into the center of the screen. As he was about to strike, something ungodly powerful whaled him in the ribs and blasted him sideways. His head thudded against the open front door. Next he was on the ground looking up at Benjamin, him and the towel-lemur both leaning into him wild-eyed.

"Get the fuck out of here!"

As if that wasn't his obvious wish. He hacked, trying to fill his deflated lungs. His cheek throbbed and he tasted blood. Finally, sucking in a desperate breath he stood back up, Then he held closed a nostril and blew a spray of blood in Benjamin's face."I hope you fucking die!"

THIRTY-TWO

"We just barge in and grab him?" Finn asked from the passenger seat, his voice nasal from pinching his bloody nose with the bottom edge of his shirt.

Gogan drove. "We knock on the front door," he said, reciting it slowly as if he were trying to figure it out himself, "and when he opens we go in fast, surprise him."

"He's been weaponizing smallpox, man. What about the guns?"

"Right right. How about knives, big knives? We can make him think we are able to hurt him and kill him."

"Are we?" Finn asked. He moved to a new spot on his shirt.

"Does he live with anybody?"

"This is no good. We need to be more subtle. I'll pretend I need information on a protein."

"Tell him you got his address off the student list on the U.T. Website," Gogan said. "It doesn't have his phone number."

"Good. So now I'm in his apartment. Worst case scenario: he has a roommate. I'll have to convince him to leave."

"Tell him you need him to go to the lab with you."

Finn bent his head trying to look up his nostrils in the mirror on the back of the sun visor. "That's going to be a tough sell." He prodded the bridge of his nose, pushed the cartilage back and forth. They stopped at a streetlight above a grassy park bordering the Colorado River. Under a fat sun people strolled, roller-bladed, canoed, and threw Frisbees. He imagined lying on a blanket next to Sarah and reading a Walter Mosely novel, he on his back and she on her stomach, under the cool shade of a pecan tree. He'd have a hand on the back of her thigh. Drum beats would drift over on a breeze and an occasional dreaded Rastafarian would squat down offering hand made jewelery. When they got hungry they'd cross the river and buy tacos downtown, joking the whole way.

"We may have to torture him," Gogan said.

"Will you?" Finn asked.

"Will you?"

Finn flipped up the sun visor thinking of dank subterranean prisons and fingernail-less men bound to chairs. "If we have to," he said, though not convinced. "How 's my face look?"

"Like something hit it." They crossed the river and climbed Congress Avenue, only a few blocks from Lance's apartment. "We must determine how to subdue him when he realizes we are not going to campus."

"We haven't even gotten him out of the apartment and you're already subduing him. We can't go to my house. My neighbor calls the cops if cars drive by too slow. Think your wife'll understand?"

Gogan sighed.

"This is fucked." Finn said. "We cannot fuck around. Forget all these cons. He'll know the stakes and will put up a fight regardless of whether he can win it or not. And we can't risk killing him."

"What if he tries to kill himself?"

"Controlling someone, even for five seconds, is not easy. I've seen cops try it. I'm convinced the uniform does half the work. Hey, that's it. We need uniforms."

"We need to knock him out." Gogan said.

Finn put his elbows on his knees and held his head in his hands.

"Do you know any doctors?" Gogan asked. "We could inject him with a...how do you call it? Something that makes him sleep."

"Tranquilizer."

"Yes, that." He parked against a curb three blocks from Lance's apartment.

Finn sat up. "I've got a friend, he's doing an ER rotation. He dug a hand into a front pocket and then the next. "Shit."

"What?"

"I don't have my phone. It must have fallen out in the fight." They were silent for a long time but it might have only been a few moments. He wanted to scream. "We're over thinking this," Finn said. "We need the army/navy on South First."

Nodding, Gogan started the car.

A hollow coat of dented, medieval plate mail holding a broad sword held guard outside the entrance of the army/navy. A Paul Bunyan type in a short sleeved red checkered flannel shirt with an unruly red beard stood behind the counter. A latex gorilla mask covered the mounted head of some mammal behind him. Long horn skulls lined both walls all the way to the back where a stuffed lion, standing upright, teeth and claws bared, swatted at some imaginary foe. It towered above long parallel racks of camouflage pants and shirts.

"Give us a shout if you need any help," the man said cheerfully.

Finn wondered who he meant—he and the gorilla, the lion, or the knight?

Gogan wasted no time. "We need pepper spray, handcuffs and a taser."

"Dude," Finn said.

The man pulled his smile down along with his eyebrows and regarded both of them. "Guess your looking for some payback," he said, nodding at the egg on Finn's cheek. Finn tucked the bloody edge of his tee-shirt behind his jeans.

"That's right," Gogan said. "We are going to subdue him, handcuff him, throw him into the trunk of my car and then take him somewhere."

"Hey!" Finn said swatting his arm.

Gogan lifted his palm to Finn. "And then we will beat him until he talks."

Finn shook his head and looked at the ground unable to meet the man's eyes.

"The guy murdered his girlfriend's parents." Gogan pointed at Finn.

The admission took Finn's breath from him and all he could do was stand open-mouthed, looking between the men. Gogan stared ahead as grim as a gargoyle. Bunyan stared back and forth between the two of them his brow furrowed and his mouth a menacing frown. His eyes tried to penetrate them. Nobody spoke. Then Bunyan broke into an easy smile. "I'm real sorry 'bout that fellas. Better be prepared then, and you're at the right place. I got a pepper spray make the devil himself cry. It's eight million on the Scoville scale. That's like a nine five on the Richter. A fucking Japanese tsunami." He ducked under the counter below a glass shelf packed with knives, the kind with gleaming blades on one side and sinister saw points on the other. He came up with two small bright red canisters the size of cigarette lighters wrapped in plastic on cardboard backing. "You should each have one. Now, note the wind if your using this outside, and—"

Gogan swept them across the counter towards Finn. "The hand cuffs."

The man stopped and nodded, impressed with Gogan's efficiency. He scooted to another section of the counter and pulled out three pairs of hand cuffs.

"Which are the best?" Gogan asked.

"Well," the man said concentrating and then finally, "for you guys, these," he pointed to the dullest pair, no twinkling shine to them, "they're the most reliable and the easiest to use, but they cost—"

"We'll take them," Gogan blurted.

He twitched his head getting Gogan's rhythm. "Okay then, the taser. I don't have that but what I can give you is a shock-stick." He went to a cabinet underneath the gorilla mask and shuffled things around.

A stuffed beaver stood at the end of the long glass counter on Finn's side. Below it on a wooden mount was tacked a handwritten sign that said. "Before you wood-chuck it away think twice. We buy guns and ammo." Someone had scrawled something along with it in blue-ballpoint pen and Finn squinted to see it. It said, "nice beaver".

"This is our best, three hundred thousand volts," the man said placing a box on the counter. He pulled out a device about sixteen inches long, a cylindrical handle with a long black tip that tapered from the handle to a dime-sized point. He searched for some batteries and dropped four size D into the handle. "Don't skimp on the batteries." He flicked a safety switch, held it up and then pressed a button. The tapered tip exploded to life, mini blue-white lightning bolts crackled encompassing it. Both of them leaned back. A man browsing shirts jerked up his head.

"All right," Gogan said, putting down his debit card.

The man looked at the card. "We're going to suggest you pay with cash."

Finn snatched the wad of twenties from his pocket.

The man hesitated. "Wait a sec," he said, "I *do* got a few more things that'll help." He hustled to the rear of the store and disappeared through hanging beads, a pirate skull and crossbones emblem on them.

He came back with a roll of duct tape and several cardboard boxes . He opened one, a box of plastic zip wraps. "These are faster and easier than cuffs. Use them first and then get the cuffs on afterwards." He slid them aside and put the next box down. It was naked cardboard, unlabeled. "That shock-stick's gotta show but this is for a pro," he said tapping the box. His voice slid into an easy clip. "It's a police issue taser and it'll drop a mountain gorilla. Just like a digital camera, its point and shoot. Fifteen feet you should be fine, go easy though you can dislocate a joint if you get to Game-boyin' the button. But hey," he said, chuckling, "maybe that's what you're looking for." His teeth were brown and scarred. "Depends on how you're fixing to finish." He pointed to a third box, the size of Finn's fist. "And this is a little present." He spread everything out on the counter and then looked at Finn. "You a veteran?"

Finn shook his head.

"Okay. Remember, taser first," he tapped the nondescript cardboard box, "zip-tie next, then duct tape the mouth. Oh yeah, and you'll get tazed too if you go to touching him while the other's still on the button. Obvious, but I gotta throw it in. If you miss with the taser, pepper spray's your back up followed by shock-stick. After the zip-tie and tape get the cuffs on and then you're off."

Jesus, Finn thought.

Bunyan looked at the wad of bills. "How much you got?"

"Four hundred, no, three eighty."

He cocked his head. "There's an ATM across the street."

"How much more?" Gogan asked.

"That again should do it."

Gogan went out and the man gathered the things into a black plastic bag. "One other thing. I need to see your I.D."

Finn hesitated then handed it to him.

The man went to a small photo copier behind him, put it under the lid and tapped a button. "Got to let it warm up." Back at the counter, he pulled a card from his wallet and slid it across the glass with two fingers. "Ted M. Burgstock", was printed in embossed matte boldface in the center of a black card with nothing else on it. Finn flipped it over. The back was blank. "There's no number " he said.

"Yes there is." He gave a scarred-tooth grin. "The name's the number. On your keypad, first ten letters."

Finn nodded. Interesting.

"I consult, four hundred bucks an hour. Call me anytime. I specialize in persuasion." The grin spread. He sat down on a high stool, put up his feet on the foot rest and leaned against the seat back.

Finn's stomach began to turn on itself and a wave of nausea rolled up his throat. He fought against images of the man conducting his sadism.

"You need a place to take him?" He asked.

Finn thought a moment then nodded.

"I thought so." The man twisted the tip of his beard in to a thick fiber and then leaned forward and dialed a cordless phone. "Yeah, its me. Yeah. Listen, shut-up. Listen! We've got," He whispered, "We've got a girl wants to go dancing. Yeah. Yeah. *Really.*"

He spun the phone up so the mouth piece was above his head, "You got a GPS?"

Finn shook his head.

"You'll need one. I've got one for you." He spun the phone back down and cradled it with his shoulder. Grabbing a pen off the counter he scribbled on a notepad, "Yeah. Yeah. fifteen, seven. Got it." Finn instinctively reached for his phone to tell Gogan to get more money, but it wasn't there. He'd forgot again about it falling out at Benjamin's. God, how he wished Benjamin were here. He'd know how to handle this abhorrent man, his sickness peeling off him like a disease.

The man got off of his stool and walked to the center of the store. He returned and stood next to Finn with a GPS unit not much bigger than a cell phone. "Three hundred for the GPS and four hundred for the coordinates." He put the notepad, he'd scribbled on, face down on the counter. "But tell you what I'll do." The man towered over him. He smelled of sweat and gasoline. Finn's nausea surged. Maybe it was the coffee, the omelet and more coffee, or where Benjamin had hit him (which throbbed now), but he knew it was none of these.

"He an illegal?" the man asked.

Finn stared at him a moment without answering.

"Or a nigger. Cause you'll get a lot less heat either way and I can do three hundred on the coordinates then." Finn stared for a moment more and then rushed out. He passed the camouflage, the flags, the knight, Gogan entering, and ran to the side of the building and vomited on an anemic holly bush in a raised galvanized tank. He gagged and then convulsed as another surge washed out.

Gogan came outside. "Are you all right?"

Finn nodded, though hanging his head and still clutching the side of the tank.

"He says we owe him another eight-hundred for a GPS and coordinates."

Finn nodded and Gogan marched back to the ATM.

Finn squatted against the building and pulled off thick mucus strings from his lips, and waited for Gogan to return.

"The ATM only let me take out four hundred more," Gogan explained upon returning.

They went inside.

"It's enough for either one but neither will do you any good alone," Bunyan said scowling. But then he brightened up pointing at the ring on Finn's finger, heavy and silver with a mother of pearl relief of two Roman soldiers side by side. "How 'bout that?"

"But it's an heirloom," Finn said. "My Great Grandfather got it in Italy chasing the Nazi's up the boot." Gogan gave him an accusing look and Finn pulled the ring off and plunked it on the counter.

"No one will ever hear you," the man said. "And I could get there blindfolded if you end up needing me. Directly *south* of it about half a mile you'll see a trail come off the only road that passes that way. About half way the trail stops dead and doesn't start up again for fifty yards. Keep going but break east or west so as not to make a trail. There's a tarp there with a couple of chairs and shovels. He handed Finn the bag.

"I don't care if you want my help or not," he said (but Finn thought it a lie), "but I need to know if you do end up going."

As they passed the plate mail knight the man called out. "Your I.D.!" Finn went back to collect it. When he reached for it the man twitched it back with a flip of the wrist. Finn gave him a harsh look of annoyance. The man leaned over the counter. "How'd he execute your girlfriend's parents?"

Finn thought for a moment. Then he shook his head. "No. It was all a lie."

The man's expression immediately transformed. He stared at him in saucer-eyed shock, blinking repeatedly mouthing some unheard vowel. Finn snatched his I.D. from the mans stalled hand, spun, and left.

"What's it all for then?" He called out as Finn passed the knight again. "You sure spent a lot."

Finn turned around. "It's for later. We're coming for you, dumbass!" He hollered it jabbing a finger towards him. Then he spun on a heel and stomped to the car. Gogan was turning around in the gravel parking lot. Finn pulled the taser box from the bag, jumped in the car and tossed the rest in the back seat. "Hurry up, we could be in trouble."

"What'd you do?"

"Go, go! Just go." Finn pulled on the plastic bag around the taser.

"Shit!" Gogan yelled, looking in the rear view mirror. They had one more point in the turn before they would be able to head straight out. Finn flipped around. The man stalked toward them waving a long barreled pistol in front of him.

Finn flung the bag down. "Keep going, I'll catch up." Finn inspected the taser for the trigger and a safety. He jammed the taser into the small of his back behind his belt and sprung from the car. He threw up his hands and walked towards the man. "Hey! It's just a joke, dude. Relax."

"You punk-ass motherfucker! I'll show you who you're fucking with!" He pointed the gun at Finn. Gogan's bumper lurched past the rear bumper of a parked car leaving him in line to drive out. The man swung the pistol at Gogan. "Stop right there!"

Biting the insides of his cheeks, Finn whipped the taser from his belt, aimed at the man's chest and squeezed the trigger. A pencil-lead thin wire raced at the man and caught him in the neck. He shrieked and swung his gun back at Finn. Finn punched all the buttons on the damn thing. A shot exploded from the pistol. Finn dove to the dirt. Then the man was down too. His limbs jerked and splashed against a puddle. Finn kept pressing buttons as fast as he could. Bunyan's hips threw his torso up and then snatched it back and hammered his head against the gravel and mud. The gun bounced from his hands. A choked moan bubbled through spit at the back of his throat. Finn eased up on the buttons. Keeping his eyes on Bunyan he went over and snatched up the gun. Then he gave Bunyan one last good jolt before he wrangled the wire free from the taser. He was about to run back to Gogan but then turned and went back to the store. The lone customer watched him as he ran around the counter and opened the cash register. Finn smiled. There sat his ring, shining like an icicle above dull copper-colored pennies.

Outside the man had gotten to his knees. Finn trained the pistol (a big one, a .38 or .44) on him as he ran by him. He sprinted down the sidewalk towards Gogan parked against the curb. Finn jumped in. Gogan pitched from the curb. "What the hell are you doing! Now we have nowhere to take Matterson."

"Now we've got a gun."

"You need to remember who our enemy is!"

Finn wanted to say that the racist redneck sadist was their enemy but he knew Gogan was right.

On the way back to Lance's apartment they cobbled together a defacto plan: wait until they were certain Lance was alone and somewhere they could attack him inconspicuously, or if that didn't happen, until darkness when they would go into his apartment, subdue him, just like Bunyan told them, and then drag him out to some field in Dripping Springs.

They parked two blocks from Lance's on Eva Street with both the side and front doors in view. Finn turned on the stereo and a Jeff Buckely song played. His angelic voice, fragile like rice paper, rose to euphoric high notes and then floated back down. *All I ever learned from love was how to shoot somebody who outdrew you,* he sang. The song made Finn feel absurd: himself, his life right then. But deep between the crevices of the notes he suspected that it wasn't absurd (or maybe the contrary, all life was absurd and *that* was normal). He was confused and couldn't be sure. He thought about how much he loved Benjamin and how he'd really like him to be there. He didn't give a shit that Benjamin had given him a solid pasting. He couldn't make sense of the idea of ties between them severed.

A deejay announced that confirmed smallpox cases stood at two. Finn switched off the radio and for a long, long time they said nothing, the windows down, the heat broiling them. Cars and trucks rumbled by and occasionally a grackle, or maybe it was a raven, repeatedly cawed. Things felt wrong, as if steel bands were tightening around them.

"He's in his car," Gogan said.

The reverse lights on a white Porsche 911 lit. "An undergrad with a Porsche," Finn said. They followed him north on Congress Avenue toward downtown. At a stoplight they pulled up behind him and then both flipped down their sun visors. Lance's pale, clean shaved face reflected in his rear view mirror. They crossed over the river, muddy with last night's run-off, and continued north to the university amid sparse traffic. On twenty-fifth street they followed him west, descending a hill toward North Lamar Boulevard that ran alongside Shoal Creek. Before the boulevard he turned into the gravel parking lot next to a mobile taco stand. Gogan parked a fews cars over and they watched him walk over to the stand, its window covers propped up on knotty wooden poles.

Maybe they should grab him right there and force him into the car. Maybe he'd get scared and talk. As soon as Finn had the idea he dismissed it. People don't take opportunities to redeem themselves, they take opportunities to protect themselves. An odor of hot grease floated in through his open window.

Mexicans in cowboy boots and jeans milled about eating lunch. Along with the aromas, their conversation floated over, but with the highs distilled out. He thought it odd that nobody smiled or laughed. A beautiful brown-skinned teenage girl hung out a window of the taco stand and gave Lance change. He gave her a pathetic grin. *I'm just a carefree young man*, it said. She passed him a white Styrofoam plate with tacos on it.

Suddenly a surrealism overwhelmed Finn. Waking up to a world with a blue sun wouldn't have seemed more unfathomable than his life at that moment. He really couldn't indulge the idea that this fresh skinned shit-kicker had something to do with a smallpox attack and that he and Gogan were the only ones on the trail to save the land of the free and the home of the brave. The Mexican's conversations and the traffic noise reverberated in his mind, as if they were not real but a distorted echo of reality. He feared his relationship with Sarah was really nothing but an echo too, a distant shout among mountains. He found himself staring at a soot-smeared Mexican in a filthy straw cowboy hat who looked to be staring back, though too far away to be sure and especially through the ripples of heat. The man sneered at Finn. (Or possibly he was squinting in the sunlight.) A gold tooth flashed and Finn thought he saw the man drag an index finger across his neck leering.

Gogan's phone rang. "Benjamin is calling with your phone," he said, showing him "Finn Barber" on the display.

Finn took the phone. "I'm sorry," Finn said.

"You all right?" For Benjamin that was an apology.

"Don't worry."

"Where are you?"

"We're fine."

"Where are you?" Benjamin asked. "I'm gonna help you, you dumb bastard."

Finn pumped a fist. A dark thrill surged within him, and with it a certainty of their collective power. He explained where they were and Benjamin told them to stay close to Lance.

"Sorry about what I said about you," Finn said. "I don't believe it. I just wanted to hurt you."

"Thanks," Benjamin said, quickly, and genuinely, but which struck Finn as odd, considering he'd just told him that he'd tried to hurt him. He handed the phone back to Gogan. "He's coming," he said. A massive grin curled up his lips.

For a while they watched Lance stuff his cheeks with tacos. *Now you're done motherfucker.* Lance wiped his face and went back to the girl at the counter and spoke with her a few minutes. Then he got into his car and continued down the hill. They pulled out and sat a few cars behind him at a stoplight at the bottom of the hill, Shoal Creek in front of them, a thin muddy ribbon in an otherwise dry bed. Finn watched the rear view mirror. Before the light changed Benjamin crested the hill behind them in a pale-blue unmarked sedan. Finn showed Gogan and he pulled a tire onto the sidewalk, allowing Benjamin between them and the cars in the left turn lane. The stoplight changed and Lance turned right. Benjamin stopped alongside them and a tinted passenger side window motored down.

"That's him in the Porsche," Finn said, leaning over Gogan. "He's alone." Benjamin gestured for him to come over. Finn threw open his door and bolted around the cars to Benjamin's window. From a radio on Benjamin's dashboard, a voice rattled numbers in static bursts. The edges of a Kevlar vest poked from underneath a white button down shirt and black plastic sunglasses rested above a forehead broken out in beads of sweat. Finn rested his hands on the open window.

"You all right?" Benjamin asked.

"I'm fine, thanks," he said, and made a move back toward Gogan's car.

"How sure are you about this?"

Finn halted. Several cars were stopped behind them. "All of this, the kid, Sarah, the connection to the smallpox?"

"Are you certain?"

A glass truck with huge panes leaning nearly vertical passed by in the turn lane and Finn pressed up tight against the unmarked cruiser.

Benjamin stared at him, waiting.

"Yeah. It has to be connected to the smallpox attack regardless that they didn't find the Interleukin sequence."

Gogan honked. "He's getting away!"

"I'm not talking about the goddamn Interleukin!" Benjamin said. "I'm putting everything on the line with this. I know what you said. I want to know. Are you convicted? Do you feel it here?" He thumped Finn's heart with a palm.

"Yeah," Finn said, and then, emphatically, "yes!"

"Good," Benjamin said. He yanked on the gearshift and the car jerked locking into drive. "Were not taking him downtown." The car lurched forward and Finn pulled his hands from the door.

"Hey!" he called out. "My phone."

Benjamin stopped. He handed Finn his cell phone. "Hey. That party at Maya's, did you fuck Jessica?"

Benjamin bringing up the incident when Maya caught Finn and Jessica (Benjamin's ex-wife) in the woods behind her house, felt like being awoke with a tub of cold water. At the time, four years ago, Finn had furiously, violently even, swore Maya made it up and he'd stuck to the story since.

His hand on the gearshift, Benjamin raised his eyebrows.

"Yeah," Finn said, weakly. "We screwed."

Benjamin flipped on his siren and rocketed ahead. White strobes beside the turn signal lights pulsed in heartbeat doublets. At the bottom of the hill the car slammed down on it's shocks and turned right. The wheel spun against the pavement and enveloped the entire intersection in a cloud of white rubber smoke.

A car horn honked from behind and Finn jumped in surprise. He stood alone in the turn lane, fifteen-odd cars lined up behind him. He ran to Gogan's car and they squealed through the intersection just after the light turned red. Far away, Benjamin's strobes vanished around a bend hugging the creek.

A few bends ahead they saw Lance's car, parked with Benjamin's behind it. They pulled onto the grass at the edge of the road a hundred yards behind them, and Finn exhaled but then grimaced from his aching rib where Benjamin had punched him, the same damn rib he'd bruised in the fight a month earlier. Benjamin stepped out of his police car, pulled his pistol from his hip and held it down at a low angle stiff-armed, ready to fire. He yelled something but the breeze carried it away. He said something again and then Lance shoved both hands out of the window. Benjamin was beside the car moving along the driver's side in a sideways gait the gun still stiffly at his hip. Lance opened the door from the outside and stepped from the car, both hands raised. Benjamin turned him and kicked his legs wide so that he leaned against the car his hands on the roof. He patted him down and searched his pocket linings, talking to him the entire time. From a rear pocket he pulled out Lance's wallet. He holstered his gun and turned Lance back, facing him. He pulled a card from the wallet, inspected it and then held it next to Lance's face. Then he put his left hand on the car hood and pulled himself close, his face just a dagger length from Lance's. It looked like a lamb being cornered by an ape. Benjamin spoke (Finn thought he could see his lips rising high off his teeth) and held the card up above his own shoulder, wagging it back and forth. *A peach fuzzed punk cruzin' town in Mommy and Daddy's Porsche,* he was probably saying. The other hand was on the roof behind Lance's head and above the open driver's side window. With it Benjamin flicked something tiny and it fell to the passenger side. They kept talking. Then Benjamin surveyed the inside of the car walking around it. He came back to Lance, cuffed him and then leaned through the window to the passenger seat. He stood up and dangled a small baggie in front of Lance's face. He pushed him back towards the patrol car and sat him in the back seat. A tremor of triumph wavered through Finn and he turned and slapped Gogan on the shoulder.

THIRTY-THREE

For half an hour they followed Benjamin, out of town and up through hills lining Lake Travis, its crisp blue fingers poking into the limestone cliffs. Finn wondered where they were going. They veered from the lake along a steep and narrow road that weaved through woods and scrub brush. A gravel driveway peeked out, the type that you'd miss on a first pass, and Benjamin pulled into it. Finn saw the mailbox had "Skully" painted on it, Sarah's fiance's house. Shit, he thought, that makes sense. It was isolated and Reece would tolerate them bringing Matterson here since he was also vested in finding the murderer's of Sarah's parents.

Thick waxy leaves brushed along the car and Finn's pulse thumped behind his ears. Benjamin parked thirty feet into the driveway and stalked back to their car. He leaned into Finn's window, dipped his chin and peered at him over the top of his black sunglasses. "What's our goal?" He asked. He was composed, didn't seem angry about Finn's admission.

"Find out what he knows."

"No. What is it that we must know?" Beads of sweat crawled down the side of his face.

Heat from the engine curled up and poured in the window while questions cascaded into Finn's mind. They needed to know who Yusif was, where he was, whether he was still pursuing Sarah, why the Interleukin-4 gene was in her cheek cells. "First, we need to know..."

Benjamin shook his head. "Only one." He held up an index finger. In the back seat of Benjamin's car, like a frightend dog, Lance twisted around to look at them.

"We must know how the Interleukin-4 is being used in the attack." Gogan said leaning over Finn.

Gogan was right of course.

"We need something," Benjamin said, "to verify his honesty. What do we know that he should know?"

"The guy who got the swabs is called Yusif," Gogan said.

"What else?"

"Matterson made the primers in two pairs but only needed one," Finn said. "One primer in each pair was a dummy primer. And that guy who helped Yusif on the bridge, he's probably Middle Eastern." Finn said it almost absently, still thinking of other questions: *Who killed Sarah's parents? What did Lance do with the swabs? Why did he receive them?*

"He made the primers at 5:00 in the morning on August 9th," Gogan said.

Benjamin slapped Finn on the chest pushing him back into the seat and snapping off his thoughts. "We're not shaking down a dealer or a gang-banger. This is a terrorist attack and that little country-fried motherfucker better be scared. You got it? Remember, don't give up any important information or connections: Names, dates, obviously the murders, the Interleukin-4 gene, and the connection to the smallpox attack. You ready?"

Finn nodded, though he couldn't imagine ever being ready.

"No weakness. No hesitation." Benjamin looked at Gogan. "Make sure you've got both our numbers. You stay here, hidden off the driveway. If anything looks fishy call us. He could have a GPS shoved up his ass for all we know." He looked at Finn. "Follow me in the car."

Benjamin turned and marched away, gravel crunching under his black boots. It all made Finn anxious, but Benjamin's decisiveness tempered him with confidence. Finn went around the car and got into the driver's seat. He followed Benjamin two-hundred-odd yards, snaking around sharp, potholed and rutted, bends. Reece's bungalow crouched in the center of a hole in the woods, exposed to the sun. Benjamin pulled Lance from the back seat, his hands cuffed behind him, and they all went to the front door. Lance looked pitiful. "What's going on," he kept blubbering.

"Shut the fuck up!" Benjamin screamed.

The outburst even startled Finn.

Benjamin knocked on the door and then tested it. It was locked. He went to the other end of the porch and lifted up a flower pot. He came back with a rusty key, opened the door, and once inside, re-set the deadbolt and pocketed the key.

The door opened into bright pine-floored living room lined with windows. A black leather couch and love seat sat in an L shape facing a flat screen television on the wall, a low coffee table between them. Benjamin kicked aside the coffee table and pushed Lance down onto the couch. He planted an index finger on his chest. "Don't move." He unbuttoned his shirt and removed his Kevlar vest while Finn went into the kitchen directly behind the living room; he didn't want to look at the kid. On the refrigerator hung a photo of Sarah and Reece holding hands on a Caribbean seawall, behind them a glassy, jade sea under a cloudless sky. He worried about the possibility that Matterson hadn't been the one that made the deleted primers, but he recalled the surprised look the kid had when he'd shown him Yusif's photo and it reassured him a little. Benjamin marched in shirtless. The thin straps of a white undershirt streched over the mounds of his shoulders. He put a pistol on the counter-top. He rubbed his nose and put a hand on Finn's shoulder, his eyes darting.

"When I said I believe in you, I meant it. But it's more than just a belief." He abruptly stopped, cocked his head listening, and Finn couldn't recall him saying that he believed in him. His eyes jerked about and Finn thought he saw his ears shift. Then he took his hand off Finn and stuck his head through the doorway and peeked at Lance. He pulled it back in. "In O-three when I went to Iraq some terrible shit happened," he said, pulling his head back in. "I made a connection to it after you left this morning. The inevitability of it all crashed into me."

"What are you talking about?"

"I'm talking about being a soldier, having orders, ones that make you feel inhuman." His tongue flicked out onto his lips and he wrung his hands. "I shot a ten-year-old girl in the back, a totally innocent unarmed girl running away from me."

Finn squinted at him, shocked and confused. "That's awful, but this isn't the right—"

"Fine." Benjamin stuck his head through the doorway for another glance. He waved a finger in the air as if a cohesive thought was pushing its way forward. "Innocent but not harmless, a very important distinction." He dug into a pocket and pulled out a tiny Ziploc baggie, half full of cocaine. "Took me years to truly understand that."

"Can you lay off shit that until we're done?"

Shaking the baggie he said, "For what I got to do I definitely need it. None for you though. Someone's got to keep their head."

He dipped the rusty house key into the baggie and pulled it out, the end heaped with stark white powder. With a forefinger he held one nostril shut, and snorted the tiny mound. He held his head back and shook it, snorting and grunting, and then repeated it with the other nostril.

Finn glanced around the doorway at the kid and he looked back, petrified. Finn would have liked to pull a pile of the delicate powder towards himself and feel the rush of invulnerability. But he knew he couldn't risk an error now. The fact that Benjamin could worried him. Benjamin sucked on the tip of the key, then ran his tongue over his gums, shoved the key and baggie into his pocket, and they both went back into the living room. He sank down beside Lance, a burst of air hissing from the leather couch. He grabbed Lance's neck and jerked it forward and down so he could see his cuffed hands. "Give us a name," he said, letting him sit back up.

Lance looked back and forth between them as if he were on a game show desperate for a hint.

Finn's stomach knotted.

"I don't know what's going on," Lance said. His voice quavered and his face distorted on the verge of crying.

"Who gave you the swab?" Benjamin said, still holding his hand on the back of Lance's neck.

"This is about the swabs? I don't know who sends them." He spoke to Finn but probed with sideway glances at Benjamin, his face hovering a kiss away.

"You don't know who sent you the swab?" Finn asked.

"I never have. They always come unmarked."

"You received others?" Finn asked.

"They come every four to six months."

Benjamin jerked Lance's head facing him. "Who gave you the swab this time? Just tell me what we already know."

"The swabs come in the mail." Lance's ruddy cheeks and polished skin nearly caressed Benjamin's beer bloated face punctured with stubble. "You mean the primers?" he asked.

Finn was surprised that he'd mentioned the primers so readily, the ones he'd taken such care to hide. "Yeah, the primers," Finn said.

"I don't know his name."

"Starts with Yu starts with Yu," Benjamin said.

"I've seen him."

"Describe him," Finn said.

"Five-ten, a hundred-fifty pounds, a black guy, foreign, African maybe. It always happens this way. I get the swabs in the mail and he gives me the primers."

"You're a fucking liar!" Finn said. He leaped towards Lance and threw a pointed finger at his face.

Benjamin clamped down on Lance's neck and he threw his shoulders up, grimacing.

"You're going to lie to us now?" Finn leaned into his face. "Cuffed in the middle of the woods. You dumbass, red-neck piece of shit! I found the two primer pairs you made." The kid looked shocked. "Yeah that's right. The one's you made in the sequencing lab at UT, the ones you tried to hide—"

"Stop!" Benjamin said, holding a palm up to Finn. He patted Lance on the chest, "Relax, son," and stood up facing Finn.

"No, no, no. You have it wrong." Lance said leaning around Benjamin. "I always make the second primer set, myself, in the sequencing lab."

"Shut up!" Benjamin said, turning back and jabbing a finger in the kid's face.

Finn, his chest rising and falling, glowered at the kid over Benjamin's shoulder.

Benjamin pushed Finn back to the front windows and whispered. "Hey idiot. You're giving up information. Stop it." He turned and yanked a white plastic zip tie from a back pocket, went to Lance, and in a burst wrapped it around his ankles and ratcheted it tight with a loud zip. Then he disappeared into the kitchen. From the kitchen came the sound of a door opening.

"The first primer set the black guy gives me and the second set I have to make in two fake sets." Tears collected in Lance's eyes making them look larger than they were. "You gotta believe me."

Finn wanted to tell him that he better pray that Sarah was not in danger but he couldn't give up information and instead gave the kid a hard-boiled stare.

"This is crazy. Dude, get these cuffs off, please." he looked pathetic. "Please." Tears coursed down his cheeks now. "I'm telling you the truth. Why would I lie? They told me it was just a DNA stability study, man. How could I have known anything else?" He squirmed and then rubbed the plastic tie-wrap against the ninety-degree corner of the couch leg.

Finn kicked his bound legs away. They stared at each other, Lance crying quietly.

Benjamin returned and placed three rusty tools on the coffee table: an ice-pick, needle-nose pliers, and a small hammer. Finn turned from them nauseated. Instantly Lance began gasping in hacked off breaths. Goose pimples drew up on Finn's arms.

"Turn on some music," Benjamin said.

"No, no, no, no, no, no, I'm telling you what you want." Lance scooted backwards on the couch.

"Shhhhh," Benjamin said, lifting a finger to his lips. "These are only for wrong answers."

Lance's face twisted into a mask and Finn felt a twinge of empathy for him. From the radio a man discussed methods to avoid smallpox.

Finn turned on the CD player and a Adele song cut off the announcer. Her voice caressed a piano melody—*It was dark and I was over until you kissed my lips and saved me*. Benjamin pumped his thumb for Finn to raise the volume. Benjamin sat on the coffee table and leaned his hands onto Lance's knees. "What gene did you copy?"

"I just sent it off, man." Lance slurped up a fat tear with his bottom lip. "I never know the sequence to the portion I send."

"You don't know much do you?"

"I know where I sent it."

"Where?"

"North Carolina," Lance said and then blubbered unintelligibly.

"What!" Benjamin yelled.

"California and Georgia."

"Why three places?" Benjamin asked.

"I don't know."

"Say I don't know again." Benjamin grabbed the crusty pair of needle-nose pliers. "Say it!"

Lance squirmed catching his breath. "Normally its only one place."

"Addresses." Finn said.

"Chapel Hill, North Carolina. A PO box. 7042. No, 7024."

"And California and Georgia?

"Pasadena, California, and Athens, Georgia. Both PO boxes, but," Lance hesitated. "I can't, we're not allowed to keep written records."

Finn went into the kitchen and found a pen and paper, came back, and they made Lance repeat the locations. It took some time. He cried and looked wretched.

"What's all this about?" Benjamin asked.

"It's my scholarship project through the Russian Academy of Sciences."

"Names!" Benjamin slapped a palm on the table top and the kid jumped back.

"Kotesky. Dr. Nicholai Kotesky he oversees the project. I don't know anyone else. I haven't met anyone else, except for the black guy."

Finn scribbled notes. "What's the point of the project?" He asked.

"We look at DNA mutation rates from PCR amplification."

"What gene did you copy from Sarah's mouth swab?" Benjamin asked.

"I, I." Lance shook his head. "Who is she?"

"The last mouth swab you received," Benjamin repeatedly poked a cheek. "What was the DNA sequence you copied?"

"I, don't, I just mailed it off."

"Turn up the music," Benjamin said.

Lance screamed and kicked at Benjamin with bound feet but Benjamin leaped up and straddled him. His broad back obscured Lance's face. Lance thrashed.

"Grab his legs!" Benjamin thundered over a blitzkrieg of stringed instruments. Finn snatched Lance by the shins with both hands and leaned his weight on them. His face rested against Benjamin's shoulders. Ropy muscles in his back flexed and then a hideous shriek pushed itself into every nook of the room. Then a shudder, like the wave in a whip, coursed through Lance's body. First Benjamin rose up and then Finn was thrown to the ground. He pounced back and hurled his weight over Lance's thrashing legs. All there was was shrieking.

Soon the spasms relaxed and the shrieks transformed into huffs, and choked cries. Benjamin sat upright and his right hand swung down, the tips of the pliers like jaws of a gar-fish covered in a sheen of brick-red blood. Finn swallowed back a surge of vomit. Benjamin stood and lifted a leg up and off of him. Lance thrashed his head back and forth, his cuffed hands still jammed down behind his ass. The lower half of his face was painted shiny in blood, a few ribbons diffusing into the neck of his tee-shirt. Finn caught a flash of bright red against clean white teeth. Finn released his legs and jumped off him. Lance twisted to his side and pressed his nose against a shoulder.

The Adele song tapered off and for a moment there was near silence, interrupted only by Lance's whimpering and the ringing in Finn's ears. From the speakers came a staccato snare like rifle fire and then Dave Ghrol's distorted guitar chugged along in a growing crescendo. Benjamin stalked about and seemed to gather fury from the music as if plugged into it. Finn felt energized too. His phone vibrated and he dug it from a pocket. It was Gogan. He told Benjamin who immediately bolted into the kitchen. Finn turned down the stereo and answered.

"Is everything okay?" Gogan asked.

"Is someone coming?"

"I heard screaming."

Benjamin came back with his pistol, planted himself beside a window and peered out.

"Everything's fine." Finn said, hanging up. "He wanted to know about the noise."

Lance's head wobbled to the side and he repeatedly swallowed nothing but air. Over a ballooned nose his eyes bulged, the left one staring, and the other its lid flickering as if unhinged. Blood continued to pulse from his nostrils.

"What do you need two sets of primers for? You doing nested PCR?" Finn asked.

Lance didn't respond.

Benjamin shook his shoulder. "Stay with us, dude. Come on!" He turned to Finn. "Get some ice."

Finn jogged into the kitchen, scooped handfuls of ice from the freezer and into a bowl, and ran back. Benjamin tugged on Lance's belt and dumped the ice between the gap and his crotch, half the cubes spilled out onto his thighs. Lance swung his head from side to side until Benjamin arrested it. "Stay with us," he said.

Lance's eyes seemed to come back from far away and he let out a howl. "Don't kill me! Please, don't kill me!" Then he blubbered, in a nasal voice, about his mother and that he would tell them everything they wanted to know.

"Why do you use two primer sets?" Finn asked.

Benjamin patted Lance's shoulder. "It's alright," he said, "It's alright."

"I use the first set to get the second set," He coughed out the words. "I have to do it that way." His nose seemed to grow with each passing moment.

"What do you mean you use the first set to get the second set?" Finn asked.

Lance shook his head back and forth moaning. "The second primer set is encoded in the DNA of the PCR product made from the first set."

Finn was confused. He paced across the room and came back. "That sounds like bullshit!"

"What time'd you make the second set?" Benjamin asked.

"What?"

"Time of day you made the second set."

"It was late. Four or Five in the morning."

"How'd you do it?" Benjamin asked.

"I make the second set in two pairs." His voice was thick now, and his nose caricatured, the nostrils nearly shut. He squeezed his eyes closed. "Each pair has a fake primer in it. I have to make it myself, and then delete the records."

"Why?" Finn asked.

"To keep people from finding my primers and cheating, I guess. They give big cash prizes for correct sequence recovery."

Finn marched around the coffee table. "Who gives the prizes?"

"A Russian foundation." Lance said something in Russian.

"Are you Russian?" Finn asked.

"No, but I studied in Saint Petersburg."

Finn went across the living room. He came back holding his hands over his eyes and trying to navigate the labyrinth of his mind. "So you find the DNA sequence of the PCR product from the first primer pair to discover the sequence to the second primer set." Finn pulled his hands off his eyes. "And you're trying to tell us that you didn't sequence the PCR product from this oh-so-mysterious second primer set?"

"I'm only supposed to purify it and send it off. I don't need to sequence its DNA."

"Doesn't that smack of a big fat lie? Some guy whose name you never know gives you PCR primers for swabs that you get anonymously. The PCR product hides a second primer set and you make that second set with two pairs, a fake primer in each one. You delete the records and send its PCR product to an address that you can't write down. And you want me to believe that you weren't curious enough to DNA sequence the second PCR product?" Finn turned around but then turned back. "And all for Russians!"

"A couple of times out of curiosity I sequenced the second PCR product."

"What was it?"

"I can't think." Lance squeezed his eyes shut for several moments and then opened them. "The horse testosterone receptor."

Finn shook his head.

"I swear to God that was it."

"Both times?"

"The other time it was the human actin gene."

Finn didn't know what to think of the actin or the testosterone receptor and the kid hadn't even hinted about the murders, or any connection to genetically modified smallpox. Anxiety that they'd over reacted crept back. Lance certainly seemed terrified enough to give up whatever he knew. But he wasn't giving up much and what he did know didn't make any god-dammed sense.

"I got used to the money. I didn't ask questions."

"And those were the only two you sequenced?" Finn asked.

"It took time. Time that I could have used doing research."

"How many sets of swabs did you get?"

"Over three years, I d—, maybe six or seven."

Finn spun around in a tight circle holding his head in his hands. He stopped, faced the kid and dropped his hands. "I'm going to give you one last chance to tell us the purpose of this latest swab sample."

Lance hung his head and shook it back and forth, groaning. "Please don't kill me. Please don't."

Finn turned to Benjamin. He looked resigned to a fight. Then he turned back and regarded the kid.

Blood gooped around his mouth and chin as he worked his lips. "I'm just a college kid. I didn't know it was anything bad."

"I'm not convinced," Benjamin said, stepping forward. From the coffee table he snatched the ice-pick by it's scarred handle. "I'm going to take out an eye."

Lance exploded into ragged sobs.

"Wait!" Finn said to Benjamin, trying to erase the repugnant image of him plucking out an eyeball. He snapped his fingers in a rapid rhythm. "Come on. Start talking. The color of the guy's shoes who gave you the primers, his hair style. The writing on the box the swabs were mailed in. Anything."

"A tall black guy always gives me the primer set. But this time it was someone different" Lance said in a gasp. "He seemed angry. We hardly spoke."

"What'd he say?" Finn asked.

"He told me to do my job, to burn the cipher afterwards. The black guy always says that."

"Who was this new guy?"

"He didn't say anything but what the black guy always says. He's like five-seven dark skinned, Middle Eastern or Indian, and skinny."

The guy on the other side of the bridge when they got the swab, the one who called to Yusif, Finn thought.

"And Dr. Kotesky, he's fat and he smokes a lot. He dresses real sloppy and he's a little intimidating."

Benjamin waved his hand indicating to keep it coming.

"And like once a year he comes to the States and visits me. I tell him how the project is going. We speak Russian and he recommends a conference for me to go to. The box the swabs come in is always a regular brown cardboard box with no return address. UPS ships it. It usually comes from far away but this time it was from here, postmarked in Austin. Like a week ago the Russian Academy of Sciences sent me seven or eight boxes shipped to the lab but its not related to the swabs."

"What was in them?" Benjamin said.

"Skin cream samples. I was supposed to pass out."

"Skin cream samples?"

"It has nothing to do with the DNA stability study."

"What'd you do with them?" Benjamin asked.

"I passed them out."

Finn pushed up next to Benjamin, standing over the kid. Benjamin fingered the ice pick.

"When?" Finn asked.

"Tuesday and Wednesday."

"This week?"

"The instructions said we couldn't pass any out after Wednesday. They were very clear about that."

"Where'd you pass them out?" Benjamin asked.

"Houston, San Antonio, Dallas and here. At shopping malls." The kid looked back and forth between them. As much as Finn could tell through his inflated face, he looked hopeful.

"What else did the instructions say?" Finn demanded.

"They're helping a start-up Russian biotech that's developing a new type of skin cream. They said they'd pay us to pass out the samples. It gave the locations."

"Which malls?" Benjamin pointed the ice-pick at the kid's face.

"Please, don't," he said, twisting away from the ice-pick. "I'm telling the truth. I swear. I swear."

"Which malls."

"I, I can't remember the names. I swear." He was crying again.

Finn held back Benjamin with a hand on his chest. "How many samples did you hand out?"

"Maybe three or four hundred per box."

Finn did the math mentally: Twenty-one to thirty-two hundred. "Tell us everything you know about the samples."

The kid scrunched his eyes closed, though they were nearly swollen shut. He hung his head down, moaning. They stood over him and waited.

"Said it was a long lasting sunblock," he finally said, "especially for shoulders and arms."

Finn yanked on Benjamin's shirt and pulled him into the kitchen. They huddled next to the refrigerator. "It's too recent to have been part of the smallpox outbreak," Finn whispered. "The incubation for smallpox is twelve days. Maybe there are other people doing the same thing and they passed out samples earlier."

"But what does it have to do with the Interleukin-4?"

"I don't know. It's only hypothetical that it weaponizes smallpox. Maybe they're using a combination of natural and genetically modified virus in case the modified one doesn't live and that's why the first case came up wild-type."

Benjamin pulled out the baggie, dug his key into the cocaine and snorted another heaping mound.

"But look," Finn said. "The smallpox cases broke Thursday and were confirmed Friday night. The instructions listed Wednesday as the last day to pass out the samples. It makes sense because the terrorists wouldn't want to risk passing out any samples if people were suspicious. The incubation time for smallpox is *very* predictable. They've been fucking dosing during the entire incubation."

"We need to get a hold of a skin cream sample," Benjamin said, marching back into the living room.

Lance's head wobbled to one side and what little Finn could see of his eyes reminded him of a fish that's been out of the water too long. "Is that what you guys wanted to know?" He slurred the words. "About the skin cream? I'll tell you everything."

"Do you have any more?" Finn asked.

"Ahh, I. Yeah. Maybe in my apartment. Yeah I think there's a few in the kitchen. I'll show you."

"Hey!" Benjamin snapped fingers in front of his face. "Did you use any on yourself?"

The kid swung his head, looking at each of them. "I tried a couple tubes."

Finn and Benjamin turned to one another and then back to Lance.

"What else about the skin cream samples?" Benjamin said.

"I handed them out. That's it."

"Hey. Wake up!" Benjamin said. "The primers. The DNA. All that shit. Are you leaving anything out?"

"No, I'm telling you everything. I swear to God."

"Get up," Benjamin said. "We're going." Benjamin picked his pistol up off the window sill. "Get up!"

Lance struggled to his feet. "I'm sure they're in the kitchen. You'll see."

"Hop." Benjamin demanded. He opened the front door and held the screen door open. Lance thumped along the hardwood floor to the doorway in teetering bounces. Finn wanted to cut the zip tie on his ankle if just to avoid witnessing his bloated face bobble with each excruciating jump. Instead he stepped back wondering if Lance were right now teeming with weaponized smallpox. Lance's nose looked like a smashed lump of clay. Benjamin must have stuck the pliers tips up his nostrils, probably snapped the cartilage.

"I promise. I won't go to the police," he said as he passed Benjamin.

"Out!" Benjamin waved him through.

He hopped across the patio and dropped down three steps in measured jumps. He began jumping towards the police cruiser when Benjamin told him to turn around. He spun around in minuscule bounces. The look in his eyes came from far away. When he faced them, Benjamin raised his pistol aiming it at his chest from six feet. "I'm giving you a moment to get right with God."

Lance didn't even try to twist away. "No, no, no." The words carried no weight. Then he simply fell over backwards like a feather on the tip of it's quill.

Benjamin strode over and stood above him. "I'm sorry," he said, "Your life wasn't in vain," and fired four quick, cracking shots into Lance's heart, the gun jumping in his hand.

Finn found he had covered his mouth with his hands. Benjamin passed by and went into the house. He returned and slapped a bright orange, rubber, dish-washing glove on Finn's chest. Finn hadn't moved.

"Grab a hand. We need to pull him out back."

Slowly Finn put on the glove. "But couldn't Gogan have looked after him 'till we found the skin cream?"

"I knew it. I *knew* you couldn't see this," Benjamin said. "Grab a wrist."

Finn's phone rang. It was Gogan.

"Tell him to stay put," Benjamin said.

As they dragged the body towards the back of the house, sounds and images sank into a thoughtless, stagnant sludge that was Finn's mind. The body passed and leaves of grass folded, tan and dead, and then behind it, rose up, dappled with shocks of crimson. A breeze lifted and dropped a tree branch beside the house, while a sparrow perched on it trilled a three-note repeat. They stopped near the edge of the woods, about fifty feet from the rear of the house and Benjamin let go of Lance's wrist. "Take your clothes off," he said.

Benjamin threw his bloodied undershirt on top of the body, then sat down and pulled off his socks. He undid his belt and slipped off his jeans and underwear. Everything got thrown onto Lance. Naked, Benjamin walked to a dilapidated wooden shed tucked into a grove of pine trees twenty feet away. Finn undressed. Benjamin returned holding a red dented gas can. Finn tossed his clothes onto the heap, his heart thumping in his neck. He could only bring himself to peek at the kid's swollen face. Benjamin shook gasoline onto Lance and the clothes. It made Lance's skin shine like a canned peach and turned the grass around him a darker shade of brown. Benjamin walked backwards making a gasoline trail in the grass. Watch out, he said, and lit a match and threw it onto the end of the trail. A delicate blue flame skittered toward the pile and then spread out above it, a ghostly dancing dervish. Finn grimaced, watching the body burn. The skin on Lance's hands began to darken while something crackled and sputtered. Just four minutes ago he'd been hopping around the living room, a healthy twenty-one year-old. A single thought echoed in Finn's mind: *Is this really me?*

Both of them, barefoot and naked, watched the body burn. "I shot that ten-year-old girl two days before the start of the war," Benjamin said. "It was murder, plain and simple. We dropped in at 1:03 a.m. along a supply-line road in the Syrian desert west of Baghdad. We dug our trench and stopped at dawn. Then we hid and waited. The attack was to start the next morning. She came by just past noon, within fifty yards, and froze. She couldn't have seen more than the top of our helmets. We hadn't had time to dig deeper. If they'd just done like they were supposed to and dropped us in at midnight. Finally she turned and bolted, screaming. I hesitated but then I had to shoot her, man. I shot an innocent, schoolgirl in the back." A wave of heat, pungent with the odor of scorched meat, passed them by. "I've never been able to forgive myself, to accept her death as a sacrifice for a few grown men trying to save their own asses." He stopped and Finn didn't know what to say. "That endless black pit opened up again, this morning when you asked me to interrogate Lance."

"We didn't have to kill him."

"That girl, *had* to die, this kid did too."

"We just needed to question him."

"Nobody trusts you and Gogan. Not even the feds. Who would have looked after him? You? Gogan? Me? He could have conned one of us and sent out a message, or worse, if he'd been nabbed by cops he could have sneaked out a message to the Russian guy, and it would have been all over for us and maybe thousands, tens of thousands, of others. Did you forget? We're on the trail of a weaponized smallpox attack. Why would we spare one person at the expense of everyone else?" He raised his eyebrows. "It doesn't matter what we think he's capable of, or if he's innocent or not. I would have traded my life for that girl's in a breath— she wasn't much older than Sophia. But I couldn't. I would have been trading the lives of all five men in my unit and possibly many, many others. Are their lives any less valuable? I never, ever expected that I'd have to kill a school girl and this morning I certainly didn't wake up expecting to have to kill some college kid." He paused and regarded Finn. "But I recognized it. You see? No, you couldn't see. That kid was dead the second you I.Ded him, man."

They went to the front of the house. Benjamin handed him a bar of soap lined with black crevices and uncoiled a green garden hose. He turned it on and let the hot water drain. He brought up the nozzle ready to train on Finn.

"Nobody can come here until it's checked for smallpox." Finn said.

"I'll call Reece after we've cleaned up."

"We should get clothes first. Here, wash my hands. And get your prints off that gas can." Finn jogged inside, and ran an old dish rag over the couch, door knob, and refrigerator. He rinsed the blood from the needle-nose pliers and put them, along with the other tools, back in a tool box in the garage. They rummaged through Reece's clothing, threw their choices on the patio and went back to grass. Benjamin hit him in the chest with a cool blast of water, and Finn scrubbed the soap into a lather.

"We have to leave, right now, for either LA, Chapel Hill, or Georgia." Benjamin said. "Book the first two seats you can find to any of those places. But first I'm going to his apartment to find a skin cream sample. I'll meet you at the airport."

"I'll go with you."

"And if we don't find a sample? And they start shutting down the domestic flights like they're doing with international ones? Just get to the airport and get the tickets. I'll be there as fast as I can."

"You're right," Finn said.

When Finn was done washing it was Benjamin's turn. Someone moved in the underbrush at the edge of the yard, and a bolt of terror coursed through Finn. But then he saw that it was Gogan climbing out from behind the leaves and branches and coming towards them, twigs clinging to his beard.

Finn cinched up a faded pair of jeans with a leather belt and threw on a black tee-shirt and, although Reece's feet were smaller, found pair of flip-flops that fit. Benjamin, on the other hand, looked like a man-child. Reece's shorts clawed at his thighs and a black tee-shirt, with "Titty Bingo" scrawled on it in various fluorescent colors, strained to contain him. Finn went up to him and abruptly hugged him. He wanted to say *thank you* but it seemed simultaneously inadequate and inappropriate and instead he squeezed him tight, and gave him a few manly slaps on the back.

"It's fucking full throttle from here on dude," Benjamin said. He pushed Finn back, "We're doing good. Now go."

Finn looked him in his eyes and he knew he'd lay his life down for him. He wanted to tell him that he loved him, but ended up saying, "Yeah. It's all or nothing." He felt moronic saying it. He and Gogan jogged to his car.

THIRTY-FOUR

Finn and Gogan slalomed between cars and trucks on Bee Caves Highway, Gogan behind the wheel. He asked Finn why they had to kill Lance and he didn't really know what to say. Benjamin was right. The cops didn't believe them and although Matterson pleaded ignorance he could have sneaked out a message. "We got all we could from him," Finn said, staring at the car-clogged highway before them. "You're right. We're in a war and keeping him alive was a risk without benefit." While Gogan considered this, Finn opened the Internet on his phone to search for tickets to Georgia, LA, or North Carolina. His Internet homepage showed an electron microscope photo of the *Variola major* virus, a gray, spiked pillow. The confirmed smallpox cases were at two, with seven more suspected. "International flights canceled, domestic curbed," read the title article. Finn checked the time. It was 4:33, six hours since he'd stood outside the San Antonio convenience store and chose to not go to Sarah. The earliest flight with an open seat bound for Atlanta would leave at 11:42 p.m., one with two seats not until the following afternoon. LA was worse. There were two seats leaving for Raleigh-Durham International Airport at 1:12 a.m., but a single open seat leaving in forty minutes. He bought it and called Benjamin.

"I'm getting on the plane to Chapel Hill in forty minutes," He said. "There was only one seat left."

"When's the next one there?"

"1:12 A.M. I'll book you after we hang up."

"Get a shotgun," Benjamin said, calmly.

"I'm hanging up. I need to book your ticket."

"A .20 gauge. Hack down the barrel and stock as much as you can."

"Okay, okay. I'm buying your ticket." He hung-up. With a credit card he bought Benjamin's ticket and one for Gogan. He insisted on taking the red-eye to LA. Moments later they pulled off of Ben White Boulevard and onto the airport exit ramp. Gogan stopped at domestic departures. His black hair was disheveled, and dirt streaked sweat ran down his face. A couple fragments of leaves still clung to his beard.

"Clean yourself up before you get on the flight," Finn said.

"We must do this," Gogan said through gritted teeth, like some half-time pep-talk. Finn leaned in and hugged him. Finn didn't know what to say. Then he sprang from the car and ran through a pair of sliding doors, Reece Skully's flip-flops slapping the concrete.

. . .

Kotesky stood smoking on the front stoop of Ledpaste's condo (or rather former condo). The police hadn't come after Youssef killed him, so for the past month Kotesky had been living there. It was much more comfortable than his hotel room. Murmurings from a radio show filtered out and mingled with bird songs and the drone of passing cars. A woman announced a total of two confirmed smallpox infections and seven suspected cases. Except for Youssef's initial difficulties, the attack was progressing as planned. Tomorrow Kotesky would be in Mexico, and homeward bound. With the inevitable travel restrictions he wondered how long it would take him to get back to Russia. (two days? A week? A month, two?) He exhaled a lungful of pale smoke and it hung languidly, shot through with thick shafts of sunlight from the orange star just now sinking below the treetops. In the stale air he caught a whiff of cooking sausage.

A pink-helmeted girl with red and white handlebar tassels pedaled by. He wondered how his son was doing, whether he was studying piano or playing video games. He threw down his cigarette butt and went inside. A radio commentator questioned an epidemiologist on the transmission mechanics of smallpox. On the stove sliced onions and potatoes sizzled next to sausages. They sputtered and grease popped. His phone rang in a tinny rendition of Rachmaninoff's Prelude in C Sharp Minor. It was a scholarship student from Boston.

"I passed out all the hand cream samples," the student said.

"When did you finish?"

He hesitated. "Wednesday."

"Are you sure."

"Yeah, yes," the student stuttered.

"And you waited so long to call."

"I'm sorry. I was going to call earlier, but—"

"Don't worry," Kotesky said. *It didn't matter now.* "Excellent work. The manufacturer saved thousands on, how do you say?"

"Marketing?"

"Yes, marketing. You'll be compensated well."

That call made seventeen. All the scholarship students had now reported in. He picked up his celebratory mug of beer and swigged a mouthful. Kotesky had predicted the first cases of smallpox would appear, two days ago, Friday September 6^{th,} and so had set the limit for dissemination of the samples to Wednesday. But the first case was found late Thursday. He wasn't worried though. It was inconceivable anyone had an idea of what was happening. Even if someone looked for the smallpox virus in the skin cream they wouldn't find an intact one, though its DNA was there, hidden in a bacteria. And even if the feds uncovered one of the sleeper cells (impossible considering the DNA encoding of information) they would have to identify one of the seventeen scholarship students who received the swabs and then uncover Rurik or one of the other two postdoctoral scientists who'd separately assembled *strain 27*, the Interleukin-4 modified *Variola major*. And then, *even* if those connections were made, the feds would still have to understand how Plan 3-27 operated. To stop the attack now, the discovering, the deciphering, the connecting, the understanding, and the reacting would all have to be done ridiculously fast. *Entirely impossible*.

While doing a shuffling dance Kotesky raised his beer and shouted a Russian drinking cheer. But then his hand stopped like an arm on a seized locomotive wheel. Beer splashed out of the mug and onto the skillet, hissing and throwing up a cloud of acrid gray steam. Sixteen of the targets held portions of the *Variola major* DNA but the one here in Austin held Interleukin-4. If the feds found any of the sixteen sleeper cells and managed to find the hidden DNA sequences they would only find the connection to the smallpox. But if they found the Austin target with Interleukin-4 they would be only a few steps away from understanding the attack.

There was a chance the feds could make a connection between Youssef and Lance Matterson, or maybe they already had. And if they found that starry-eyed farmer it wouldn't be long before he'd be crying out the details of the DNA stability study along with the skin cream samples. Kotesky cursed Ledpaste, that reckless sadistic asshole. The main reason the feds might find Matterson would be while trying to solve the murder of the target's parents that Dahoud had ordered. So, it was possible they could find the interleukin-4 gene. And if someone understood the implications of the interleukin-4 then the attack could be derailed in one swift (if not highly improbable) decree. If the vaccinations were canceled, the attack would be lost in an instant.

He put his beer down and dialed Lance Matterson. His voice mail answered and Kotestky hung up. He called again. Voice mail again. If the feds had found Lance they could have a trap set, could be staking him out. He thought about calling Jassim but couldn't depend on him for a task like this. He needed Youssef to cooperate. He dialed him. When he answered, a siren was blaring in the background.

. . .

Since the moment Cemile Yilmaz had died Youssef had been zeroing in on the one who'd called the police and caused her death, that cunt Sarah Dougherty. He had poured over all the email accounts of hers that he'd breached, as well Reece Skully's online accounts he'd also broken into. He hacked into phone records with help from a contact with connections to the F.B.I. Soon he suspected she would hide somewhere in New England. He immediately bought a bus ticket to Boston. He had $80.00 when he arrived on the morning of August 11th, and survived by doing odd jobs, begging, sleeping in youth hostels or in fields behind elementary schools closed for the summer. He was dirty, and thin, and it felt urgent again, like old times, when he'd staked out the mid-ranking Hamas officer discussing limited disarmament, the one who's throat he'd slit from behind as he pissed in a restaurant urinal. But this time he would be looking into Sarah's quivering green eyes while she explained to him why she had called the cops on the Lamar Street Bridge when he had made it oh-so-fucking clear that her parents would die if she involved the police. All he'd needed was a fucking mouth swab. Who would call the police over that!

Three days ago he got his big break when she'd emailed Finn Barber (one of several people whose email he'd been monitoring). And there was a generous bonus: He was coming to be with her today. He could even be here now. Maybe Youssef would do like they say here—two birds with a single stone. Just this morning he'd identified the very house where she was living and now he crept between hedges toward it. In dusk's light he could just make out silhouettes of chairs, tables, and shelves in a dark living room. He made his way to the back of the house, peering into an empty bedroom on the way. Sarah had called the police and given Ledpaste the reason he'd needed to kill Cemile. Maybe like most Americans she didn't give a goat's balls about her family. Maybe she even hated her parents. But she should have known, with her parents lives threatened, other lives were on the line too. Why couldn't she have just done what she was told?

At the back of the house he rolled down a ski mask, smashed a window on the back door, and stuck his hand in and tried to open it. Fucking dead-bolt! He kicked, and kicked the door until it exploded in splinters from its jamb. He ran into a bedroom, flung open drawers, and threw shirts and lacy panties on the floor. From a jewelery box he snatched a few bracelets, and rings and jammed them into his jeans' pocket. He shook out the box's remaining contents on the floor and then hurled it across the room. That was when the house alarm sounded. The fat undulating boom branded itself onto his brain. He jogged outside and tossed a necklace and a bracelet on a stone walkway. Rushing back into the roar he threw open a corner door in the dining room. A narrow set of stairs curved down into darkness. He closed the door behind him and hurtled down the steps. In a cramped, dirt-floored cellar, a window, nearly blocked by leaves, passed a frail light. Below the stairs and beyond—under the kitchen—the ground was three or four feet higher and crisscrossed with ducts and pipes. It was better than he'd hoped for. He rolled onto the ledge and shimmied underneath the aluminum ducts and to the very back into the pitch darkness. He pulled a napkin from his pocket, ripped off two pieces and jammed them in his ears. From another pocket he pulled a pair of Sarah's ivory-colored, lacy panties and drew a deep breath through the crotch. His cock tingled and began to stiffen. He unzipped his pants. Then he felt his cell phone vibrate. *Dammit!* It was the fat Russian. Youssef hesitated but then pulled a napkin from one ear and answered.

"Tariq. Youssef!"

He was about to say something but then stopped and just listened.

"You must go to the student's apartment."

Youssef hung up and replaced the napkin. He re-zipped his fly. He thought he had fallen asleep because when the alarm stopped he snapped to, alert. He pulled the napkin from his ears. For ten minutes he heard voices and the footfalls of at least three people. Then the door opened to the cellar and the stairs creaked under a large person's weight. A light switch was thrown on. The person descended but he could not see him. He imagined a stiff-booted patrol cop laden with a Kevlar vest, gun, and cuffs. A beam of yellow light raked the crawl space around Youssef. He pressed himself into the dirt. Against the bricks above a shoulder the beam cast a shadow of the duct between him and the cop. Then the stairs groaned again, the light was turned off and the door shut. He waited a couple of minutes and then shimmied out from under the ducts. Above, people still trod. A power tool buzzed and hammer blows reverberated. After five minutes the foot traffic stopped and voices came only from the front of the house. He tip-toed up the stairs and put his ear to the gap between the door and the floor. Soon the front door clicked shut. He counted to ten and then opened the cellar door and listened. He had sixty seconds before the motion sensors would reset. He shut the cellar door and then crawled, staying below the window sills, towards the front of the house. Once there, he stood up between the front door and the fireplace pressing his back against the wall. He peeked through a bay window. Sarah's auburn hair fluttered as she turned left out of the driveway in a little hatchback, followed by a cop car. The same faint and pleasant odor as in her apartment in Austin lingered here. Right here, next to the front door, Youssef thought. *When she returns and opens it, it will swing hiding me. And then she will be all mine.* He grinned and indulged himself a moment of mental pre-celebration.

. . .

Youssef can't be trusted anyway, Kotesky thought. So he didn't redial Youssef after the first call disconnected. This he would have to do himself. He put his wallet, and phone—things that could easily identify him—on the kitchen counter top. He picked up his gun from beside the stove, and left. Twenty minutes later he stood in front of a wide staircase in an interior hall outside the front door of Lance's apartment, one in a four-plex. It was sunless and stifling. He put his ear to the door and thought he heard water running. He gingerly placed his hand on the knob, turned and pushed it. It was bolted. He stepped back and surveyed the hallway. He yanked up the welcome mat, but found only dust below. Near the entrance, sat a potted and dehydrated ficus. Nothing below it either. Above it hung four narrow mailboxes. He opened the one labeled Matterson and peered down inside. At the bottom a key shone in the thin light. He took it. Slowly, he inserted the key and retracted the dead bolt. He took his pistol from its hip holster and held it ready while he millimetered the door open and peered inside. A television sat on a metal table in front of a futon. He widened the opening, stepped inside and shut the door. He crept towards the kitchen, careful not to make footfalls. The water (he heard it clearly now) was only the toilet running. It came from behind a partially closed bathroom door in a hallway leading from the back of the kitchen. Kitchen drawers stood open, utensils and cooking ware scattered across the counter. *What a slob.* He tucked his pistol behind his belt.

Then the bathroom door swung inward and out stepped a man, or beast rather, in shorts and black tee-shirt. Kotesky leaped backwards and knocked a pan from the stove. The man was twenty years younger than him and jammed full of muscle. He burned into Kotesky an apish ferocity. Kotesky's vision tunneled but he never wavered his gaze from the man's eyes. A single thought creaked through his mind. *Is the gun set on safety?*

The man smiled ever so slightly. "Kotesky," he said, with the slow cadence of solving a riddle. He glanced sideways into the bathroom, low towards the ground.

Kotesky shot a hand to his hip for the pistol and the man exploded like a charging silver back. Kotesky lurched backwards tugging on the pistol. The man crashed into him and white nebula exploded in Kotesky's head. He was on the ground, the man on top of him. The steel of the gun was still in his grip and he pulled the trigger frantically. 1,2,3,4,5...He found himself struggling to breathe beneath the gorilla's weight. He struggled to his feet, panting. He lowered the gun and shot him once in the back of the head. Leaving Matterson's apartment and getting back to the condo seemed to happen as if in a haze.

Once back he called Hernando Sepulveda, the MS-13 boss in Miami.

"I've got a job for you," Kotesky said. He paced in the narrow kitchen holding a bag of ice to the back of his head.

"Russia!" Hernando cheered. Then he directed something in Castellano away from the phone and people in the background laughed.

"It's a twenty-four hour job."

"*Tu* plan is no go smooth, huh?"

"Four jobs actually," Kotesky said, trying not to sound too pissed off.

"*Cuaaaatro,*" he sang the number out. "*Bien, bien.*"

"The three I gave you. Remember? Rurik in Chapel Hill, North Carolina and the other two, in Pasadena and Georgia."

"Si, si. The, how you say? *Para emergencias.*"

"Contingencies. That's right. And a woman."

"Little time is pay more."

"Triple, four times, I don't give a fuck. The faster it's done the more."

"A woman?"

"Don't get chivalrous on me. Sarah Dougherty. Those first three are easy but this is tough job. She's in protective custody, federal, so use your connections." He gave Hernando details on Sarah and her case. "Find her. This *has* to been done right now."

"Of course, *patron.*" Hernando said. "No you worry man."

THIRTY-FIVE

Finn waited to check in for his flight, bouncing from foot to foot behind a Greek family lugging a phalanx of suitcases. They boisterously argued with the attendant and amongst themselves. Four endless minutes passed before they finally checked their luggage.

"Finn Barber," Finn said, leaning around the family as they collected their carry-ons. A man with black-gelled hair took his I.D. and clicked a keyboard. After a moment he squinted at what he read and then leaned over and called to a woman standing on the other side of a luggage scale. She went to his side.

Finn's pulse surged.

The man pointed at the monitor and registered the woman's uncertain response. He turned to Finn. "You got a doppelgänger?"

The flight Sarah booked must have come up too.

"You booked a flight to Providence, Rhode Island, which leaves in an hour and a half, *and* one to Raleigh-Durham," he checked his watch, "Which leaves in twenty-two minutes."

The earth beneath Finn's feet softened, and he stepped backwards to accommodate it. Sweat distilled through his skin and prickled at his pores. Sarah was in Providence. In five hours he could be holding her, breathing her in, rubbing her feet, her calves, thighs, stomach, breasts, neck. They could have sex over and over. Maybe it was a sign since the flight hadn't left yet and he was here in the airport, a sign that he should go to her instead—

"Sir, where are you going?"

"I'm," Finn looked at him, the woman, and then her nervous customers waiting, unattended, in the adjacent isle. *If Benjamin finds a skin cream sample, and it's found to contain weaponzied smallpox, what I do will be irrelevant. Besides, they've already passed out all the skin cream samples. What good is following the thread now?*

"Sir, which flight?"

"I'm..."

They all looked at him expectantly.

"I'm, I'm going to North Carolina." He'd said it quickly and it felt wrong.

Benjamin would find weaponized smallpox in the skin cream, and then they would find the connection in Chapel Hill, he told himself. The government would step in and he would be with Sarah within two days.

While dodging passengers on the way to the security gate, he quietly chanted, *soon I'll be with Sarah, soon I'll be with Sarah.*

Finn slumped into his airplane seat, breathing heavily from his jog through the airport. A matronly woman sat to his right. He pulled out his cellphone and began searching the Internet.

"Excuse me."

Finn looked up at a young man, a flight attendant.

"All devices must be shut off now."

Finn nodded and fiddled with a few buttons while the man moved on, down the aisle. He started browsing again but then felt the woman watching him. She raised her brow. "It's very important," he said.

"So is our safety."

He stood up and went to the bathroom. Sitting on the toilet, he continued searching. The jet engines revved in a pitched whine. He found a biochemistry Ph.D. student, Rurik Montokov, at the University of North Carolina working under a Russian Academy of Sciences scholarship. He was the only student affiliated with it. The plane lurched sideways and he grabbed the stainless steel sink and braced himself. He searched the California Institute of Technology in Pasadena, California—one of the other places that Lance had sent Sarah's DNA sequences. Again, he found a single graduate student working under the same Russian scholarship program. He leaned back against the wall. Could it be, he wondered, that easy. He searched the Internet for Rurik Montokov's address. "Sir!" a man yelled, through the near edge of the door. "Please take your seat for take-off." The engines screamed. "Did you hear me?"

Finn ignored him.

"Sir!"

"Yes," Finn finally said, pocketing his phone and opening the door. He definitely didn't want trouble with security now.

...

The grass around the body was burnt like a halo. Detective Mulveny prodded the corpse—more a smoking pile of ash now—striking at it with a twisted limb. It found something substantial and arced with tension. The corpse, like a marshmallow that had fallen in a campfire, was charred crisp outside but still fleshy inside. If he'd been infected with smallpox you'd never be able to tell now. He chipped away at the cracked layers where the chest should be and a thin twist of smoke curled out. The cop next to him said something.

"Do what?"

"That's some sick shit, lieutenant." Her voice was muffled, stripped of its treble by a biohazard suit: pure white rip-stop nylon with latex gloves, respirator, booties, and full hoodie with a plastic face cover.

Mulveny turned his head but it swiveled more than the god-damned space helmet and his view in one eye was cut off. He cocked his head motioning behind him. "The shed?"

"I went through it quick. Nothing obvious."

Mulveny shuffled towards the clapboard shack with its warped door hanging open. A cop, also in a biohazard suit, squatted and took a swab sample for a smallpox test from the handle of a dented, red gasoline container sitting in the grass thirty-odd feet from the body. The doorway to the shack swallowed the sunlight. He stepped inside, careful to lift his feet over the baseboard, not to catch a nail. The pitch rendered him blind and a stale hovering heat pierced his suit. A faint, tangy odor of gasoline filtered through his respirator. He reached out and found a shelf, the old wood chalky and with deep furrows. His vision returned slowly and he made out pottery, garden tools, gloves, and pots for plants. He pulled a cell phone from a pouch pocket in the front of the suit. It was to be used on site and incinerated later. He checked a slip of paper and dialed a number.

"Hello," a tired voice said.

"Detective Deyermand. This is Jim Mulveny with Austin—"

"What? I can barely hear you."

Mulveny repeated himself.

"Look," Deyermand sounded annoyed. "I told Finn I can't do a thing on the Sarah Dougherty case until this smallpox subsides."

"Barber? When did you talk to him?" He shouted through the respirator.

"That nut came to my house this morning going on about weaponized smallpox."

"Weaponized?"

"Look, we're chasing a million leads with this, but I promise after it calms down I'll send—"

"We have another body. At Reece Skully's house. Skully got a call that his place was contaminated with smallpox."

Deyermand was silent.

"Mulveny!" Someone called him from outside.

"I'll call you right back," Mulveny said, and hung up. He cursed himself for not putting on a wireless headset before climbing in the suit.

A biohazard suited corporal, silhouetted by the sunlight stood in the doorway. "I have the interview notes," he said.

Mulveny gestured for him to continue.

He opened a notepad. "Skully said someone called warning him— he won't give the caller's name. The call was four minutes long, started at 4:54, and originated from a land line at a convenience store at the corner of 2222 and Bullick Hollow Road. It's a mile from here. He said the caller told him not to go to his house that it was infected with smallpox and that someone had been killed there, someone Skully didn't know. The caller told him to go down to the station, give his alibi and clear his name."

"He said 'killed'?"

"Skully said, the caller said, 'killed'."

Mulveny checked the time on the cell phone. It was 6:47 and that body must have been smoldering at least two hours. He picked up a bowl off a shelf, swiveled it and thought he saw something move. He poked a couple fingers in and touched something, something wet possibly. He raised his fingers to the bulbous projection of the respirator and inhaled. He couldn't smell a damn thing below the odor of gasoline. He couldn't believe it or understand it. This whole fucked up case with Sarah and Finn and Reece. Now it was back, and someone else was dead. He squatted, inspecting an old knobby-treaded truck tire leaning against the wall. The details of Sarah's case twitched in his head like the mosquito larvae in the squalid water resting in it.

"Put a priority material witness warrant out on Finn Barber."

The corporal scribbled on his notepad.

"Find the pay phone that call was made from. See if there's a camera on it, and look for a witness to ID the caller."

On his cell phone, Mulveny punched in the number for the central desk at the police station. He wanted to ask Benjamin Black about Finn Barber. Those two were tight as a tick.

"Alivia, it's Mulveny. Connect me with lieutenant Black please."

"Just a moment."

Mulveny pressed the phone into his ear, against the papery hood. Static hiss cut in and out. He swiveled the mouthpiece away from his face and spoke to the corporal. "Call Deyermand in San Antonio, the one on the Dougherty case, and find out what he knows. And get Barber, *now.*"

"Black's in his cruiser," Alivia said, through the phone.

"Where?"

"His GPS isn't transmitting."

"Shit." Mulveny stamped his foot.

"Should I connect you to his cell?"

"Yeah." The phone rang but voice mail answered. "Benjamin, it's me," he said. "Call me. Now." He hung up and turned to the corporal, "Find Black too."

The corporal stood poised to write. "One other thing," he said, "Channel Seven News is setting up at the top of the driveway."

"God dammit! I'm gonna kill who ever leaked this."

"There wasn't a leak. They've been staking out the mobile bio-hazard lab since the first smallpox case broke."

Mulveny picked up another bowl, looked inside and then back up at the guy. "Then let's use them. Fix them up a photo of Barber and tell them he's wanted for questioning in a murder. Also, get dental records on him and check it against that briquette outside."

The corporal hustled around the back of the house towards the driveway. *Weaponized smallpox,* Mulveny whispered the words to himself. He left the shed and cast around trying to spot a neighbor's house, or any source of potential witnesses. But trees, bushes, and brush barricaded him.

. . .

During the flight Finn tried to mentally prepare for his arrival, but the variables prevented him from forming a plan beyond renting a car, buying a gun, and finding Rurik.

At 12:29 a.m. the seatbelt sign darkened with a terse chime and he was the first to stand. It was 11:29 in Austin. It felt as if he had actually lost time. In the hallway connected to the plane he shimmied past the passengers and then jogged down the terminal, through baggage claim, and finally outside. In ten minutes he sat behind the wheel of a sedan in the rental car parking lot. On the Internet he found several Chapel Hill addresses for Rurik Montokov. He repeated aloud the most recent address to himself, "905 Dawes, 905 Dawes," while searching for it on an Internet map.

He emailed Gogan the name of the Cal Tech student and then on the keypad, texted out an email to Sarah on the account she'd created using Benjamin's name: *Tortuously, regrettably, I can't come (you must believe me). I have no time to explain. Nothing less than flabbergasting! But very soon I will hold you, tell you every unbelievable detail. I am fine. I will come as soon as humanly possible, you must trust me. I love you as much as anyone can love another.* He felt both sick and faint writing it.

He thought of adding that she was somehow connected to the smallpox attack but assuring her she was infection free. (He didn't know what the feds had told her when they'd done a smallpox blood test the night before.) He decided not to add it. Next he searched for a local Walmart store and then headed there. While driving he called Benjamin and got his voice mail. "I'm in Chapel Hill. I think I've found the guy who got the Interleukin-4 sequence. I'm going to get a shotgun now."

Finn switched on the radio and it wasn't thirty seconds before a commentator announced four confirmed smallpox infections and between twelve and seventeen additional suspected cases. A discordant buzz from the radio—an emergency warning tone—jarred him and he lowered the volume. A synthesized voice followed. *Smallpox vaccinations begin tomorrow morning in Durham, Orange, and Wake counties. All residents with last names beginning with M to P report to local clinics, beginning at 7:00 A.M. The immunologically compromised, elderly, and children under two are not advised to take the vaccine...* He shut it off.

He parked below an anemic street light at the edge of an expanse of macadam outside Walmart, went inside and bought supplies. He came back, tossed three plastic bags into the trunk of his rental car and laid down a shotgun in a camouflaged soft case. He fished a hacksaw frame and blade from one of the flimsy bags. Attaching the blade to the frame, he tightened it down with the wing-nut. He unzipped the gun case, pulled out the gun,—a twenty gauge pump-action—and put it on the car's plastic bumper with the barrel hanging off. He put the hacksaw on the barrel above the end of the chamber to hold the shells. He drew back the blade in a slow pull. It chewed into the black steel. A minute later the end of the barrel clanged off the asphalt. He dragged an arm across his forehead and slung sweat to the ground. Next he chewed six inches off the butt with a hand saw and then took a cordless drill and punched a large hole near the new end. He'd seen it in a James Cameron movie once. While slapping mosquitoes he poked a three-foot length of rope through the hole, knotted it, and then draped it over his left shoulder. It hung too low so he retied the knot and cut the excess. This time it swung just above his jean's pocket. He put on a black windbreaker. In his reflection in the car window he couldn't tell that he was strapped, not unless he jerked suddenly and made the gun swing against the jacket.

He put the gun on the passenger seat, covered it with the windbreaker and checked his cell phone. It was 2:47 a.m.. *Benjamin's in the air, and on his way.* He started to leave but stopped. He slung the shotgun over his left shoulder, put on the windbreaker and got out. From the trunk he opened a box of shells and shoved five in. The red plastic shells' heft and the guns' solid mechanical movements soothed him. For several moments he stood, gun in hand but yearning to hold Sarah. He tried to ignore the thoughts and practiced hanging his arms naturally at his side and then snatching the gun. He whipped it out from behind the jacket and pressed it against his ribs below his right pectoral. He flipped the trigger safety to off and let the gun hang again. He scanned the parking lot and didn't see anybody.

Benjamin would arrive in about four hours, perfect timing. They would knock on Rurik's door just after daybreak when Rurik and any others inside would be sleepy and slow. Meanwhile he would find the house and gather any clues about Rurik without exposing himself. He strolled toward the store, toward parked cars. He stopped between a sedan parked on the right and a hulking Hummer glistening to his left. He turned left. Emulating Clint Eastwood in Fist Full of Dollars he let his arms hang down and undulated his fingers. Then he snatched the shotgun, whipped it from his jacket and pulled the trigger. It belched, punched him in ribs, and the Hummer's rear window exploded. He bent over coughing and trying to regain his breath. Straightening himself he whipped the gun out again, steeled his stomach, and pumped off three shots, deflating both tires and pulverizing the left side of the trunk.

A door to a car three slots over burst open and a man in a Walmart vest careened headlong toward the store. Finn turned and raced the opposite direction, to his car. As he squealed off he thought the man was watching him from the store entrance but then an instant later thought it only a shadow. Once on the highway he dialed Benjamin. *I'm going to scout out Rurik's house,* was the message he planned to leave.

Thirty-Six

Benjamin's phone stopped ringing but nobody spoke. "Benjamin? Benjamin!" Finn said. Did he have it turned on during the flight? Surely, it's too soon for him to have landed in North Carolina. "Can you hear me? I'm heading to the guy's house. There must be a bad signal. I'll call you—"

"Where's Lance Matterson?" a deep, accented voice asked.

"Who is this?" Finn pulled the phone from his ear and confirmed that he'd called Benjamin.

Nobody spoke.

"Who is this!"

"You tell me where Lance Matterson is and I'll tell you where Benjamin is."

Finn felt his head and neck flush. Benjamin must have left his phone at Matterson's apartment when he went for the skin cream samples. It must be the Russian whose name he wrote down, the one the kid had mentioned.

"I know where you are, Finn Barber, and I am sending my people after you."

Hearing his name stunned Finn mute. Then he realized it appeared on Benjamin's phone when he called it. The Russian couldn't know where he was. It must be a bluff. "No," he paused, trying to recall the man's name. "I'm coming after you." He saw he was passing an exit he needed to take and jerked the wheel. He swerved across a lane and onto the exit ramp just before grass separated it from the highway.

"You better leave Chapel Hill and protect your bitch, Sarah. I sent the nigger after her."

Finn's head floated. "Don't fucking touch her!" He slammed on the brakes and pulled onto the shoulder at the end of the exit. "I'll fucking kill you!" He pulled the phone away and saw that the call had ended. He redialed Benjamin and voice mail answered. Immediately he dialed Detective Deyermand.

"It's Finn Barber."

"Un-fucking-believeable," Deyermand said.

"You have to move Sarah from Rhode Island."

"U.S. Marshals handle—listen. We have an APB out on you. Turn yourself in."

Finn paused. "They're trying to kill her."

"You should know you're listed 5150."

"What?"

"Psychotic and armed."

"I don't give a shit, You're obligated to protect Sarah."

"Finn, turn yourself in."

"The terrorist, the one who's trying to kill Sarah, has my friend, Benjamin's, cell. Finn fished out a folded sheet with the notes from Lance Matterson. His name is Nicholai Kotesky, take this down too: 512-37—"

"Benjamin Black?"

"Yeah. APD. He works with Mulveny."

"He's dead."

Finn hesitated. "You're a liar."

"Shot."

"That's a weak trick, Brian."

"Six times, all with powder burns in a UT student's apartment, downtown."

Finn didn't, or couldn't, respond.

"Mulveny told me."

"It couldn't be him."

"I'm truly sorry, but for your own safety..."

They could be pin-pointing me right now, this moment. Finn hung up. His stomach felt as if it were being pumped with helium. He arched his neck and shrieked. Hot tears streamed down his cheeks. He punched the roof. The interior light flashed and then burst.

An image of Benjamin as they left Reece's house hung in his imagination. He had turned and looked back at Finn, somber, before ducking into his police cruiser. *It's all or nothing.* That was the last thing he'd said to Benjamin. How stupid.

Then an image of Benjamin prone and pocked full with black rimmed bullet holes kidnapped his imagination. He wanted someone to suffer. He wanted blood, Yusif's, the Russian's.

As boys, he and Benjamin had built castles of sand in Benjamin's back yard.

Move! A thought demanded. *You have an APB on you.*

They used to jump off their rope swing and into the muddy red, clay creek, down the hill from Benjamin's house.

Move!

As soon as they could drive they'd done late night dough-nuts in suburban front yards in Benjamin's four-wheel drive Jeep, fleeing when the houses' flood lights filled the air with light. They both drank a potion of all Finn's parent's liquors thrown into a canteen and got sick on alcohol for the first time together. On their senior class trip to the Bahamas they sneaked Alison and Dawn into a vacant hotel room, and had sex in the darkness, each couple trying not to be too loud or obvious, but not succeeding.

He can't be dead. It's Benjamin.

In the dark Finn clawed for the phone. Finally he grabbed it off the passenger-side floor and dialed Benjamin. His voice mail answered.

He wiped his nose and spoke. "I'm coming for you, Nicholai Kotesty, I'm going to rip out your veins."

How many hundreds of times had they played pick-up soccer games with Mexicans in Austin, and then grilled steaks on Benjamin's back porch while Sophia played tea with her dolls? *It's my fault. I brought Benjamin back into this.* He drove forward and stopped at a stoplight, looked at the floor and cried over the past and kept going into a future that would never come, a future where he couldn't tell Benjamin how he found Rurik and the weaponized smallpox, how they'd saved thousands of lives, a future where they wouldn't sit down over a beer knowing that risking Benjamin's career, his pension, Sophia's future, had all been worth it. His thoughts jerked to Sarah. He accessed the Internet on his phone and texted to her email. *Drop everything. Leave immediately! They're after you again. Don't go anywhere predictable. Email me when safe.* He couldn't lose both Sarah and Benjamin at once: his past, present, and future.

He saw the stoplight was green. *How long had he been there?* He pulled forward slowly checking the street name but stared dumbly at the sign. The letters were marks without any relation to sounds. In the rear view mirror something approached. It took him several moments to understand that it was a motorcycle and it was nearly upon him before he realized it was a cop. The light was red now. Immediately he turned right and then right again, into a subdivision of boxy houses. His phone rang. It was Deyermand. He silenced it. *Don't do it. Don't do it,* he murmured to the cop. But the motorcycle took the turn too, staying close to the curb some hundred feet or so, behind him. Then he turned on his flashing lights.

NOOOOOOO!

Finn exhaled in a measured breath and parked next to the curb. He watched the cop in his rear view mirror, a shadow of him on the bike raced from far behind, joined him as he passed under a street lamp and then shot ahead, only to be erased in the glare of the next lamp. *You shouldn't have pulled me over.* He wiped tears from his face. The cop stopped behind Finn and pushed out a kick stand. The bike leaned over and thumped still. *This is the end of the line. Benjamin's dead. You've got an APB out on you. You'll spend the night in jail and then be flown back to Austin. Then it'll be all up to Gogan in Los Angeles.* The cop grabbed a receiver on his shoulder, attached to a curly-cued cord. He spoke into it. Colors flickered about Finn, red, and blue, then red again, and then a flash of white.

The shotgun, beneath the windbreaker, hugged Finn's body, its hacked barrel against a buttock. Breath came in ragged gasps. *You gotta go at it whole hog.* A feeling encapsulated him. The same feeling from a month ago, stuck in his car on the Lamar street bridge as Yusif and his partner had hurtled toward him. *It's fucking full throttle from here on out.* Those were Benjamin's last words to him. He couldn't be that coward on the bridge again. Never again. *The cop'll find the APB any second.* Finn put his hand on the shifter, still in park. *No way I'll out-run a motorcycle.* The cop continued speaking into the receiver on his shoulder.

M*ove!*

I have to smash his bike, run it over. Any second he'll find I'm listed armed and dangerous and unholster his gun. Then he'll shoot me if I flee. And I'll be a simple target if I wait until he's off his bike to run it over. He's innocent, though. But thousands of people could die if he stops me, maybe tens of thousands. What had Benjamin said? *Why spare one at the expense of everyone*? Finn saw a vast plain of corpses, shoulder to shoulder, and fairly eating him alive with steady eyes.

Here's your window, your moment. Act! "Forgive me God," he whispered. He popped the car into reverse and then stomped the gas pedal. The cop jerked his head up. In a crunch of metal he went down below Finn's line of sight and the car bucked and lurched up in the back. Finn flung open his door and rocketed to the back of the car, the hacked-off shotgun low. The front wheel of the motorcycle hung just above the ground at a shallow angle spinning steadily. White, red, and blue strobes pulsed angrily against the asphalt. The cop moaned.

"Your hands! Show me your fucking hands!" Finn scurried toward him in a low shuffling gait, his ass just a foot-or-so off the ground. He held the shotgun inches from the ground and parallel to it and trained the muzzle on the cop's face. The car had ridden up on the motorcycle's back tire and pinned the cop beneath it. He turned himself inside-out trying to get from underneath the wreckage.

"You don't have to do this."

"Get your hands out!" The barrel was inches from the cop's face. Finn cast about for his hands but everything melted together in the pulses of light and their shadows. He pressed the shotgun into the cop's neck, just below his helmet strap, took his left hand from the gun and jerked on the cop's left arm, pinned against the ground. It popped out and Finn replaced his hand to the pump action, and backed a step away.

"You can get help," the man said, pulling his right arm from below the car bumper.

"Keep your hands where they are." For a moment they stared at one another unspeaking. His eyes no longer held the fear he'd seen in his rear view mirror. Now they only looked uncertain. "You don't understand," Finn said. "I'm sorry." He inched back to the man looking only at his hands resting on the pavement above his head. Again, he pressed the muzzle into the man's neck. Then he popped the button on his gun holster squeezed between the cop's hip and the ground. Left handed, he thought. He fished a revolver from the holster and slung it along the pavement behind him. Then he pivoted and blasted the front motorcycle tire. The gun seemed to echo like a cannon, and the tire spun like a wayward ferris wheel, twisted spokes grating against the front fork. Immediately he turned back to the cop. His hands hadn't moved. Finn stood up still training the gun on him. Only the heavy lull of insects and tree frogs filled the air now. "Take off your Kevlar," he said.

The man leaned on an elbow and undid the Velcro straps. "You'll never get away."

Mentally, Finn tabulated his shots: four in the parking lot, and one here. He didn't want to change to the revolver and risk fooling with the safety, so kept the empty shotgun aimed on him. He watched as the cop jerked and pulled the vest from himself. "The cuffs," Finn said. Next, he had him unclip a set of keys, his radio, and a heavy black flashlight. Then two shadows of Finn appeared, over the cop, crisscrossed like bandoleers. They came from floodlights on the corners of the house behind him.

THIRTY-SEVEN

Finn jumped into his car and screeched ahead, the acceleration slamming the door shut. He left the subdivision and crossed over the highway on an overpass. Just beyond it sat an old-time convenience store at the bottom of a hill. *Benjamin's dead.* He swung into the front of the convenience store, his headlights illuminating a mix of gravel and asphalt. He drove around back where the gravel cracked and gave way to patches of tall weeds. He jammed the car between weeds, put the Kevlar vest on, replaced his tee shirt, and slung the shotgun rope over his shoulder. He was shoving shotgun shells into his pockets when his phone rang. It was Gogan.

"They killed Benjamin," Finn said.

"I know. I am very sorry. You are on the news. They know you are in North Carolina."

"You need to find Sarah. She's in Rhode Island."

"Domestic flights are canceled too now."

"They're gonna kill her!"

"Finn, listen to me. You cannot stop. It is just you now. You must keep going. I'm driving to Los Angeles. We should not talk. They could be locating you now with GPS. Abandon your phone and do not give up," he said before hanging up.

A shadow cut across the parking lot below a street light. Finn spun and leveled the gun. Nothing moved. He squinted into the darkness. A man stood at the edge of a clearing between him and the exit ramp. Finn held the shotgun low against his hip, afraid to move. The veins in his neck thumped. Something moved but it was not the man. It was low to the ground. It scurried directly towards him. Long snout, bushy tail, delicate trot. A fox. It scurried between the logs and around the store. He snapped his head back to the man, but he wasn't there. Now it was just a sign post. Finn turned and followed the fox.

Under brash moonlight the fox crossed the street, then turned (was he looking at Finn?) before disappearing down a narrow cross street pressed on its sides by dense brush. Finn crossed to the side street but then pushed into the foliage and sank down, crunching twigs. He pulled his knees up and rested the shotgun on them. An animal drone dropped a veil of noise that made Finn feel a bit safer: Cicadas, crickets, frogs, two owls calling to one another. Anxiety for Sarah commandeered his mind and he fought for space to think. He checked the map on his phone. Its battery was nearly dead. He deactivated the GPS on it.

The fox was right. He needed to continue down this alley, cross two more streets and at the third intersection he would be just two houses south of the target. He wished he were with Benjamin swigging pints. He wondered if Rurik Montokov knew he was coming. The Russian on Benjamin's phone had known he was in Chapel Hill. He may have warned Rurik. Finn had no idea how many people lived with Rurik: other terrorists, brothers, sisters, wife, roommates, children. He didn't know if he was armed. But he had to assume he was well armed and alert. And Finn had no idea how he would get into the house at this hour, 3:35 a.m. He decided he would circle the house looking for clues as to the number of people living there. Then he would try to determine where Rurik might be sleeping. He thought about waiting outside until morning when he could approach without arousing suspicion but every second could be an innocent life lost and a higher chance he'd get arrested. But if he went in haphazardly and failed more lives could be lost.

"Here we go," he said to Benjamin. He jogged up the hill. Beyond it the lane sank back down, continued straight and turned to gravel. Narrow driveways crawled between trees to unseen houses, a few illuminated with incandescent light that filtered through the woods. Something jingled. At the top of the next hill a silhouette of a large dog, a Retriever, perhaps, stood at the corner of a chain-link fence poking from the woods. As he neared, the dog began barking.

As if by divine messenger a plan swooped down on him. He didn't like what it entailed, but he appreciated it's creativity. It's just a dog, he told himself. It's life is inconsequential compared to a weaponized smallpox attack. He angled towards the animal and from a pocket in his windbreaker he thumbed shells into the shotgun. The dog barked happily, standing with its paws near the top of the fence. Her belly was exposed. Finn placed the shotgun against his shoulder. He started to feel despicable over what he was about to do, so before he could regret: The gun snorted and the dog blew backwards and to the ground. Finn jumped the fence and went to the dog. Blood, black in the moonlight, leached into the grass. He lugged the dog over the fence and climbed back. Grabbing two paws per hand, he heaved the dog over his shoulders with its belly against his neck. He jogged up the remainder of the hill but the dog jumped and slapped against his shoulders. He squeezed the legs tighter and changed his gait to keep the dog from bouncing. Warm blood oozed down his neck and against the Kevlar vest. *905 Dawes, 905 Dawes.*

At an intersection he skidded to a stop in loose stones. He had to approach the street sign to read it. Not Dawes. He started jogging again and climbed another gentle hill to the next cross street. Dawes. He freed one hand and pulled the cop's flashlight from the small of his back. He fussed with it a few moments with a single hand before finally turning it on. He raked the beam across the gravel behind him. It was dotted with drops of blood, infrequent sure, but enough to make a trail. He cut off the flashlight, and walked ahead, through the intersection going a hundred yards before turning and retracing his trail. He crossed back through the intersection again but just beyond it left the road, climbed across a drainage ditch, and forced himself through dense brush and into the yard of a house on the corner, one house from the Rurik's.

He crossed the front yard of the first house, and then climbed the stoop of 905 Dawes. He plopped the dog on a welcome mat. He ran his hands around his belt feeling for the police radio but it was not there. The dog's tongue, gray in the porch light, hung limp over the muzzle. He didn't think it was easy to tell the cause of death in the moonlight. He zipped up his windbreaker, covering the shotgun. The mailbox to the left of the stoop listed the inhabitants as Montokov. He drew a deep breath, and let it out, repeating, *full throttle,* a whispered mantra. He told himself that he trusted himself to face what lay beyond that door. He pressed the doorbell, paused, and then pressed it repeatedly, and then knelt next to the dog. It was 3:48 a.m. *God, don't let them recognize the dog.* Vibrations of someone coming to the door drifted toward him. The stoop light came on. A curtain covering a window at the top of the door slid to one side.

"Help!" Finn shouted, as loud as he dare. "My dog's been hit by a car."

The curtain swung shut and Finn hoped to hear the door unlatch, but he didn't. He shouted a few more times and was planning to run around to a side or back door and enter by force when he heard footfalls and the the curtain slid open again. "Please help me," he said, cradling the dog; its head wobbled on a forearm. The door cracked open, a bearded, narrow-faced man in his thirties behind it.

"I need to call my vet," Finn said.

The man's eyes widened, but his mouth drew up in a tight knot and he seemed angry even. But then he eased the door open slightly more. Finn looked to see if he had a weapon but could only see his one hand on the door. He wore cotton pajamas with no shirt and light from inside traced him rendering him gray.

This man was connected to the executions of Sarah's parents. He was part of the group now trying to murder Sarah, and connected to the person who'd shoved a muzzle into Benjamin and pulled the trigger six times. He was a terrorist, and he had succeeded, or was attempting to create and spread weaponized smallpox. Finn allowed vulgar rage to caress him, thanked it even for the power it imparted him. The man turned to the back of the house slightly, but still kept his eyes fixed on Finn, and yelled something, likely in Russian. "Come to the bathroom," he said in English, opening the door further. In his right hand he held a revolver. When he saw Finn look warily at it, he said, "Sorry," and lowered it.

Finn stepped over the threshold and launched the dog carcass at the man's chest. He deflected the dog but still tripped backwards and crashed to the floor, taking down a small table and lamp. The gun clattered against the floor and slid toward a couch. Finn bounded over the dog and toward the man, who was now on his knees. He stomped him in the center of his chest with a heel. A sharp shriek came from the back of the house. Finn pivoted and kicked the man's head. He managed to deflect some of the blow but it still pushed him several feet across the floor. Finn spun and snatched up the revolver and jammed it behind his belt, at the small of his back. He cut the patio light, shut the door, flipped the deadbolt locked, and jacked the pump action in the shotgun. Thoughts pinballed across his mind. The scream had sounded like that of a little girl, likely at least a mother and a child back there, likely calling the police this very instant. *If he pushed Rurik down the hall they may have enough time to make the call. They may have already called after he first rang the bell. They could be armed. If he went for them alone, Rurik could escape.*

"Rurik!" He said. He trained the shotgun on the man. "Nobody dies unless you fucking lie. How many people are here? If you lie I'm killing the girl. How many!"

"Two.

"Where?"

"What do you want?"

"Do they have a gun." They could be talking to the police right now, Finn thought. "Get up!"

Rurik stood.

"Get them out here."

The man's face was set in a defiant frown. Finn turned him and kicked him from behind, through a kitchen and down a dark hallway. "You cooperate, no one gets hurt."

Rurik called something out.

"No fucking Russian!" He punched the muzzle into the man's spine. "Get them out. Now!" Finn kicked a door open. Bathroom. Another door. Child's room. He flipped on the light. Empty bed. He pushed Rurik down the hall to a closed door, and made him open it and turn on the light. Master bedroom. Finn thought he heard a muffled whimper. "No one gets hurt. As long as you cooperate," he said to the unseen hiders. They could be in a closest or below a queen size bed against the far wall. Finn stepped backwards and pressed himself against the hall wall, in case the hiders had a gun. He kept his muzzle on Rurik.

"Let them go," Rurik said.

"I'm not here to hurt them. Just make them come out. I'm getting fucking scared!" He had to get them out now and he had to risk losing control.

"I followed protocol," Rurik said.

Finn jumped to the ground and from the hallway scanned under the bed. Two people. He bolted into the room, to the side of the bed, and snatched it from below, his shotgun swinging down on its rope strap. The frame rose up and against the wall. Its speed stunned even himself. A woman and a child lay huddled together. The girl shrieked.

Finn pointed the shotgun at them. "Make her shut up!"

She clamped down on the girls' mouth.

"You want me. Let them go," the man said.

"Did you call the police?" Finn asked the woman.

She looked over at the man. Was she glaring at him?

"If I'm surprised by the cops, I start shooting." Finn enunciated each of the next words, "Did anyone call the police?"

The woman shook her head.

"Any noise, any tricky shit, or I catch anyone lying and the girl gets shot first." Finn looked back and forth between the man and the woman assessing whether they believed him. Even he didn't believe himself, that he could shoot an innocent girl. But thousands of other innocent girl's lives could be at risk. He thought of Benjamin pushing Sophia too high on her playground swing. "And no fucking Russian." He looked at the man. "Any more guns in the house?"

"Just the revolver," the woman said.

"How many cellphones?"

"Two," she said.

"Where?"

"There," she motioned to the nightstand, "And in the kitchen."

Aiming at the mother and daughter, Finn crossed the room and grabbed the cellphone. For a minute or so he fooled with it until he found the recent calls list. The last outgoing call had been over six hours earlier, at 9:21 p.m. There were four unanswered incoming calls in the last twenty minutes. Undoubtedly Kotesky. Finn had gotten lucky that the ringer was silenced. He shoved the phone into a back pocket.

"Everyone get up." He directed them single-file into the kitchen, father-first and then mother, with the girl clinging to her.

Once in the kitchen he searched the outgoing calls on that phone as well, found no 911 call, and then smashed it under a heel. *Think, think, think, think.* He needed to verify that the man was indeed Rurik. Finn pulled the police handcuffs from his back pocket. "Put these on him," he said to the woman, holding the cuffs in one hand and keeping the shotgun aimed at the man and close to his chest. "Hurry up."

Gingerly she came to him and took the cuffs.

"Behind his back."

She clicked them closed.

Finn made the man walk backwards to him. He grabbed the handcuffs and squeezed them, ratcheting them closed several more notches.

"I need an I.D.," he said to the man, pushing him back to his family.

"Please, just let them go."

"Where's the I.D.?"

"I'll do what ever you want if you let them go."

The girl monkey-clung to the mother and cried but it seemed to come from far off. A lush field filled with thousands of flaxen-haired girls lying down in summer dresses filled Finn's imagination. His mind's eye zoomed in as if airborne and he saw that under their lacy dresses all the girls were swathed in ripe smallpox boils. "Get your Daddy's wallet," he told the girl.

"Go on," the mother said.

"And come right back," Finn added. He wiped his face. His hand felt slimy and he pulled it back. It was smeared in blood. He must have looked a pretty mess.

The girl came back still sobbing and handed the wallet to the mother, who handed it to Finn. He pulled out a University of North Carolina student I.D. He was Rurik Montokov alright. He tossed aside the wallet. "In there," he said, waving the gun barrel toward the living room.

He marched them single file over the dog carcass, and sat them on a couch. Rurik scooted to one end by himself. The girl's sobbing crescendoed on seeing the dog and the mother shielded the girl's eyes. At the front were two bay windows covered by maroon curtains. Finn checked to make certain they overlapped. He flipped the light switch off, leaving only weak light to filter in from the kitchen.

Just then a beam of light brightened them from outside, washed scarlet through the curtains. It panned across the room. Finn threw himself down and aimed at the girl. He jacked the pump action and expelled a shell (for effect). Certainly the beam was a police search light. Nobody breathed. The girl whimpered. The light faded and after a long, taught silence Finn spoke to Rurik, "Start explaining." He pulled a chair out from a desk and sat down.

"I followed the protocol, to the syllable," Rurik said. Then he began speaking in a measured monotone. "At the lab I will receive a single glycerol stock of a bacteria along with instructions for its growth conditions, the number of DNA samples to expect, and the size of the circular DNA sequence resulting from the fragments ligated together..."

"Shut up! Tell me about Sarah Dougherty,"

Momentarily, he looked confused. "I never heard of her. It's the truth. I did everything that was asked of me."

"Tell me about the DNA sequence. The one you got from Austin."

"My family has nothing to do with this. Take me and—"

"No!" Finn glowered at him. Then he took a calculated risk. "Your samples weren't received."

Rurik hung his head. "I sent the DNA certified mail. The receipt's in the bedroom." He looked up, "My uncle has a huge piece of land. He'll sell it for me. I'll give you all the money. Just leave my family alone."

"I don't care about your fucking money."

Rurik said something to Finn in Russian.

"No fucking Russian!" Finn tried to think.

"Who are you?"

"Tell me about Kotesky." Finn had to move it along. The police may knock on the door any second. He found him himself taking air in shallow breaths.

"I don't know who Kotesky—"

"I know you received DNA sequences and they're connected to the smallpox attack."

The man looked over to the woman and then back to Finn.

"I don't think you understand your position, family man." Finn went to the mother and girl and waved the muzzle in the woman's face. She gripped the girl against her chest and a pang of empathy for her hit

Finn. "I don't care about your life, or your family's. I need to know what you did and what you know."

"They set me up. You've got to believe me." His voice showed traces of cracking. "They had me engineer the virus, though I didn't know what I was doing."

"What did you make?"

"A man told me to assemble multiple DNA sequences. I received them in the mail and put them in the bacteria they sent me. I didn't know what they were."

Finn backed up from the women a few steps.

Rurik gained speed like a boulder crashing downhill. "I wanted to go to the police, but they threatened to kill...they threated me. I lost my brother and father in a terrorist bombing in Moscow after Perestroika, and my mother suicided. I could never risk my family here."

"What'd you make?"

"I could not be certain that it was unethical, only secret. You have to believe I had no intention of being in a terrorist attack." He began to tremble.

"I don't need to believe anything."

Rurik looked at the woman. "I'm sorry," he said, his face melting into a frown. He turned away from her. "You understand?"

"What was it?"

"You shit piece!" the woman shrieked. She continued in Russian, took a hand from the girl and balled it tight, and whaled at his head.

"Stop it!" Finn kicked at her feet.

Rurik jumped up from the couch and backed away. "Of course I was suspicious," he said. "I hid copies of the DNA pieces I had assembled even though they threatened...ah, they forbid it."

"Now I see," the woman said. "The revolver, the paranoia, your lies."

"Shut up!" Finn said.

Rurik's face wrenched as if he were before a firing squad. He started, paused, and started again. "Kill me if you want, just don't hurt my family. They had nothing to do with it."

"What was it?"

"I sequenced the final assembly, and..." He dropped his head. "It was smallpox. I made smallpox."

"Was it wild-type?"

"But it's impossible that it's connected to the attack. I put it in a bacteria. Smallpox won't replicate in bacteria."

"Were there any other genes in it?"

"It had a foreign gene."

"Which gene!"

Rurik squeezed his eyes tight and then released them. "Interleukin-4."

Finn spun around in a tight circle. "The entire smallpox genome plus interleukin-4."

"In a B-A-C cap."

"A what?"

"A bacterial artificial chromosome. It's a circular piece of bacterial DNA. With it you can insert a large amount of foreign DNA into a bacteria. It's always passed on to daughter cells."

"Why would you do that?"

"I don't know, but it's harmless. The smallpox DNA alone cannot infect even a single human cell. And it can't replicate without the viral proteins."

"You never went to the police?"

"I planned on it, once I could protect my family. I swear."

Finn wondered whether to believe him.

"Why isn't someone from Homeland Security here if you think I'm involved in the smallpox attack?"

"If you want to save your family now you have to tell me *everything* you know."

"I did send the bacteria, to a friend, a bacteriologist. I asked him to identify the species."

"What'd he say?'

"He couldn't identify it. But he found it is related to two separate species: An agro bacteria that causes tree tumors and another one that lives on human epidermis."

Finn thought there was a small chance he was lying, but he couldn't have known about the Interleukin-4 gene unless he'd sequenced it. Lance Matterson had claimed the same sort of ignorance, more even. The wife looked startled but cautious and she held the girl tight. Though she may be incensed with Rurik she was smart enough to keep quiet. Finn motioned for Rurik to sit back down on the couch. Finn needed to think. He tried to speak as calmly as possible. "You may not save yourself but you can save your family so keep telling the truth."

Rurik nodded, a pitiful frown etched across his face. He wouldn't look at the woman.

Finn decided to trust what he was saying unless he could catch him in a lie. Finn began slowly, "You put the interleukin modified smallpox into a bacteria that lives on human skin? A functionally dead virus though."

"Yeah. Obviously this can't be part—"

"Where'd you send it?"

"A California biotech. Epicor Neutriceuticals."

Lance Matterson had passed out skin cream samples sent to him from a biotech company. Skin cream, Finn thought, with weaponized smallpox stuffed into a bacteria that lives on human skin. *Think, think, think, think.*

"I assure you, it cannot infect anyone," Rurik said. "It's a naked piece of DNA. It can't enter a cell or replicate. Only an intact virus can do that."

Finn considered what he said, trying to relate it to everything else.

"I don't know," Finn muttered. He paced the room, stepping neatly over the dog each time. He told Rurik's daughter to bring a laptop computer to him.

She went to the back of the house, came back, and gave him a laptop. Finn turned a desk to face the three of them and put the laptop on it. He opened an Internet encyclopedia and searched "smallpox vaccination". The vaccine was made from a live virus called vaccinia, a pox-type virus closely related to smallpox, but far milder. Vaccinia didn't cause sickness in humans. But it did infect skin cells at the injection site and formed a single lesion before the human immune system shut it down. The key was that vaccinia was related enough to smallpox that it conferred complete immunity to it. "You said the smallpox DNA needs viral proteins to replicate. The vaccinia virus, it's proteins, could they be related enough to smallpox to replicate its DNA? It's a live virus vaccine."

Rurik exhaled. "Theoretically. Maybe. But that is irrelevant. The smallpox DNA cannot replicate in bacteria."

"What was the name of the tree-tumor-making bacteria related to the one you put the smallpox in?"

Rurik thought a moment. "*Agrobacterium tumefaciens.*"

Finn searched it on the same Encyclopedic website. It caused plant tumors by inserting some of its DNA into the plant cells. He scrolled down to a section titled "Agrobacterium in humans". A study in the National Academy of Sciences said *Agrobacterium tumefaciens* attached to and inserted its DNA into several types of human skin cells. Finn jumped up from the computer. "The bacteria you put the smallpox in is also related to a skin bacteria."

Lance Matterson had said the skin cream was specifically designed for shoulders and arms. The smallpox vaccine was given in the shoulder. Finn stopped and turned to Rurik. "If your bacteria injects the smallpox DNA into a human skin cell, one that later becomes infected with the live virus vaccine, then the vaccine proteins could replicate the smallpox DNA. The smallpox will replicate, package itself, and erupt from the skin cell: a fully intact virus."

Rurik knitted his eyebrows down while Finn mentally reviewed his logic.

"No!" Rurik said. "It's a vaccination. The person would be immune to the smallpox."

Finn spun around in a couple of tight circles. "It's not smallpox. It's interleukin-smallpox. The Australian group inserted Interleukin-4 into a mousepox virus and the mousepox vaccine was useless against it." He covered his mouth. "Oh my God. Oh my God. The Interleukin-smallpox won't replicate until the vaccine is given. Then it'll explode all at once. The cases on the news now are just a decoy attack. They can't have Interleukin in them or it would give away the true attack. The vaccinations kick-start the interleukin-smallpox on the people who've used the skin cream. Oh my God. The vaccine starts the fucking attack!"

Rurik and the woman stared at him as if looking into him, and for an instant Finn had the distinct suspicion they were embedded deep in glacial ice. "The vaccine starts it but no vaccine can stop it," Finn said. "And the vaccinations start this morning. We have to stop them. You'll come with me. We need to get to someone in Homeland Security, as high up as possible."

"Who will listen to us?"

Finn checked his cell phone. "It's 4:47 right now. When do the vaccinations start?"

"Seven."

"Where are your car keys?"

"On a hook next to the kitchen door."

"Tell me everything I need to know to get into your lab and get the bacteria containing the smallpox."

"Get my card key from the nightstand. My lab key is hanging on the key rack in the kitchen."

Gun shot blasts and glass exploded behind Finn. As if someone had whaled him in the back with a sledge hammer he crashed forward and onto the coffee table. The girl clung to her mother. The gun blasts kept coming, 4,5,6,7,8... Finn gasped. Rurik threw himself over the girl and woman but then crumpled on top of them. The gun shots stopped for a moment. Finn found himself on his back on the floor, the shotgun across his chest. The girl whimpered but her mother's head hung limp at an awkward angle. Hunched over, he scrambled through the kitchen doorway. More glass breaking. Wood cracked and something heavy thudded, like the front door being smashed open. Headlong. The master bedroom. He launched himself into a closet and between hanging clothes. He pulled the shotgun across his chest. More glass shattered, but closer now—the bathroom or back door. He darted a hand behind the kevlar vest and up his back. Pain clawed at his lungs through the back of his rib-cage. Leaned from the closet and cut the bedroom lights. Moonlight and cicadas. Finn's blood became slush.

Then the room went hot white and a gun blast deafened him. Then two more. The light came on and before he could think, he jumped out of the closet barrel first and pulling the trigger. The blast kicked a hole in the wall just in front of a squat Hispanic man, his face swathed in black tattoos. He sprung away. He crashed a shoulder into the wall while popping off his pistol. Staccato. Pop-pop-pop-pop. Finn pumped and pulled the trigger. He hit the tattooed man's abdomen. But Finn's stomach exploded. Crashing backwards. The shotgun falling from his hands. Raking breaths. Searing stomach.

The man struggled to a knee, a blood stain the size of a soccer ball spreading across his belly. He brought his pistol up and toward Finn. Finn found himself rhino charging. The pistol went off. Finn was on top of the tattooed fuck, hands around his throat trying to squeeze it flat. Sharp silence. Except—soft thuds of the man's punches on Finn's face. More gun blasts. Inside the house now. Finn released. The tattooed man reached for his throat and sucked in breaths. Finn swiped a radio off the nightstand and brought it down on the man's face: once, twice, three times, four, five, six. Finn wobbled to feet. He dragged Rurik's revolver from the small of his back. Click. And then Blam! A hole in the man's heart. Finn leaned against the wall for just a moment—watching for movement on the man's tattooed face and listening for anything from the front room. He jumped the body and went into the bathroom. He crouched in the tub. He peeked around the back wall of the shower with the revolver trained on the open doorway. Movement in the living room. He slipped a hand under his Kevlar vest and pulled it back out. Bloodless. Cicadas and tree frogs. He held his breath. The front screen door banged shut. He nearly jumped up for a chase but then squatted back down suspecting a trap. He waited several minutes. No movement. He crept toward the living room. The girl, the woman, Rurik: all sprawled on the the floor, motionless.

He turned and went out the back door, lurching through yards. He climbed a fence and careened down a vine covered ravine to a skinny stream. Dug his cellphone from a pocket, called Deyermand and got his voice mail. "The vaccine launches the true attack," he said, panting. His phone beeped, signaling a nearly dead battery. "The one using weaponized smallpox. The current smallpox cases are just a decoy to initiate vaccinations. You must stop the vaccinations. Check the laboratory of Rurik Montokov at the University of North Carolina, Chapel Hill. The weaponized smallpox is in *Agrobacterium tumefaciens*, engineered to grow on human skin and insert its DNA into it. Epicor Neutraceuticals, in California, made ..." The phone shut off. He searched pockets for the phone he had taken from Rurik's nightstand. It wasn't there.

He bent down, slurped handfuls of water and splashed water on his face. Under moonlight he took off the wind breaker, washed off the dog's blood-stains and put it back on, threw his cellphone into the shallow water—he couldn't risk using it later and being located by the police—, climbed the other bank and emerged into a quiet suburban neighborhood. Gauzy light filtered through the tree tops. He scraped out a shallow pit in pine needles and dropped in the kevlar vest. He pulled the windbreaker over Rurik's revolver and walked out onto the streets trying to orient himself using his memory of the Internet map.

Eventually he found a thoroughfare and walked into town, shades of gray having given way to tones of warm yellow and orange. A white banner with red lettering hung on a stone cathedral announcing "Vaccine Site". He came to a café and went in and asked for directions to the library. It wouldn't be open for twenty minutes, so he ordered a coffee. Lance Matterson said he had handed out two to three thousand skin cream samples and who knew how many others like him had done so. He'd only created a small part of the genetically engineered smallpox. There could be many more who made other parts of the interleukin-smallpox, who also passed out thousands of skin cream samples.

Once the library opened Finn got online and sent an email to Sarah:

These smallpox cases are a decoy attack created to start a vaccination campaign. It will launch a weaponized attack. Trust me! I'll explain it all when I see you. In two weeks (the incubation period of smallpox) the real attack will erupt. Once started it will swamp any precautions, or quarantines designed to contain it. Stop everything and get out of the country. This is serious. Emailing me back is secondary to getting far from the United States.

He sent a similar email to everyone on his contact list, and then an email with all the biological details to Gogan.

Three other people were using computers and a man with dreadlocks and layers of threadbare, homeless clothes sat nearby reading a magazine. A librarian passed Finn pushing a cart of books. He surveyed the unknown (and unknowing) faces and a naked loneliness stole over him. He well knew how they would react if a ragged stranger told them to avoid the vaccine, to leave the country. He asked the librarian for directions to the highway.

. . .

Youssef had rushed into position between the front door and the fireplace over twelve hours ago. He was dizzy with exhaustion. His feet throbbed. He eyed the couch across from him, and then the motion sensor hanging in the corner of the room, between the ceiling and the wall. He shifted his weight from one foot to the other, and cursed the bitch for not coming home. He imagined being with Cemile again. Hadn't he fulfilled his *bayat*? God could not deny him entrance to heaven, could he? Her smiling face, filled his imagination and he smiled back. He tried to coax himself into waiting another half hour but couldn't. If Sarah had cameras installed like in her apartment in Austin, within half an hour the sun would offer enough light for filming. He broke vigil and strolled to the kitchen. The motion sensor flashed an angry red light. He opened the refrigerator door and scanned for liquids, unscrewed the interior light bulb, and grabbed a two quart container of milk. He took the clear plastic pill case from his pocket,— the hydro-cyanide pill Ledpaste gave him when they first met— separated the caps and dumped it's blue powder into the milk. When the alarm blared its rolling siren, he didn't flinch, though it sounded harsher than yesterday. He swirled the milk and put it back, screwed the bulb back in, and shut the refrigerator door. Then he reopened it and slammed it shut again. It bounced open and he slammed it again. He kicked and slammed it bellowing under the blare of the alarm. Food and bottles toppled and a head of lettuce rolled across the kitchen floor. He stood for a moment breathing heavily. Then he replaced the lettuce, up-righted the toppled bottles. He took the milk out, popped the cap, threw the other blue pill into his mouth and washed it down. He replaced the milk then slumped down with his back against a cabinet, exhaled and smiled, sinking into Cemile's coffee eyes.

THIRTY-EIGHT

Finn jogged down a weed-choked overpass embankment to the shoulder of a highway, just outside of Chapel Hill. He yearned to go north to Sarah. But would she believe him? Or could he find her before she read his email and left the country? At that very moment, while he kicked at pebbles and cars whizzed by, the vaccines were being injected, the weaponized smallpox was silently exploding. He saw Benjamin from yesterday afternoon, screaming at him about how he didn't truly know commitment, and in that instant Finn accepted that he had only one option: He had to return to Austin. He had to take Benjamin's daughter, Sophia, with him.

He turned around and jogged the mile or so back into town, back to the library and began typing another email to Sarah. He yearned to tell her to meet him back in Austin, but overland (now that all domestic flights were canceled) to Texas could expose her to the virus for many days. The Internet encyclopedia had said that smallpox wasn't contagious until the days just before the lesions arose, but who knew how the interleukin-4 would alter that. He typed out a message urging her to head for Canada and to then search for a Canadian flight to Mexico City where they could meet. Then he went back to the highway, the southbound lane this time, and stuck out a thumb.

Finn leaned against a cement wall at an Alabama truck stop and listened to Gogan through the heavy plastic of a pay phone. Gogan had read the email and was now driving to Washington D.C. to convince politicians of the weaponized attack. Finn told him to leave the country. "They don't move on dimes," he said, "Get out and save who you can."

"You cannot do this. It's your country."

"No body can stop it now."

A day later Finn arrived in Austin and raced to the downtown library to check his email. There were over a thousand responses to his mass mailing. He leaned into the monitor, eyes devouring the addresses, searching for one from Sarah. Many forwarded a small article from the Raleigh News and Observer: "Texas Fugitive Assaults Chapel Hill Motorcycle Patrolman". Others contained an Austin American Statesman article: "Austin Detective Gunned Down in

Downtown Apartment". Finn's mother had sent three emails a day imploring him to turn himself in. But not one email from Sarah.

Half an hour later he sat under the shade of a live oak on a bench across the street from Sophia Black's kindergarten. He watched Jessica, Sophia's mother, arrive, park, and enter the long brick building. He thought the chances slim that she would believe him sane if he tried to explain he and Benjamin discovered a weaponized smallpox attack that will be initiated by the vaccine. But he *would not* leave without Sophia and he'd use the revolver if he had to.

When Jessica emerged with Sophia a few minutes later, he intercepted them at the car. Jessica looked at him with startled, blinking eyes.

"Hi, Uncle Finn," Sophia said, clutching her mother's hand.

Finn gave her a tense smile.

"The *whole* force is after you," Jessica said.

"I'm so sorry about Benjamin," he blurted, nearly at tears. They hugged, Finn keeping his hips back. He didn't want Jessica to feel the revolver behind his belt. Kneeling, he gave Sophia a long squeeze.

"Can we get in the car?" he asked Jessica.

Jessica cast about, furtively. "I need to get home."

"I'm still me. Listen. I have a lot to tell you, and not much time."

She unlocked the car, and started to put Sophia in the back. He couldn't tell if Jessica was ignoring him or not.

"If I get arrested it'll be too late."

She stopped buckling in Sophia. "Five minutes."

"Just you and I," he said.

She sent Sophia to a sandbox near the kindergarten entrance. She climbed into the front, and Finn sat in the passenger seat. They rolled down the windows letting out the dense heat. "Please hold your judgment and just listen for a sec." He gave her a reassuring smile and stalled, trying to collect his tactics, set his limits.

"Well?" she said.

"Benjamin did some bad shit."

Jessica's expression switched to unimpressed.

"He got tangled up with some drug dealers. He still owes them a lot of money, and these aren't people who care if he's dead, Jess. They'll be coming for Sophia. If not today, tomorrow or the next day. But they're coming, and soon. I'm sure of it."

She looked at Sophia, climbing a red plastic slide. Finn searched her eyes assessing whether she was buying it. "I can get the money but it'll take me a least two weeks. I swore to Benjamin I'd protect Sophia."

"How much did he owe?"

Finn picked the highest figure he thought she'd believe. "Just over a quarter million."

"A quarter million?"

"We have to take her to Mexico. It'll buy me the time I need."

"The police can protect her."

"Maybe," Finn said. "Maybe not. It's cops he owes."

She cradled her head in her hands. Then she jerked her head up. "Then I'll get a lawyer and go to the chief. I'm not hiding." She enunciated "hiding" as if it were a disease.

"You'll lose his pension."

"They'll never let it leak." She leaned out the window and called Sophia.

Finn reached down and pulled out the revolver. Before Jessica saw it he dropped it on her lap and thrust up his hands in surrender. "It's loaded," he said. "Kill me now, or come with me and Sophia to Mexico." He felt his chin quivering. "I won't risk her life." He wanted to ask her if she knew what Benjamin meant to him. "If you don't kill me right now I will pick up that gun and take Sophia and after that I won't even allow you to stop me." They glanced between each other and the gun lying on her thighs. Her chest rose up and down. He wanted to hug her, squeeze her, for her to trust him.

"Finn, I'm not going to kill you."

"I can't have you trying something sneaky later."

"Get it off of me." She wouldn't touch it.

"I pulled you in the car, threatened to kill you and you wrestled the gun from me. I'm wanted for murder and assault. It's a slam-dunk defense. I swore to Benjamin I'd protect her or die trying." They were both quiet for some time.

She handed Finn the gun. "At least were vaccinated."

Finn halted while tucking the gun behind his belt. "You haven't used skin cream, a free skin cream sample, have you? Or Sophia?"

She furrowed her brow, annoyed. "No. Why?"

He hugged her. "It's nothing. Forget it."

"Hey, not so hard."

Seven hours later the three of them drove over the muddy Rio Grande and into Nuevo Laredo. It was 10 p.m. Tuesday September, 10th. Eight smallpox cases had been confirmed across the United States. The next afternoon Mexico sealed its border and not a half hour after that he began hearing talk of Americans being rounded up and deported back to the U.S.

In a dreary coastal town thirty miles south of the border the three of them hid out in a dingy motel while Finn went into town to supposedly arrange for Benjamin's debt money. He promised a fat little fisherman the equivalent to five years of his wages for a trip to Belize. "We'll be safest on the water," he told Jessica.

While they waited for the fisherman to prepare, Finn spent a couple nervous days slipping between phone kiosks, an Internet café, and a local bank, plundering his retirement account. Every few hours he would slip into an Internet café and check his email for a message from Sarah that never came. He kept calling his mom.

"I'm so sorry about Benjamin," his mother said. "Where are you?"

"I'm still in North Carolina. Listen—"

"Is it true what the papers are saying there?"

"Promise me that you won't take the vaccine."

"Honey, everyone's taking it right now."

"Mom, Listen to me. You have to get out of the country."

"I've spoken to a lawyer. He's the best in Philadelphia. He's got connections in North Carolina."

"Do you remember getting any skin cream samples within the last few weeks, free ones, hand outs."

"I don't know," she sounded annoyed. "Look, we can help if you don't have health insurance."

"You have to leave the country and you have to take as many people along as you can. Dad, Henry, and Meghan. This smallpox will get a lot worse."

"We can't just drop everything."

"You have to!"

"I can send money. We'll arrange everything and you'll get a fair..."

The fat fisherman rapped on the glass to the phone kiosk. He pointed to his watch. Finn's mother continued.

"Mom!"

She halted, mid-sentence.

"I love you. I love you so much. Tell Uncle Jim, and Aunt Liz, and Tow-head, and of course Meghan and Henry, and Dad. The fisherman rapped again and rattled off something urgently. "Tell them what I said, that the smallpox will get much worse. Tell them to leave the country. I love you, Mom."

The fisherman slid the bi-fold door open and tugged at Finn's shirt sleeve. Finn slumped in his seat. The phone bounced off the floor and swung from its cord.

They lazed up and down gentle swells, the fisherman joking and laughing, using hand signals and simple Spanish. Finn twisted scenarios around in his mind, of how he would meet up with Sarah. After a few days they docked in some ramshackle town and resupplied. Nervous that the rumors of Americans being deported were true, he popped into an Internet café. Then he saw it: *Benjamin Black,* the fake account Sarah had made. He threw his chair back and pumped a fist in the air. "Yeah!" The four of five people in the café stared at him. He jumped towards a woman a few seats away and squeezed her arms while barking triumphs. She laughed with him. Then he sat down and read the email praying she was coming to Mexico City.

She had heeded his warning, she wrote, did not return to the house. In fact someone broke in late Sunday night, the 8th. She thanked him and said the police still prohibited a cell phone. She even had to leave her laptop computer in the house. He raced over the text searching for clues to her whereabouts. She did believe him about the smallpox attack and she would be leaving the country but there were just a few things she needed to tie up.

He threw his hands up over his face. "No!" The blunt syllable clanged against the quiet people on headphones, and against the waves lapping the dock outside.

Leave Leave Leave Leave now! If you are reading this you are wasting time. You taught me to act in the present. Do it yourself. If I'm wrong you will only have wasted a couple of weeks. Go directly to Canada this moment. Then try to meet me in Mexico City. You don't need money. I have my retirement fund.

In another fishing village a few days later, the fisherman returned with a newspaper and news that gringos indeed were being rounded up. Using high school Spanish, Finn deciphered that although the smallpox had kept growing, the number of new cases was decelerating. There were six additional infections between September 11th and the 13th, for a total of fourteen cases, but only four more had arisen by September 16th. This is what he expected, a lull before the weaponized assault.

Pundits regaled victory against the terrorists while Finn dreaded September 21st, twelve days post-vaccination, the incubation period for normal smallpox. But September 21st passed with no bad news. On the 22nd Finn dared the slightest of hope. But on the 23rd in the port city of Merida the fisherman went into town and returned with a solemn face, and the day's paper. A photo encompassing the entire front page showed a boy, his entire face blossomed in ripe smallpox boils. Finn couldn't read the article but he understood the title: "¡Epidemia!" On September

22nd 8,179 cases of smallpox had exploded in the United States.

"*Salud,*" Finn said, snapping from his stupefied state and pounding his chest for the fisherman.

The man shook his head, pointing to the coast, "*Fuera,*" -Go.

Showing the fisherman his, Sophia's, and Jessica's forearms, he said, "*Mira,* no sores." He offered more money.

The man made a pistol with his hand, put it to his temple, and pulled the trigger. "*Policia, me matarán.*" The police would kill him if they found him harboring Americans. Finn begged, and finally the fisherman relented, though he made it clear that nobody was to ever come on deck during the day.

They continued south and Finn turned his attention to making it to Belize and waiting out the smallpox attack there. When he connected with Sarah they would figure out how to meet up, he reassured himself. Then he told Jessica that Benjamin had not owed any drug dealers, but rather they were fleeing a weaponized smallpox attack. Sitting on the thin cabin bed cushions and facing one another, Finn explained. "This burst of 8,000 cases is from the dormant virus in the skin cream being activated by the vaccine. There'll be a second lull and then another burst of cases, but many more: people who contracted the weaponized virus directly from the people sick now, even before they had symptoms."

"How many?"

"Who knows? Wild type smallpox has a reproduction rate of 3. Who knows about the Interleukin version." They were quiet a while, holding on as the boat shifted over broad swells.

"When will it end?"

Finn shook his head.

"Where are we going?"

"South." He reclined on the bed, relieved to finally be honest. It seemed possible, he said, that with ruthless quarantines the weaponized attack could be contained, that the cases would diminish after the second round. He started to think that his assault on the cop could be defensible. The emails, and the phone call to Deyermand proved that he figured out the strategy of the attack. At the least this would carry some weight with a jury and he'd be given leniency even if convicted. Then, feeling guilty, he chased away his selfish thoughts.

One evening after refueling they puttered away from a village of zinc-roofed, clapboard shacks crowding a rocky cove. The old fisherman had been getting lax and letting his three refugees come above deck with the last vestiges of light. Children kicking a soccer ball on the shore stopped and waved as they left the cove and for the next six hours Finn laid next to Sophia on the deck playing "Spot the plane." They saw nothing but twinkling stars and an occasional faint glow of a satellite racing around the planet, but not a single set of blinking plane lights. He wondered when he would see Sarah again. The next morning they chugged into the Mexican port city Chetumal, on the border with Belize. They thanked the fisherman but knew better than to try and shake his hand or hug him. Finn imagined that he'd be furiously hosing and scrubbing down the entire boat in a few minutes. Finn bribed a border agent and the three of them made it into Belize.

They discovered that after the initial explosion of more than 8,000 cases new ones dropped off dramatically. There were less than 200 new infections on September 26th, and there had been no new infections in the United States yesterday. It was September 28th, nineteen days post-vaccination.

The next morning, in the first wisps of light, Finn stood before a newspaper vendor, Jess and Sophia still asleep in the simple hotel room. The front page of the Belize national paper proclaimed, "United States: 42,435 New Smallpox Cases!". They had exploded the previous eighteen hours. Even a few seeped into Canada and Mexico. He raced back to hide in the hotel room. At 8:30 p.m., half an hour before the Internet café down the street would close, he scurried out.

Outside, alone, he went directly to the Internet café, a conspicuously pale dot floating among a sea of brown and black. People swerved around him or stopped and stared, or even shouted for him to leave. He searched for an email from Sarah but didn't find one. He felt like dying.

Two khaki-clad policemen entered. Finn quickly closed his email account and watched his periphery as the attendant behind the counter spoke with them. She pointed in his direction. Finn looked around but there was nowhere to go, except through them.

"You be showing me your passport," one said, in a thick creole accent. All eyes smothered Finn. "Be coming with us, then" the man said. Neither one touched Finn.

Three hours and half of his retirement account later, the two cops gave him one more day of freedom and a promise to kill him if they ever saw him again. He, Jess, and Sophia, hustled onto a night bus bound for Belize City, a filthy town crawling with hungry people and emaciated dogs. He skittered around docks laden with the stench of fish guts, urine, and rotting trash, bluish in the moonlight, and knocked out a deal to leave that morning, on a fishing boat bound for Brazil. His retirement account had lasted him to the ripe age of thirty-three.

For several weeks the three Belize fisherman and the three of them bobbed around the Gulf of Mexico fishing and occasionally camping on deserted islands. If the fisherman were afraid that any of them might harbor the virus they didn't show it. Every few days they'd pull into a port and sell their catch, stock up on block-ice, gas, and booze, while Finn and the women stayed below deck. Mostly, Finn stayed drunk with the fisherman.

One day while fishing north of Cartagena a Colombian coast guard patrol boarded and discovered the three of them. They hauled Finn, Jessica, and Sophia to port, shackled them to the bed of a pickup truck, and for the next three days the sun and the rain took turns on them. They dragged and bumped along from the sweltering coast and up into the dismal windswept Andes. During the day they were thrown stale food and at night they slept in the truck bed, Jess and Sophia covering themselves with a mud-caked blanket, and himself with a ripped, synthetic fiber sleeping bag. Nobody touched them or got closer than they needed. Everywhere they went people gave the truck wide berth and stared. Once some adolescent boys threw rocks at them. Another time a fight broke out and a crowd struggled with a man coming at them with a gasoline can. Mostly, they did what little they could to guard their lives.

On the night of the third day they were unshackled by a man in a sterile suit (egg-shell white in the moonlight) and pushed at gunpoint into an expansive square beside the road. It seemed the square was lined with dozens of the rectangular black voids. The three of them were separated and Finn shoved into an eight by four foot iron cage. Finn dropped his torn sleeping bag in a corner. He thought he heard Sophie bawling and called out, telling her not to worry. He was very worried.

His cage was solid metal with vertical iron bars in the front and just tall enough for him to stand erect inside. That night in the crisp air he heard people coughing, talking quietly, or deliriously shouting in English. He didn't sleep, but kept quiet, either pacing to stay warm or staring at the stars, pinholes in a shroud high above.

At first light he saw the cages were lined up in a rectangle, side by side, all facing inwards, in the remnants of an old stone-tiled town plaza. There were 127 cages and nearly all appeared occupied, piles of drying feces and urine stains at the front. Charred buildings surrounded the cobble stone square and a few black tree stumps jutted up at irregular intervals. A woman in the cage to his right told him they were heading to a quarantine camp for Americans and that several in the cages had smallpox.

Every day was the same except for the first few when they added some more people. The only person ever outside the cages was a man in a sterile suit who drove over a suspension bridge once a day and dished out milky gruel and water from pots in the trunk of his dented sedan. At least twice a day Finn shouted to Sophia and Jess, telling them they were tough, that they would all get through this. During the nights he shivered while wrapped in his sleeping bag or paced until his feet ached, and during the day he slept at the front of the cage in tepid rays of sunlight. Normally in the early evening when everyone was awake and trying to stay warm there was a lot of chatter but by the second week it had diminished to sporadic murmurs. The woman next to him had not spoken for three days. Finn spoke little himself.

On day twelve, as every day, Finn watched the shadow of a burnt tree stump hit the stone joint signaling lunch time, but today lunch didn't come. *He's just running late.* The entire shadow cleared the joint. Hunger gnawed at him. People banged their cages but things eventually grew quiet. It must have been three hours later when he saw the tension wires on the suspension bridge bounce from the weight of the food car. The decrepit sedan pulled into the center of the plaza and Finn sighed with relief. However, instead of pulling out pots of stew the sterile suited man removed what looked like two scuba tanks attached to a black hose. He strapped them to his back and when Finn realized what the man was holding his mind went black like outer space. On the tip of the nozzle danced the blue translucent flame of a flame thrower. The man came directly at him. Finn scrambled to the rear of his puny cage pressing his spine into it. He couldn't tell if he was yelling or not. But others shrieked and struck at their cages.

The man stopped and with a noise like crashing surf, a bright orange fire ball exploded from the nozzle and into the woman's cage pushed up against Finn's. Finn curled into a ball. Immediately his cage went from clammy to scalding. Then the man turned and walked by. Finn crawled to the bars and watched him. The man blasted another cage. He twisted the nozzle and moved the flaming jet of liquid up and down, and side to side. Flaming drops fell to the stone at his feet. He passed a few more cages and then stopped and torched another. Then a man, also in a hygienic suit, rode in on a horse. He climbed off the horse, opened the cage next to Finn and went in dragging a rope with a large iron hook on the end. The rope attached to the horse. The man came out and guided the horse forward pulling the woman's charred body from the cage.

Pieces of clothes fell off and lay smoldering. A powerful scent of burnt hair struck Finn. He felt sick, and would surely have vomited were there food in his stomach. He fixed on Jess and Sophia's cages. All his muscles tensed until the flame-thrower man passed them. The two men dragged out seven bodies and piled them in the center of the plaza. They doused them with kerosene and lit them into a pyre.

The torching happened again on day twenty-two but this time there were only two. Sophie and Jess were safe.

On day thirty-five several armed white-suited men let the rest of the prisoners out, everyone gaunt, and wide-eyed. Immediately Finn rejoined Sophia and Jess, hugging and reassuring them. The sun shone strongly as they were marched past empty storefronts, streaked black with soot above windows and door ways. A few were intact, their painted signs bright, the shelves still lined with products as if they'd been closed the night before and never reopened. Every few hundred feet tall signs on new posts displayed a skull and crossbones over a simple drawing of a pox-covered face. A few mangy dogs ambled along with the group. They trudged along for fifteen minutes, and stopped before a large concrete building: an abandoned hotel.

An American, in jeans and a sweater, spoke through a megaphone. "Congratulations," he called out. "We're the lucky ones. We've escaped the epidemic and managed to stay alive. All of you will now spend one month in this facility, an interim quarantine." He motioned to the building behind him. "You'll have beds and be permitted to socialize, but if you try to escape the Colombians *will* kill you. Although Colombia has had only a few cases of smallpox it is under martial law and as Americans we have no rights. After one month you'll enter a general detention facility where you'll have more freedom. Best of luck." People shouted questions. *How many have died? How long will we be imprisoned? Are we safe from smallpox now? Can I see a doctor?* The man turned and left.

After the month they were crammed into the bed of a pickup truck that clacked across the suspension bridge, a spindly creek far below, twisting like a varicose vein. They emerged onto a dusty brown plain dotted with craggy rocks and stubby windblown plants. Half a mile away lay an encampment. A thick rectangular concrete wall encircled it. Razor wire ran its length along the top and a tower with armed guards stood on each corner.

Once in the camp, a former penitentiary, Finn quickly caught up on the news.

The information that trickled in told of the world trying to create a cage where no bars existed. Canada and Mexico bombed and cratered highways leading to the U.S. and patrolled the borders with their armies. After the explosion of the interleukin-smallpox Canada was overrun with fleeing Americans, and Mexico, after initially trying to make a stand at the border wall, was forced to abandon troops and civilians and scratch a new line in the sands of the Chihuahuan desert two-hundred miles south of the Rio Grande. They patrolled with helicopters and infrared, dogs, and radar. A sun-glazed woman told Finn that in this zone the Mexicans (with international aid) had shot or bombed anything heading south, "an inch tall and with a heart beat". She related stories of shelled American convoys and skirmishes in the desert. "Millions dried up in that hell-hole," she said, "somehow I didn't."

The electrical grids became erratic sometime in October and all Internet, and phone contact with the United States was soon lost. Boats, freighters, or cruise ships, filled with fleeing Americans were forced to return by foreign navies patrolling the Caribbean, Atlantic, and Pacific coasts. Hawaii, smallpox free, had petitioned and received protection from Japan—Alaska, Canada.

Rumors were that in late October, planes full of politicians and the very wealthy, left the U.S. headed for impromptu quarantine camps in Europe. On October 26th a jumbo jet crossing the Atlantic was intercepted by British and Spanish fighter jets and forced to land in Seville, Spain for refueling. It was told it would be escorted back to the United States. But after landing the doors opened and people began streaming from emergency slides. They were all killed. Two days later China, Japan, Britain, and Germany began bombing U.S. airports, aircraft, and runways, civilian and military.

The United Nations had been shipping in petroleum explicitly for food harvesting, until the freighters started getting attacked and the petroleum hijacked, first by pleasure yachts loaded with armed men and then later by U.S. naval vessels. Russia and Britain began escorting the petroleum shipments with nuclear subs and destroyers. But in early November when, in two separate incidents, stowaways (including three who later died of the Interleukin-smallpox) were discovered hidden on the U.N. tankers, the petroleum shipments were suspended. Instead the U.N. launched a massive food aid campaign, parachuting down food staples from cargo planes.

"It's a black hole," one man told Finn. "Nothing comes out, and whatever goes in vanishes."

. . .

Ten months later, Finn squatted in the dirt against a wall, squinting against the chilly sunlight. It glanced off the high plains sand and was whisked along by one of the tireless gusts of wind. His face was tight, dry and the skin on the corners of his mouth cracked. Across the yard guards stood on each corner turret holding AK-47s lazily across their bellies. Finn stroked his wiry beard and then pulled it up and chewed on it. A sharp blast of wind flipped his hair across his face and threw up some dirt, stinging his eyes. He turned his head and tightened his scarf against his neck. On a sketchpad resting on his knees he penciled in a few more details. People mulled about in the yard, some alone kicking stones, others chatting. A group of women knitted and men played cards. They were certainly a sight, their sad-sack faces, wind-burnt and sunken-cheeked, and the men with their scraggly beards. Their clothes, ripped, patched, and restitched, hung off them.

Finn closed his sketchbook and scuffled along kicking stones. He didn't feel high so much as just normal, not obsessing about Sarah, not wondering about his mother, and father, his sister, cousins, Gogan. In the cafeteria he plopped down onto a scarred wooden bench and laid his sketchbook onto the empty table. Men and women had lined up along the edge of the cafeteria, out the door and into the yard. Finn wasn't hungry. For the moment, the cocaine was still working. It didn't matter anyway. That miserable watery slop they pawned off as soup wouldn't dent anyone's hunger here. Anyway, it wasn't a question of satisfying hunger but of stemming the slow wasting. The line crept along, and he reached into his back pocket and pulled out a folded piece of paper. It was his Bukowski poem. *Your life is your life*, it began.

Don't let it be clubbed into dank submission.

Be on the watch

There are ways out

There is a light somewhere

It may be faint but it is there.

He unfolded the bottom half and stared at a dog eared photo of Sarah (and that French guy) on an Afghani mountain. She had a carefree smile and he could hear her roller-coaster laugh. People began sitting down with their trays filling spots in the long, empty tables. He would sit there and wait for Sophia, or until the coke wore off, and then get his share. Sometimes, the servers were so stingy that only by waiting you'd get a decent bowl with several chunks of grisly meat in it. Sometimes all you got was broth and then you'd be in for a tough twelve hours after that, unless you had money and could find guards willing to sell potatoes or jicama. And right now he had no money. He waited, touching up the knitting women in his sketch-pad.

Eventually he assumed Sophia was eating in the east hall. He stood up, crossed the cafeteria and picked up a lunch tray at the end of a short line. The murmur of people slurping soup and crunching on stale flat-bread filled the place. Beyond the open doors the wind whirled dust and plastic wrappers.

Two guards burst through a set of double doors next to the kitchen, storm troopers in heavy black riot fatigues, plastic knee and elbow pads, black gloves, molded plastic face shields and shiny, laced, black boots reaching their knees. The cafeteria hushed. Everyone swiveled to watch them, and everyone near them cowered. Both the men held short black batons. They walked differently than the prisoners. They stepped with certainty and meaning. Finn held a tray with a bowl of soup, some lucky chunks in it. The two men turned and came his way. He put his tray down and his wrists behind him. His plan was working.

The miracle, the 31st of July, sixteen months ago, the day he and Sarah intersected, it's all led to this. It saved his life, (and please God Sarah's) and now it may kill him. He'd survived the worst of the war, or epidemic, or whatever you call it, but now he has to find Sarah and go to her.

The jackboots handcuff him, frisk him, and haul him into the director's office.

"Mister Barber," the camp director says from behind a rickety wooden desk. He rolls the last 'r' on Barber. A neat mustache covers a harelip. One of the jackboots pushes Finn into a lone chair in front of the desk.

"When this was prison of criminals I have much violence. Fighting and noise all the hours. But we have food, we have town, restaurants, stores, whores. There is life. I even leave and see family. Now I stick here with gringos and the disease. I no permitted to leave. And each time I am thinking they will break the quarantine but each time more disease or more gringos coming. But no so much money. Nobody want pay for gringos and sick. So how we all live here? *I* make us live here." He thumps his chest. "*I* make us grow food, yet even coffee." He waves his hand toward a window overlooking a rocky plain, snow-capped mountains on the horizon. "But this is no sufficient. We are no surviving without selling cocaine." He nods at Finn and raises his eyebrows. "Before you purify much but every time now less and less. You want I give more business to Cooper?"

Janeen Cooper's a chemist and the only person in camp other than Finn who knows how to purify cocaine. Finn and Janeen work separately. They're supplied the raw extract to purify into pure cocaine powder for sale. But since Finn has started purposefully slowing down his cocaine purification he knows the director has been shunting more extract to Janeen. But she has too much, and on top of that he has her training someone. Finn heard one of her batches caught fire. Finn sits hunched and with his cuffed hands behind him. He shakes his head. "I'm purifying as fast as I can."

The director scoffs. "Without cocaine you no helping your women."

He means Jessica and Sophia. He's right of course, but Jessica does make a little money working on the farms outside camp. He and his fellow Americans are all the same now. Everyone's lost family, friends, freedom, and those are the lucky ones who've made it. Now they're all scratching out an existence. The game's been reset.

The director shakes a cigarette from a crumpled package. "I know you more mister Barber. I know you a killer. I know you attacking police. I hear much. Is my job." He holds up a cigarette, offering it to Finn and then reaches over the desk and sticks it between Finn's lips. "They say you slowing down on purpose and then you going to kill Cooper. Make new deal with me. Good for you. Good for business." He shrugs as if the logic appeals to him in its practical simplicity. He lights Finn's cigarette.

"I don't hurt other American's stuck in this shit-hole," Finn says.

"Maybe you not eating without the money." He twitches an eyebrow.

The coke has worn off and now hunger chews Finn's stomach lining. A headache pulses behind his right eye. "I have something for you. In my back pocket." He leans forward and pulls out the photo of Sarah. With his hands cuffed behind him he holds it out above a hip.

Other than glancing at the photo the director ignores it. Pensively, he taps ashes into a plastic cup. "Maybe you think Cooper want kill you first. You slow down. No more—how you say—competition." The director rubs a hand across his face. He looks as tired as Finn feels. "Is no important. You must purify more cocaine. You make twenty-five kilos in four months, for the half pay, and must teach a student." He nods as if he finds it fair, and then focuses on Finn. "I protect you here.

Is my job."

"You hardly feed us. We have no doctors."

The director holds out his arms. "You are illegal. You come with disease. You have luck we do not burn everybody. And remember food is little in the total world." He calls toward the hallway for a guard.

Finn shifts his weight, and takes some of the pressure of his cuffed hands where the chair back pinches them. It would take him six months to purify twenty-five kilos. Without the extra money surviving would be grim (precarious rather) and especially for him—he'd give most of the money to Sophia and Jess. He wouldn't want them to suffer for his agenda. "I won't do it," he says.

The director leans forward and plucks the dangling cigarette from Finn's mouth. "Maybe you want solitary *reclusión*. Where you have much time to reconsider." He tosses the nearly full-length cigarette into his plastic ash cup.

"Do what you must," Finn says. "I do the right thing. I don't concern myself with consequences."

The director looks angry. "If you survive *reclusión* then you go work with new arrivals at the cages. *Very* dangerous."

Finn fixes his eyes on the man's black pupils. "*Patrón*," he says. "There's no real safety in life."

They regard one another, the director working his lips as if he's about to convey something but not finding the words to express it. The director calls for a guard and in a moment one comes in. The guard lifts Finn, still clutching the photo behind him. The director glances at it.

"Please," Finn says.

The director takes it and holds it up, looking at it.

"The woman in the photo," Finn says. "If you can find her—"

"Everyone always asking me to find people." He holds it close, inspecting it. "Like if there were a directory." He sighs. "There is nothing can I do." Tucking the photo back into Finn's hands, he says, "You will have much time to decide."

"I decided long ago, before you ever knew me."

The guard pushes Finn out and down the hallway. "If you find her I'll make forty kilos," Finn calls out.

The director yells something and the guard stops. They both turn to see the director outside his door. He saunters over. "But you are working as fast as you can. Right?" He smirks and Finn can't help but smile with him.

"You have persistence Barber. You will make, how you say, a square of me." He puts his hands on his hips.

"A sketch? Yes, yes, absolutely."

For a moment the director holds a proud stance, looking beyond Finn as if posing. "You make a painting. Then you make forty kilos."

"And you find her."

Almost imperceptibly, the director nods.

Three months later Finn sits on a plastic chair down the hall from the director's office. He has purified nearly twenty kilos, frequently going days without sleep. A guard cuffs him and takes him down a hallway past several doors before knocking on one and entering. Inside the director looks up from his computer monitor, the bay window beside him. Finn sits and the guard leaves. Outside gusts of wind blow trash across the dirt road leading to the camp. Beside the window hangs Finn's charcoal sketch: the director framed by ragged mountains.

The director goes to an old gray upright file cabinet and slides open the top drawer. He shuffles papers. "From now ahead I pay you full price for purification."

"Just tell me. Is she alive?"

The director spins around and slaps two sheets of paper on the desk.

Finn thrusts himself up and over them. His eyes consume the papers. "It's in fucking French!"

"Sarah Dougherty," the director says, tapping his finger on one.

"Is she alive!" Finn felt he would faint.

He came around the desk and put a hand on Finn's shoulder. "No, she is no live."

Finn wobbles. The director supports him and then Finn leans into his shoulder. Finn slumps back down into the chair and on top of his cuffed hands.

"Since eight months she is in Quebec, Canada, in quarantine camp. She die of the disease since a month."

Gently at first, Finn begins dropping his head on the wooden table. Soon he is hammering his forehead on the edge, faster and harder.

Then the director has Finn's head in his hands and he's yelling something in his face.

"Huh?"

"You are father!"

"What?"

"The boy has three months. You are the *Papá*."

"How do you know?"

"I know this. Look. The boy, his name." He shakes one of the papers.

Finn absorbs the name while staring at the blotchy fax paper. He says the name aloud, like a spell, "Finn Benjamin Dougherty."

The director holds up an envelope. "And they make a fax to me of letter Sarah has written." The director collects the papers and puts them in Finn's cuffed hands along with envelope. It's fat. He opens the door and a guard comes in and takes Finn by the arm. The guard tugs Finn out by the elbow, and Finn looks back over his shoulder. "I make 50 kilos," he shouts from the hall. "In three months. Then you let me go!"

Natalia Weedy

TODD LEVINS studied molecular and cell biology at Penn State University, but soon after graduating hightailed it to Austin, Texas to be a rock star. Well beyond the point of clear failure he slunk back to the security of a research laboratory in Durham, North Carolina. But no sooner could feel himself turning to stone. He sold all his possessions and set off on a two-year sojourn of South America. The first draft to this novel he wrote in eight months while on the Caribbean coast of Colombia. He lives with a dog in Durham, North Carolina.

24991202R00167

Made in the USA
Charleston, SC
10 December 2013